BY LIBERTY STOWE

The Vogel Springs Collection

Steady Now
Bottled Up

The Holiday Collection

The Holiday Mixtape
The Holiday Headline

Steady Now

Liberty Stowe

RUPERTBOSSIER PUBLISHING

Paperback: 978-1-964011-13-4

Hardback: 978-1-964011-26-4

EBook: 978-1-964011-14-1

Book Cover by Dana Nicole Joiner

To all those who had to get lost...
before they could find their way home~

Content Warnings

Although *Steady Now* is a Small Town Romance, it is crucial to note the story includes foul language and sexually explicit content, making it an 18+ read. Other notable triggers are parental neglect, child abandonment, and mentions of drug use.

Playlist

- RIDE OUT IN THE COUNTRY *Yola*

- PARIS, TEXAS *Lana Del Rey, SYML*

- READY TO LET GO *Cage The Elephant*

- A THOUSAND MILES FROM NOWHERE *Dwight Yoakam*

- THUMBING MY WAY *Pearl Jam*

- AMARILLO BY MORNING *George Strait*

- NOSE DIVE *Post Malone,* (Feat.) *Lainey Wilson*

- YOU PROOF *Morgan Wallen*

- WHERE I FIND GOD *Larry Fleet*

- TROUBLE *Cage The Elephant*

- READY TO RUN *The Chicks*

- FISHIN' IN THE DARK *Nitty Gritty Dirt Band*

- IN COLOR *Jamey Johnson*

- BABY'S GOT HER BLUE JEANS ON *Mel McDaniel*

- OCEAN FRONT PROPERTY *George Strait*

- SHOES UNDER MY BED *Buck McCoy*

- YOU AND TEQUILA *Kenny Chesney, Grace Potter*

- DEEPER THAN THE HOLLER *Randy Travis*

- WHEN YOU SAY NOTHING AT ALL *Alison Krauss*

- I'M STILL A GUY *Brad Paisley*

- I'LL TAKE CARE OF YOU *The Chicks*

- NOW THAT YOU'RE GONE *The Raconteurs*

- COME BACK *Pearl Jam*

- STEADY NOW *nilu*

- SOMETHING IN THE ORANGE *Zach Bryan*

- GENTLE ON MY MIND *Johnny Cash, Glen Campbell*

- DANNY'S SONG *Anne Murry*

- HIDE MY GUN (Feat. HARDY) *Post Malone, HARDY*

- JUST BREATHE *Willie Nelson, Lukas Nelson*

- PINK SKIES *Zach Bryan*

- TAKE ME HOME, COUNTRY ROADS *Lana Del Rey*

- I NEED YOU Tim McGraw, *Faith Hill*

Welcome to
Vogel Springs
STAY A WHILE IF YOU CAN
EST. 1872

Wren

Chapter 1

running on empty

"**O**h my God, I thought you were dead."

Death. That's one solution.

"Where are you?" Anderson's high pitch tells me he's really actually worried about me.

I glance out my window as big, round, golden bales of hay fly by to the horizon. "I'm not sure. Flat. Open. Big Sky. Hay bales."

"So, basically anywhere from Iowa to Abilene. Then let's back this up. Where have you been the past three weeks? Have you been back home yet?"

"Sure. Mom and I went shopping, had a lovely time. Dad and I went skeet shooting, and after, he gave me Gran-Gran's heirloom necklace."

"You little bitch. You haven't been home yet. You've been hiding all this time."

"Not hiding, Anderson. Just..."

"Running?"

"Let's go with... driving." I glance up, into my rearview mirror, at the eighteen-wheeler on my ass who thinks he wants to pass me. I push the accelerator to the limit of my next-to-limitless Maserati GranCabrio V8 and make a decision for him.

"Dammit, Wren."

"Okay, okay. Denver. Taos. Santa Fe."

"Are you headed home now?"

No way in hell.

"You can't run forever."

"Who says?"

"Me, for one, because if you needed an escape, I thought you would have come to me. Instead, it's been crickets since that last text."

Wait a minute. "I didn't text you."

"No. You didn't."

Phillip. My heart flutters as it pitfalls to my stomach. Damn, those half-assed, tainted flutters. Even my butterflies know something went wrong there and hesitate to fully take flight. "Phillip texted you? Why? When?"

"A week ago. He said he and your parents were worried. He wanted to know if you were with me."

I fight the panic clawing up my throat. "What did you tell him?"

"The truth. That I didn't have a fucking clue, and I hadn't heard from you. I was a good little boy, so don't you think it's time you tell me what happened?"

"Did my dad call?" My voice lingers. It echoes through my head at a hauntingly familiar, child-like pitch.

The roar of wind speeding down the highway with my top down fills the silence of my best friend's absent answer. "Wren, whatever happened, he wasn't worth it."

Yes, he was. *I wasn't.*

"So you went and got a little bit broke up with... Is that it? Chickie, you get thrown, you get right back in the saddle. Or whatever bullshit you Texans say. I tried to tell you he was a cad from day one."

He did.

Anderson is nothing if not intuitive, even when he's wrong.

And I can't say he's entirely wrong this time. If he knew what happened, if I had told him... I guess that's the reason I didn't.

My eyes drift from the call screen to my windshield and out the window at the endless blue of wide-open spaces. Even with the frenzy in my head, and the broken flutter in my heart, there is something so calming about the miles I've traveled. The roadside, even the pastures, are arrayed in wildflowers of every color.

"Again, if you wanted to run away, you should have run to me." Anderson is as persistent as he is intuitive.

"It's not a bad idea. I'm not that far from Austin."

"I thought you didn't know where you were."

"I'm in Texas. These are Texas road signs. Anywhere I am, I'm sure I'm close enough."

"Not quite, Wren. Doll, I'm not in Austin. I told you three weeks ago I'd be in South Padre for sea turtle season."

"Sea turtles?"

"It's a thing. They have like a million babies in the sand. It's a big deal every year on Padre island."

"You hate nature."

He blows a loud huff into his phone and lowers his voice. "It's Hansen's thing."

Hansen? I scroll through my mental list of Anderson's torrid flings. "Please tell me you're not dating somebody named after a boy band."

"I think it's precious."

"I could see how you would. Okay. Padre, here I come."

"Obviously." Anderson hangs up. His classic move. We never say goodbye. It keeps our conversations ongoing, alive, and always active.

I love that about him. He is the only constant in my life, even when I try to duck away from him.

Guilt creeps in, and I feel a little bad for the eighteen-wheeler I crushed. Pulling into the right lane with a sigh, I slow down and let him have the win. The sun is brighter, pelting through my windshield, and I need to pull over and stop soon to pee anyway.

Maybe one rest stop, 'Here I come,' first?

Something pops.

A raucous rattle.

What is that sound?

On second thought, I don't think the sound is my problem.

The loud rattle that just ricocheted off a foreign-to-me-popping sound simmers to a dull, terrifyingly sustainable clattering as I continue to press my accelerator to no avail.

I check the rearview for cars on my ass. Crap. I let the only one in sight fly by me with honors. Dammit. *What's happening to my car?*

I take my foot off the accelerator and listen as it slows and sputters to a dull roar. It's coasting to a quiet hissing sound.

Is it the heat? Did I literally burn rubber?

No. This is definitely a problem.

Kicking off my platform sandals, placing the ball of my bare foot on the accelerator, and pressing as hard as I can, my car only climbs to a painful twenty miles per hour.

I have no control over the speed whatsoever.

Pull over, Wren. Just pull over.

I try to coach myself into doing the safe thing, only there isn't anything in sight but open road with barely a shoulder to pull onto. Maybe I can coast to something?

My controller system, car-computer-thingy flashes with every engine light and warning button available to it. *Nice touch, Maserati.* I wasn't certain something was dire just yet. Thank you for making my car have a panic attack before I do. Now I know.

And... the screen goes black.

So much for OnStar. And Bluetooth.

The sun bears down on my chest, and I sweat in my tank top. Turning the air conditioner off in ninety-plus-degree weather may have been extreme. Still, sounds are coming from my car I can't explain.

Now it feels like someone opened an oven door and put my head inside, and not in the suicide way. No, the extreme heat and burning way.

However, cutting the air and now the radio off have given me some semblance of conserving whatever energy I'm coasting on, as I drift down the first exit I see. And it's an exit to nowhere I see.

I kill the engine next to a rather charming hay bale. Charming in the sense that someone had to make it or bale it... thus, a sign of life.

Oh, it's fine. Everything's fine.

I've never worried about this sort of thing. There's always someone around to help. Any minute, a kind stranger will pull up, or a family taking the exit will drive right to me.

Maybe the eighteen-wheeler will feel guilty for flipping me off and turn around to come check on me. He has to know I'd be behind him again by now. Shit.

WrenB: Do you have Triple A?

Anderson: Come again?

"Mas...er ...a...ti!" I scream into my phone, enunciating as slowly and clearly as possible for the third time.

"And what year is your Mazda?" The lady on the other end of the line is trying to help, but the connection is terrible.

That, and my ear is being seared by my hot phone. It's going to burn my flesh before she gets my location. I'm shocked the thing hasn't completely overheated.

"It's not a Mazda. Who cares? Could I just get someone out here as soon as possible?"

"The closest tow service is ninety minutes away."

"I'm so sorry, ma'am. You're breaking up a bit. I almost thought you said ninety minutes."

"Yes, that's correct."

"Umm. With all due respect, a heat stroke will take me out in less than ninety minutes."

"Ma'am, we'll get a rental car your way so you don't have to wait for the tow. Do you have anyone in mind for a mechanic you'd like to be towed to while I look up the available rental car?"

Sweat drips down my back as I process what the woman just asked me. "I'm so sorry, but I have no idea where I am. You're asking me to abandon my three-hundred-thousand-dollar car on the side of the road—which, at this point... for a restroom, I'm one thousand percent okay with—because I really have to pee. But no, I don't have a mechanic in mind."

"Looks like Bass Pit Stop is about seven miles away. It's showing as the closest repair shop that's open. Would you like me to let them know you're coming?"

"Yes, please, and thank you very much."

"I'll transfer you to the rental car. They pick up within a ten mile radius."

"But wait... Is there one within ten miles?"

"Hold please."

Tears. Should I just start crying? Would that make something work out? Although, at this point, I've sweated out every bodily fluid available to me.

"Easy Ride in Rockridge. It's a fine day to rent. How may I help ya?"

"Oh thank goodness. God bless you, a local."

Good job Wren. Way to let the young chipper man, and possibly the last human you will ever speak to again, know that his Southern accent is so thick you recognize him as someone within a ten mile radius of burning hell.

"Local as you can get if you call Rockridge home."

"I can't say that I do, but I'm positive I'm missing out. Thank you for answering. I'm afraid you're my last hope. I was transferred from Triple A, and I need to be picked up and driven to my car, which should be towed to the mechanic within the next eighty-six minutes. Are you within a ten mile radius of me?"

"Where's the mechanic?"

"Umm. I don't know, but she said it's called Bass Pit Stop, like Bass Pro Shop, I'm guessing."

"Oh sure. Yeah, you're just outside of Vogel Springs."

"Vogue what?"

"Vogel Springs. It's just a town over from Rockridge."

"Is that a problem?"

"Nope. You're within the ten miles of us."

"Thank you so much." I wipe the sweat off my brow in pure relief, marking the official end of my panic mode. "I'm so relieved. It's funny, normally I'm such an easy going person. I get accused of going with the flow too much... it's just, there was no flow here in... what was that again, Vogel–"

"Springs, ma'am. And, I assure you there's plenty of flow in that town."

Ugh. Whatever that means.

"I said the miles weren't your problem. But, ma'am, we close in five minutes. It's a half-day today."

"What? What does that mean, like a bank?"

"No, like we hit our quota yesterday and 99% of our bookings are out for the weekend after being picked up this morning. Cars won't return until Sunday night. So it's a half-day today."

"But it's Thursday."

"Yup."

"Okay, you said 99%, so you have at least one car left, right?"

"We don't stay open for one percent, and even if I could get to you in five minutes, you've got about what, eighty-one more minutes before the tow truck arrives, if he's on time. Our rules state that we only give courtesy rides to the vehicle, meaning I can only drive you to your vehicle at the auto shop. And your vehicle won't be there until I'm home enjoying my half-day off."

"So...Wait! I don't understand... there's nothing I can do?"

"You can wait for the tow truck and in seventy-nine minutes from now, ride with him and your car to Bass Pit Stop. It's the best shop around. Hud will take care of you. Good night."

Click.

Please add, terrible judge of character to my list of attributes. That and no bladder—as in, mine will burst any moment now.

And, who the hell is Hud? What kind of name is Hud? I can't possibly want him taking care of me, not after my luck in these parts.

Of all the times for Anderson to escape. Damn Hansen and the sea turtle he rode in on.

Priorities: Restroom.

I Google 'Bass P'… and my search is inundated with all the Bass Pro Shops in West Texas. Awesome.

How about trying 'auto repair Vogel Springs, Tx'?

"Hot dog!" I shout to my hay bale friend, and press call on the number for Bass Pit Stop like my life depends on it. My bladder's life does.

The truth is after the array of uncanny events from On Star, Triple-A, and Easy Ride—Bass Pit Stop is my final lifeline. He may just be the most important phone call I make. Please don't let him be closed.

"Bass Pit. This is Hud."

"Hud." My voice is a breathy combination of recognition, relief, and… a bit awe-struck over his deep, sexy voice. "Hello?"

Now I'm clearly hallucinating from the heat and from having to go so badly. *Say something, Wren.* I take a breath to respond, but my phone responds for me with a blinking dead battery symbol just before the screen goes black.

"*AAAAAAAAAAAH!*" A beat goes by as my scream bounces off the white rock hills. The hay bale does not respond.

Hud

Chapter 2

hot snowflake

Sick of guess-what-the-hell-I-mean-texts, I dial my cousin, who owns Texas Towing. "Very funny, dickhead." Travis is constantly jerking someone's chain. It can get old, especially on an afternoon as hot as this one, when I'm busy.

"It's not a joke," he says. "I'm pullin' a Maserati GranCabrio—"

"Fuck," I groan.

"Woah, man. We got a lady on board."

I stalk to the shop refrigerator, snatch an icy cold can of soda, and pop the top. "Would that be the same lady who told Triple A she drives a Mazda?"

"That wasn't me!" A woman shrieks over Travis' Bluetooth. "The lady I talked to kept saying Mazda, and I kept telling her it's a Maserati. What's the big deal anyway? A car's a car, right? Engine. Four tires. Stopped running. Needs fixed."

I choke on my swallow and sputter.

When I finally clear the acidic soda from my nostrils and wipe the sticky syrup from my upper lip onto my shirt sleeve, I yell back, "Do you realize the difference between a Mazda and a Maserati?"

"I feel certain you will soon enlighten me," she snips.

I cover the phone while I finish clearing my windpipe, but I can't throttle the nasty laugh that gurgles out. "Ma'am, the difference between what you drive and a Mazda is the difference between Secretariat and a plow horse."

"What?"

I close my eyes and shake my head. This woman has so much money, she doesn't know what she's got. "Lady, you're driving one of the fastest, finest, most expensive automobiles in the world and I can't even *imagine* what you did to break a vehicle like that, but getting parts for a Maserati GranCabrio can take days. I mean—*days*. Maybe weeks." And fuck only knows what they'll cost, and I've got to pay when I order them and wait for her to pay me.

"Days? I don't have days."

"Darlin', you're driving a Maserati. You've got nothing but time and money."

"Don't call me darlin'," she huffs. "How condescending."

Oh, brother. I roll my eyes. A snowflake. This woman isn't offended by me saying she has nothing but time and money. She doesn't like being called darlin'.

"What would you like for me to call you?" I've got a few choices in mind.

"My name is Wren Baldwin. And if you don't have the right part available, all you have to do is send for it from Dallas. That's where we got it. They have the parts."

I polish off the soda and crush the aluminum can in my hand, chunking it into the metal trash can. "Miss... or Mrs. Baldwin..."

"Miss," she interrupts.

"*Miss* Baldwin, depending on what's wrong with your car, the Dallas dealership may have to send to Italy for the parts."

She. Hasn't. Got. A. Fucking. Clue.

'Don't call me darlin', how condescending... You can just send for it.' I may throttle her before this is over.

"We'll be there in a few," Travis interrupts. "You two can fight about it then." He disconnects the Bluetooth.

Great.

I take pride in keeping my place clean for the customers, but it's still a friggin' garage with a Ram diesel mud truck up on the lift, an old Chevy farm truck I just finished changing the oil on, and I told Mrs. Sanderson she could bring her Buick by this afternoon since her air conditioner's not blowing cold enough to suit her.

I'm wearing half the grease and grit that Ted Spencer's mud truck had on it when he brought it in this morning, after mounting three of his four new tires, and Little Miss La-tee-dah Baldwin is about to waltz in here all high and mighty, sneering with her nose turned up, going, *"Eeewwww. Yuk."*

Fuck.

Oh, man. I'm in love. Look at that thing.

Travis pulls up to the shop with a brand new, pearl white Maserati GranCabrio convertible in tow. What. A. Beauty.

I can't take my eyes off of it. Looks like she's got a white leather interior. Who in the hell buys white leather? It's impossible to keep clean. But I guess if you can afford a Maserati, you can afford to hire people to keep it clean.

What did she do to this car?

How do you ruin a three-hundred-thousand-dollar vehicle with a V-8 engine that'll go from zero to sixty in four seconds? That thing tops out at around 200 miles an hour. Did she suck a small animal into the manifold?

I'm lost admiring the automotive masterpiece when the passenger door on Travis's cab flies open and a pint-size woman with wild strawberry blonde hair jumps out before he comes to a complete stop, beelining for the front door as fast as she can go, clenching her thighs together.

That sight prompts an unexpected laugh.

I'm waiting inside the air-conditioned lobby, holding out the restroom key, trying to throttle my chuckling, when my nightmare swings the glass front door open.

She stops abruptly, staring from the key to me, her jaw sagging.

"You need to go? Right?"

She keeps staring.

I jiggle the key in front of her face. "They said you were desperate for a restroom. Here's the key." I tilt my head toward the ladies' room. "You're safe. It's clean."

Still, this delicate woman stands rooted to the spot, gaping at me with wide, hazel eyes, pink pouty lips... so pink they're almost stained red from her time in the sun. Long, wild, wind-blown hair falls below her shoulders.

No way in hell I can stop this grin any longer.

She looks like she's been through the wringer. "Are you okay? It's Wren, right? The Triple A people said you needed to go." Once again, I rattle the key. "Go."

She takes the key cautiously as if I might bite her, her focus cemented on my eyes.

Is she afraid of me?

Little freckles dot not only her nose, but her cheeks and shoulders. And I can only guess I'm staring at a few new ones after her time in the sun. There's not a cloud between Amarillo and the Gulf.

Watching her scurry to the ladies' room, I've got to give her this: Little Miss Wren Baldwin is the human embodiment of her car—rich as hell and fucking beautiful.

Wait.

What's that white streak trickling down the middle of her calf?

I laugh out loud again. *She's got a fake spray tan.*

"Dude. What about the chili pepper, plus hot car, plus chick didn't you understand? Duh." Travis pulls my attention away from staring at the ladies' room door where my new, obnoxious but drop-dead-gorgeous customer disappeared. He blabbers on as he helps himself to a free soda. "I tried to warn you. The car and the chick are both smokin'."

"To each his own."

Travis lifts his baseball cap, wipes his sweaty forehead on his shirt sleeve, and lowers his voice to whisper. "Horse shit. You'd have to be blind *not* to think she's a total babe." He elbows me and winks. "And you can get under the hood of both."

"Are you fifteen? She's a customer."

Travis snickers again. "You tellin' me you wouldn't like a taste of that?"

I aim my arm at the ladies' room. "That is a rich, spoiled brat who won't be in town long enough for anyone to get under her hood even if they wanted to. Which I don't."

Wren

Chapter 3

no lifebuoy

Peeing a lake's worth? Expected. I stand from my seated position and peer around. A restroom this clean? Totally unexpected. I didn't even have to put paper down on the seat.

I catch a glimpse of myself in the medicine cabinet-sized mirror that looks freshly polished. Stunning. I'm dirtier than an auto repair shop restroom.

To be fair, this one is oddly immaculate.

I brush stray hair from my face and pull the sticky, wet strands from the nape of my neck, trying to fluff my wavy locks a little. Forget the hair. I should be checking for pit stains, splotches where my skin caught on fire out there, or got pecked by buzzards.

That's when it hits me... also unexpected: Hud. Six feet plus of tall, dark, handsome asshole.

Good night.

Who knew Bass Pit Stop housed the town sex pot and, apparently, my car offends him. His eyes. Holy moly. Now, those are offensive, if not dangerous. Frosty gray, set off by long, dark, thick eyelashes that I'd pay money for. Dark brows—his bronzed skin—everything about him draws your eyes to his. It's criminal.

Too bad he's an absolute ass.

One would think bringing someone business warrants a decent attitude, at the very least. So much for hospitality. I try to calm my thoughts along with my wild hair.

Get it together, Wren. The only mechanic in town is being an obnoxious brute for no reason. I'm still light-headed from my 90 minutes in what felt like 175-degree heat, and to hear him tell it, my car needs an Italian engineer to get back running.

As my dad would say, I've been caught with my pants down. My failure to plan... *bla, bla, bla*—bastard. I do have a plan, Daddy, and it involves a V8 engine that I need running ASAP.

I ignored Anderson's original invite to South Padre weeks ago because it felt a little too close to home. I wanted to be as far away from Dallas as I could get. And now, I break down even closer.

If I hadn't had life errands to return to, I'd still be in Colorado or well on my way to San Francisco. Maybe Napa. Anywhere but Texas. Turns out the state is not as big as they say.

My stomach turns.

I don't know if I'm hungry or getting an ulcer again. I take a deep breath. I'm miles away from anyone who could recognize me. I can enjoy that win. My car will be fine. It's made to run. It just needs a little tune-up. I'll catch up to Anderson, and we'll pick another place to go after Padre.

I lean toward a bottle of grapefruit and vanilla hand soap. I can't help but smile over the image in my head of the grease-covered bar of red Lifebuoy soap that is supposed to be there.

Ahh, that's actually kind of—

Three quick, loud raps on the restroom door make me jump. "You fall in?"

Ugh. That voice does nothing for me now. I open the door to find Travis, the tow trucker, standing in my way.

"Oh... sorry... I, uh, got another ding and have to head out. Just wanted to make sure you didn't need a ride to the rental car place." His eyes are tracing me up and down. There's the grime and grease I expected to find in the restroom.

"The one in Rockridge?" I hit the bathroom light off and charge confidently toward him.

"That'd be the only one we got around here." His voice trails off as he steps back from crowding my space, glancing over his shoulder so he doesn't trip.

"Yeah, well, apparently that one closes around like, eight a.m. so I'm afraid you and I are both off the hook."

A low chuckle surfaces from the garage, where I see Hud standing above a computer. At least the jerk has a sense of humor. If only that means he's an exceptional mechanic.

"Alright then. You okay here?"

"She's fine, Travis." The voice answers for me, the deep, smooth one I remember from when I called the shop.

"Don't worry. You're in good hands with Hud." Travis salutes in Hud's direction and heads out the front door to his tow truck.

"So I've heard." I can't help the hint of sarcasm that laces my statement as I watch Travis start the tow truck and drive my last lifeline away—the lifeline I waited ninety minutes for, standing by my car in the heat like a buzzard circling its prey, waiting for it to die.

Only I'm not sure who was the vulture and who was the prey in my scenario. Again. Heat stroke.

"Any luck?"

"Excuse me?" Hud looks up from his computer with serious eyes.

"Can you get the part?"

"The part? Lady, I don't even know what you did to the damn thing, much less what part or parts you might need, and I've got three cars in front of yours before I can take a real look, or even begin to run a diagnosis."

He steps toward me from the computer.

I step back and swallow a breath.

"You want a water?"

I look up at him in recognition of what he offers, still processing what he just said about my car. My gaze shifts to all the cars parked in his garage in mid-service, and I take a defeated step back to sink into a lobby seat across from his desk. "I'll take a Coke."

He huffs and shakes his head as he walks away from me.

"I mean... a machine. If you could direct me to a Coke machine, I'll be fine." I press my lips closed as a bright red familiar can presents in front of my face, silencing me.

The can of Coke is ice-cold and dripping.

I look up to thank him as a drop of sweat slides from the can onto my chest. Damn him and his on-hand Coca-Cola products. I can't catch a break. "Thank you."

Hud shakes his head as he turns back to his desk.

"What's so funny?" I have to ask.

"Nothing. You're just very specific. Like your car."

I take a long swig of the best Coke I've ever tasted in my entire life, trying to hide the smile creeping across my face, but it advances into a chuckle.

"What's so funny to you?" he spouts, still facing me from where I originally stopped him in his tracks.

"It's just that my car may be the only specific thing about me. Sorry—I wasn't being a butt, just jonesing for a Coke. Have you ever been so hot that a Coke's the only thing that sounds good?"

"Every day of the summer." He doesn't smile, but his face looks like it wants to.

"Or you know, when you've been sick and can't keep anything down or haven't eaten for days, it's like a Coke is the first thing you want on the day you feel better." I take another sip to shut my aimless chatter.

The truth is I'm exhausted, I have to be dehydrated, and it just feels good to sit down for a second now that I'm in, well, a version of civilization.

I don't have my druthers yet, and I'm certain when I come to my senses, I'll charge my phone and figure out what to do next.

Hud looks toward my car, then types something else into his computer. "Where were you headed?"

A small laugh escapes as I answer, "South Padre?"

"I see," he smirks.

"Why? Is the spring break in me that obvious?"

"No. It's not the season." Hud shifts his gaze from his computer, right into mine. There are ten feet between us, but his stare is so intense I can feel it. "I'm thinking more along the lines of turtles. Arribada," he says.

"Arribada?" Shit. My voice is breathy again. How the hell does he know about the sea turtles?

"It's Spanish for arrival by sea. Kemp's Ridley sea turtles. They're native to Texas. We're the only state where they're native. Thousands of female Kemps travel through the Gulf every year to nest on South Padre. They return to the same spot every year." A piece of dark hair drapes down the side of Hud's forehead as his grey eyes stay locked on me, unmoved by the distraction.

"Right. That's exactly why I was going. How'd you know?"

"Because it's their season, and you look a little old for spring break." Hud returns to his keyboard.

My God. I don't know whether I'm offended or impressed.

This guy is smooth, and I should probably keep him away from Anderson with all his turtle talk.

Shit. Anderson. He's probably worried sick. I slide my dead phone out of the pocket of my cut-offs. My eyes drift from my dull black screen to Hud. My bottom lip twitches.

Is there a chance I have too much pride to ask? Absolutely not. "Umm..."

"Here." Hud opens his desk drawer without acknowledging me further and pulls out a bright yellow cord. He walks slowly around the desk toward me and plugs it into the outlet by my chair.

"Thank you. Really."

"It's not mine. People leave them here all the time."

"Lucky me."

The ding of his shop bell slices through the tension and I look up as a middle-aged man in jeans, boots, and a cowboy hat waves and steps toward Hud.

"She ready yet?" The man asks with a proud inflection in his voice.

"I'll let you be the judge." Hud tosses the man a set of keys from the desk drawer. "Come on back, Mr. Wilkins."

Happy to discover the charger works, I drop it and my connected phone into my lap to let it get enough juice to turn on, watching as the customer follows Hud into the main garage.

My eyes drift up to the muted TV in the corner, and from my peripheral, I think I see Hud look back at me as he holds the door open for the man.

Still here. Where does he possibly think I could go?

My eyes tire of the silent news station on a loop. I glance around the well-kept lobby. It's retro and modern at the same time—clean, like the restroom. Business cards fill a bulletin board, all neatly thumbtacked in order—as if they were posted with pride.

The bulletin board hangs above a gumball machine. It looks like it has the good big gumballs, the ones that were worth your whole quarter when you were a kid.

Text messages begin to filter in, dinging in my lap louder than Hud's shop bell:

Anderson: Call me back. Where are you Wren? Don't make me worry!

Anderson: P.S. Your father called.

No, he didn't. He never does. My phone battery is only three percent and I don't think I can reach this little yellow cord to my ear. I'll give it more time to juice up before I relieve my best friend.

He deserves to worry a little longer after that last text. That was a low blow.

A yawn escapes me, and I slump deeper into the theater seat-style chair. Maybe they were theater seats once... if this town was ever big enough to have a movie theater.

I yawn longer this time, as I allow my eyes to close, agreeing to rest them for a minute.

"Call me back. Where are you, Wren?" Anderson's messages replay in my head. They've been the theme of our friendship lately. *"Don't make me worry... Your dad called."*

Him, worrying about me. If I'm tired of it, I know Anderson's got to be exhausted... I'll make it up to him. I've just got to get...

"Wren! Where are you going? You can't just take off!" I don't want to leave Anderson. He doesn't even know why I have to yet.

"*I don't give a damn! No daughter of mine is going to cause all this hell, make a mockery of me, and not show up the next day. I want her ass in the chair, at that desk come Monday morning, or that's it!*" Daddy always gets what he wants, except from me, and that's why he hates me.

"*I'm sorry—Wren, please. Let me explain. Don't cut me completely off. There's nothing I could do. It's better for you this way, too... your dad—*" A door slams in Phillip's face and I stand alone on the other side of it.

Hud

Chapter 4
break or brake?

Taking a break from mounting tires, I check on my little nightmare. She's fallen asleep, curled up like a pretzel in one of those old theater chairs I bought for the lobby. She's drooling. Her long, tangled hair drapes to the seat. Poor kid. Part of me wants to empathize with her, but how can I?

I have no idea how women think.

Women. Shit.

I'm not filthy rich and I've never been stranded in some strange place because I don't go wandering off to parts unknown, and I keep my vehicles running. But then, I know how.

She doesn't. That's not her fault. Maybe I was too hard on her.

I try to put myself in her place—stranded in the middle of nowhere, her cell phone's dead. Gotta pee like a racehorse.

That brings another surprise chuckle from my chest. Damn, she was cute walking with her thighs squeezed together, trying to keep from wetting her shorts.

I'd have pissed on the side of the road. No big deal. She should have—would have saved herself a whole lot of misery. But I guess she's a lady. Ladies don't squat on the side of the road with no toilet paper.

I catch myself chuckling again.

Wren Baldwin. Who the hell named their daughter Wren? Maybe it's a nickname.

Anyone who drives a car like that must exist on a whole other plane of life from the rest of us.

For some unknown reason, I think of that movie, *To Kill a Mockingbird*, where the guy tells his daughter 'you can't know a man until you walk in his shoes.' I don't know Wren Baldwin. I can't even imagine walking in her little platform sandals, having the money to buy a Maserati.

We're all products of our upbringing. *Upbringing*.

I wipe sweat that's stinging my eyes. I'm doing everything in my power to preserve my upbringing. What was handed down to me, I want to hand down to mine. But it's getting harder by the day.

Maybe that's it.

Maybe, on first blush, rich little Miss Wren Baldwin and her shiny white Maserati represent everything I'm fighting. Maybe I had my hackles up from the mention of Maserati.

"Hud?"

I glance from the KM3 I'm mounting to the voice. Ted's right on time. "This is the last tire. You can have her back in just a minute." I should have had his new tires mounted thirty minutes ago. "I'd have finished sooner, but I got sidetracked."

Ted hooks his thumb over his shoulder with a smug grin that produces his dimple. "Let me guess. Sidetracked by that Maserati?"

"Yep."

I get busy tightening the lug nuts on this last tire, the pneumatic wrench whirring as Ted steps closer to admire the luxury, Italian-made convertible, yelling over the high-pitched whine of the wrench, "Damn, man, that thing looks brand new! What's wrong with it?"

I holler back. "Haven't had a chance to check it out!"

"Who's the owner?"

The wrench falls silent. "From Dallas. Broke down driving through. Travis towed her in."

Several seconds of silence linger as I gather the last lug nut, and Ted harrumphs. "Speaking of Dallas—are you still?"

"Yeah."

Ted takes a step closer. "I gotta say it, man. Lots of people are excited about that plant being built here."

I straighten and meet Ted eye to eye. "Then let them sell their land for it."

"But you've got the water, Hud."

Letting the wrench slide to the floor, I take a step toward the chunky owner of this mud truck, feeling my pulse pounding in my neck. "That fucking company has the money to build their own reservoir, so they can build it somewhere else. Anywhere else. I'm not selling land that's been in my family for a hundred years."

Ted's round face is frozen, his dark eyes wider than normal. As he steps back, holding his hands up in surrender, I realize my fists are clenched.

"Sorry." I open and flex my hands, taking a step away to pick up the wrench. "Give me five minutes, Ted, and the truck is yours."

Ted's not my enemy. He's a friend. We grew up together. He's just warning me what others are whispering. I've caught the hushed mutterings in the cafe a couple of times. It's been in the paper.

A company that makes batteries for electric cars wants to build a plant outside Vogel Springs and for whatever reason, the cock-suckers have decided my property is the only suitable spot to build.

"It's okay, Hud. Whatever you decide. I just thought... maybe you didn't realize."

"I realize. I'm not trying to keep people from having new jobs, I'm just not going to sell my land so it can happen." I find a clean rag to wipe sweat sliding down the back of my neck. "When Dad passed, the one thing he asked of me was, 'Don't sell the land.' I made him a promise. I intend to keep it."

Ted nods and tugs on his pants, which have slide below his belly, as I divert this dead-end conversation. "Are you going to enter this truck in the Mud Bash?"

"Yeah."

I take in his Ram 2500. "She's a good one, but let me give the suspension a once-over ahead of time. Just to be sure. It'll be on me."

"Ten-four."

"Get a drink out of the fridge. I'll wrap this up and get your keys."

Ted heads to the office to pay.

"Don't worry about it today. We'll settle up tomorrow."

He turns around to give me a curious stare.

"If we go in the lobby, we'll wake Tweety Bird. She looks like she needs the nap she's having."

"Tweety Bird?" Ted steps to the glass lobby door, peering in at Wren.

"The owner of the Maserati. Her name is Wren. I think she's on the verge of a breakdown herself."

He whistles again as he twists his neck. "Damn, man. Which one is the hottest? The convertible or the owner?"

"You asked what happened to the car?" I aim my arm toward the sleeping beauty. "She did, I'm guessing."

Wren
Chapter 5
Local Flair

"Wren." It's a man's voice in a tunnel, then a loud snap in my ear.

"My God. Did you make that sound with your fingers?" I scootch up from apparently making myself at home in the lobby seat. One leg is stretched in front of me, and I use the hand previously tucked under my neck to wipe what feels like drool off my chin.

I must have dozed off. Hud's face is right beside mine, and he obviously knelt down here to wake me. I am so embarrassed.

"There you are. Look, I've got two left in front of yours before I close shop for the day. I'm hoping to at least run your test so we know what we're in for, but I can't promise. And even if I could, you've got a while yet. Why don't you head across the street and grab a bite to eat? There's a cafe with anything your little heart desires."

I sit up straight, moving away from him.

He straightens, standing above me. "Can't have you loitering around here anyway. Bad for business." Hud tilts his head as the corners of his mouth lift into a smile.

Bad for business, my ass. Have you seen my ass? Okay, Wren. Get up.

You're drooling, you have sweat stains under your armpits, and your stomach was probably growling the entire time you napped, which may be why he woke you.

Yikes. I stand and stretch and grab my tote bag, glancing through the garage area at my beautiful traitor of a car.

"Don't worry. She'll be here when you get back. And do come back. I usually close at six, but I'm so backed up, you've got 'til about seven at least. That's when I lock up. Just want to warn you, in case you get to shopping or..."

"Oh, are there great shops around here?" I can't help my hopeful smile.

"No." Hud shakes his head. "Not at all."

His shop bell dings as the door closes behind me. It's becoming an all too familiar ding.

I wince when the sun hits my face, realizing I left my sunglasses in the tow truck. And when Hud mentioned a cafe across the street... he meant the cafe across the street—as in the one and only.

A wide smile spreads across my face as I take in the tiny town. Old-fashioned brick storefronts connect with colorful flowers in hanging baskets that withstand the heat to greet me.

Wow. This place is like a storybook.

Old men are having coffee on the porch of what looks like a hardware store to the far left, and a red pickup truck full of high school kids with gear packed for the lake whistle and shout from the truck bed as they speed away from the four-way stop.

There's not even a traffic light. The small, dull, lifeless town is anything but dull and lifeless. It springs to existence in front of me. Was this going on the whole time I was drooling in the repair shop?

Four middle-aged women shut their car doors and head into a place called Mueller's. Their studded handbags, big hair, and jewelry make me smile from across the street.

Mueller's Cafe. That must be the food place.

Beyond the stretch of local shops and what might be a post office lies a back road connected to the four-way stop boasting the town's coveted sign, "Welcome to Vogel Springs. Stay a while if ya can!"

The backdrop for the sign is what catches my eye, more than what feels like a personalized welcome. A beautiful Victorian-style home stands tall, demanding, and slightly out of place with the typical houses I would expect to line the backroads of a middle-of-nowhere town like this.

In other words, the town might not make the map, but that beauty would.

A look to my right conjures up a Dollar General Store. There's a first for everything, and I'm down for a pair of sunglasses. Pivoting on the ball of my platform sandals, a second wind has me all but skipping next door to check out the town merch.

Ding-a-lingggg!

If this town were a Christmas movie, seventeen angels got their wings today from my part alone. Does every door in every shop in this town have the exact same bell?

Beaming from ear to ear below a bell that sounds identical to the one at the Pit Stop, the Dollar General, and now the cafe, I step into Mueller's, breathing in a whiff of home-cooked deliciousness.

It quite nearly brings me to my knees. I'd forgotten how hungry I was.

Well, I remembered in the Dollar General when I purchased three bags of sour straws, two packs of peach gummies, a Cow Tale, a handful of banana Laffy Taffies, and a Tootsie Roll Pop in each available flavor in addition to three pairs of sunglasses. And a phone charger.

In my defense, they're all still in their bags and wrappers. Should any of the natives have cause to peek in my tote, they'll think I robbed the place.

My eyes widen as I stare up at the Specials' board. The 'Please Seat Yourself' sign is lost on me, as they had me at chicken fried steak. I especially appreciate that it's written in permanent marker as if it is the daily special always.

As hellacious as this day has been, I feel as if I've stumbled into heaven. A heaven of air conditioning and white gravy. Yum...

Still staring, I neglect to notice I'm the 'Chicken Fried Steak' sign for others, as in everyone else in the cafe. My eyes drop and graze the onlookers. Granted, it's not a lot of people. I must be here in that awkward, 'well after lunchtime, not quite dinner rush' slot.

A pair of muddy work boots in front of me step back, forcing me to sidestep another man wearing striped overalls tucked into similar weathered boots. He shoves his wallet into his deep pocket after, apparently, picking up the tab for him and his buddy.

Railroad guys, I can tell by the logo on their caps. Atchison, Topeka, and Santa Fe railroad tracks crisscross West Texas with freight trains almost long enough for people to eat lunch at their crossings. I may have once or twice.

The rude one who backed into me doesn't even look my way, while the other grabs a toothpick and makes a show of eyeing me up and down as he chews on it like a piece of hay.

"Y'all be good now. Martha, Genevieve." The men walk out, grabbing their packed to-go meals, and a woman in her fifties or sixties waves at them from behind the kitchen window.

I listen as she hollers at her kitchen staff, asking why they're "Eight-six the Housemaid Ranch Dressing," and she's got to go uptown to buy the nasty bottled stuff before dinner shift.

I can't quite guess her age, as her voice is older, gruff, and wise, but her energy is younger than the waitress's, who's been eye-balling me since I walked through the door. That one dusts her hands on her apron and goes back to her task as if she has no intention of helping me. Her almost black hair is gathered in a low ponytail that hangs down one shoulder, and her dark blue eyes are round and scolding with each calculated glance she lifts my way.

Before they catch me staring back, I notice a shadow box frame with a T-shirt folded neatly inside. The shirt is light green with a faded pink sunset that has Vogel Springs written in cursive across the front.

The shadow box frame is dusty, and I can barely make out the handwritten sign that has 'size small only left' above a large twelve-dollar price tag.

"I'll take it." I announce to the cafe in general.

"Excuse me?" The scowling dark-haired waitress looks up from marrying the bottles of ketchup.

"Ah, what's that, hun?" The woman yelling behind the open kitchen window looks at me, and the kitchen staff's eyes follow. You could hear a pin drop in the once-noisy cafe.

I look around and smile, pointing to the framed shirt. "I'll take one of those. In a size small."

There's a beat of silence.

The kitchen door swings open, banging back and forth, as the charming older woman flies out of it, dusting her hands on her waist-tied apron. Grey strands of hair interrupt her low black bun, pulled tight behind her neck, as she forges toward me. Her top-heavy body moves almost gracefully through the space she commands so well. "Well hell, honey, why didn't you say so?"

Her boisterous smile lights up the cafe, and I seem to score a point with the staff behind the window, as they are now off the hook with the ranch dressing they are out of.

"Genevieve, get over here and ring her up while I get this thing down."

"Can't. It's the last one. It's just for display."

"Oh, my God. Are you kidding me? Display for what? It's the only one we've got left. I've been trying to get rid of the damn thing for the last fifteen years."

The older woman climbs onto a step stool from behind the cash register, opens the case with a key, and reaches to pull the folded T-shirt from the boxed frame. "Now I've got a reason to order new ones. I'm Martha. Owner. Who might you be?"

"I'm Wren, and I'm starving."

"Ah. The Maserati."

"News travels fast."

"You have no idea, sweetheart. Glad you're gonna' to eat. Can't have you sporting my shirt if you've never tasted the food." Martha holds the shirt up and flips it over where the writing across the back reads: 1st Stop MUELLER'S CAFE. "It's got Mueller's on the back. That alright?"

"Well, it wasn't my first stop, but... close enough." I smile brightly.

"Oh, that's right. Hud was obviously your first stop. I mean, Bass Pit Stop."

"Yes." I nod an innocent smile, and Martha winks not-so-innocently.

The cool-eyed waitress in the background scowls even more deeply.

"What are you waiting for Genevieve? Get her a menu and take her order," Martha snaps.

I nestle in a wooden booth with a white and green checkered tablecloth. God Almighty, I hope this is the kind of place that leaves the potato skins on the ends of their fresh-cut French fries.

A menu plops down in front of me via a set of light purple, coffin-shaped acrylic nails, an old-school heirloom silver ring, and a couple of rubber bands and friendship bracelet-style rings.

Goth meets 90s Revival/ 'I used to be popular, too, in high school' is the vibe Genevieve gives off. That, and the daggers she shoots from her eye. Does she hate her job that much?

She death-stares at me. "Hud sent you over here?"

"Well, ah, it's the only restaurant in town, right?"

"And he's the one and only Mr. Fix It." She grabs my ketchup and salt and pepper caddy and centers it in front of me, robbing me of the ketchup bottle I assume she's taking to refill.

"He's a good one, right?" I ask humbly.

"Oh, he's the best. Just ask Rosalee."

"I'm sorry?"

"Nothin'. You know what you're havin'?"

"Umm, yeah, but mechanic, I mean—he's a good mechanic, right?"

"Yes. He's annoyingly the best." She delivers this as if it's a bad thing. Then again, she hasn't smiled once. "What'll it be?"

I look up at the chicken fried steak sign once more and catch Martha's smiling face landing on mine from the kitchen.

My belly is so full it's almost busting out of my new Vogel Springs T-shirt. I've developed a food baby since I freshened up and changed into the vintage-T.

I'm practically hobbling back to the shop, but man, that was good.

I pause at the four-way stop to look in all directions as a faint train whistle blows in the distance. Cicadas begin to sing, announcing the sun's impending departure. No offense to Anderson, but music like that, accompanying a West Texas sunset, may fascinate me more than sea turtles.

I turn at the sound of a loud thud across the street to see Hud stepping out of his shop, pulling the side garage door shut.

Guess he's locking up already.

"You weren't going to wait?" I shout from halfway across the street. I'm almost to him.

Hud turns to face me as if he already knows my voice and expects me there.

It hits me—déjà vu-like. Walking across the street and calling out to him feels like the most natural thing I've done—like I've done it before. I continue my stride toward him.

"You eat?" He asks, eyeing my new shirt closely in recognition.

An expression I can't stifle raises the corners of my mouth.

"Not the chicken fried steak?" he asks with pinched brows.

I nod.

"Liar. Where's your doggie bag?"

"Clearly we've just met." Sure. I'll play. "Sometimes I forget to eat, but when I remember... look out." I smile awkwardly.

My confidence in sharing either backfired, or broody-britches doesn't want to play anymore. I tilt my chin up to the open garage. "Any news?"

"No." And now he's back to being curt. Very curt.

"O...kay..."

"My machine doesn't speak Italian."

"What?"

"I put your car on the computer but so far, the two aren't communicating. I'll try again first thing in the morning." Hud turns to the side door with a ring of keys and locks the bolt.

"Tomorrow, then?" My voice comes out shaky.

"That's what I said." He looks at me over his shoulder, and his grey eyes soften. "We'll see what we're in for tomorrow." Hud nods.

It's not promising, but it's reassuring that he'll do what he can.

It stings that I don't have an update or better news to end the day, but what could I honestly expect? He's the only shop. He's busy. I'm lucky he can get to me tomorrow.

Hud reaches one arm up and pulls down a lever, closing the main garage door and the final glimpse of my Maserati.

I get a slight sinking feeling at the realization that I have nowhere to go, and I'm frankly embarrassed to ask the guy that thinks I'm some entitled brat for advice. Ugh. Why didn't I solve this sooner?

Screw it. I'm too exhausted to be humiliated. "Do you mind pointing me in the direction of a hotel?"

"Next town over."

I tilt my head in sincere confusion. "There's not one in this town?"

"Nope."

"What about when people come vis—"

"Nope."

I point to the large Victorian home diagonal to us. "A B&B?"

"Yeah. Good luck with that." Hud starts walking toward a large truck parked off to the side. It surprises me a little to watch him turn away from me to leave. "Come on. I'll drive you to the motel."

"Oh, that's okay. I can call an Uber."

"You could…" Hud raises an exaggerated eyebrow, and crickets literally chirp behind me.

"Oh. Got ya."

"Yeah, unless you're lucky enough to ding somebody in Austin who's bored enough to spend fifteen bucks just so they can make ten. Then you'd be waiting an hour or so for them to get here…"

I take a few timid steps, bridging the gap between us, and look up at him. He's so tall. And, still, alarmingly gorgeous. "Are you sure you don't mind?" It comes out softer and more hesitant than I intended.

I must look like a puppy dog trying to beg. Hud has this quality about him... even though I'm miffed that he's rude for no reason, I don't have it in me to inconvenience him. I don't know why, but I don't want to make something—anything—more difficult for him.

I suppose my car is exactly that: an inconvenience.

Now I am, too.

"Get in." Hud opens the door to his navy blue Ford-whatever-ton truck. It is massive, and very tall, like its owner.

I brace myself on one platform sandal, the straw base of my wedge wavering as I hike my other leg to climb in. I may have done better crawling up on all fours.

At this point, I have to consider my previous conversation with myself. For example, why am I worried about inconveniencing Hud, as opposed to climbing into a giant truck with a six-foot-two or three stranger who has already shown disdain for me?

"Choices, Wren. It's the choices we make that define a person." My dad's mantra cascades through my brain.

Is it? Or are we all just wired a little differently?

I push off my leg to hoist myself into the passenger side when I feel the base of my sandal tilt. I can't release my grip on the handle I'm holding onto for dear life, so I reach for the nearest thing I can grab with my other hand.

My fingers press into Hud's forearm as I swallow a gasp.

He must have stepped behind me when he saw me start to topple. Close behind me. His skin is hot to the touch on the palm of my hand, and I feel the heat of him standing so close.

Maybe I'm just feeling the heat of the day settling into night. Even with the sun going down, it still feels like 90 degrees out here, with no breeze whatsoever.

"Sorry." I catch my breath and turn my head in the direction of his extended forearm, not realizing how close his face is to mine.

Pulling myself up into the truck has put me much closer to his height. I think of anything I can say to break the tension or not be made fun of by him. "So this is what the weather's like up here?"

He lifts an eyebrow, helping me the rest of the way in. "Didn't know you needed a ladder."

I take a deep breath to relax as he closes my door.

Note to self: When eye level with the mechanic, do NOT look directly into his eyes. Talk about being thrown for a loop. Try being thrown from a horse.

His gaze is so intense. His beautiful eyes, almost silver...

Wrong thoughts. Please don't kill me and leave me for dead on a dirt road. Those are the proper thoughts when accepting a ride from a stranger in a truck the size of a modular home. Again. Wired differently.

Wren

Chapter 6

sound of bacon frying

The ride is quiet, but not an awkward silence at all. I keep my eyes locked on the window at the passing scenery. I'm quite curious when given the opportunity, and I don't want to nose around the cab of his truck and start asking nervous questions.

The two-lane highway whips past us as Hud drives with one arm on the wheel and the other propped in his window like these roads are second nature, and he could drive them blindfolded.

I fail to notice when the sun completely disappears, and all I see from my window are stars... Huge, bright, shining stars that give the song, *Deep in the Heart of Texas*, true meaning.

I grew up with these stars, but they were upstaged by the Dallas skyline.

Here, they are indescribable. Relentless in their pursuit, matching the truck's speed as they follow us into the black night. It's the first peace I've felt in weeks. Honestly months.

"It's just around the curve here. Rockridge is about a mile or two away. We're getting close." Hud breaks the silence for my benefit.

"I wasn't worried." The silence is awkward now. "Have you lived in the area all your life?" Here I go.

"Umm. I grew up in Vogel Springs if that's what you mean. I have also left town before."

"That's not what I meant. Family? Do you have roots keeping you here?"

"Roots you could say. My family's been here for four generations. My folks are gone now. They left everything to me. Land mostly. The Pit Stop, that's mine, and it doesn't *keep me*, I keep it."

"Let me guess, you became a mechanic because you've always been good with your hands."

Hud hikes a shoulder. "No. I believe that everything can be fixed, including your car, and I like to know what makes things tick. Your turn."

I look down at my hands lying sheepishly in my lap. I didn't expect him to trump me. "Although I may not be familiar with these particular parts, I'm just as Texan as you are, only by way of Dallas City Limits."

"I see. And roots?"

"None that would keep me there. Just the kind that—"

"Sent your car speeding down the highway to me?"

"Something like that."

I turn to look through his window as the lights of the next small town replace the black night. Hud's signal clicks on, and he turns us into a friendly-looking motel behind a large sign that reads: Rockridge Inn and Lodge.

The surrounding area is packed with cars, and several young men walk about in matching ball caps.

Hud scans the parking lot as he slowly inches his way through. "I don't think I've ever seen more than three cars parked at this place at once," he offers.

The largest truck I've ever been in slides into the only parking spot left with one smooth stroke of the wheel. Hud hops out, and after I realize he's not dropping me off but walking to my side to help me out, I'm determined to slide or crawl out before I embarrass myself again.

Hud sees my feet hit the ground, then he strides into the lobby of the motel with me racing to keep up. My painted red toenails pinch the pads of my sandals to keep them on as I all but run behind him.

A line of parents and teens in matching ball caps disperses toward the exit with take-out menus and local restaurant coupons as Hud and I make our way to the front desk.

"Fresh out of rooms. Sorry you two."

"Oh, no. We're not... together." I vomit my words fast and loudly at the short, grey-headed man, and he rightfully looks to Hud to continue the rest of the conversation, as I must seem crazy.

"Yeah, surely you have a single room. It's just for one." Hud nods toward me.

"No vacancy. The ball tournament cleaned us out. They'll be here 'til Sundy' evening. Some will check out Saturday by three, if they lose the heat. You're welcome to check back then."

I look up at Hud stunned and take a step back.

The lobby door dings.

That sound I enjoyed so much today infiltrates my ears as a forest-green-baseball-capped pre-teen slips through the lobby door with his kid sister.

The bells taunt me as the door sways shut again.

Ding, ding, ding. I. Have. No. Place. To. Go.

This isn't fun and games. A complete and total stranger just took his time driving me somewhere, and nothing is available.

This is... not how this is supposed to go.

I try to take a breath, but there is simply no air.

"Wren?" Someone says my name, but I can't hear anything or focus.

Dammit. What did I get into? Breathe.

Uh... Why can't I breathe?

Short, quick inhales and exhales pump from my lips, and I don't know if I'm helping myself or on the way to hyperventilating.

The lobby goes dark. I hear muffled words, but nothing is as loud as my heartbeat.

The bells muffle in the background as hot air hits my face from the parking lot.

I have no idea what's happening or what just happened, but I am one thousand percent in Hud's arms and being carried, bridal style, back to the truck.

Oh. My. God. Wow. Wren.

Just. Wow.

Realizing the summer air I feel is only on one side of my face, I come to understand my other cheek is plastered to a hard, warm chest.

I look up at Hud, his brow furrowed and face terrified. Our eyes lock.

"Hang on. Let's get you to the truck." Those words. That voice. He is my real lifeline today.

I shift modestly in his arms, mortified at what could have resulted in me needing to be carried, but Hud grips me tighter, letting me know he's got me and it's okay that he's carrying me.

I shock the hell out of myself when my body accepts the kind gesture as truth, and I nestle my face into him.

Into his smell.

His clean T-shirt smells freshly laundered, the soap on his skin, the summer on his skin. He smells like what women want men's cologne to smell like. Clean, fresh, rugged.

What? Did he shower before he locked up?

Is there some magic man-spa behind garage bay number two at the shop? Could be. The restroom was cleaner than the one in my apartment, and I have a cleaning service.

The door to the truck clicks open, and I'm gently hoisted inside.

Hud's grey eyes look me over quickly, then search my own as he reaches around me for the seatbelt.

I know that's what he's going for, but apparently, I need some other security. As his upper body surrounds mine in reach of the belt, I place my arms around him in an embrace so tight that I don't think he can pull away, even if he wants to.

Ever so gently, Hud releases the seat belt and closes his grip around me instead, hugging me tightly back. As if that wasn't humiliating enough.

As if I didn't just cause scene enough in a motel lobby to have to be carried back to the truck, I begin to sob uncontrollably on his shoulder.

Someone, please stick a fork in this one and pray she's done. What is happening to me?

I feel the stubble of Hud's face pressed to my cheek, and warmth settles all around me as he holds me tighter through not just tears but a crying jag. I try to catch my breath and attempt to calm myself.

"Steady now." He takes a deep breath and whispers them in my ear. "Steady now. You're okay."

Those words.

I mimic his action in effort to calm myself, recognizing it's not the first time he said that. My chest rises against his as I suck in air.

He said those words to me when I lost it in the motel lobby. I'm flooded with an awareness of him. Hit with curiosity and a selfless hope that I've not embarrassed him as much as I have myself.

Having no idea what came over me, I loosen my grip on his upper body and lean back into the truck seat where he placed me. "Thank you," I whisper in his ear.

He pulls away from where I had his face barred to my cheek and looks me in the eye. My heart skips a beat as he maintains his penetrating stare for a moment longer, then returns to his original task of manning the seat belt and buckles me in.

When the passenger door slams, I almost wither in self-destruction over what I just did, but something clicks, a calming from inside and I count the steps Hud makes until his door opens and he is back by my side. He looks over at me and I don't hide.

"Are you okay?" he asks in earnest, like a lifeguard who just pulled someone from the deep end.

I stare back at him with no response.

"Wren?"

"Yes. I... I'm okay. I'm going to grab my phone and get a place to stay and..." My voice cracks.

The embarrassment catches up to me, and I'm on overdrive trying to make what happened better. I reach for my tote bag and begin digging for my phone.

The ignition starts, the air blasting, cooling us, and Hud's hand covers mine, stopping me from grabbing at my phone.

Without a word, he pulls out of the parking lot, and the next thing I hear is a dial tone coming through his truck's Bluetooth.

"Hud, what's going on baby? Are you still at the shop?" It's an older woman's voice I recognize. A kind voice that smoked most of its life.

"Hey Martha, thanks for answering this late. No, I'm driving back from Rockridge. I need a favor. Is Sheldon's old spot above your place still empty? You don't have another renter do you?"

"Been empty since he left. Why?"

"I've got a friend here who needs a place while we get her car fixed. There's no vacancy over here in Rockridge. Some baseball tournament."

"She wouldn't be the prettiest little strawberry blonde this town ever saw wearing a Martha special in support of Vogel Springs' own Mueller's Cafe, would she?"

Hud looks over at me as I beam down at my shirt.

"Umm. Yeah," His eyes are still on mine. "Martha, that's her."

"Any friend of yours is a friend of mine. Plus she seemed like good people to me. She ate everything on her plate. You can't get more honest than that."

"I'm not sure how soon I'll have her car running, but Rockridge'll have a vacancy in a day or two, when the ball tournament's done."

"Give me fifteen minutes. The room gets cleaned once a week with the restaurant. I just got to get fresh linens out and some toiletries for her. That, and I hope she doesn't mind waken' when the biscuits rise. It gets pretty loud up there when the staff arrives to open for breakfast."

"Thanks Martha."

"See ya in a bit."

Hud hangs up and clears his throat.

"You like to fix things, huh?"

He cuts his eyes at me with a smile. "Well, I don't know if that was me as much as Martha. My granddad always said, there's nothing that clean sheets and a brand new bar of soap won't fix."

I stir and finally wake to the smell or sound of bacon frying. I can't be sure if it's not both.

Dishes clank in the kitchen and a country song I can't quite make out blasts from a *very* early morning, radio show.

It must be the kitchen crew below opening the restaurant.

My goodness, would they start breakfast this early? What time is it anyway? I pull the sheets down and search the room. Clean sheets. I smile at the memory of last night.

One would think the horrors of my nut-job behavior and complete loss of sanity would be what resurfaced. Instead, looking around the tiny, cozy apartment, what I remember first is Hud coming up the stairs with Martha and me.

Hud listened to everything Martha told me, from how to turn the shower on, to how and when to use the hot plate.

He stood beside me the entire time and made sure I was settled, the same way he walked me into the Rockridge Inn. He walked with me and waited by my side as if I was his responsibility.

I've never experienced that before.

I sit up in bed when I feel my hand on my phone. Thank goodness I didn't lose it in all of yesterday's chaos. I've got to call Anderson back.

Oh, shit, Anderson.

Chapter 1
about last night

The red LED lights on my alarm clock blink 5:30 a.m. when my eyes open, like they've been trained to do since I was a kid feeding stock. I don't need an alarm. Five-thirty is my body's default setting, even when I don't fall asleep until way after midnight, like last night.

It took a couple of drinks to get my lids to close.

She cratered.

I don't recall ever seeing a fireball fizzle as fast as Wren did when she learned the motel was booked up. No rooms in the inn.

She tried to be brave, biting her lower lip to keep it from quivering, but all hope drained when it hit her: she had no place to sleep—not even a car to sleep in.

That pretty little rich girl got her first taste of what homelessness feels like, not that I'd know, but I recognized it when I saw it and for some reason I still can't figure out, I never felt sorrier for anyone in my life, witnessing her meltdown.

First, she broke into a cold sweat, little beads pebbling on her upper lip. She paled and trembled. Her hazel eyes darted about in sheer panic as she backed away from me and the desk clerk, as if one or both of us would devour her.

Her eyes couldn't settle on anyone or anything, no matter what I said, until I grabbed her shoulders tightly and forced her to face me. Like talking to a skittish colt, I kept saying as soft as I knew how, "Steady now. Woah. Everything's going to be alright. Wren. Everything's alright."

It's what I've heard all my life. Steady, now.

Still, she fainted. Passed out. Thank God I caught her and she didn't bash her head on the tile floor. Yesterday was just too much for her, breaking down in the middle of nowhere, waiting for a tow, finding out she had no place to stay.

After getting Wren calmed, I called Martha, who was happy to rent her Sheldon's old apartment above the cafe until she's ready to leave town. Fifty bucks says she's arranged for a rental car and will be on her way to the sea turtles before noon.

I sneak a peek out my second-floor bedroom window blinds, straight across the street to Wren's room. No lights on. She's not up yet. I shouldn't be surprised. She was probably more exhausted than me when she finally got settled.

Turning on the coffee, I head to the shower. Maybe get rid of this friggin' hard on that I went to sleep with and woke up with.

What is it about her?

Even though she'd been sweating and fretting all afternoon, the faint fragrance of what has to be the world's most expensive perfume stuck in my head as I carried her in my arms. She was so... vulnerable. So beaten down. I hated it, for her.

She can be haughty as hell and flighty as a butterfly, but for some reason, ever since she made me laugh—watching her scurry into the ladies' room, fall asleep in the lobby, and fall apart at the motel—shit, I can't keep my mind off Wren Tweety Bird Baldwin.

No biggie.

She won't be here long enough for me to worry about it.

In the meantime, my first priority is to find out what happened to the Maserati and order her parts.

It's ridiculous, the time you'll invest in someone when you've decided to keep your distance. If I had a nickel for every time I've thought about her as I check under the hood of her Maserati, I could probably own this car. The realization hits me when I glance over my shoulder at the sound of her sandals clicking across the garage floor.

She's bright and chipper compared to last night, but I'm afraid I'm only going to have to disappoint her again. "Sorry to tell you this, darlin', but..."

She inhales sharply, summoning my eyes to meet hers.

Dammit, they're all fiery again. Didn't take long for me to go straight into dick mode. I straighten and hold up my hands in self defense. "Sorry. Just a habit. I don't have good news for you."

Her head tilts back so our eyes meet right when the printer begins to hum. "What does it say?"

You'd think I was holding a pregnancy test by the fear in her eyes. I challenge myself to look from the printout to her and drop the bomb. "It's your catalytic converter."

She blinks. "My... what?"

"Catalytic converter."

Her whole body sags. "I take it that's not good."

I feel a grin coming on. "No, it's not."

She glances around the shop, as if looking for help. "Well? Can it run without one? Maybe just remove it? Like tonsils?"

Again, the laugh her naivety evokes rumbles from my chest. "What did your car tell you yesterday?"

She tucks her chin with a pouty face. "That it won't run without it."

"Some cars can. Yours can't."

And there it is.

I watch panic crawling up Wren Baldwin's throat, turning it scarlet. Her cheeks flush and her eyes begin to dart about the shop like a bumble bee trying to decide what flower it wants to settle on. Sweat beads on her forehead, even though it's not hot this early in the morning.

"Woah. Steady, now. We'll figure out how to make it as painless as possible."

"Painless? How can you possibly make it painless? It's already painful. Being stranded so close to..."

"I'll get on the phone with Dallas and do my best to get the part here overnight."

"But what if they don't have it, like you said? What if they have to—"

"One step at a time. We know it's your catalytic converter. In the scheme of things, it could be a hell of a lot worse."

She takes a deep breath and nods. "You want to eat?"

I thought the car's diagnosis would silence this chatterbox, but she's got grit. This time, she denied the panic and forced a big smile.

My brows climb. "Do I want to what?"

"Breakfast. I woke up to the smell and sound of bacon frying and I don't think I can focus until I get some." She turns to head back inside the lobby as I look from the open hood of her car to her, trying to hide my confusion.

Wren opens the door from the garage into the lobby, peering back at me. "You don't have the part, right? Car can wait. Bacon cannot."

As we leave, I hold the shop door open for her and lock it, turning the lobby sign to closed. I hadn't opened the bay doors yet.

What am I doing, closing the shop when I just opened it?

Anyone who needs me knows I'll be across the street.

I cook some, but mostly I take advantage of living a few yards from the best cafe between Llano and Austin. Martha Mueller and I trade. She feeds me. I keep her cars and refrigerators and anything that breaks down running.

It's perfectly natural for me to walk across the street when I'm hungry, just not right after opening up.

"Morning Hud," Martha calls from behind the counter as we enter. Several tables are already full and I nod good morning at one friend after another.

"Hud, who ya got there?" H.D. Keesler asks from several tables away with a wide smile that shows off his new veneers. H.D.'s got to be crowding eighty—maybe ninety. I'm no judge of age, but those shiny white veneers are oddly out of place in that leathered face. Still, H.D.'s proud of them.

Placing my hand on the small of her back, I guide Wren to the table. "H.D., guys, this is Wren Baldwin."

Again. What am I fucking doing?

"Wren, this is H.D. Keesler, Bill Farnsworth, and Adam Simms. H.D. owns the hardware store. Bill, as you can see, is a Sheriff's Deputy, and Adam is the high school coach."

She grins and nods. "Nice to meet you all."

Bill tips his white Stetson, and with his mouth full, Adam mumbles into his napkin, something akin to, "You, too."

They're all dumbstruck by this shiny little beauty.

"Wren's car broke down yesterday. It's in the shop."

"The Maserati?" Bill asks.

"Yeah."

They all exchange glances.

"Nice car, young lady," Adam says, this time without a mouth full of breakfast.

"Thank you," Wren smiles graciously and looks up at me. "Hud's going to fix it."

Shit.

"He can do that," H.D. says before Martha cuts him off asking, "The usual?"

"Yeah, and I'm buying for this one. Whatever she wants. Excuse us, guys."

I gesture at a window table where I can keep an eye on my shop in case a customer tries to come in, pull out a chair for Wren, who sits daintily and crosses her legs, soaking up her surroundings. "I woke up smelling this place."

Look at that. Yesterday, I had no idea she could smile this much.

"I couldn't help myself," she says. "It smells delicious."

Not as good as you do, darlin'.

"Smells like blueberry muffins," Martha says. "How'd you sleep?"

"Like a baby." Wren's honesty blurts out.

"Good. Hud'll take care of you and your car." Martha sets two thick white ceramic coffee mugs on the table in front of us, each steaming with the aromatic liquid. She pats my shoulder motherly. "He takes care of everyone. Do you need sugar?"

Wren quirks her brows and cuts her eyes from Martha to me. "Sugar?"

"For your coffee, dear."

Wren's cheeks flame crimson. Cute as hell. She wears her emotions on her skin. "Yes, please. And creamer? And a blueberry muffin?"

She should never play poker. Her hazel eyes are the windows to her soul. She asks for cream and a muffin with hope swimming in them.

"Coming up." Martha nods and turns her thick back to us.

Wren's attention moves from Martha to me as her eyes narrow. "That seems to be a familiar refrain around here. 'Hud will take care of you.'" She rests her chin in her hand, her elbow on the table, staring into my eyes. "Do you take care of everyone, Hud?"

Abruptly, she moves her hand, tucks her chin, and stares at the table for a long beat.

Wren fidgets with the metal napkin holder between us, her freshly washed hair falling in waves around her face, glistening coppery as the morning sun beams through Martha's front windows. This light brings out the amber in her eyes more than the green, and those freckles across her nose and cheeks are more pronounced this morning than they were yesterday.

At last, she lifts her eyes to meet mine sheepishly, and whispers, "I guess you do. Thank you. For last night. I'm so sorry... I just..."

"Had a meltdown," I say over my coffee mug, trying to hide my amusement.

"Yeah."

"Don't worry about it." I set the empty cup down, wave at Martha for a refill, and cross my arms, leaning on the table. Our eyes are no more than a foot apart as I tell her, "It happens to the best. You'll get through this and life will go on. Call Hertz in Austin. They'll have a car here by noon and you can be on your way to South Padre. If they won't bring a car to you, we'll find someone to drive you to them."

What are you doing, Hud?

Getting her the fuck out of here. It's what she wants, anyway. "Leave me your phone number and I'll call you when the Cabrio is fixed. Voila. Easy-peasy."

"Right..." She runs her perfect pink fingernails along the rim of her coffee cup, which she hasn't touched, her gaze everywhere but on me.

I lean back in my chair, feeling my brows pinch together. "You don't trust me?"

"No. No," she stutters, as her eyes finally meet mine again. "That's not it." She lifts a dainty shoulder. "I just... If it's only going to be a day or two, I thought I'd stick around. I mean, why not? Maybe explore."

"Explore what? You're lookin' at it. This is Vogel Springs."

"Well, anyway. I thought... Martha and I worked everything out. The apartment's great. I'm happy to pay whatever she asks for the days I have to stay."

I throttle a snicker. She could buy the place if it was for sale.

I scratch my cheek, studying her, trying to get inside that pretty little head. Is this the same woman who didn't have days to wait just yesterday afternoon? "You've already seen all there is to see."

She pushes back in her chair and wags her shoulders defiantly. "Tut, tut. I know there's more to this place than what little I've seen. You've got a school, right?"

"Yeah, I told you, Adam's the coach."

"So I bet you have a library, then."

I nod as I glance around the cafe. Where the hell's Martha with my refill?

"Playgrounds and parks?"

"You haven't touched your coffee but I need more. Be right back." I take my cup and walk around the counter to pour myself a refill.

Martha is taking breakfast orders at a booth in the back, crammed full of people I don't know. I zero in on the booth. Suits. Suits. Suits.

I snatch a little container of creamer and a blueberry muffin on my way back to the table, setting both in front of Wren. "Okay, you got me, we've got a library and we even have a swimming pool," I say dryly.

She pours the creamer into her coffee. "I love a swimming pool. I can soak up the sun while I wait for my car. What about a theater?"

Genevieve Landry cuts a glance back and forth between me and Wren as she slides a plate of ham, steak, and eggs in front of one of the suits. Our eyes meet, and Genevieve hightails it back to the kitchen.

"Hud?"

"What?" I bring my focus back to the little bird in front of me. "Oh, yeah, the theater. Well, what's left of the only theater that ever was is in my lobby. You napped on it yesterday." I fight to squash the grin that wants to hijack my face, remembering her curled up, drooling on herself in that seat. She was shiny in her disheveled state and even shinier this morning. And she still smells like million-dollar-an-ounce perfume. Clean. She smells clean even when she sweats.

Wren's smile shows a little dimple in her left cheek as she says smugly, "I thought that was a theater seat. You can just feel the nostalgia and adventure on it."

"Sorry, Hud," Martha appears beside my shoulder. "Jessie's running late. Just me and Genevieve. We're swamped." She wipes stray hair from her forehead with the back of her hand, nodding at our table. "See you helped yourself." Martha peers at Wren as she refreshes my coffee, again. "You look quite at home here in Vogel Springs, Miss Wren Baldwin."

Wren flashes Martha the happiest look I've seen her wear yet.

My face freezes as my heart *thu-thumps* loud in my chest.

I glance around at the people I call friends, who are all ogling this beauty across from me with some combination of curiosity and envy. If I noticed one table of suits a few minutes ago, there are two more now, and if Genevieve gives me the side eye one more time—

Fuck. What am I doing?

I gulp Martha's refill and clomp my cup on the table, telling Wren as I stand, "If I were you, I'd be calling Hertz to get to Padre Island. Ask anyone, your car is safe with me. I won't damage it or swindle you."

Martha's mouth gapes as I look from her to Wren. "I forgot something." My sanity. "I've gotta go. Wren, enjoy your breakfast. Martha, don't let her pay."

What have I been doing, thinking about her? She's a shimmering mirage in the desert that will disappear in the blink of an eye.

Crossing the street, trying to put as much distance between me and Tweety Bird Baldwin as fast as I can, my phone dings in my hip pocket and I pull it out.

My best friend, Cal Cooper.

CalCoop: WYD

> **HudBass: Working**

CalCoop: U got Maserati in garage? WTF?

> **HudBass: Long Story**

CalCoop: I've got time

> **HudBass: I don't**

CalCoop: Headed UR way

> **HudBass: 👍**

Cal and I go back to grade school. We played high school football and basketball together. Cal was an exceptional talent. Good enough to play football for UT on scholarship.

Now, he's in the NFL.

But his roots run deep in this rocky soil. His family still lives here, so Cal is in and out a lot. He was raised by his Aunt Tiny, who is anything but tiny, and the only person in these parts who can rival Martha Mueller as a cook.

That would be something to see. A cook-off between Martha Mueller and Tiny Cooper.

CalCoop: What's with the 🍌🌰

HudBass: 💩

CalCoop: 😂

W hat happened? What did I do wrong? Moreover, why do I care?

One minute we're chatting about lobby chairs, and the next thing I know, he's striding across the street like his shop is on fire.

Even Martha notices. "The boy got a burr in his saddle all of a sudden."

I'm watching Hud, who is looking at his cell phone as I answer Martha. "Yeah."

Martha shakes her head and pushes her glasses up on the bridge of her nose. "No telling. Hud's had a lot on his mind lately with everything going on."

"Everything going on? Like what?"

I feel it now—some mystery surrounding this handsome mechanic with icy gray eyes. My eyes beg for an answer from Martha, and I surprise myself, the way I did last night.

Vulnerable is the last word that would ever be stitched on the ass of my monogrammed panties, but Vogel Springs seems to bring it out of me.

Or is it him? Does he bring it out in me?

Martha's forehead wrinkles and her mouth draws into a thin, hard line. "Just... stuff. Nothing for me to go into."

"Is he like... going through a divorce or something? Wife or kids sick?"

She shakes her head softly. "Hud's never married. You want another muffin?" She's diverting this conversation.

Okay, for now, but I'm not through with this line of questioning.

I take in my already almost-eaten muffin. "Yes, I'll take one more to go. You should sell these things you know. They're delicious, especially warm like this."

Martha's head tilts back as she cackles loudly. "I do sell them, dear."

"I mean, like, mass-market them. They're awesome." I do my air quotes. "*Martha Mueller's Famous Blueberry Muffins*—I can see them in stores everywhere."

She chuckles. "Thank you dear, but I have my hands full with what I've got right now. What about coffee? You need more coffee?"

I glance across the street at Bass Pit Stop as the overhead garage doors slide open noisily, exposing the inner shop.

Martha catches me. Dammit.

Pouring my refill, she says, "Hun, anybody over the age of eighteen has a past." She follows my eyeline across the street to Hud, then tucks her chin. "And good-looking especially doesn't exclude that. I'd lay my odds that you have one, too."

Martha's eyebrows rise emphatically as she taps my hand in a comforting, motherly way and I feel the heat of a nasty grimace from the server who waited on me yesterday. What is her problem?

Her dirty look sears through my periphery as Martha squeezes my hand. Her pudgy hands are warm and comforting, and I can't explain why or how in the world Martha Mueller feels like a home I never knew.

She says, "I've known Hud for a very long time. All I can tell ya with good conscience is, I wouldn't bet against him for nothin'. You take that for what ya' will, and I hope to see ya' for supper."

A kitchen bell jingles, signaling food in the window, and Martha disappears into the crowd of breakfast diners. A loud ping startles me, and I dig in my tote for my cell phone.

Anderson: Status report please.

    WrenB: ☕ + Waiting

Anderson: ✈

My gaze arcs to the cafe's front door as it swings wide with an entourage of men and women entering. One man aims his arm at the back of the cafe, and the group follows him.

All in suits. All carrying briefcases.

They don't wait to be seated but instead troop between tables to a booth in the back.

They don't belong here.

Those people are from Austin or San Antonio or Houston or Dallas. They walk quietly while I wait for Martha to return with my muffin to go.

When she does, she cuts her eyes at all the suits, and I detect a go-to-hell glare. "Do you know them?" I ask.

"Some of 'em."

"What are they doing here?" Something about their entrance feels ominous, like a black cloud just settled over this wonderful cafe, casting a shadow on everything.

Martha tilts her head toward them. "They're a bunch of vultures circling. Waiting on their prey to die."

Like me, yesterday. "Martha? What's going on in this town?"

Between Hud's abrupt, unexplained exit, these people who don't belong here, and that server's incessant frown—something's not right.

Martha shakes her head in what I already recognize: with her mouth tight, the corners of her eyes crinkling. "Just small town stuff, sweetie. Nothing for you to worry about."

Leave it alone, Wren. You'll find out soon enough.

Muffin in hand, I step outside and sit in the morning breeze on a bench outside Mueller's Cafe. The sun is high enough it doesn't hit me as I face Bass Pit Stop, and stare across the street.

Martha has soft cushions lining the bench seat and back and oversized hanging baskets of pink petunias sway from the balcony overhang.

Honestly, they don't realize it because they live here, but Vogel Springs could be a section of Six Flags Over Texas or Disneyworld. It's idyllic with its red brick buildings lining Main Street, its four-way stop, and its old brick street.

Even Bass Pit Stop is picturesque.

It's inside an old brick building that I can only guess was at one time a filling station where the owner's family lived upstairs. It has an upstairs with a balcony, like the one outside my new apartment over Mueller's Cafe.

Does he live up there? No. He's got a house somewhere.

Maybe he uses it for storage or his office. Maybe he has a shower and bed up there.

Who knows? And why in God's name am I obsessing over this rude mechanic?

Because he's handsome as hell with dark hair and light eyes fringed with long black lashes. Crazy, strong arms that reached out and held me.

Shit.

I wouldn't feel like such a stalker if Hud hadn't done a complete one-eighty. Emotionally available last night. Cold shoulder this morning.

Ugh. The last thing I need is a complication. As Anderson always says, "Keep it simple, stupid."

I've got a feeling Mr. Hudson Bass is anything but simple.

On that note, I should probably get up from the bench perfectly situated across from his shop, where I am certain I look to be staring at the man while he works. Stalker.

I walk across Mueller's Cafe's porch to the next porch of what looks like a dress boutique. I can't really tell. It's closed. But there's a lot of lavender in there. I step back from peeking through the window to see their sign on the door. *The Purple Polka Dot*. Makes sense.

The next one down leads to the last storefront, *Amaryllis By Morning*. Cute. A florist, I'm guessing. I step down from the string of shops and find myself at the edge of the four-way stop, facing that glorious monstrosity of yesteryear.

Looking up at the dark purple, teal, and forest green trimmed Victorian, I can't help but be curious. Its wrap-around porch puts this one on Main Street to shame.

I pass the *Welcome to Vogel Springs* sign to get a closer look at the home and notice it has its own sign in the front yard.

FOR SALE

Hud

Chapter 9

one bite at a time

"**Y**o!"

"In here!" I call over my shoulder to the familiar, friendly voice.

Cal saunters through the lobby door into the shop and wolf whistles. "Ooh-wee! Damn, man. What. A. Car." His arms are folded over his chest, which is about as thick as a frigging redwood and just as hard.

"Yeah." The Cabrio's up on the hydraulic lift. "Gotta remove the catalytic converter." I step away to back-slap my friend, and nod at the pearl-white beauty on the lift. "Can you believe she's got 444 horses?"

A smile takes over Cal's face. Martha says he looks like Idris Elba, only with dimples. "Damn, man."

"Yeah. But there's nothing easy about her. I've got to remove panels to reach the exhaust system."

He surprises me, drawing me into a firm embrace. It's been a while since we've seen each other, with him in training camp, though we text a couple of times a week. Cal Cooper is the only man I know who makes me feel small—all six-foot-six, two-hun-dred-fifty pounds of him. This past year, he started braiding his hair. He doesn't do it. Someone does it for him. To each his own.

"Take a break?" he asks.

"Might as well. The new part's either in Dallas or Italy. I'm waiting to find out." He follows me into my office, which bridges the lobby and shop. "Have you been by Tiny's yet?"

"No, man, I just drove into town."

I clock a new Bentley Continental parked in front of my shop and nudge my head toward it. "That your new ride?" I let out a wolf whistle of my own. "Not shabby."

"Yeah." He grins and tilts his head at the Infinity, Range Rover, Cadillac, and Lexus parked in front of Martha's. "Shitload of cars over there. What's going on? A convention of assholes?"

I growl. "I don't know exactly." I ease into the chair behind my desk, directly facing the cafe. "But I'm thinking those fuckers are here about this."

I sail a Federal Express envelope at him, which he catches like an NFL receiver would, even though Cal's not a receiver. He's a linebacker.

He cuts his big eyes from the envelope to me and narrows his gaze. "You haven't opened it."

"I had to sign for that fucker. I've got a sneaking suspicion I know what's in it."

"Another offer?"

"I've heard them whispering eminent domain."

"Idiots wouldn't dare."

Leaning back in my chair, staring at the ceiling with my hands locked behind my head, I take in a deep, long breath and let it out. "Why else would I have to sign? I don't know. VoltEdge is huge. Tesla's got that new place in Austin needing God-knows-how-many electric batteries a week. I don't know."

My friend's stare is heavy and level. "They offered a shitload, Hud. You'd be set for life."

My mouth puckers automatically and I shake my head, refusing to look at that envelope in his hand. "Can't do it. I promised."

Cal snorts. "Your dad never imagined how much money that land would be worth when he made you make that promise."

I lean my forearms on the desk. "He didn't make me. The land's been in our family for four generations. You don't think they thought about selling out during the Depression? During the drought of the 50s, when my granddad went to work for the railroad just to pay the property taxes? It was the last thing Dad said to me: 'Son, don't sell the land.' I can't do it."

He shows me his palms. "Hud, man, it's okay. You don't want to sell it, that's enough for me." Cal tosses the cardboard envelope on my desk and points. "But open that thing."

"After I get the catalytic converter out."

He laughs loudly. "How do you eat an elephant?"

"One fucking bite at a time."

"So changing subjects, what's this I hear about you and the owner of the Maserati?"

I groan. "Nothing. What do you mean?"

His brows shift high. "You two trying to check into the Rock-ridge motel and you showing her around the cafe this morning."

I snort. "Are you spying on me?"

"No, but my best man has a new babe. I ought to at least be able to answer questions tossed my way."

"Who the hell told you we tried to check into a motel?"

He grins out of the side of his mouth and flicks his eyebrows. "I have my sources."

"Her car broke down. She had no place to stay. I drove her into Rockridge to get her a motel room, but they were booked up. So I brought her back to Martha's. She's staying in Shel-don's old room."

"Not what I heard. I heard you carried her like a little baby from the motel lobby to your truck."

I moan, tipping my head back. Cal giggles like a school kid. "No, man. My nephew's playing ball in that tournament. He saw you, called Tiny and of course, she called me asking ques-tions. So don't try to blow smoke up my ass, friend. Kids don't lie."

"But they have vivid imaginations. It wasn't what he thought."

Cal hikes one brow. "Out of the mouths of babes." He tucks his chin, staring a hole into me. "You telling me, you didn't carry her in your arms?"

I close my eyes and sigh. "Because she had a panic attack. She collapsed when she realized she was stranded in a strange place with no place to stay."

"So, Hud to the rescue." He keeps chuckling and aims his arm at the ceiling. "You have a place right up there. You coulda' brought her back here."

"And where would I have slept?"

And that does it.

Cal lets out a cackle like I haven't heard from him in years, his shoulders shaking, slapping his thighs. "I've known you since we were six years old, man. I got radar and it's pinging all to hell. Something's cookin' between you and Miss Maserati."

"Wrong. She's a customer. You sound like Travis." My face falls flat. Wait. "Travis. He's the fucker feeding you full of this bullshit, not your nephew."

And the laughs keep coming. "Travis called me as soon as he left your shop yesterday. Said when Miss Maserati saw you, she froze in her tracks. Said you two made goo-goo eyes at each other, even though you couldn't stop clawin' at each other about her car. You know the sounds cats make when they—"

"Get out, man. Go. See Tiny."

Fuck. Me.

"Headed that way." Cal keeps chuckling as he leaves, aiming his arm at me. "I want to meet this girl of yours. See for myself if she's as hot as Travis says she is."

She is. But I won't admit it. "If I have my way, she won't be here long enough for you to meet her."

"Bullshit. Tiny's expecting you for lunch."

"I wouldn't miss it."

The phone rings as Cal folds himself into his Bentley and drives away.

"Mr. Bass, we'll have to order the catalytic converter for Miss Baldwin's car," a woman says. "We don't have one here in Dallas. I emailed the manufacturer, but with the time difference, I probably won't know anything until tomorrow."

It is what it is.

"Send me the bill."

"Oh, Miss Baldwin's car is under warranty. I'll be sure to let you know when the part is on the way."

"Thanks."

Hanging up the phone, I stare at that evil envelope. Don't be such a pussy. Open the damn thing.

"Martha, give this to Wren for me." I refuse the urge to glance upstairs. The cafe has finally emptied.

Martha looks up from wiping down the counter. "She's out exploring. If you want to wait, I bet she'll—"

"I've got to get back." I hand over a note I scrawled for Wren, explaining about the part. "Cal's in."

A playful smile rises across Martha's face and I swear her brown eyes twinkle. "I saw him."

As I head for the door, Martha says, "What did you think about the crowd this morning?"

I turn. "You know what I thought."

"What's going on Hud?"

My heart drums in my chest. "You know what's going on. They're here to convince the county judge and commissioner's court to file an eminent domain claim on me. Fuckers drove here to eat right across the street from my shop to try and intimidate me." Blood rushes to my temples. I feel my pulse in them.

"I'm sorry, Hud. I know what the land means to your family." She knew both of my parents, and I love her, but the sudden, sympathetic way Martha's looking at me—like I'm some poor, abandoned dog that needs to be fed—rankles me.

I take a step toward her. "Don't start planning my funeral just yet. I'm not rolling over and dying for them."

Chapter 10

sliding meringue

Whoops. I'm the last one here. Restaurants hate that, but maybe Martha won't mind. I can get it to-go if she needs me to.

"Wren, you made it back. I was going to worry if you let it get all the way dark. How was your day out and about town?"

"Perfect. I discovered so many hidden gems. Before you know it, I'll know all the best-kept secrets."

I hear Genevieve scoff in the background. Martha shoots her a fiery glare as she says, "Genevieve, why don't you bring our girl a menu?" Martha's gaze settles back on me. "You've got to be famished, unless you're sick of the place already."

"Are you kidding me? I haven't even started on your pies. That's what I'm having for dinner tonight, unless I'm too late. I can get it to-go and take it upstairs."

Martha brushes stray gray hair off the side of her tired face. "You get over there and sit your rear right down." She motions toward the corner window seat. Martha knows me well already. "You got anything against chocolate, Wren?"

"Never."

Martha putters away and I look out the window over at Bass Pit Stop. I haven't seen Hud since he fled before breakfast was served. His lights are on inside, but I can't see in. His main garage bay door is closed. Funny, you'd think I'd be peeking over for a glimpse of my car.

Is it odd to miss his voice? I haven't heard it since it changed this morning. He went from coffee and blueberry muffins to a nervous wreck that couldn't flee our table fast enough.

Typical.

Men seldom do the morning after. I chuckle to myself at the reference to my motel meltdown in his arms as if it were a night we shared together. Apparently, it was just as alarming to him.

A plate plops down in front of me. It's chocolate cream pie. Genevieve slams it down so hard the meringue slides off the top.

"Thanks. I think."

"I take it your car's not fixed yet."

"Still waiting on a part."

"Anything to drink?"

"I'm good, thanks."

With that, Genevieve is off. I bite into the most delicious pie I've tasted. It's so good, my fork with the bent prong doesn't even detour me. She hand-picked this utensil especially for me. Again, what is her deal?

"You can head on out if you want, Genevieve. You worked a double for me again, and for that, you know I'm grateful. I'll take care of your side work. Go on and cash out." Martha calls from the kitchen and heads back into the front of the house to Genevieve.

"Hey." Genevieve, the young woman of not so many words, unties her apron strings and tosses her checkbook of cash, receipts, and an order pad on the counter. "About all the doubles."

"Look, if I can't get a hold of Jessie... If she doesn't show up in the next day or two with a doctor's note, I'll get somebody else. I promise."

Martha doesn't want to see Genevieve unhappy. Better get a blindfold.

"Rosalee's back." Genevieve stares directly at Martha as if she has some sort of upper hand.

Martha unleashes a loaded breath, drops her head, and shakes it from side to side.

"It'll only be for a little while. She can just cover until you get Jessie comin' back around."

"It's never just a little while with Rosalee. How long has she been back?"

"Day or two. Stayin' with me."

"Hud know yet?"

Genevieve cuts her eyes at me as if to catch me eavesdropping, then back to Martha and shakes her head. "I don't think so. He's been busy."

"Yeah? And he's gonna stay that way. He's got too much going on right now for—"

"Just what does he have going on?" Genevieve has a bite in her voice as I hear her words fly in my direction.

I make sure I'm absorbed in the slab of chocolate in front of me as opposed to the view across the street or the now-awkward moment of what I sense is Genevieve challenging Martha.

"Let's just say he's got a lot on his mind right now, and Rosalee doesn't need to add anything to that." Martha grabs Genevieve's cash-out sheet and begins tallying to pay her out.

"I don't understand why you can't just give her another chance."

"This whole town's given Rosalee chance after chance. Don't you dare suggest otherwise. Hell, you're preachin' to the choir to bring me and Hud into it. We've given her more chances than you could dream up, and I know damn well, more than she'd bother to tell ya."

"Fine." Genevieve swipes the cash Martha lays out for her and combines it with her tips.

"I'm just telling you. I don't know what ideas Rosalee has come back through town with, but if I know Hud, it ain't gonna' go like she thinks." The cash register bell dings as Martha slams the drawer shut and Genevieve pivots to exit.

If I know Hud. Martha's words I've been living by and feeding on.

The truth is—I. Don't. Know. Hud.

I guess every town has a bad boy, even the smallest, and if Genevieve's unfounded beef with me and her allegiance to this Rosalee tells me anything, Hud may be theirs.

I wipe chocolate out of the corners of my mouth with my napkin and lay it over my empty plate. Again, I have not disappointed Martha, eating everything on it. Grabbing my tote bag, I pick up my plate to bring it to her so I am not one last table she has to bus. "Thank you, Martha. That hit the spot."

Martha's look is far away as she brings her eyes back to mine and starts the process of raising her cheeks to smile. She pushes her glasses on top of her head. "Hey wait, Wren. I nearly forgot." She bounces the cash register drawer back open, lifts the cash tray, and pulls out a note.

My name is written across the top of the folded sheet of paper. I don't recognize the handwriting, but my heart stops for a second anyway. Whoever wrote it, it can't be good news.

"Hud dropped this by for you a bit ago."

"Ah. Thanks." I nod and take it from her. "Night, Martha."

"Night, Sweetheart."

I turn away from her toward the back, to my upstairs entrance. Walking slowly, I open the note to read as I go.

> Wren,
> No part in Dallas.
> They'll let me know tomorrow
> when they can get it from Italy.
> Hud

That's it?

Guess I'm wrong about him having any interest in me, or wanting to make a move. What am I even suggesting? *Make a move.* Apart from starting out as a medieval tyrant, the guy was nothing but kind and a complete gentleman to me last night. I guess that's why I thought... Right, that a man I've barely known for two days wants to... what? Secretly ravish me?

Jesus, Wren. He was just being consoling. You were that much of a basket case in front of him—he had no choice but to calm you down. I don't think I'd considered the obvious before. That he was simply calming me down. It felt so natural to be in his arms when the most unnatural thing I could imagine was happening to me.

Pitch a fit and a damn good one, for Daddy's sake? You bet. But a nervous breakdown in front of a stranger? That's not usually in my arsenal.

That's another thing. Martha's a total stranger as well, and look how I'm latching onto her kindness.

My father's right. There is absolutely something wrong with me.

Of all my escapades, and even the whoppers I've pulled, getting hooked on the idea of a complete stranger—I need my head examined.

I trudge the remaining stairs to the door leading to my cozy little space. It's been just as embracing as Martha.

The knob turns behind me as I lock and bolt the door. It makes me giggle that I even bother. Habit, I guess. But here, in Vogel Springs, I've seen no reason whatsoever to do so. I'm surprised the door has a deadbolt on it.

Everything is just as I left it as I survey the charming space. And, maybe that's all this is. It's inviting here. Vogel Springs, the little apartment, Martha.

Hud is just something I confused with a traumatic situation and the atmosphere of this place. He's just a dude with a lot on his plate.

Still, I can't help but wonder what all is on his plate.

Overhearing Martha, it may be much worse than being stranded and waiting on a car part.

Let's get real. I have money. I'm not stuck anywhere. I guess that's it... I have never been stuck before, or stranded. Hud made those things feel okay, even when I was terrified. Hud made it feel nice to be stuck somewhere.

I pull my heavy waves into a ponytail on my head as I stare out my window into his shop. The lights are still on. Later than usual for him. Again, take it easy, stalker.

After what I've been through, what I'm running from—a delicious stranger who smells like that, looks, and feels like that when he lifts me off the ground or opens the car door—is the last thing I need.

I recognize a ringtone that can snap me back to reality like no other, and I race to answer my phone. "Oh, thank God it's you. If you knew the conversation I was just having with myself."

"Would we still be friends?" Anderson's voice is the perfect combination of coy and astute. He has his own brand of satire that keeps me going.

"Knowing your sick, demented mind, we'd be better friends."

"Do tell... is it the mechanic? The tow truck guy? Rental car fellow?"

"I'll stop you there."

"Oh, come on. Give me something. I'm in line for a ride share at the airport. It's now the worst line in life."

"You're not home, yet?"

"Who cares? Back to baby chicken. Tell me everything."

"Oh, please. Who do you take me for? Don't answer that. I'm just saying, there's nothing to tell. I messaged you the play-by-play, including my meltdown at a roadside motel in the middle of nowhere... Can you believe that, Anderson... Even *they* didn't want me."

"Well, you seem pretty set up now."

"These people are kind. That's all."

"Dorothy, you're not in Denver anymore. It's hot down here in Texas. I, for one, know what that does to people. That kind of heat puts a little itch on your skin, sweat starts smellin' like sweet perfume, and before you know it—"

"God, stop it." I glance up just as Hud's light goes out across the street, and my heart skips a beat. "There's nothing there, Anderson. Here. I mean, there's nothing here. My car will be fixed in a day or two, and I'll be happily on my way.

"You'd know that if you'd bothered to block certain numbers like I asked you to. If you had, I'd head straight to you, making a stop off in Austin. As it is, I'm afraid I've stayed here too long and I won't risk being found at your place. If they're calling you, they suspect I'll be there soon, if I'm not already."

"Well? Don't you have it all figured out?"

"Certainly not. But I should get on the road as soon as possible, regardless."

"I didn't block them for your own safety and my entertainment. Don't you want to know what they're after? Honey, I give everybody equal opportunity to show their ass and make a complete fool of themselves. Ergo, I never block anyone as a rule. Knowledge is power, baby."

"B.S. This coming from the guy who is notorious for saying, 'What you don't know can't hurt ya,' or 'Ignorance isn't just bliss, it's sheik,' and my favorite, 'I love a stupid man.'"

"Well, I won't say you have me there, as those are life lessons in love and relationships, not life in general. Hey... what's that?"

"What's what?"

"Do you have a better pic of that fabulous Victorian in the background of the welcome sign? Give me that front and center, please."

The many pics about the town I sent Anderson while he was on the plane must be coming through. It makes me chuckle to think the place is so small, yet I found a trillion things to take pictures of.

"Hello, gorgeous! Wren? Are you sure that's in that town?"

"It's behind the Vogel Springs welcome sign, dumbass."

"And, is that a for sale sign I see out front?"

"Judge, I talked to a lawyer. It's a private business, not a water line or highway. You don't have legal grounds for eminent domain. And get this straight: my land's not for sale." My arm swings wide. "This is Texas, for crying out loud. There's land everywhere. You come after me with eminent domain and you'll have one fucking long fight on your hands."

Slamming down the phone, I squeeze my pounding temples. I'm going to have a stroke, and I'm too damned young for that. "Dammit!" I yell at no one there.

After leaving Cal and Tiny yesterday, I came back and opened the damned FedEx envelope. It was exactly what I thought it would be. I have forty-eight hours to agree to sell, or the county will start eminent domain proceedings and their forty-eight hours started from the time I signed for the damned envelope.

They can shove their deadline and FedEx envelope up their collective asses.

I didn't wait until the courthouse opened at eight. I called the county judge at home. Woke the fucker up.

I'm one of the largest landowners in the county, but most of Bass land doesn't have an inch of topsoil on it. I grow hay on what is decent ground because there's not enough of it to do anything else with. This is rocky hill country. The only animals that thrive on it are white-tail deer and the only livestock anyone raises are sheep and goats.

My dad made a decent living raising them, but I'd rather tinker with engines than stinking sheep and goats, so all I do with the land now is grow hay to pay the property taxes. It's mine. It's nobody's business what I do or don't do with it.

But Cal was right. With what VoltEdge is offering, I could sell and be set for life.

Then what would I do? I'm not like other people. I've got no desire to gallivant all over the world doing absolutely nothing. I like work. I like fixing things. And I can't imagine living anywhere else.

Besides, I made him a promise. We Basses keep our promises.

I slump into my desk chair and stare at the ceiling in my office, my hands locked behind my head. It hits me as my gaze darts around the ceiling—I'm exactly like Wren was the other night. My eyes can't be still. I'm a caged animal searching for a way out. And there's no way out.

I'm facing a long, drawn-out, expensive legal battle and the wrath of about half the people in this county who want to turn this place into Austin or San Antone, just to hold onto what's mine.

The other half of Friedensburg County feels like I do. We're happy with it, just as it is. We don't want to be citified.

Get up, man, and go to work. Get your mind off of this shit. I still haven't removed that catalytic converter.

I rub my eyes with the heels of my hands. Another long-ass, sleepless night drinking and staring across the street at little La-tee-dah Wren Baldwin in her new apartment right across the street. She was over there happy, giggling on the phone with someone. Once she got past her meltdown, that pretty girl hasn't got a care in the world.

What the hell is she still doing here? She should be splashing on the beach right now. And what was I thinking, putting her up across the street?

That's just it, shit for brains. You weren't thinking. I get stiff every friggin' time I'm around her. Her smell. Her eyes. Her plump lips. Her freckles... I can't deal with Wren Baldwin, the county commissioners, and VoltEdge.

I head to the garage, pretty sure the Maserati people tried to hide the catalytic converter to fuck with mechanics. It's time to get it off. Speaking of getting off.

I'm standing under the Cabrio, arched over backward, trying to reach this slippery little motherfucker when I hear, "Enlighten me. What, exactly, have I done wrong?"

Great. Speak of the devil. She slipped into the shop unnoticed.

Guess I was too focused on my task to hear the lobby doorbell or the *click, click, click* of her sandals.

Glancing over my shoulder, I see Wren standing with her legs braced, her arms crossed, glaring at me. Spoiling for a fight. "What are you talking about?" I ask and keep working.

"A note? You left me a note? I invited you to eat breakfast with me and you left before it was served. Rude. R.U.D.E. And then you leave me a *note*?" Her voice climbed an octave during that little tirade.

"Your catalytic converter is somewhere in Italy."

She stomps in those platform sandals across the garage, stopping smackdab in front of me, holding up the message I left with Martha yesterday. She stretches her arm up and out, but she's not tall enough to shove it in my face, which is what she'd like to do. "Yeah. As I said, I got your note." She shakes it at me.

I stop working to face her. "Glad you can read." She is so small. Like a wren. I was wrong, her name fits her perfectly. A little songbird with bright red toenails. If she knows what's good for her, she'll take the hint and walk her tight little ass back to Martha's. I'm about to...

No. I go back to working overhead.

"Hud?"

I turn to her soft voice. It's not angry or condescending anymore.

"What?" I bite at her.

Her eyes are pleading as her lips quiver. "What happened? We made a truce. I thought... we were... friends."

My brows hit my hairline as I snark, "Friends? You're not going to be here long enough for us to become friends." My head and heart pound like a marching band as I tuck the wrench in my hip pocket and stop working. Okay. Let's get this over with. "As a matter of fact, why are you still here, Wren?"

After a drawn-out mutual glare, she averts her eyes, peering through the open bay doors at Mueller's Cafe, chewing on her bottom lip.

I wait for a response, lost in those lips. That mouth. I can only imagine what her mouth could do. Does she have any idea how beautiful she is?

Sure, she does. She's wearing a tight tank top designed to show off luscious round tits with a turquoise necklace hanging strategically over her cleavage, close enough to force my gaze to dip down.

Staring at her breasts, my mouth waters. My cock strains inside my jeans.

Her hands flounce above her head, coming to rest on her hips. "What am I doing here?" Fire shoots from her eyes. "I'm waiting on a Fucking. Catalytic. Converter."

I bend my knees so our eyes are level, almost whispering, "It's not going to be here for days." I aim my arm at the cafe, feeling flames shoot from my eyes as my voice booms, "Go, Wren. Now. Call Hertz. Your sea turtles are waiting."

I turn my back to her, resuming my vain attempt to reach this goddamned converter. Those Italian engineers had a mean streak, hiding this bitch from anyone with man hands. My heart drums in my ears.

You told her to go. Are you sure that's what you really want?

Yeah, I answer myself. She needs to go. The sooner the better.

My body freezes as small hands slide around my middle. She rests her warm face against my back, pulling me into her, nuzzling her nose in my back. "Steady now," she whispers. "Everything will be alright."

I close my eyes. I can't believe she said that to me.

My hands are over my head in the Cabrio under-carriage. "Wren. Don't. You need to leave."

"No." Her hands glide up my torso, pulling me hard against her, and I feel those perfect tits press into my back. My cock swells as she stands on tiptoes and whispers at my shoulder. "I don't know what's going on. But I'm not leaving. Not right now."

I drop my hand to cover hers. "Don't, Wren. You don't know what you're doing." *To me.* She doesn't know what she's doing to me. She hasn't got a fucking clue how close I am to...

"Hud." She slips around me and slides her hands up my pecs, her head tilted back, her beautiful moss-colored eyes staring into mine with a pained expression. Those pink lips tempt me. Her tantalizing fragrance and... Shit, I'm looking right down her tank top.

God help me.

I yank her to me, lifting her off the floor as my mouth finds hers, finally tasting her, and from somewhere deep inside me comes a feral growl as I tug on her hair, tilting her head back, demanding access to her mouth. I'm fucking out of control with her tongue on mine, my hands sliding over her soft skin, inhaling a scent that is uniquely her.

I slip my fingers through her long, silky hair, pressing her mouth to mine as I devour her. My free hand cups that perfect little round ass, pulling her up and into me. I'm so fucking hard.

"Hud," she whispers breathlessly. "What's happening?"

"This." I trail my tongue down her neck, nibbling, as I lift her higher. "This is happening."

I've got her feet off the floor, hoisting her higher so she can slip her legs around my waist, and I carry her toward the apartment stairs. Before I know it, my hand is under that tank top, slipping under the little bra, gripping a firm, perfect-sized breast, teasing her nipple with my thumb.

She whimpers into my mouth.

Now, I've got to taste it.

I slide my hand underneath that little lace bra and take her tit into my mouth, sucking on her pink nipple, and Wren rolls her hips into me. Her head falls back, her hair tickling my hand as she moans, "Oh, Hud."

My fingers find their way inside her shorts, sliding her panties aside, and fuck if she's not as wet as I am hard. I'm having her. "Dammit, Wren. I want you so fuckin' bad. I'm going to—"

"Oh! My! Gawd!" A man's voice thunders through the garage, and I freeze. "What in the holy hell?" he yells.

Wren stiffens and pushes against my pecs. "Anderson?"

I peer over my shoulder, still holding her, with her legs tight around my waist. I've got one hand in her shorts, my dick's throbbing, and my heart's pounding.

All he can see is my back. I'll keep it that way. "Anderson?" I bite out, peering from the beauty I'm holding—the gorgeous woman I was just about to carry to the edge of ecstasy with me—to a man glaring at me from beside the Cabrio. "Who the fuck are you?" I demand from our particularly compromising position, which, again, I hope he can't see.

"Hud, wait," Wren says. "He's my best friend." Her legs ease their grip around my waist.

Dammit. Shit. Hell. No.

Against every instinct in me, I remove my hands from her body and lower her to the floor. Fuck. Me.

I wish.

Wren's cheeks flush crimson as she yanks her bra and top down—my body hiding her from this son of a bitch—before she steps around me to face him.

I turn with her to get a look at this interloper.

Her sweet ass is rubbing against my aching cock, but in her defense, she's too focused on being caught almost in the act to realize what she's doing to me. Still.

"Anderson, what are you doing here?" she demands.

He steps closer. "Obviously, I came to see you." He's about my age. Nice enough looking guy. Thin, tan, very blonde, light blue eyes. Something tells me he's never been caught in this position with Wren or any other woman.

So this is the best friend.

My head is still spinning, and my heart is about to pound out of my chest and if I don't get a release soon—if I don't get to slide my cock inside of Wren's warm, wet, waiting wonderland—I'm going to implode. Or explode. My hands are gripping her shoulders now. I can't seem to make myself let go of her. As I open my mouth to suggest he come back at a better time, before I can get a word out, we hear, "Yo! Woah, brother."

I groan and give up, letting my head tilt back. "Cal."

He takes a long stride to us, and Wren backs farther into me. Shit.

Please. Everyone get the hell out of here so we can finish what we started. What we both want.

"So this must be little Miss Maserati." Cal flashes a smug, caught-you-red-handed grin, as he approaches and extends his hand to Wren, his gaze sweeping from her tousled hair to her feet. "My best friend is not only a liar—he's rude. I'll introduce myself. I'm Cal—"

"Cooper." Anderson chirps from the other side of the garage.

Cal hadn't noticed him over there. He came into the shop through the lobby while Anderson, apparently, walked in off the street through the open bay doors.

What were you thinking, trying to take her in such a public place? Easy answer: You weren't. You let your dick do the thinking.

"Well, butter my biscuits. In the flesh. The great NFL linebacker Cal Cooper in little Bumfuck, Texas." Anderson pulls his gaze from Cal long enough to smirk at Wren and wag his finger. "Shame on you. If only I'd known, I'd have been here sooner."

Cal swings around on his heels to face the voice, taking in Anderson, fashionably dressed in a Burberry shirt and slacks. He cocks his head to the side and folds his arms over his enormous chest. "And you are?"

"Anderson Sofitel."

Their eyes are locked onto each other.

"As in *the* Sofitels?"

"Yes."

I rub my hand over my face. Great. Now we're one big happy family.

Fuck.

It's for the best. I didn't need to go there, anyway. One time might not be enough. I might never want to come back. Best to back away from my little songbird. She's only going to fly away. I clear my throat and kiss the top of Wren's head. "I hate to break up the party, but I've got work to do."

Wren's head tilts back as she peers up at me. "Hud?"

I shake my head. "Go with your friend. I've got work to do, anyway."

Wren

Chapter 12

realtor check

"**W**here are we going?"

"Realtor."

"What?"

Anderson speeds down a two-lane highway I've never been on, as if he knows exactly where he's going.

"Careful with this thing, grandma. If it was way more expensive and went a million more miles per hour, I might have PTSD from my last highway venture."

"I'm so sorry my slightly dated Audi falls short of your recent experience. Story of my dating life."

"Okay. Talk. Seriously, where are we going?"

He snickers. "Oh, that's rich. You... telling me to talk. You're gonna talk real soon and you're not going to stop until you answer *all* of my questions about what I walked in on. However, right now, I can still smell him on you. That and the visual is a little too hetero for me. We'll just let it breathe while you stew and fester in it, and I run potentially the most important errand of our lives."

He cuts his eyes from the highway to me. "Now... fix your tousled hair and your lipstick. Try to look a little less man-handled before we pull up. I can't have the realtor thinking I'm responsible for that."

"Trust me. They would never."

"I resent that."

I check my hair and face in the passenger mirror, processing my flushed cheeks and the buzz on my lips from mere moments ago, clearly more lost in the feel of Hud's hands on me than what Anderson just said about a realtor.

Wait. What?

"Anderson. Seriously, I'm elated you came here for me, even though one could argue your questionable timing, but where are we going? And what's this about?"

"Oh, chickie, I didn't come here for you. Well... not entirely. Maybe a little." He reaches for his phone in the console and holds it up. "I came here for this..."

My jaw drops as we speed down the highway, and I stare at Anderson's home screen. It's a picture of the Victorian house behind the Vogel Springs sign.

"Wait. That's not the picture I sent you. Where's the for sale sign?"

"It's a pic from the realtor and the for sale sign is gone. Let's just say it's in escrow."

"Oh, be realistic."

"Honey, I'm being as real as I can get if this place has all the realtor says it has."

"And what am I supposed to do?"

"What you do best. You can decorate it."

"A gay and straight bestie home renovation show... because there aren't enough of those on HGTV."

"Bitch. This is real life, no cameras please. It's going to be a real B&B." Anderson pulls into the drive of a modest real estate office. "Our B&B."

"What?" My head spins around like the girl in *The Exorcist.*

"You said it yourself, there are no hotels in Vogel Springs. What else are they going to do with the damn thing? Stare at the empty place until someone bulldozes history? Let's go make some instead. Wait here. You look like the tart you are with your mouth agape. I'm going to say hello and get the keys."

His car door slams and my mouth stays agape. I turn to the reality of the real estate agency as the door swings shut behind Anderson's entrance. A Bed & Breakfast? Is he serious? Here in Vogel Springs, where I...

Butterflies flutter me back to the shop, and what made my lips swollen. I lift strands of my hair to my face and they smell like Hud, from when he ran his hands through them, hoisted me up, and pulled me into him—the second time he carried me like I'm a feather.

My legs were wrapped so tightly around his waist that I barely had to adjust to feel him hard against me. What the hell was happening there? It takes my breath away, remembering the sounds he made into my mouth. The way he tasted when his tongue took over mine.

I only meant to console him, the way he consoled me, but... *Good. Night.* Something sparked between us, and I would have been naked before him in mere seconds had Anderson not shown up.

Something shifted, and now my association with Hud's shop and Vogel Springs is no longer solely about my car. At this moment, it seems the very least about my car.

So much for strangers. So much for keeping it simple... shit. Anderson? A B&B diagonal from Hud after I let him very nearly take me in his shop?

Forget the exorcist. Let's go back to the stalking I'd been doing from my apartment above Mueller's. Buying the Victorian makes me seem full-blown *Fatal Attraction.* Except for fatalities and the whole rabbit thing. I don't know, though. I may just kill Anderson for this.

I watch as he steps out of the building and flashes his dashing smile at a beautiful realtor in her forties. Her dark hair coiffed perfectly by her ear, curling under her fabulous earrings and the jacket over her pantsuit... I'd love to ask where she bought it. Her perfect makeup, nails, and bright red lipstick complement her dark complexion. Leave it to Anderson to find the best of the best, even in a town this small.

Anderson gives her an air kiss on each cheek, and she waves goodbye as he marches back to the car with a file folder. Oh, brother. He's serious.

Anderson shakes the new house keys at me excitedly, then stalls before turning on the ignition. "Look. I know you are hell-bent on running. Also, what you do best."

"I was still for two years, thank you very much." I turn away from his enthusiasm, laced with personal digs, to face the window.

"All I'm saying is you don't have to go that far. Haven't you ever heard, 'You can drown in a teacup of water.' Now that's a BAMA-ism right there. BAM!" He starts the car.

"I must not be fluent in your native Alabamian tongue, as I don't follow."

"It means you don't have to wade out to the deepest part of the ocean to drown. You can tip over in your own bathtub face down to do the trick. It's much quicker and easier. You've been focused on how many miles you could put between you and the situation you're running from, and those are just miles, Wren. When I look at you and this town... you and Hud—"

"There is no me and Hud, and what do you know about the town? You just got here."

"Please. Right now, this minute, you are the farthest you've ever been from Dallas, your father and—"

"Don't say his name."

"Right. Less is more. I'll stop while I'm ahead." Anderson looks both ways to turn onto the highway and back at me again with a wink.

"Oh, you're ahead alright, I'm just not sure on what." I blink back up at him.

"Okay. We have our keys, we're about to see inside our next adventure. We have eight miles back to town. Talk! About the town, and that beyond-glorious mechanic who almost made it under your hood. Oooh, and his stunning friend. This town grows NFL players? Get to chirping, chickie."

We settle into my favorite window seat at Mueller's, with the perfect view of Bass Pit Shop. It's become a habit now—if you can create one of those in a few days. I'm glad Anderson doesn't call me out on it or ask any questions.

He's too busy checking out the local fare.

Good God, hasn't he seen enough? Hell, he just bought some of it.

Wren, get ready, baby because it's about to be the Anderson Sofitel Show. As if it hasn't been all day.

I smile, reassuring myself. It's a good thing. It's actually great. Not only am I honored and overwhelmed that he came here for me, not to mention how I can't even begin to unpack his plans for us and that house—but, this is good for now. It's my distraction from what keeps me looking out the window and across the street and yearning to be back in that garage in his arms, under his unbelievable chest, his stare, and his touch. Every bone in my body wants to be under that man, and oddly, it feels like it belongs there. What is wrong with me?

"Hi, there. Would you two like more time to look?"

"Well, hello, doll. How are ya today?" Anderson oozes Southern charm. He can't help it. When in Rome, he'd say, if I could read his mind.

Sadly, I can.

He's just rolling in this place until he's deep fried, covered in gravy, drizzled with honey, and dripping with Vogel Springs. *Please, don't embarrass me.* I practically live here above Mueller's for the time being, and I don't want to annoy the staff enough for them to spit in my dinner.

"I'm dandy, how about yourself?" The ash, almost-platinum blonde waitress with roots showing is pretty, regardless, and her narrow blue eyes sparkle at Anderson as she turns on charm of her own.

I haven't seen her before. Maybe she's Jessie, the one who keeps missing shifts.

"I'm Anderson and this is Wren, if you haven't met her already, with all her loitering between here and the Pit Stop."

"Nice to meet you Anderson." Her smile remains, but the sparkle in her eyes dissipates as she turns to me with a laser focus. "Hello, Wren. I can't say I've had the pleasure." She pauses long enough to look me up and down. Her smile widens confidently across her face. "I'm Rosalee."

Hud
Chapter 13
reality check

What. A. Dumbfuck. I can't believe I did that. We're lucky we got caught by her best friend and mine, not the Sunday school class or the county judge. After our conversation yesterday morning, it wouldn't surprise me to see Judge Nelson come stomping into my garage at any time.

It's time for me to pull my head out of my ass and deal with reality. Wren will leave when her car is fixed, which might give her another week here at the most. I'm guessing Anderson the Interloper will whisk her off to parts unknown. Hell, maybe he already has.

Involuntarily, my gaze gravitates to the second-floor window across the street. Face it, man. She won't be here much longer. You can't go there and then let her go. It'd be a goddamned knife in the heart.

She's different.

I never expected a woman like her to get under my skin, but I can't deny it. Not after that. My only means of self-preservation is distance. She needs to stay away from me, and I need to stay away from her. With time, I'll forget that little wren ever flew into my birdcage.

Time heals everything. I know it does.

Now that I've had time to process it, I realize we were lucky to be interrupted. Instead of being pissed, I should be thanking Anderson and Cal. If I'd carried her upstairs... if I'd gone there... shit.

I can't let myself think about it. Besides, I've got way bigger problems than my current obsession with her. I could lose our family land if I don't take their eminent domain threat seriously.

I didn't at first.

It was too absurd to be real. It was just their bluster trying to scare me. But those papers are proof I need to hire the best land attorney money can buy.

No doubt the county commission and VoltEdge have an army of high-priced lawyers. My scalp tingles as it sinks in. *They're really going to try and take your family land away from you.*

You don't have time to dick around with matters of the heart.

"Steady, son." I hear Dad in my head. "Stay calm. Use your brain."

I need to find out why my land is the only land they want.

Yeah, I've got a spring-fed lake on the property, but a company like VoltEdge would suck it dry in no time. There has to be some other reason for a company to be so tunnel-focused on one piece of land. What is it?

That's got to be job number one.

"Yeah, thanks. So I have to send an FOI request and you'll get back to me? How long does that take?"

"Hard to say," a woman with the US Geological Survey tells me. "It just depends on how many records we have to comb through."

"And cost?"

"The first two hours of our search time is free but you'll pay for the time after that, plus the report itself normally costs fifteen-cents a page."

"Okay, I'll send this request later today. Email is fine, right?"

"Yessir."

I hang up the phone. I've got a sneaky suspicion that there's more to this land lust than meets the eye. The county judge and commissioners may or may not know about it, but I'm convinced VoltEdge has deeper reasons for wanting Bass land.

Maybe I've got some minerals they want.

I've done my studying. The minerals used to make batteries for electric cars are rare. My Google search says there are few manganese mines in Texas, the nearest outside Llano. What if VoltEdge found something on my land that they need? I researched. Companies like VoltEdge use satellite imaging to scan for minerals all over the world, but when they conduct hyperspectral imaging on American soil, the USGS requires them to file a report.

God bless America.

"You got your shit together now?"

I straighten from resting my head in my hands, elbows propped on the desk, to see Cal holding a to-go box from Martha's. "You haven't eaten."

"Love you man, but fuck off." He'd walked out with Anderson and Wren and left me alone yesterday to finally get that catalytic converter off her car. Cal knows me. He gave me time alone. But for whatever reason, he's decided time's up.

He drops the to-go box on my desk and jabs his finger at me. "Naw, man. You lied to me. Straight out lied to me."

I meet his gaze. "No, Cal, I didn't lie to you. I lied to myself."

We share a long, drawn-out stare before Cal tweaks his mouth to the side, takes in a deep breath, and nods softly. He sinks into the chair in front of me. "Yeah. Guess I know about lying to yourself. But you admit now—you like Little Miss Maserati?"

I groan and rest my head back in my hands. "Yeah."

"Go for it, man. She's obviously into you or she wouldn't a been lettin' you carry her upstairs like that. I froze in the fuckin' lobby with my jaw saggin' to the floor. I saw her legs wrapped around you." Cal tries to stifle a chuckle but he can't. "By the way, how'd that happen? I mean, the garage wide open and all? Mmm, mmm, mmm. You gonna' ravage a woman, at least lock the damned doors." He keeps trying to throttle the chuckle that refuses to be controlled. His shoulders are shaking.

"Obviously, I wasn't thinking. She just... we just... damn, man." My arms swing wide. "It happened. What do you want me to say?" I stand, shoving my chair back with my legs. "I've had time to cool off and think about it. It was best you two interrupted us. I might not be able to come back if I went there. She's different from any woman I've ever been with."

My best friend covers his mouth with his fist and clears his throat loudly, interrupting. "Speaking of different than any woman you've ever been with."

My gaze snaps to meet his. "What?"

He tilts his head to the side while lifting his brows. "When's the last time you heard from Rosalee?"

I scroll through memories like thumbing through a pile of cards. "I can't remember."

Cal leans back in his chair and locks his knuckles together. "But you still get Connor at least twice a month, right?"

"Yeah. Usually more than that. He lives with her parents in Rockridge. Rosalee's lost, man. She's on drugs. Where are you going with this?"

He hikes his shoulder. "I just..."

My jaw falls seeing the mother of my son sashaying across the street, making a beeline for my front door. "What the?" My eyes snap back to Cal's. "She's here."

"That's what I was about to tell you." Cal nods at the to-go box. "Working at Martha's."

"Hud?" Rosalee presents herself inside the lobby, and our gazes hold.

Part of me cringes. She was so beautiful once. She looks ten years older than the last time I saw her. The other half of me gets mad looking at her. It was her choice to mess with drugs and get hooked. I did everything I could to stop her. "Rosalee."

She smiles. "So good to see you, Hud." She ignores Cal, walks to me, and wraps her arms around me, planting her face in my chest.

My eyes meet Cal's, who holds up his hands with a mocking grin. I can't find it in me to hug her back. Instead, I grip Rosalee's shoulders, pulling her off of me. "What are you doing here?"

She bats her long, fake eyelashes. "Staying with Genevieve."

"Why?"

She draws back as her blue eyes flash. "Well, aren't you the welcome wagon."

"What do you expect? First you run off with Connor, then you dump him on your parents. What do you do with the child support you get every month? Buy drugs? Because it damn sure isn't going to him."

"Screw you, Hudson Bass. You're just as big an asshole as ever."

"And you're just as messed up as the last time I saw you." Holding her at arm's length, I scan her body up and down, noticing sores still on her arms. Her skin is dry and pruney, and her cheeks are sunken in. It amazes me that people like her do speed, knowing what it does to their bodies. She does own a mirror, right?

"How long since you had a fix, Rosalee?" I bend down to get in her face. "You jonesing for some meth?"

My neck whips to the side as she slaps my face open-handed. Not the first time. She can still pack a punch. My fault for getting in her face.

"I expect you to help me with Connor for a while. Genevieve doesn't have room and my parents—"

I cut her off mid-sentence. "I'll be glad to keep him all the time. Sign over custody."

She turns and flaunts her shoulder. "You wish. I'll drop him off when I come into work tomorrow."

Cal stands. "Wait, Rosalee."

She turns, glaring at him.

"Why's your ass in Vogel Springs in the first place? Last I recalled you couldn't wait to get out. What brings you back now?"

She answers with her upper lip curled and her teeth clenched. "None of your business."

"Mmm, mmm, mmm, Sweet Rosalee. Back in Vogel Springs." He turns to me, scratching his cheek. "Chickens come home to roost."

"Screw yourself, Cal Cooper."

He chuckles, and his deep dimples show. "Good to see you too, Rosalee."

She holds the lobby door open as she leaves, turning back to face me with a murderous glare. "I'll drop your son off when I come to work tomorrow."

"Like I said, as far as I'm concerned, you can just leave him here."

She ignores the remark and stalks back to Martha's. Her sashay is gone.

What I'm looking at is the old Rosalee, puffed up and clawing like a wet cat because things didn't go the way she planned.

Rosalee's like that. She's a planner. Conniving. Manipulating. I don't know what she has up her sleeve, but she's got something. She hates Vogel Springs. She'd never be back here of her own free will. I'll talk to her folks. Maybe Connor knows.

Cal swears. "The boy would be a damn sight better off with you than her."

"Connor's not with her, Cal. I told you, he lives with her parents and they love him. He loves his grandparents. They're good to him and he's their blood. But I know for a fact, they aren't getting the child support I send. They've told me. So I make sure he has school clothes and haircuts—whatever he needs. I take care of Connor financially, but you're right, he'd be a lot better off living with me full time."

Cal hikes a brow. "You willin' to raise him full time?" His eyes lock on mine with a look there's no escaping. It's a question he already knows the answer to.

"Yeah."

My eyes swell as Cal's Aunt Tiny drops a second plate of hot-grilled biscuits before Anderson and me.

I used to forget to eat, but between Martha and now meeting Tiny, I'm afraid I can't avoid it.

Anderson reaches for her homemade apricot jelly while I stick with the blackberry that coated my first food-porn-worthy hot biscuit. Jesus.

No wonder they don't have a doughnut shop in Vogel Springs. These biscuits are pastries of their own, and I haven't even touched the savory option.

I'm sitting between Anderson and a vat of cream gravy made with peppercorn and coffee grounds, and I think Tiny said the small basket at the end of the table was full of deep-fried banana fritters.

Cal reaches across me for one and tosses it on Anderson's plate. "Go big or go home, Alabama."

"If you think I haven't had a banana fritter before, Cooper..."

"I said you haven't had one of Aunt Tiny's. I can guarantee that." Cal grins widely, watching Anderson lean in for a bite.

My dirty, tacky, degenerate bestie brings the round fried fritter to his lips and pauses, their gazes cemented together. "Cal. I assure you I always go big."

"Hush you two. Not in front of little girl," Tiny laughs.

I don't even know her, and I already love her laugh. It's boisterous and feminine as it erupts from her large bosom, demanding attention. It ends in a giggle as if begging the question of all who hear it if they thought something was funny, too.

It's a contagious laugh that Cal was raised on, I'm learning.

It's not hard to ascertain why Anderson likes him so much, why I'm struck by him... how he and Hud... are best friends.

Tiny finally sits and takes a biscuit. We're more than halfway through breakfast, and the large but spry woman has yet to sit and enjoy. Aunt Tiny is anything but Tiny.

She smiles as I watch her beautiful hands reach for a biscuit. "Now, little girl, pass Tiny the blackberry preserves, and tell me all about it."

"Oh, me?" It's hard to swallow a giggle. I'm so shocked that I could be of any interest at this table. Cal and Anderson must have already mentioned me to Tiny.

I take a moment to study my bestie with his infectious smile, blonde hair, and blue eyes. His chiseled jaw and nose.

How does he do that? Anderson makes fast friends with anybody. He has a natural ability to make himself at home, whereas, these last few days, I've felt like Vogel Springs made me feel at home. It insisted.

My eyes drop to the table as my smile evaporates.

Three.

It's been three days since Hud grabbed me like he couldn't resist having me, took my breath away when he told me he wanted me, and then avoided me like the plague.

Tiny turns and throws me a wink. She must know.

"Little girl, if you only knew how I couldn't wait to have you over. I had to meet Miss Maserati in the flesh. Now, I figured I'd get the skinny on you before anybody else, seeing as how Cal is such a sports car enthusiast, but you must have arrived right before he got back. And Hud's been such a stranger lately, I had to wait 'til Cal brought him over to hear all about it."

Cal clears his throat loud and obvious, right before I detect a kick under the table, and Aunt Tiny snaps, "Cal Cooper. I was talking to Wren, not you, and I was referring to her car and just how uncanny the events were that brought her to us. I didn't say nothin' about that boy losing his mind over her."

Her glare softens as she turns from Cal back to me and flashes the prettiest smile I've ever seen. "But I can certainly see why he did."

I turn the color of her strawberry preserves, and my heart rate goes into overdrive.

Did he? Is he? Is it possible Hud lost his head over me?

"Honey, sometimes, men take a little bit longer to figure it all out. Eve didn't eat the apple first just because she was tempted...

she realized what it was before Adam did. Hud might need a second or two, 'cause he's in the eye of the storm right now, but he'll come around." Tiny tucks her chin and lifts her brows as her eyes bore into mine.

"Seems like you might have been in one of your own, before something stopped you in your tracks." She gives my hand a reassuring squeeze. "Now I don't pretend to know what it is, but I won't pretend that the whole town's not wonderin', including myself."

Glancing around the room, I realize the boys have left the table.

Cal appears to be showing Anderson around Tiny's yard. He'd mentioned the peach and pear trees that surrounded her place.

"All you have to know is, whatever your secret is, it's safe with Tiny, if you ever have to share it. And as for Hudson Bass, I've known that boy since he was this high." She holds her hand even with the tabletop. "And when I saw what crossed his eyes at the mention of your name, I knew right then and there..."

She purses her lips, her gaze darting high in the room, before rejoining mine. "I wish I could say I don't mean to be presumptuous, but Cal would tell you I'm lying. So I'll just say it. I believe your Maserati mishap was the good Lord telling you to stop and smell the roses. And maybe it was His way of tellin' Hud to do the same. You just think on it."

The kitchen door swings open as Anderson and Cal reappear, with Anderson carrying a fist full of roses he cut for Tiny from her own beautiful yard.

Cal reaches into the cabinet to hand Anderson a vase. It's like they've known each other for years.

As Anderson arranges his vase of flowers, he asks with an inquisitive eyebrow, "Aunt Tiny, how long will it take me to grow a peach tree or two?" He's got his wheels-turning face on. They may not know it yet, but I do.

Cal belts out a boisterous laugh as Tiny's head tilts back, and she joins Cal in cracking up. "Anderson Sofitel, I had you pegged as a smart man. You could've talked all day and not said that."

"She means, you can't plant a peach tree and get peaches overnight. They take years to produce fruit," Cal chimes in, and I love how Anderson's fruit tree dilemma is just as important as anything else we could be discussing at this table.

"No Cal, that is not what I meant," Tiny says. "He doesn't need any peaches or pears. Anderson, when you bought the old Vogel place, did they fail to tell you there are a couple acres of pecan trees in the back? Why do you think I've been feeding you so well? A trade for a trade, hustler. You listen to Tiny, and come late fall, we'll have some pecans to shell."

"Shell and sell! Will I have that many?" Anderson asks, all eyes and ears, like a good little entrepreneur.

"We'll see. Depends on the kind of shape they're in. They've been neglected for a while."

I sit back and marvel at their banter.

Late fall. The idea of it.

I'll have my catalytic converter in a matter of days. That's the only thing definite right now. Yes, Anderson bought the Victorian, and for a song, as it is so badly in need of repair, but he lives in Austin.

He's less than a hundred miles away. It's a realistic business venture for him. I see the path he's carving out as they speak.

I'm afraid I still may be an outsider in this equation.

Worse, I feel I am especially an outsider in Hud's world. His absence from this breakfast solidifies just that.

By 2 p.m., I'm itching to stretch my legs and catch some rays. There's not much we can do in the Vogel House yet. Cal with Anderson to meet with the building inspector.

Gauging how full I still am from another Southern breakfast, I may need to run off a biscuit or three too many. Between Martha and Tiny... *Good night.*

A walk to the pool and a few laps should do my pale ass some good.

The clothing boutique by Mueller's didn't carry swimsuits when I asked on my first day here, and it's not a great idea to go to a public pool with children present in the suit I wore in Taos.

I hesitate as I look across the street at the Dollar General next to the Pit Stop. Ugh. It's my only option.

When I begin to walk discreetly over, I beeline toward Anderson's Victorian, all but hide in the brush, then dart across the street, already almost passing the dollar store, just so anyone who sees me is clear I am under no circumstances looking for Hud, nor slumming around his shop.

A brighter pink one-piece than I would normally be caught in later, and another pair of sunglasses I couldn't live without, and I'm opening the gate to the pool.

I pay two bucks cash, and apparently, I'm good for the entire day. I can't hide my smile. I already adore this place.

I take a swim test, swimming the length of the pool so a high school lifeguard can give me permission for the deep end, and then I continue my laps, hopefully soaking up some color.

I've felt naked without my custom airbrush tan spray made to match my skin tone. I haven't seen the can since I left the resort.

Asking Martha if they have a tanning salon in Vogel Springs that specializes in custom color airbrushes didn't seem high on the list. Asking Hud if I could rummage through my car, coming up with a can of spray tan that he could shame me for, was even less appetizing.

Freckles dotting frighteningly stark, white skin and some vitamin D it is.

I hop out of the water and decide to dry off before I can no longer boast about my pale white skin but instead nurse a sunburn.

It's hard not to think about Hud. However, it is paramount to recognize what and who has not crossed my mind, and for that, to Anderson's credit, I have Vogel Springs to thank.

Still, missing someone you don't know—but know you want to be with—is a new kind of torture.

Yearning for someone who's less than a hundred yards away at all times is an additional torture of its own.

Pity what it's come to after days of stomach flips at the memory of his mouth moving on mine, his hands finding their place on my body, and feeling his need for more when he pulled me closer and looked directly at me with his darkened, grey eyes. Now I'm reduced to the assumption that I will, at least, get to see him when my car is ready.

Or will he simply leave me a note that we're square and the keys are in the dash?

I shake my head as I start to pack up Martha's towel and my Dollar General knick-knacks.

"Hey, ma'am, you dropped this."

I look down, pulling my tote bag strap onto my shoulder to find a little boy with the cutest face smiling up at me with my sunscreen in his hand. "Thank you so much. I didn't realize I hadn't grabbed it."

"You did. It just fell out of the top of your bag when you shoved your towel in."

What a little gentleman. "Well thank you, again. You're a skin-saver."

He giggles at my goofy humor and walks with me as I head out the gate, peering up at me with the happiest of smiles. "I get it. Instead of a lifesaver. Who are you?"

"Who am I?"

He hikes his shoulders. "It's just, I've never seen you here before, and I know everybody." He flashes an irresistible smile. "I really do."

"I'm Wren."

"You're still a stranger."

I have to laugh. "Yes, I am. What's your name?"

"I'm Connor."

"Nice to meet you, Connor."

"You too, Wren. Guess we're not strangers anymore."

I almost melt. Who is this kid? He's beyond charming.

Cute as he can be with his full head of thick brown hair and sparking blue eyes. "Did you swim?" He's not dripping wet and doesn't seem like he went swimming.

"Nah, I just stopped by to say hi to some of my friends. They get upset when I've been back in town for a couple of days and don't stop by. Especially Annie. She's the swim test girl."

"I see. So you were making the rounds?"

"Yeah, I'll probably swim tomorrow. I've got stuff to do today."

"Got ya. Me too, I think." My stomach growls. "See. Told ya, I've got to eat. Guess I did swim off my breakfast."

"Your breakfast? It's after lunch, and gettin' closer to dinner time."

My stomach growls again, and I join Connor, laughing with him like a little kid. "On that note, I'm headed to Mueller's. Where are you headed, Connor?" I enjoy his company so much that I neglect to wonder where his parents are.

Yikes. I am a stranger-danger.

"Well, I was headed back to my dad's." He points to Bass Pit Stop, and my heart falls to the ground. My entire body freezes stiff, and I stare at the garage where my Maserati sits. "But I could eat. I'll come with you to get a snack."

Connor motions to Mueller's, and I turn to ask, "Is that okay with your parents?"

His parents. Hud is his parent. My heart has stopped. What the entire fuck?

I thought I'd thrown a lot of curve balls in my life. Hell, I am a curveball, but this is... this is...

"Earth to Wren!" Connor tugs on my arm. "Watch what I can do." He jumps up on an old round pipe rail that runs down Main Street in front of the shops lining the street.

I watch in amazement as this nimble, adorable little boy—who can't be but seven or eight—walks the small round pipe like a tightrope artist with a smile that breaks my face.

"Yay!" I clap my hands and Connor beams like he just won a gold medal as he jumps to the ground. "My dad taught me. Hurry," he says. "Let's go. Martha has me a snack, no matter what time I'm hungry." His small hand grabs mine, and he halts us to look both ways before crossing the four-way stop.

I follow him willingly, partially entranced by what I just discovered, and entirely entranced by this adorable, tiny human.

Connor pushes the cafe door open, bells ding, and a small after-lunch crowd looks up in classic Vogel Springs fashion.

"Mommy, Mommy!"

Air leaves my lungs when the warm little hand lets go of mine, bypassing tables, booths, and Martha to throw his arms around Rosalee's waist and bury his face in her apron.

My heart crashes and shatters on the hardwood floor.

Rosalee looks down, patting his thick head of hair, and brings her eyes back up, glaring at me. She stares as if she just won a prize or the joke—at my expense.

An unexpected numbness falls over me, and I have no idea what to think.

I simply feel suffocated in the town I thought I'd made my own, the same way I felt at the firm with my father and Phillip, in the life I thought was my own.

My ears begin to ring as it hits me, watching Connor in his mother's arms. Twice now, everything I hoped for—I didn't lose it. I never had it. Phillip belonged to someone else, like Hud belongs to Connor and Rosalee.

I suck in a breath, finding a strength maybe I never knew I had, and a bright smile beseeches me, spreading across my face, forcing me to follow suit. My eyes twinkle toward Martha, and I hold up my tote bag of swimming gear as if it's a shield or houses some excuse for why I can't sit and eat, say hi, or control my own body and emotions right now.

"Be right back in for a bite, Martha. Just gonna get rid of this swim gear." With that, I head for the stairs, but instead, escape out the side door of Mueller's Cafe.

I don't run upstairs to my room above the restaurant because it doesn't feel like it's mine anymore.

I don't run anywhere near Rosalee's sneering glare because it is one I do not know or understand. I'm apparently out of my league here by default.

Air. I just need air.

Anderson was right, not about the miles and running, but about the teacup of water. I'm face down in my own bathtub. Drowning. Thank God Mueller's has a door to the alley. Emergency exit is more like it. That's what it is for me.

My tote bag full of swim gear slides down the brick wall as I release it and continue fleeing behind the brick buildings lining Vogel Spring's Main Street.

My oversized tank top is a short dress that drips with the water from my swimsuit and still-wet hair.

I don't want to be seen by anyone.

I just want air.

Out of nowhere, strong hands wrap around my waist.

His legs encompass my stance, and I walk backward as he presses my back firmly but gently against the bricks and drops his face to the top of my head.

Tears burn down my cheek at the feel of him—my body's recognition of something I crave—the smell of him surrounding me again.

"Steady now," Hud says in that rich, smooth tone as he breathes into my hair, holding me tightly.

I don't move other than to melt into him.

I can barely breathe, much less speak.

I've never been so overwhelmed in my life.

"I'm so sorry." He breathes wildly into my hair as if he's trying to calm me and absorb me at the same time.

Hud steps back slightly to see my face without loosening his grip on me. Then firmly, with what feels like truth, free of explanation, he growls, "It's not what you think. I... It's just. Not."

Chapter 16

an explanation

I glance over my shoulder from under the hood of a GMC diesel with its check engine light on to see something I never expected. But I should have. Connor Bass has never met a stranger, and neither has Wren Baldwin. I let him go to the swimming pool after lunch. Now he's walking home with her.

She told me she loved a swimming pool. I just never put it together that this might happen.

I straighten to watch Connor trying to impress her by walking the old hitching rail that lines the street in front of Mueller's and the hardware store. The merchant's association voted to keep it for historical reasons, even though it hasn't been used in a hundred years. I grew up walking on it. So has Connor, first with me holding his hand until he got the hang of it. Now he walks it like a pro. Little show-off.

Wren is applauding him.

Again, why am I surprised to see them laughing and talking, heading my way? *Guess you've got some 'splaining to do, Lucy.'*

Wait. No. They're not coming here. They're going into Mueller's. Together. With Rosalee on duty.

I groan. Living over the cafe, I'd assumed Wren knew about me and Rosalee by now. But she wouldn't know about Connor. Shit. Rosalee will eat her alive.

I've got no customers. I yank down the bay door, stride to the front door and lock it—and all but run across the street to Mueller's, taking the porch steps in one giant stride, my heart pounding faster and faster. I've avoided her since that moment. I owe the woman an explanation. I'm sure she's wondered why I've kept my distance. But so has she. We both knew we didn't need to go where we were going.

But still, I need to explain about Rosalee and my son. I owe her that.

Stepping into Mueller's, Connor's got his face in a chocolate milkshake, and his mother leers at me with a smirk that I want to wipe off her face. I can only imagine what Rosalee said to Wren when she walked in with Connor.

I turn to Martha, and she tilts her head, indicating the alley door. I head straight for it.

"Where ya' going, Hud?" Rosalee's taunt drips with contempt.

Doesn't deserve a response. I stride across the cafe and out the back door. There she is. Wren is too absorbed in her emotions to hear me come out the back door or feel my presence as I take quick, long steps toward her. Her head is bowed, her gaze on the ground. She startles when my hands grip her waist and pull her into me, inhaling her. "Steady, now..." I whisper, as I walk her back to the wall.

With the words, Wren softens in my touch, leaning on me. Tears flow down her cheeks.

What have I done to this beautiful woman? I would never hurt her, not on purpose. But obviously, I have. "I'm so sorry."

Nothing. She says nothing. She just cries quietly as I try to absorb her. Her. I've missed everything about her. I didn't want to let go of her that day. I wanted to yell at Anderson and Cal to get the fuck out. But I didn't. Maybe I should have.

No. Logic tells me I did what I was supposed to: Let her go. She doesn't belong to me. She doesn't belong here.

I can't allow myself to have her because she'll leave in a matter of days. Yet, watching her hurt, all I want to do is comfort her—erase the pain I've caused. I've got a legal battle looming over me, and Connor is living with me. I've got too much baggage for a pack mule to carry. How can I pile it on top of this delicate creature?

And again, I know, even though her heart is breaking right now, she'll leave and when she does, she'll forget a country boy like me in a week. It is what it is.

I ease my grip on her to step back and take her in one last time. I want to remember Wren Baldwin when I'm an old man. The golden tan she drove in with is gone, revealing perfect porcelain skin, dotted with adorable freckles. Why would she ever cover up that skin with a spray?

Like warm honey dripping over new spring grass, her eyes peer up at me through a veil of tears, searching my face for answers. All I want to do is carry her across the street, up the stairs, lay her across my bed, and make mad, passionate love to her. But instead, I cup her face in my hands, adoring her, tracing her delicate chin with my thumb. My fingers run gently over her perfect brows and along her cheekbones, etching the curves of her face into my brain, my eyes devouring her the way my body wants to.

I outline her perfect lips with my fingertips. The only thing I can offer this little beauty is, "Wren, I... it... it's not what it looks like." My eyes beg for her to understand, knowing I'm asking the impossible.

I lift her off the ground to command her mouth, to feel what I felt in the shop the other day one more time, like a damned addict—and stop myself. It wouldn't be fair. A goodbye kiss would make both of us more miserable.

Instead, I press my forehead to hers, inhaling her one last time, unable to find any words. I kiss her forehead, lower her to the ground, and head back to the shop.

I'm not going to reopen. Screw it. I need to get out of here. This shit is killing me. Where's Cal when I need him? Normally, if he's in town, he's at the shop every day. Underfoot, like when he walked in unannounced the other day, just as I was about to...

Dammit. I pull my cell phone from my hip pocket.

HudBass: Where RU?

CalCoop: Shopping

HudBass: 😞 ?!

CalCoop: Need 2 catch up

HudBass: No 💩 Need U bro

I glance across at Mueller's. Rosalee. I'd like to pick her up and throw her back to wherever she came from. I can only imagine what she said to Wren. Not to mention, she's a half-assed mother. I'm going to finish Jack's diesel and get out of here. I fish out my phone again.

HudBass: Not today. Out of here

CalCoop: WTF??

HudBass: Taking Connor 🎣

CalCoop: Catch u tomorrow

HudBass: K

Wren

Chapter 17

his way or the highway

My car broke down. I felt an attraction to a stranger, and I fell in love with a quaint town. That's all that's happened here. It's not earth-shattering or course-changing.

I dove into this because I lost my own agency when I lost my wheels. Once I get my car back, things will look different.

Scratch all that. They already do.

One last glance across the street at the Pit Stop that comes up empty-handed, and I can't pop out of bed fast enough.

I'm out of here.

Even Anderson's too absorbed. What happened to South Padre? We are way past the phenomenon of sea turtles.

I throw open the small closet to find my carry-on staring up at me. Apart from the toiletries I took out that first night, between Vogel Vintage, The Purple Polka Dot, and the Dollar General, I've barely opened the darn thing. Imagine that. Me, dressing myself for a week at a shabby chic, purple-obsessed boutique and second-hand store while accessorizing at Dollar General.

Reaching for the handle, I toss the bag on my bed before my heartstrings tug at the very shops I'm making fun of.

I have actual memories of this place. It's insane.

Not to mention the haunting memories that kept me awake all night. I swear, I smelled him and felt him before I realized he was holding me.

And the way it felt to be held by him again... the reminder was almost painful under the circumstances because he still felt so good and so right.

Then grey eyes searched so deeply into my own, as if they were trying to tell me more than he could. As if he had to make me understand.

But I don't understand this at all... not what's going on, not the attraction or longing I have for a person I clearly don't know at all.

I think I was crazy enough, tossing and turning in the heat of the night, to think he might walk over and find me again. And when he didn't, it made me mad to wonder why he hasn't yet, under these unorthodox circumstances. He was determined to avoid me, then so determined to make me see him that second, as if to trust him, and for what? What does it matter?

"It's not what it looks like..." I mock his words out loud.

"Then, what is it, Hudson Bass?"

Either way, he appears when he wants. He gives what little he wants, and damn me if the little he gives isn't a lot. It's certainly enough to keep me thinking about him, even when I've sworn off this ludicrous idea of him.

That's it, exactly. It's his way or the highway, and I choose the highway. It's never let me down before. My Maserati did. But hey, that's what rental cars are for.

I'm getting the fuck out of here before I'm caught packing up, staring out a window, and talking to myself above a cafe of strangers.

"Knock. Knock. Knock."

"You've got to be kidding me."

"Well now, we know you're in there, doll. Open up." Anderson's voice is recognizable from anywhere. Wait. We?

I crack the door open to find Anderson and his new appendage, Cal, standing above me.

"Oh, brother. What do you two want?"

Anderson marches in and looks around. "Well, sister, for you to put your suitcase away, for one. I'm not fussing at you Wren, just perhaps stating the obvious. How far did you think you were going to get with no catalytic converter?" Cal is charming, if not soothing, even when he's being a butt.

"Actually pretty far, as soon as you get me to a rental." I turn pointedly to Anderson. "The one in Rockridge, or you can drive me to Austin for one, but I'm leaving. Today."

"Oh, and just fuck your Maserati? I mean, I know it's a special car, but last I checked it couldn't drive itself to you."

"Next year's MC20 Coupé and MC20 Cielo can."

"Cal." Anderson shakes his head at his new bestie. "What, you want to spend an exorbitant amount to have it delivered to God-knows-where you plan to land next, just because you can't survive on RC Cola and MoonPies for a few more days until it's fixed?"

"Shut up."

"See? You can't, can you? Because not even you know where you're planning on going next."

"I know enough to get gone."

"About that. Wren, I don't think you know everything, and I'm certain you don't know enough to understand." Cal reaches for my suitcase and sets it back in the closet.

"Why are you two always together? You're attached at the hip."

Anderson and Cal share a look.

I roll my eyes and charge through the small apartment. "Who cares. I'm leaving. With or without your help."

Anderson shakes his head and raises a new shiny key ring. "I guess I'm just supposed to shove four thousand square feet of our future and Vogel Springs' official, one-and-only bed and breakfast up my ass?"

I gasp. I can't help being proud of my best friend. He may be as impulsive as I am, but he has a straight-A student follow-through on what he puts his mind to.

"You got it? They gave you the permit?"

Anderson nods slowly, his sparkling eyes on mine. This is something to celebrate.

"This bitch walked into the courthouse with a long shot, and left with the permit and the promise of a liquor license for the nonexistent dining room, just so he could serve wine someday, which is damn near impossible in these parts." Cal shakes his head in admiration. The NFL linebacker is beaming at Anderson.

"Nonexistent, yet. We'll have one. And it's not hard to get a license to sell wine, especially if you plan on having a vineyard."

"Please don't tell me there's a shovel waiting for me in your car. A tiller?"

"Nope, but we do have a surprise for you." Cal motions for me to follow, and we leave my suitcase right where it started the day—back in the closet.

One hundred-plus-year-old wood creaks below my wedge sandals with every step I take inside the living monument.

Sunlight pierces through the old uncovered windows, illuminating all the work yet to be done. Past my footsteps—the wood creaking and Anderson and Cal's faded conversation on the porch—I feel a serene sense of peace.

This place.

This house, or home as they call them, is not at all what I expected.

It needs way more work, yet being inside evokes the same awe-struck feeling I had when I crossed the four-way stop to look up at its magnificence that first day. And although it's very different from anything else in this town, it, too, evokes the same feelings of a home I never knew.

It kind of takes my breath away.

As I step toward the kitchen, bypassing what has to be an original stained glass window, my curiosity peaks. I almost want to run out back and find Tiny's promise of pecan trees and Anderson's hope of a vineyard before I even see the upstairs.

This place is perfect. It's perfectly Anderson.

Is it odd that I feel pride for my best friend?

It doesn't take a once-stunning Victorian home in desperate need of attention to do that. Even on our worst days, I am always proud of him. "Ah, ha ha ha! I knew she'd love it."

Cal peeks through the front door frame as Anderson enters the house to join me, phone in hand, and he waves with it, motioning to Anderson. "I've got to split. You two alright in here? Nobody's afraid of ghosts?"

I look back and smile at Cal, the impression the house made lingering on my face and in the air.

"Good. Just can't have one more reason for your chickie to fly the coop. Later." And Cal is off.

"Fly the coop? What's with all the bird references? I get it. My name is Wren. You call me chickie sometimes, but I've heard it around town more than Maserati."

Anderson bursts out laughing. "You really don't know, do you?"

I cock my head toward him with an emphatic look.

"Vogel Springs?" Anderson tosses his hands in the air dramatically.

I shake my head.

"Vogel is the German word for bird. My little Wren landed in a town named after birds." Anderson slides his hands into his khaki pockets and rises on his toes.

"You bitch! You didn't know that until the realtor told you. Or Cal did." I rip a dusty sheet off an old chaise lounge and threaten to drape it over him.

"Hey, speaking of things you don't know." Anderson's serious voice interrupts my attempt at horseplay. It's a very serious voice, as in he very seldom uses it.

The hair stands up on the back of my neck, and I immediately toss the dusty sheet aside, all ears.

"About, Hud—"

"Let me guess. It's not what it looks like."

"No. It is. The hot mechanic you can't keep your hands off of has a son. I just think there's more to him than you think. At least, that's what Cal tells me."

I chew on the side of my lip while Anderson takes a pregnant pause, testing to see who will break first. My very own curiosity shocks the hell out of me. "Rosalee? Are they married? Separated?"

"No. High School sweethearts. Cal said she was beautiful, practically Miss Vogel Springs, but spoiled rotten. Hud was the only genuine thing she had going for herself. Her parents were older when they had her, and she's an only child. They doted on her and gave her anything she wanted until that turned into getting high and her next fix."

"No!"

"Yes ma'am. Former homecoming queen has a bit of a drug habit she can't seem to kick."

"And Connor?"

"Cal said Rosalee fled after graduation for greener pastures. She and Hud stayed in touch throughout college, off and on. Let's say young Hud was caught in her Venus fly-trap. Then, one day she says she's pregnant and it's his."

"That must've been really hard for Hud."

"You have no idea. To hear Cal tell it, the guy's a saint. I'm not trying to make you cream your panties here, but Hud is the only stable thing that kid's got. Well, him and the grandparents."

"Rosalee's parents?"

"Yeah. I think he predominantly lives with them, not her. He goes between them and Hud. Cal says this is the first time Rosalee's been back in years—other than to drop him off. Her dad's had Parkinson's for a long time and Cal suspects that's taken its toll."

"So... she's looking for Hud to..."

"We'll see. Cal's looking into it. Don't talk about it with Hud."

"Talk about it? What are you even talking about? You got here days ago and know more than I do about the guy. As if I were ever given the opportunity to talk to Hud."

"Look, I'm not trying to delve into what keeps you up at night or what makes you sing like a canary—"

"Please. No more bird jokes."

"I am trying to help my business and renovation partner clear her head with a little relief. You may do what you want with it, but I'm asking you to stay... for me. Look at this place. I can't do it alone. I came here for you Wren, but I truly found something for me, and I can't imagine attempting it with anyone else but you."

I dive into Anderson's chest and hug my true blue with all my might. He's right about everything he's suggested since the start of my escape charade.

He hugs me back tightly. If Anderson makes me realize anything, it's that I count, too. We both do.

Men will come and go. Circumstances change daily, but who I am and what I seek counts for something, and so does my place as his person.

I smile brightly at Anderson and let him show me everything throughout the house.

Yes, I am all in.

I meant it when I said I was, but in terms of Hud, I can't accept Anderson's explanation via Cal's intel at face value. I can't be all in with that one.

One, because Hud isn't asking me to be. He's not asking anything of me.

And two, this isn't the first time I've been pushed over or out by a significant other and *their* kids.

What does that say about me?

Chapter 18
fishing

"**D**addy, Daddy! I got a fish!"

I glance over my shoulder to see my son leaning back, reeling in a flopping, fighting fish with a smile that makes me forget everything else. I had the lake stocked with bass and catfish a couple of years ago. "Good job. Bring him in, buddy." I rest my fishing pole on the bank to join my son, standing over him as he cranks his rod furiously, trying to pull his catch to the bank and out of the water.

Connor is one hundred percent focused on this battle with the fish. He lets out a gigantic sigh. "He's not very big." His voice drips with disappointment as a little perch pops out of the water with a hook in its mouth.

"That's okay." I grab his fish and work the hook out of its mouth. "How about we put him back and let him grow some more?"

"Yeah," Connor mumbles. "He's too little. His parents would be sad."

He makes me chuckle as I squat and ease his little perch back into the water.

"Dad?"

"Yeah, buddy."

"What happened yesterday?"

The muscles in my neck tighten. "What do you mean?"

"I mean, I heard Momma and Genevieve talkin'. Do you know that lady, Wren?"

Fucking Rosalee. I cut my eyes from the bait bucket to Connor, hoping to divert his attention back to fishing. I came here to forget Wren. And VoltEdge. And his mother. "You want a minnow for bait this time? Or a worm?"

I catch him out of the corner of my eye, studying me as I squat on my haunches, resting on my heels beside the bait bucket.

Connor says, "She's nice. I met her at the swimming pool."

"Good. Now let's get back to fishing. Minnow or worm?"

"Worm."

"Minnow's better, if you want to catch a big fish, like bass or catfish or trout. What do you say?"

He nods. "Okay. Minnow. I don't think Momma and Genevieve like Wren."

He's really going there, and I don't have a clue what to tell him. "Wren's a nice lady whose car broke down, and she can't leave town until I get it fixed. And I can't fix it until the replacement part gets here, which should be this next week. No need to worry about her or what your mom or Genevieve think of her. She'll leave as soon as her car's fixed."

He peers at me through crystal blue eyes, eyes exactly like Rosalee's were when she was young, eyes that catch the sun's reflection off this clearwater lake. "Momma said you like Wren. I heard her say you and Wren were, you know..." His voice trails off as he shrugs one shoulder.

I have a flash vision of drop-kicking Rosalee's ass over a goalpost.

I stand. "I do like Wren. But like I said, she's just passing through. A customer. There's nothing between us and she won't be here much longer, anyway. Now, let's get back to fishing. Okay?"

"Yeah." He digs the toe of his tennis shoe into the damp earth at the water's edge. He still wants to pursue whatever he overheard yesterday.

I nudge him with my elbow and wink. "Bet I can catch a bigger fish than you can."

A smile hijacks his face. This kid loves a challenge. His dark hair glistens in the morning sun and I realize, for the first time, my son needs a haircut. "Bet you can't," he beams.

"You're on."

"Hey, Cal." Connor waves and races to Cal, who exits his Range Rover after parking in front of my parents' old house. The one I grew up in. The one I left when I opened my shop.

He had sense enough not to bring his Bentley down here. The quarter-mile dirt lane to the homeplace is too rutted for a low-riding car. With his NFL salary, Cal has a stable of vehicles. The Bentley just happens to be the latest.

I look up from frying fish to see Cal scoop up Connor, swing him around, and hold him high, at arm's length. "Damn, boy, we're going to have to put a rock on your head. You're getting too big."

"I'm the tallest in my class."

"I'm sure you are." He sets Connor on the ground and bends over, resting his huge hands on his thighs, their faces not a foot apart. "Wanna do your Uncle Cal a favor?"

"Sure."

"Will you run inside and get me something to drink? Like a Dr. Pepper or Coke?"

With a nod, Connor takes off, bounding up the steps to the cement porch that stretches across the front of the house.

Using Mom's cast iron skillet, which is probably older than me, I'm frying the fish we caught this morning on a camp stove I set up in the front yard.

Cal steps close and asks quietly, "What's up, man?"

I shake my head, my focus on turning the frying trout. "Don't feel like talking about it anymore."

Cal draws back. "Sorry I couldn't be here yesterday."

I show him the palm of my hand. "No need to explain."

He narrows his coal-black eyes, twisting his neck, studying me. "You pissed?"

"Why would I be pissed?"

He aims his arm at me as he steps back. "Yeah, you're pissed I didn't come yesterday. I was in Austin, man. With Anderson."

My focus leaves the fish to meet his hurt look with one of surprise. "Anderson?"

"Yeah."

So that's where he's been. I should have snapped that first day, the way they scoped each other out. "What's up with you and Anderson?"

He hikes a shoulder.

We've never gone there, but I've always known, and I'm sure he knows I know. Some things men don't talk about. I don't give a shit what his preferences are, and he doesn't care what mine are. Cal Cooper is the best friend anyone can have, and I'd take a bullet for him any day.

"I like him," Cal says. "Anderson is... different. Quirky. Smart as hell. Fun."

I nod. "Glad you have someone. He seems like a nice guy. Wren is crazy about him."

"Yeah. About Wren," he says.

I feel my lips tighten along with the muscles in my shoulders. "Don't go there."

The screen door slams as Connor calls, "Cal, here's your drink." Connor makes it from the porch to Cal in under two seconds, holding out a can of Mountain Dew.

Cal grimaces. "Oh, man. Mountain Dew? Yuk."

Now, that's a look of disappointment on an eight-year-old face. Connor's big smile melts. "Ahh. We don't have Dr. Pepper or Coke. I thought you'd like this, cause I do."

"You got some iced tea?"

"Yeah."

"Sweet?"

Connor cuts his eyes at me and I nod. He answers, "Yeah."

Cal hands the can back to Connor, who takes it. "How about you drink the Mountain Dew and get your Uncle Cal a glass of iced tea instead? Me and your dad need to talk."

"What about? Wren?" Connor takes a long, innocent gulp of the Mountain Dew, his eyes glued to Cal, who snorts and guffaws, picking him up and lifting him high again so they are eye to eye—Connor still gripping the aluminum can.

"Now why would you say that?" Cal asks.

"'Cause that's what Mom and Genevieve were talkin' about yesterday. My dad and Wren."

Cal cocks his head. "What about your dad and Wren?"

Connor shrugs as he dangles in the air, and it's all I can do not to laugh out loud watching him hanging there, so comfortable in Cal's grasp. "I don't know... something about how they've got something going on."

They both turn their heads, looking at me as I take the remaining fish out of the frying pan and turn to the old picnic table, setting the filets on a large platter covered with paper towels. "Lunch is about ready."

Turning off the propane burner and taking the fish platter in hand, I summon them with a nod. "We've got fresh fish, Martha's potato salad, coleslaw, and hush puppies. Let's eat."

His little belly bulging, Connor turns on the TV to watch cartoons and settles on the couch. As much as he's run this morning, with his stomach full, he'll be asleep in ten minutes.

I put dishes in the sink and clear the table while Cal grabs two beers from the refrigerator.

"Let's go outside," he says.

"I told you. I don't want to talk. I did, for a minute. But it passed."

He hands over a cold one. "Too bad. I'm here. You're gonna talk."

Connor, on the couch, already has his mouth open. Sleeping like a baby. The window air conditioner is aimed straight toward him, so I draw a thin couch blanket over him.

Sitting at the picnic table, I take in my family's homeplace. For my money, there is no place prettier than the Texas Hill Country; not that I've been all over the world like Cal and probably Wren and Anderson, but I've traveled enough to know this is where I want to be. My father's grandfather settled here after the Civil War, raising sheep and goats. The small rock cabin they first built is a skeleton that sits maybe a hundred yards from the lake, which is spring-fed with a limestone bottom, cupped in a ridge of white rock hills that are dotted with live oak and cedar.

The water is crystal clear, not dirty brown, like manmade stock ponds.

This house my dad grew up in, and so did I. It's a shotgun house built of native rock with a red tin roof. You go through the living room, through the dining room, into the kitchen. Taking up the left side of the house are bedrooms and a bath. The bathroom still has a clawfoot tub.

They built a big den and master bedroom and bath across the back when I was a kid. A native rock fireplace sprawls across the den's back wall. When lambs and kids were born too early, when winters lingered on for too long, Dad would bring the newborns inside, put them in a big cardboard box lined with a wool blanket, and set them in front of the fireplace so they'd survive.

He and I cut enough firewood in the summers to last the season. Connor and I need to start doing that. I need to bring him out here more often. Who knows? Maybe I'll move back if I don't lose the place.

Rambouillet sheep and Angora goats—I grew up with them. Nothing... I mean, *nothing* stinks worse than a billy. I still have the smell of billy goat piss in my nostrils. But I can't imagine not having this place.

"So talk to me." Cal interrupts my thoughts. "What's on your mind?"

"The thought of losing this." We sit beneath a sprawling, live oak that shades the front yard, one of countless on the property. I peer at the canopy above me. This tree could have been here when my family arrived. "I let my deadline pass. The county will sue me for eminent domain."

Cal nods. "Fuck. I understand how you must feel."

My mouth draws tight. "Thanks. But I don't think you can. Not really. No one can."

He nods. "Okay, I accept that. Maybe I don't. But I know you, and I know what's bugging you is more than the land."

My gaze leaves the oak canopy to meet his as I concede, "It's everything. It's the land. It's this convoluted whatever it is with Wren. It's fucking Rosalee and the way she treats Connor." I glance at the house to make sure my son can't hear. "Her showing up out of nowhere like this and working at Martha's doesn't feel right. And she's trying to poison Connor about Wren."

Cal leans close, lowering his voice just above a whisper. "Wren doesn't mean anything to you. Why do you care what Connor thinks of her?"

"I never said she doesn't mean anything to me."

He grins and aims his finger at me like a pistol, pulling the trigger. "Gotcha."

I finish my beer, reach into the ice chest beside the picnic table, draw out another, twist off the top, and hand it to Cal. I pull another for myself. "Look. I already admitted to you, I like her. But she's leaving. And I'm not going to let myself get any more attached than I already am."

Cal grins, showing off perfect, pearly white teeth. "What if she doesn't leave?"

'What if she doesn't leave?' What does that mean? She *will* leave. She's got nothing keeping her here. When he threw that out yesterday, Cal hiked his giant shoulders and grinned, adding, "Just sayin'."

Smartass. Why'd he say it?

"Dad." Connor shoves my shoulder, rousting me from my ponderings, as we drive back into town. "Can I go swimming this afternoon?"

I glance at him, with his wide eyes and his brows lifted high with eager anticipation. "Sure. But let's get the ground rules clear. If I say you can go to the swimming pool, that means nowhere but the swimming pool. If you want to go to a friend's house afterward, you come to the shop and ask. I'm giving you freedom because you're getting older and Vogel Springs is a safe place, but I want to know where you are all the time. Understood?"

"Mom doesn't make me do that."

"I'm not your mom. I'm your father. My rules. Now let me hear you say it: you don't go anywhere without telling me."

"I won't go anywhere without telling you."

"Good."

We pull up in front of the shop, and Connor bolts for the café before I can get out of the truck, calling over his shoulder, "Martha's biscuits and gravy! You want some?"

"I'm good. Thanks." Ordinarily, I'd join him for breakfast, but I don't like the new wait staff. And I'm avoiding Martha's new upstairs tenant.

Unlocking the shop, my first order of business is to brew coffee. Connor and I got up and left first thing. After closing the shop early Friday, I figured I needed to open early. I don't want to get behind on work, and I don't want to lose business by not being here during normal business hours. The doorbell jingles.

"You didn't ask me if you could take Connor for the weekend."

I glance over my shoulder to see Rosalee standing a foot or so inside the lobby with a fist resting on her hip, an elbow out. I go back to making coffee. "I didn't have to. It was my weekend. Remember?" I feel my upper lip curl as I turn around to face her. "You don't even know what weekends are mine, do you? You've farmed him off on your parents for so long you don't know shit about him. Go back to work."

I turn my back on her, hearing the bell over the door jingle, signaling she did just that. Good. Stay the fuck out of my hair.

The doorbell jingles again and I'm about to take her head off when a man says, "Special Delivery. From Italy."

My gut tightens. Her part is here. It won't take long to put it on, and Wren Baldwin will be gone. "Put it on the counter."

"You need to sign for it."

Some parts are harder to take off than put back on. Not this ornery little bitch. The new one is fighting against going in as hard as the old one fought against coming out.

"Can I watch TV upstairs 'til the pool opens?" Connor is behind me.

"Sure." I can't take my eyes or hands off the converter.

"Whatcha' doin?" He's beside me, peering up at the under-carriage of the Cabrio.

"Putting the part back in Wren's car."

"That's her car?"

"Yeah."

"Fancy."

"Um-hum. Gotcha, you little bitch."

"Got what little bitch?" He steps closer, craning his neck back to look up at the underbelly of the car on the lift.

I drop my gaze to meet his. "You can't say that word."

"You just did, Dad."

That wins him a full-frontal grin. "Do as I say do, not as I do."

"Huh?"

"I shouldn't have said that word. Sorry. I finally got the converter to go where it's supposed to go." I step back, looking at my son.

"Want to go with me to test drive it when I get it all put back together?"

"In this car?" His eyes become big blue saucers, which keep me smiling.

"Yeah, I need to make sure everything runs right before I give it back to the owner, but I can't do that 'til I put everything back together."

"Can I watch TV in the meantime?"

"Yeah. Give me about thirty minutes. Maybe an hour."

I go back to the Cabrio. All those panels that had to come off before I could reach the catalytic converter now have to go back on. I haven't just been under her hood; I've had my hands on every part of this baby, the way I wanted my hands all over its owner. I remember the first time I laid eyes on both of them and chuckle quietly, remembering Wren. What a vision. Both of them. Yes, I'll remember these two, the car and the owner.

As Connor heads for the apartment stairs, I call out. "When you come back down, bring two towels. This thing has a white interior, and I don't want our butt prints on it when we give it back."

She runs like a top as I take the Cabrio through Vogel Springs and onto the highway, my focus pegging between the highway ahead, my rearview, and the information panel on the dashboard.

"What's this?" Connor shoves an aerosol can in my face.

I draw back, tucking my chin, to see it. "No idea. Where'd you get it?"

"It rolled out from under the seat when you put the pedal to the metal."

"Read it."

I cut my eyes at my son as he holds the can close to his face, his lips moving as he tries to read the fancy writing. Damn, he's entertaining.

"T... R...O... Pez... Tro-pez Spray Tan."

"Tropez Spray Tan." A laugh bubbles up from my gut as I tip my head back. It's the kind that won't stop. Goofy girl. Paying money to cover up that beautiful skin. "Put it back under the seat, son. She might not appreciate us finding it."

My left forearm rests on the door, and my right hand is on the wheel. This car is smooth. I see now why it costs so much. I check the rearview and up ahead. The highway is empty. "You want to see what kind of pick up this thing has?"

"Yeah," Connor croons. "Stomp on it."

I goose the Cabrio, and she takes off like a rocket. Blows your hair back. I'm pegging ninety before I know it, so I back off the accelerator, cutting my eyes at my son. "This car will go from zero to sixty in four seconds." I've been trying to teach him a little about engines. "She's got four-hundred-forty-four horses under the hood."

"That's a lot, right?"

"Yeah."

"Wow, Dad. Do it again."

"Better not. I need to get back, put the car on diagnostics one more time to make sure everything's right before I give it back."

Connor peers at me with a little frown. "So, this means Wren is leaving?"

"Yep."

"Awww. I'll miss her."

Me too, buddy. Me too.

"Dad, will you drop me by the pool on the way back? I can swim in what I have on." He beams again. The kid's got one hell of a rebound rate. He wags his shoulders with a smile to die for. "Everyone will see me in this car."

The computer gives a clean read and my work on the Maserati is officially finished. My fingers feel numb as I text the car's owner.

HudBass: 🏎 **Ready**

WrenB: Now?

HudBass: 👍

I'm on my back on the creeper, underneath Gerald Spivey's mud truck—he and Ted are competitors—checking his suspension, when I hear the already familiar sound of Wren's platform sandals on the garage concrete floor.

Click, click, click. "So, she's ready?" The tone is chirpy.

I answer from under the mud truck, "Yeah. Give me a minute."

All Wren can see are my legs, thank God, because my skin tingles at the sound of her voice, and now my face feels like lead, and there's that familiar uptake in my ticker. I don't remember dealing with it before Wren Baldwin hit town.

She's leaving in a few minutes like I knew she would.

"I'll wait in the lobby. I need to pay." *Click, click, click.*

I call out to what I'm sure is her back if she's still in the garage, "The warranty people pay."

I need time to get my gut in check. This. Is. Goodbye.

"You mean, I owe you nothing?" she asks. Her sparkling eyes are on mine, and she smells so damn good. I breathe in that fragrance for the last time, I remind myself, as my eyes drink her in as inconspicuously as I can. She's not at all the heartbroken mess I comforted in the alley a few days ago. Wren Baldwin looks like she sashayed out of one of the women's fashion magazines I keep in the lobby for my female customers. I bet Rosalee and Genevieve despise her for her natural beauty.

And you want to talk about rebound rates? Wren's is as fast as her car.

Mine isn't. I stretch out my arm to offer her keys over the counter. "Your car's under full warranty. They pay me, not the car owner."

She reaches slowly and cautiously to take the keys from me, as if she wants to be sure to get the keys but not touch me. What do you expect? You did manhandle her, then drop her. The room suffers an uncomfortable silence.

Wren looks at her keys, not me.

But all I see is her. God, I want to grab her. How stupid would that be? *She knows how you feel.* She's cutting her losses and leaving. For a woman like Wren Baldwin, there will always be greener pastures.

"Come on, I'll walk you to your car." I hold the door and walk with her to the pristine Cabrio. I always give them back the same way they come to me. Dammit. Except, she didn't come to me with those towels in the front seats. I glance at Wren apologetically. "I took it for a spin to check it out. Connor went with me."

Her focus shifts from her car to me as she smiles beautifully. "Did he like it?"

"Loved it." I reach around her to snatch the two towels. Turning around, she's in my face and in my space, staring at me with her head tilted back, those beautiful eyes searching my face... looking for something... as the silence lingers.

I can't speak because I don't know what I want to say. Everything. Nothing. I'm overcome by flash memories—cradling her in my arms like a baby, striding from the hotel lobby to my truck, kissing her like a deranged madman, tracing the contours of her face. But, dick that I am, all I can manage to say is, "You be safe out there."

She drops her gaze to the ground, staring at her perfectly manicured red toenails with the gold ring around the second toe on her right foot, and slowly lifts her delicate, proud chin high, meeting my eyes with a direct gaze. "Thank you, Hud."

My heart is about to rip apart as I do my best to smile. "No. Thank—"

"Hudson Bass, you selfish horse's ass!"

I turn to see Eleanor Adams stalking across Main Street toward me, looking like the wicked witch in *The Wizard of Oz*. The real estate lady is drawing closer, aiming her arm at me like a spear. "I just heard the county's going to have to spend hundreds of thousands of dollars to sue you, so we can get thousands of new jobs. Why don't you think of someone besides yourself?"

"Mrs. Adams, go back where you came from."

"If I have my way, we'll run you out of town." She swings that arm like a javelin, with the meanest, nastiest snarl I can remember on anyone's face. "I'm going to tell all of my friends, 'Don't trade with Bass Pit Stop.' We'll boycott you."

She taps her chest. "You realize, this lawsuit will make my property taxes go up. All your friends, their property taxes will go up, because the Commissioner's Court has to fight you."

I take a step toward the railing banshee. "Then tell your commissioners to drop it, and your taxes will stay the same." One step closer, and I bend a little to get in her face with my own narrowed squint. "Matter of fact, Mrs. Adams, why don't you call VoltEdge and tell them they can put their plant on your property?"

Before she can snap back, behind me I hear, "Hud?"

Turning my back on the shrew Eleanor Adams, I watch Wren close her car door and scoot the automatic seat forward with a sweet smile. "Goodbye."

She pulls onto the street, and my fucking heart hits the sidewalk.

Wren

Chapter 20

on the road again

My blinker ticks like a time bomb at the four-way stop until I turn right and gun it to the highway.

The wind blows through my hair, and my freedom washes over me. Freedom of having my car back, and the freedom of the open road I've missed... but for the first time in a while, I don't feel that I have to be on it.

I give my Cabrio as much gas as she'll take, testing her to the next exit. She drives like new.

Guess I have Hud to thank for that.

His pause in walking me to my car. He stalled several times.

Hudson Bass, I've got you.

He didn't think I'd do it. He didn't think I'd leave without putting up a fight.

Well, I'm not leaving, Hud.

But I'm not fighting for you. I'm fighting for the Vogel House and Anderson's new project.

My blinker ticks on again as I exit to head back down the highway to the Vogel Springs exit I just fled. And if he sees my car flash back through town, right before his eyes, then so be it.

It's none of his business. I'm none of his business.

Hud made it very clear to me that he could keep away from me, so much so that he didn't bother to ask if I was staying.

Sure, it's an odd question. Whose best friend flies back from vacation to entertain them while their car is in the shop, stranding them in 'Mayberry,' where they proceed to buy a dilapidated historical marker to turn into a bed & breakfast?

In all fairness to Hud, how could he have known? Much less guessed something as insane as that?

But, again, and as they say in my favorite gangster movie, 'If you're not looking for me, I'm not looking for you.'

But he did... look *at* me. It made my heart swell and my head spin, and with all the confidence I exuded in my exit, I can't deny that I ached for him.

I wanted him to ask. Hell, I wanted him to beg. Beg me to stay, ask where I was going next, tell me he'd miss me, that he has missed me, and—

Enough.

He said none of the above. He wanted to. I could see it in his grey eyes as they looked me over and landed time and time again on mine. But something kept him from it. Maybe I just wasn't worth choosing in the end.

I've been there before.

I brake before taking the exit to my destination. My car halts on the shoulder the same way he paused to look at me before I said goodbye.

Am I making the right choice coming back? Staying?

"Just try not to make a fool of yourself on my watch." My father's words intrude on my thoughts—words he said over and over when Phillip and I parted ways, and dear old Daddy wondered what I would do next.

The biggest hit was that it didn't matter what I did as long as I didn't embarrass him any further.

The thought of Phillip doesn't give me a heart flutter this time; it releases a coldness in my veins, and a fear rushes over me, one that makes me wonder if I'm not about to make a fool of myself in front of Hud or Vogel Springs, even.

Anderson always thought I was habitually on the run. I hear him in my head, 'When something doesn't go Wren's way, she does what she's best at and runs away.' My best friend is very perceptive, but he fails to see the true talent in my actions: I'm very good at not hanging around where I'm not wanted.

For most people, that doesn't pertain to your home, job, or father—but in my case, those have always been ground zero for that sentiment.

What if Hud truly doesn't want me here, either?

I should respect that. It's his town. I know he wants me... but that doesn't mean he wants me to stay.

My eyes drift from my windshield to the tiny world before me that presents as an idyllic small town. But there's nothing small about what I've experienced in Vogel Springs.

I click my tongue on the roof of my mouth, contemplating whether I should veer left or not.

The same part of me that feels drawn to Hud also feels drawn to Vogel Springs, this home I've never known.

I turn the wheel and forge ahead.

A parade of contractors, plumbers, an electrician, and a landscaping truck, all of which must have exited before me, lead the way back into town.

My adrenaline returns, along with my confidence, as I follow them, making a personal bet they are stopping at the Vogel House. Anderson doesn't play.

Something's happening to me as I pull up behind all the work trucks and park. I suggested it was confidence before, but I can think of two other "C" words for the feeling now coursing through my veins as Bass Pit Stop teases my peripheral vision.

Cocky and Conceited, with capital Cs. If it looks like a duck, walks like a duck, and quacks like one... let's just say Hud Bass has no clue what's in store for him. Just in case he missed my brilliant exit, I'm going to make sure he witnesses my homecoming.

This little duck has decided to waltz straight over in broad daylight to her old residence to get her things. That's right. I'm going to get my stuff to move into my room at Vogel House.

Anderson, Cal, and I scoped out the bedrooms upstairs, and the building inspector approved them for living conditions. They just need a fresh coat of paint, Anderson's vision for window treatments, and maybe a bathroom remodel.

As I strut over in plain view of Hud and all who work at the cafe—and let's be honest, in front of everyone in Dollar General, The Purple Polka Dot, the post office, the florist, and anyone in Vogel Springs who's not visually impaired, taking a moment, I consider the dramatic effect of my impending actions. All of Mueller's will see me walk down with my suitcase and assume I'm finally leaving town. That plays.

But rolling my signature carry-on down the porch, into the street, and across the four-way stop to Vogel House seems a little theatrical. However, if this duck could be a fly on the wall inside the Pit Stop to see Hud's face when I do it, it would be worth the all-star cast award.

My little safe haven has never looked so empty. I'm going to miss the smell of bacon. I won't, however, miss sleepless nights and raising up on my elbows to peer through the window at a particular auto shop directly across the street.

As I reach for my carry-on handle, my heart sinks at the thought of Martha.

I wasn't planning on saying goodbye to her. God, Wren, you goober. You are practically, if not literally, moving next door.

My race down the stairs to the cafe is met with Martha holding her arms out for me. "I'm gonna miss those platform chunks clomping around up there between lunch and dinner shifts." She hugs me tightly.

"You didn't tell my secret, did you?" My eyes search as far as they can as I whisper in Martha's ear. I can't see them, but I can feel Rosalee and Genevieve's eyes on me, enough to know they're somewhere in the vicinity. I've developed radar for those two.

"Honey, I'd say your secret is safe with me, but I reside in Vogel Springs." She chuckles, and I reluctantly pull away from the hug. "I will tell ya I don't think the cat's out of the bag just yet, as I haven't seen enough jaws drop or heads roll—but believe you me, they will, and you just hold yours high."

"My head or my jaw?"

Martha laughs loud enough for all to hear. "Both, darlin. Both."

She pauses as she takes me in. "I'm just so excited for ya. I can't wait to see the place. I'd tell ya to make sure you and Anderson aren't strangers, but I have a feeling I'm cooking your breakfast, lunch, and dinner up until he opens to compete with me."

We share another laugh and she squeezes my wrist. "I can't believe I'm saying this, but I really am going to miss you, kid. I don't know what it would have been like if you did decide to leave us for good, with your car being fixed and ready."

She looks at me sincerely and holds my gaze, letting me know she means it. I'm blown away by Martha's kindness and generosity. I have been from the beginning, but this moment makes all the difference in the world for me.

I hug her tightly again, which has to look like a true goodbye to anyone watching.

A deep breath and sigh later, I make my walk of pride to Vogel House, rolling my custom pink Louis Vuitton teal palm tree printed carry-on behind me.

Eat your heart out, Hudson Bass.

Hud

Chapter 21

that's what you get

I let out a loud groan, hurl my empty soda in the metal trash can, and tromp to the shop fridge, pulling out a cold one when the third sad sack song comes on about some guy crying in his beer because his girl is gone. Shit. Fuck. Hell. I turn Pandora off with a vengeance. Silence is golden.

Yeah, it's early, but between Eleanor Adams' shrieking and Wren driving off without a hug... a few last sweet words... not a tear in her eyes as she left me standing on the street with that witch yanging on me—I want a drink. Screw everyone. Maybe I'll close the shop early again.

Gerald got his truck and left right after Wren. I glance around my empty shop, and the hair on the back of my neck stands on end. It's like someone hits me with a cast iron skillet as reality sets in. I'll be damned... they're going to run me out of business for trying to hold onto my family land. *'I'll have all my friends boycott you.'* She isn't *going* to have her friends boycott me. It's already started.

I'm going to be broke. I'm an outcast in my own hometown—and nobody told me. Not until just now. It never crossed my mind people would hate me for trying to protect what's mine.

I chug the cold beer, drop the glass bottle in the trash, and reach for another. Twisting off the top, I drain that son of a bitch, too. And grab a third.

They can all fuck themselves. I'm not selling. If I have to, I'll sit out there and starve to death. As I stare straight ahead at my empty bays, my scalp tightens while I mindlessly peel the label off the sweaty beer bottle with my fingernails. What am I going to do?

My eyes dart around the garage. Other than Wren, who was a Triple A call, and my regulars, I haven't had much business lately. I've been so preoccupied with VoltEdge, Rosalee and Wren, I don't guess it registered. Until just now.

Typically, somebody would be driving up for an oil change, or for a set of new tires, or a brake job. Somebody else would be calling, needing me to find out why their check engine light is on or their brake lights aren't working. I never realized how I took my business for granted. I haven't had but two customers all day. Gerald and Wren.

Wren. She left.

I take a deep breath and sink down to sit on the steps to the apartment. Okay, then. Be pragmatic. I paid off this place with my inheritance money, so I have a roof over my head, even if I lose my homeplace.

I can always take a job doing something. Work for the railroad, maybe. Hell, go to work for some dealership, maybe in Rockridge. I'll get by.

"Daddy!" My gaze finds Connor's voice. He's breathless, running through the garage, stopping right in front of me with a smile as wide as Bracken Cave. "Did you see all the trucks in town?"

What I'd give to be his age again, full of curiosity and sheer enjoyment about everything. He's so innocent. "No, buddy, I haven't seen what's going on. I've been back here."

He aims his arm at the street. "There's a parade going over to that old house."

"The Vogel House?"

"I guess. The old, big one over there." He points at the four-way with one hand and grabs my hand with the other. "I've never seen so many trucks and people in town. Come look." He's hopping up and down on his toes. "Come on."

I heave a sigh. I'd rather go upstairs and go to bed. But that's not an option. He's not taking no for an answer. "Give me a minute, will you, bud?"

His eyes meet mine, then drift to the beer bottle in my hand. "You're drinking beer in the afternoon."

I set the beer bottle on top of the refrigerator. "I was."

"Why?" His little brows knit together as he peers from my hand to my eyes with worry. For me.

It makes my heart hurt. His mother is an addict. He doesn't need a father who's a drunkard. My shoulder shifts high. "I'm done."

"Then come on, Dad. Don't be a party pooper. Come see what's going on." Connor tugs my hand, and I'm overcome by the need to hug him.

I grab and lift him high, hugging him tight against my chest. "I love you, buddy."

He hugs my neck and whispers, "Love you, too, Dad," then pulls away, pressing his hands against my chest. Enough affection. "Come on and see what all's going on."

What has him so excited? "Okay, okay." I let him lead me through the lobby to the street.

"Look." He points to the four-way, beaming with pride like the circus came to town.

Damn. Maybe the circus did come to town. The Vogel House is swarming with every kind of contractor known to man. Looks like several trucks with lumber, a couple of plumbing company vans, and a couple of others I can't recognize.

So, the Vogel House has been bought. They'll paint it, for sure. I hope. Something besides that God-awful purple.

I can't even guess what all kinds of contractor trucks are over there, but half a dozen workmen are going in and out—and my jaw falls half a foot. I'll be damned if that's not Cal's Range Rover and Wren's Maserati parked in the driveway. What the fuck?

I just watched her pull out of my parking lot and head out of town, dragging my damned heart behind the Cabrio.

Connor drops my hand to jaunt across the street. "Hey, Wren." He darts toward little Miss La-Tee-Dah Baldwin.

I catch myself not breathing. She's back? She didn't leave?

"Hey, Connor." Wren stops rolling her suitcase down the street to bend low and hug my son.

"Where ya going?" he asks loud enough for me to hear.

I can't hear her answer, but she says something and gives him a tight squeeze before her eyes drift over his shoulder, catching my wide-eyed, what-the-fuck stare. And just like that—she turns her head away like I'm not here—not worth looking at—and goes back to rolling that pink suitcase down the street and through the four-way.

Well, fuck me running.

Wren

Chapter 22

"honey I'm home"

“**B**ro! Wait up.” I hear Cal call from the porch of Vogel House toward the Pit Stop. I can only assume Hud is still standing there with his mouth agape as I make my way to the steps. I want to turn and look back, but I can't.

When I thought I was out of Hud's view, I looked up briefly to make sure Connor made it back across the street, but I didn't bring my eyes back to Hud's.

Obviously, Hud was watching him. Connor didn't need my extra eyes, but I guess my gut instinct took over. A gut instinct I denied when it came to locking eyes across the distance with Hud again, or running over myself to explain. I puff out a breath as Cal runs past me.

It seems that is what he's going to do right now. He's going to Hud to explain. Explain me, and why I'm still here. Yikes. This is not quite how I intended this part to go.

Oh well... look around, Wren, it's going. I'm in awe of the people dedicated to their tasks at hand. Mere moments ago, there were only trucks pulling up. Now, what looks like expert craftsmen have fallen into place, working alongside each other.

Pounding hammers, electric saws, and the all-but demolition of the kitchen attack my senses, but in the most progressive way. It's almost calming, all of this racket in my ears.

It means it's real.

I've never been so proud of Anderson for sticking to something. He's great at what he does, but his family rarely gives him the opportunity to showcase it.

This. Is. His.

"Hi, honey! I'm ho-me!" I shout above the construction and quickly learn I am not invisible, nor are these kind gentlemen who are wearing earplugs and holding power tools deaf.

At least seven pairs of eyes from the first floor alone land on me, standing just past the entryway. One wouldn't say they landed, would they? Not when they continue to move up and down my body.

My goodness, between Hud feigning a blind eye and the modest Dollar General one-piece I've been sporting to swim with kids, I think I forgot I was a woman. According to these fellas, I've still got it.

Anderson sashays to the rescue and pulls me down the front hallway. "Don't worry chickie… it works both ways. You should see the crew up stairs. I can't help but stare unapologetically. I mean, I am paying them."

"Anderson." I slap his arm—the one wrapped around mine—as he leads me up the stairs.

"Look at this banister... all original wood." His eyes dazzle as he points mine toward everything he's excited for me to see again as if we've never done the walk-through. I guess it's more about what he wants me to envision, and I have to hand it to him, I like what I see. "I think I'm going to like it here, Miss Hannigan," I say, looking up at him to match his smile.

"Right this way you little orphan, let's see if there's gin in one of the bathtubs." Anderson whisks me up to the second floor. Men are above us on ladders, already peeling down century-old wallpaper.

"Speaking of gin in my bathtub... is my room ready for tonight? I mean, are you still crashing at Tiny's and I was supposed to stay at Martha's, or am I cleared to move in tonight? Hence my belongings in the suitcase in your entryway."

"Darling, if you think I'd stand in the way of you being my first customer–"

"Oh, don't you dare make me pay. Aren't I part-owner or designer or some shit? I thought we had paperwork, Anderson Sofitel. At least I thought that's what you were drawing up behind my back. God knows you've forged my signature as many times as I have."

"Once, young lady... to save your life."

"It was to save me from the wrath of my father."

"Same thing."

Anderson spins me around by my shoulders and covers my eyes. "Now, don't peek, yet. Wait for it... take a step forward."

He removes his hand, acting as my blindfold. My eyes open in sheer shock. The walls of the dainty little room have been stripped, and rolls of wallpaper samples, material specs for drapes, and all things Anderson overlap the built-in bookshelves, vanity, and insanely beautiful woodwork on the cabinetry and armor.

A large bay window ordains the center of the room, and I recognize it as the main decorative window on the second floor from looking up at the house so many times. My smile rises, and I turn my head to meet Anderson's. "I can't believe my room is the focal point!" I'm practically squealing.

"Well, Matilda's room, and you have complete artistic freedom to make it look just like this." Anderson waves a newspaper clipping in my face."

"Matilda who? Wait, where's my bed?"

"It's under all the fabric samples. You'll find a twin mattress complete with your favorite memory foam topper. Matilda Adelaide Vogel." He slaps the front page newspaper article, clipping back its 1987 date. "I need this..." He pauses for effect, brings his hands together, then pulls his arms apart, spreading them across the room. "To look like this." He points profusely, tapping his finger on the newspaper clipping and the photo of the room showcased in the newspaper article.

A newspaper article titled *Vogel's Victorian Ghost Spotted By New Owners*. The story reads, 'Matilda appears again, claiming her bedroom in Vogel House, Vogel Spring's Victorian Home Landmark.'

"A ghost?"

"Not the ghost, the boudoir. This article, in 1987, is the last look of Matilda's original bedroom from the early 1900's. It is the only room in the house that has entirely original features, and this photo is our key to making it look exactly like it did when she was here." Anderson moves to the fabric samples.

"Because that's not creepy enough? Why don't you just have a seance and invite her back? Or maybe you're banking on the fact she'll come running once she sees her favorite curtains hung." I look around the room, feeling something between appalled and uneasy.

Anderson is deep in thought, eyes searching between a solid velvet plum and a scarlet red print. "Damn it, and isn't that the bitch of it. The newspaper is black and white. I'll never get the colors just right."

"I don't care about colors. What's the story with this ghost?"

He dismisses me with a backhanded wave. "Oh, I don't know, read the article. She jumped out the window and hung herself on her petticoat when her daddy wouldn't let her marry the black overseer. Or, she climbed in the walls where they hid the silverware from the Indians and they forgot about her or some shit."

"Oh. My. God. I can't with you."

"We'll, you're going to have to. Your name is on the deed next to mine."

"Anderson. We don't have a B&B because you just got us canceled before we even opened."

"What. Too soon? I shouldn't add it to the home tour?"

"My friend, it will never be the right time for your candor. First off, this is not an Antebellum home, it's a Victorian. We are quite past the Civil War here, and well into the 1900s. Second, I'm not going to touch the offense to Native Americans you provoked with your slang and slander, as well as being additionally off on their timeline."

"I could add a trigger-warning to the brochure."

"Stop it. I demand you address the ghostly elephant in my room."

"Keep your platforms on. It'll be fine. I'm still at Tiny's for now, but my room will be ready by next week, and you can sleep soundly knowing I'm snoring under my face mask across the hall. You should get one. They're like blackout blinds for your eyes. Add some pink ear plugs, and it's see no evil, hear no—"

"Next week? What about tonight? And the rest of this week?"

"Honey. It's no different than you being above Mueller's cafe. You don't think that restaurant's not full of ghosts of its own? You slept through that. I need you. Here. To open the door at five thirty in the morning when the first of the carpenters, electricians, plumbers, and whoever else pop in to start their day. Think of it this way, you won't have to wake to the smell of grease."

"Yeah, that means I won't wake up to breakfast prepared either."

"**B**ro, wait up!" Cal yells across the four-way as I stand dumbstruck, watching Wren disappear behind him, pulling her suitcase up the steps of the old Vogel place.

I guess that's what he meant when he said, 'What if she doesn't leave?'

Why didn't he just come out and tell me?

Thump. Thump. Thump. My heart pounds in my ears as I stand like a concrete statue staring at Cal as he barrels toward me like the NFL linebacker he is, and for the first time in our lives, I'm wondering if I even know him any more.

"Hey, Cal." Connor's beside me with his head tilted back, trying to make eye contact with a man who stands six-foot-six. "Wren's gonna live over there now?" He points to the old Vogel place.

Cal answers Connor with his eyes on mine. "Her friend bought the place. It's going to be a bed and breakfast."

"Bed and what? What's that?" You've got to love his curiosity as he peers from Cal to me.

"It's like a hotel," I tell my son.

Connor croons, "Cool," and cranes his head back, looking up at Cal. "Are you gonna live there, too?"

His question goes unanswered. I don't think Cal hears him. He's too focused on our drawn-out stare. I feel my gaze pinch tight as my jaw locks up. *Why didn't you tell me?* It hits me during our staring match how little we've seen each other since Cal met Anderson.

No, you don't know him anymore.

I've lost him, too. As the corners of my mouth drag down, I nod at Cal and shift my gaze to Connor, ruffling his hair. "Run upstairs, son. You can watch TV for a while."

"K." He's off. Not a care in the world.

"Why didn't you tell me?"

"Bro, I didn't know for sure she was gonna stay. Plain and simple." I'm looking at worry, maybe even a little fear, in his eyes. He knows he screwed the pooch, not telling me.

"You knew Anderson bought the place. Real estate doesn't change hands overnight."

His arms swing wide. "How was I supposed to know he could make it happen that fast?"

I feel fire come into my eyes. "You've known. And you didn't say a word. Not a fucking word, even when you had the chance."

Cal takes a step closer, our gazes still locked. "Listen, man. You've done nothing but insist the girl means nothing to you, so what are you mad about?"

My gaze narrows to a squint. "I never said she doesn't mean anything. I just know she won't stay."

"But she is!" His voice booms. "She's helping Anderson with the renovations and designs."

"*Then* she'll leave." As I turn my back on him to tromp into the shop, I not only feel Cal's eyes on my back, I spot Rosalee and Genevieve gawking from the cafe porch. Knowing them, they're taking a video. They'll post it on TikTok or Instagram—NFL great Cal Cooper caught arguing in the street.

He yells at my back. "Fuck, man. Why don't you give her a reason to stay?"

Rosalee heard that.

Cal follows me into the shop, glaring as I sit behind my desk. He shakes his head, his cornrows swaying. "Naw, man. We ain't ending this conversation this way. You and me... we go back too far for this shit."

Our gazes lock yet again. "Yeah, we do. We go back too far for you to keep secrets." My thumb drums my chest. "From me."

More glaring.

Cal nods. "Okay, man. I'm sorry. I just... you know... it all happened too fast."

"Not good enough, Cal."

He bends over, resting his weight on his palms spread across my desk. "Bro, I didn't know for sure that she was staying. I swear."

He's not a liar. I know that. He deserves the benefit of the doubt. I suck in a deep, bitter breath. "Okay. Give me a minute."

Cal straightens, snickers, and wags his head demonstratively. "You know less about women than me, and I'm a gay man." He aims his arm at the four-way. "If you want her, give her a reason to stay. Dammit, man, you're not an idiot. Why do you think she'd parade her suitcase right down Main Street, in front of you, if she didn't want you to notice? She wants to get under your skin."

He slaps my desk with his open palm. "Stop feeling sorry for yourself over this land shit and focus on what's happening. There's a woman across the street who's crazy about you. If you want her, man up."

I cock my head and cross my arms over my chest in wonder. "I know she's not your type, but have you *looked* at Wren Baldwin?" I stand, aiming my arm at the Vogel House. "She's a fuckin' maneater. I guarantee that woman has had every man she ever knew fall at her feet. If I go running over there begging her to stay, she adds one more heart to her charm bracelet. And the next thing I'll see is her dragging that fucking pink suitcase right back down the street, in front of me, tossing it in the backseat of her Maserati and driving off, waving, 'Goodbye, sucker.'"

I slap my desk with my open palm, too, our faces not but a couple of feet apart. "Because Wren Baldwin. Will. Never. Stay. In Vogel Springs." My back straightens as anger overtakes all of me. "Why would she? She can live in Paris or London or Hawaii or… wherever the fuck on this planet she wants to live. Why would she stay here?"

His black eyes spew fire back as he takes a long beat to answer, chewing on his upper lip, studying me. "Because, shit for brains. She. Wants. You."

He turns his back and strides for the door.

"Wait, Cal."

He stops but doesn't turn, giving me his back. "I'm sorry. With Rosalee and VoltEdge and Wren—I just need a little time. I know you're not a liar."

Cal comes back to my desk. "About Rosalee. Is Connor gonna live with you full time now? Did she give you custody?"

"Hell, you know as much as I do. She hits town saying her parents can't take care of Connor and she's staying with Genevieve, and Genevieve doesn't have room for both of them so she expects me to help her out. You heard the same thing I did. I'll take whatever I can get. I'm assuming Connor will be with me at least until school starts." It smacks me in the face and drops to my heart. "And then, I'll probably lose him again."

"One day at a time," Cal says. "We good?"

"Yeah. We're good."

"Connor." I call up the stairs and grin hearing his little feet bounding downstairs obediently. When he reaches the garage floor, I ask, "What's really going on with your grandparents?"

I tried to get in touch with Stan and Vickie the day Rosalee appeared unannounced and several times since, with no success.

Connor shrugs and digs the toe of his tennis shoe into the step. "Granny fell and broke something. She can't take care of me or Poppy, so she called Mom and told her to come home and stay.

To help out." His voice trails off. "I heard Granny on the phone, telling her."

"But your Mom's staying with Genevieve, right? Not her parents."

"I guess."

"Does that bother you? Not being with your mother? Staying with me?"

His eyes light up. "Are you kidding? I love staying with you."

I grab him for the second time today, lifting him high, holding him against me so we're eye to eye. "What do you say, we go see an Astros game? I've got some business I need to take care of in Houston. We can take a little vacation."

"Yes!"

"I'll ask your Mom."

I pissed her off by taking him for the weekend without asking. It's only fair I ask her permission to take him out of town.

Legally, I have to. Rosalee has full custody of Connor. My name is on his birth certificate. He's Connor Bass. But we never married. I'm what the court calls a non-custodial parent, meaning I pay child support and I have visitation rights, but she runs the show. I'd be out of line to take Connor off without asking his mother, even though she disappears for months at a time, leaving his actual custody arrangement between her parents and me.

We walk across the street to Mueller's. They aren't any busier than I am. Maybe the boycott hasn't started yet, after all. Maybe everyone's slow.

Seeing Rosalee wiping down tables, I swing Connor up and carry him, sitting in the crook of my arm as I approach. "Is it okay if Connor comes with me for a few days?"

She straightens, and her topaz eyes narrow suspiciously. "Where're you going?"

"I thought we'd go see an Astros game. Maybe the Houston zoo. Just have a few days together, father and son."

Her eyes snap to Connor, who pleads, "Please, Mommy? Please?"

She purses her mouth as she shifts her gaze from Connor to spear me.

"Thought we'd swing by your parents on the way out since Connor hasn't seen them in a while."

"They aren't at home."

"What do you mean?"

"I mean Daddy's Parkinson's has progressed and Mamma slipped on the stairs. She cracked her hip. They're together in an assisted living facility."

"Forever?"

"I don't know."

"Where?"

"Marble Falls."

I set Connor to the floor. "Ask Martha for a soda." As he runs into the kitchen, I ask Rosalee, "So does that mean Connor's here to stay? I need to know. I need to make arrangements for school."

Her snicker drips with contempt. "I'm not giving him to you."

"So, he's just uprooted from your parent's house? Where his bedroom is? Where his toys are?"

Rosalee purses her lips. Doesn't answer.

"So what are your long-term plans?" Our gazes hold tight.

Feels like that's all I've done today: endure one stare-down after another. First, old lady Adams, Wren, Cal, and now Rosalee. The stars are misaligned.

Rosalee goes back to wiping tables, avoiding my eyes, as she snips, "I haven't made up my mind yet. When I do, I'll let you know."

The hair stands up on the back of my neck. She can take him and run off to Austin, Dallas, El Paso—wherever the hell she wants. And she knows I can't do anything about it.

"He can live with me from now on, Rosalee. I'll keep paying child support. He doesn't get what I send now, anyway. You can have it. Give him to me. I'll raise him."

Her brows shift high with a sneer. "What? The two of you are going to live in a one-bedroom apartment over the garage?"

"If I have him, we'll move back to the homeplace. He'll go to school here in Vogel Springs the same way we did."

Her head tilts back as she cackles. "You're pissing that land away out of pride. Had you agreed to sell it, you'd have something. But eminent domain? They'll give you pennies on the dollar and you'll be living above the garage for sure."

My voice ices over like my heart. "I'm not losing the land. And I won't lose my son." I just made up my mind.

Here comes another haughty snicker—this one from Genevieve, on the other side of the cafe. Eavesdropping.

I hadn't seen her when I came in. "Rosalee, let's talk in private."

She cuts her eyes behind me—to Genevieve no doubt—but she follows me to the back door. I hold it for her, and we step outside. Before I can close the door, Rosalee starts in. "Come to your senses, Hud. You're going to lose the land. And Connor is mine. You never had him to begin with."

"I've spent more time with him than you have."

She may be clean right now, but she won't be for long. She never is. If Rosalee runs off with Connor and her parents can't help take care of him, he'll be subjected to her druggie lifestyle and friends. *No fucking way.* "I'll sue you for custody. Prove you're an unfit mother."

She slaps my cheek. Hard. *Damn, she always did like to do that.*

My cheek stings as Rosalee launches into another rant. "If you had the sense God gave you, you'd take the county's money. As it is, you think you've got the money to fight the county—and me, too? Good luck, Mr. Bass. Or should we start calling you Mr. Ass?"

Another fucking staring contest. "Can he come with me to Houston or not?"

She glowers for a long beat, deciding. She's weighing her options. On one hand, there's the fun of sticking it to me. On the other hand, if she has Connor, she can't party after work with Genevieve.

I watch her eyes as she calculates. *What to do? What to do?*

Finally, Rosalee blows out a loud huff and waves me away. "Fine. Yeah, you can take him."

I open the door, stepping into the cafe, calling, "Connor, let's go!"

He barrels through the swinging doors from the kitchen, hollering over his shoulder, "Bye, Martha," and races with his eyes bouncing between me and his mother, his smile the size of the sky. "Are we going?" He bounces up and down on his tiptoes.

Rosalee gives him a big smile with open arms. "Yes. Come give Mamma sugar first." She pulls him in for a squeeze.

Fake. All fake.

I know why he can go with me. Because she doesn't want him. She never did. But she'd run off with him in a heartbeat to spite me.

That's. Not. Going. To. Happen.

I wake to the sound of power tools, sawing, hammering, and stabilizing the beautiful wrap-around porch that is so uniquely Vogel House.

I slam my face back down to my pillow and pull my other pillow over it. I can't imagine why I muffle my groan when there is no possible way they can hear me over all that noise.

A few days ago, it was a collection of noises that represented progress and a bright, fun future. Now—it's my day—my mornings, my afternoons, and my evenings. Anyone who suggests remodels are quick, painless, and easy is either lying or they've never done one.

Not even with money are they easy.

I better get dressed. The porch guys have been showing earlier and earlier since they don't have to be let in. Fifteen minutes from now, five to eight more people with more power tools will be standing at the front door waiting for my greeting smile to *Open Sesame.*

I slide into my shorts and the cleanest tank I can find. Between the Vogel Springs laundromat and buying new ones at the Dollar General when I'm high and dry, I'm not always sure what's freshly laundered.

Hopping into my shoes, I turn the knob to face the...

"Anderson." He stands in front of me with a look on his face. *I know this look.* "What are you doing here this early? You haven't made it here before eleven o'clock since we started this whole charade where you pretend we're in this together. What's wrong?"

"Okay. I may not be the earliest riser. I may... really be enjoying the hospitality at Tiny's, but we are absolutely in this together. Starting, like... the day after tomorrow."

"What?" I push past Anderson out of Matilda's 1900s cedar door with the skeleton key knob into the hallway.

"I have to go to Austin. Check in with the family. Make some appearances, and explain my latest transaction. Our latest transaction. So, see, I'm taking one for the team. I'll be back in two days or less. It's in the bag. We got this."

"I've already been holding down the fort—"

"Yes, but you do it so well." Anderson follows me as I charge down the wooden stairs.

"What am I supposed to do here by myself with all these men?"

"Is that a trick question?"

I pivot at the bottom step and look back up at Anderson, making an event out of rolling my eyes.

"Cal's going to check on you. Don't worry."

"Does he have one of those paranormal activity detector thingies? What about Matil—"

"*Ahhh!*" Anderson's hands fly up to his ears. "Don't say it. Don't say her name. I'm warning you. If you get that in my head I'll never move in and sleep next to you, and the reason won't just be because I'm gay." Anderson walks past me toward the front door with his ears covered like a child. "Be right back!"

And with that, the front door closes behind him.

"Honey, I hear ya, but I can't side with ya on that one. I could never be too mad at Anderson. I've had to hire extra kitchen staff to handle the lunch rush from all your workers over there." Martha nods toward Vogel House, swishing the pot of fresh coffee she peddles in her hand. I can't help it, but my eyes dart across the street at her words, 'over there.'

The Pit Stop has had the Closed sign facing the public since I waltzed my suitcase over to Vogel House, and Connor came rushing over to say hi.

The last time Hud turned the sign to say Closed during business hours was when I forced him to head to breakfast here with me.

Funny, as I bring my eyes swiftly back to Martha's, I can't help but wonder if I didn't force him to leave town. Is my staying such a bad idea or a hindrance to him?

I haven't bothered him. I haven't had the opportunity. I've proved that's not what I stuck around for. If he wants freedom from me, he has it.

I'm so deep in my thoughts that I don't notice Martha stepping away to refill another table's coffee, stab a ticket, and return to me with my ham steak, hash browns, and fried eggs.

"Any more from Matilda?" Martha's eyebrows dart up. She's as intrigued by the Vogel House ghost as I am.

"I can't be sure. I mean, I don't want to be naive to it, but how much of what goes bump in the night is just the creaky old house adjusting to all of the construction? So nothing that crazy since my first terrifying night, but I'm definitely missing a scrunchy, my face wash, and I cannot keep ear plugs."

"What?" Martha manages the word out of a giggle.

"I'm telling you, Anderson bought me a pack of like, thirty pink ear plugs, as a joke, and I started using them the first night. I had two in my ears, a couple in my makeshift nightstand drawer, and the little package of the rest on top of my suitcase. Not one ear plug in sight. Not one rolled under my mattress or my pillow case. And the entire new pack is gone. Crazy, right?"

"Sounds like Matilda has a sense of humor. I don't know, you might want to ask Genevieve about her."

My eyes drift up to a staring Genevieve, with Rosalee's prying eyes not far behind hers. I hadn't noticed them.

Because having a ghost in your room—scratch that living in a ghost's room—makes these two bitches' death stares far less scary. Or maybe I'm just that into catching up with Martha, so they don't matter to me.

Genevieve's eyes widen, and I can tell she's being put on the spot.

"Genny, isn't it your great aunt and uncle that last occupied the place? That'd be the couple that the article was about."

"I wasn't even born then Martha, how would I know any more than the article?"

"Well thank you for announcing what a relic I am. Hell, I remember pouring them coffee, same as I just did Wren."

I smile at Martha as everyone's attention filters out the window to two more work trucks headed to the Vogel House. I let out a long huff. "Duty calls." With my napkin tossed onto my half-eaten breakfast, I exit to face my day.

Good night, it's hot. It's barely after two in the afternoon, and if it gets any hotter in this place, I'm going to lose my mind.

Who knew they could make it back in the 1980s with only a window unit or two instead of sparing the expense of truly renovating a Victorian home complete with central air. I don't know much about global warming, but the fact that my tank top is tied in a knot almost up to my ears and I'm still dripping with sweat may prove something.

One guy left.

Jerry, the carpenter, is wrapping up.

Could you wrap it up a little faster there, buddy?

I finally caught a break with some of the crews finishing early and others leaving early, promising to return bright and—what's that word again, right, early—with different parts and more power tools tomorrow morning. This will be the first time I've had the place to myself since I moved in.

Apart from my roommate, Matilda, obviously.

I could nap, wake up, and do some yoga. Maybe I could actually get some of my work done.

Come on, Jerry. Speed. It. Up.

"Uh-huh. I totally agree." I walk toward the ice chest in the middle of the kitchen to grab a water bottle from the ice. Maybe I just want to stick my head in it. Did I mention Jerry's a talker?

I keep shrugging and saying, 'Yup,' and 'Uh-huh' to his endless stories, and I've tried walking into another room six times in the last half hour. The guy just keeps reeling me in with one story after another.

He's not a bad-looking dude if he would learn to keep his mouth shut. Or get a clue.

Trying to step away multiple times, I've even said, I had to go take care of something upstairs. He just keeps gabbing.

Perhaps I should head upstairs anyway. The silence might speed him up and let him focus on the kitchen door frame he's readjusting. It was so weathered, the original door wouldn't close. He had to remove it and shave some off, and now he's reworking the door frame to fit.

On the bright side, I get the feeling he's close to being done, and I don't like the idea of being upstairs and not knowing if he left or not. Matilda's shady enough to contend with. I can't have some of our crew walk in on me in the bathtub when I thought they already left.

"Yeah, my buddies and I head down to Rockridge to shoot pool at Hawk's all the time. You should check it out, if you'd like to take a break and cut loose."

Great, another story begins. Let me guess, 'one time me and my buddy'... blah, blah blah, and what's with all these bird names? Hawk's? Jeez. "Yeah, I'll have to check that out." I throw him a bone before I yawn, yet another hint.

"How about tonight?" His breath is behind me. It's close, hot, and literally on my neck. What?

He must have swung through the door frame when he stepped off the ladder. I wasn't standing this close to him before. I take a swig out of my water bottle to distract the situation and divert him back to a normal social distance. From me.

"What's that?" I ask.

He still hasn't moved from my space, and as his eyes drift from mine down my body, then back up to my bare stomach, the hair stands up on the back of my neck and scalp.

Great. The Rockridge Casanova. This guy thinks he's God's gift.

"Tonight. You outta' come out and put back a few. Relax after a tough, hot day." He emphasizes the word hot and bites his bottom lip as he looks me up and down again. He takes a step closer up beside me.

"Oh, I... um... I'm not off the clock yet. I've still got a lot of work to finish. So—" I take a substantial step away from him and turn to face him, hating how my voice cracked, showing I'm flustered.

I'm not flustered. I'm pissed off. "So, if you're done for the day, I'll go ahead and lock up and see you tomorrow."

What is this guy's problem?

I can't take another step back. He's practically cornered me in the kitchen. I mentally tug at the knot that ties my tank top high under my bra, exposing my stomach, but I don't pull it down. I don't want to draw attention to it or confirm that now—I am scared. It might fuel him further.

"I don't have to be done. And we don't have to go to Hawk's. We can relax and kick back here."

The gall this man has, speaking to me this way in my own home.

We hired him. The fucker. Where's Matilda to knee him in the balls when I need her? He takes another step toward me and props his hand by my head to lean against the wall above me. My final step back lands me against the wall, as I suspected.

"I really do have to get back to work. Anyway, thanks so much for reconfiguring the door. I've heard that's the real difficult part."

That's it, Wren. Keep it jovial, like it's all fine if he just leaves and walks out now.

His other hand takes a place above my head. I swear to God, if he touches me or leans in any closer, my favorite shoe will meet his crotch. He stinks from working in the heat all day, and his rotten breath smells like whatever he ate for lunch, and if Matilda can't show her sorry ass right about now, then I'm going to have to. "Okay, Jerry, that's enough."

"You're a spicy little redhead, aren't ya? I'm just playin' around after a hard day." His shit-eating grin brings acid to my throat. Jerry's eyebrows rise, and a corner of his mouth lifts to a fucked-up smile. The piece of shit is turned on by my refusal to play.

"Back off!" I shove with all my strength against his chest. "I said, get off of me!"

Jerry flies across the room.

Wait, I didn't do that. No way could I push him that hard.

I draw in a quick breath, seeing a tall shadow—a stance I'd recognize anywhere. "Hud!" My heart races in pure relief.

"She said get off of her, Jerry. You never could take no for an answer, could you?"

"Awe, hell Hud, we were just havin' a little fun." Jerry tests the back of his hand on his upper lip to see if he's bleeding as he calls up to Hud from where he landed on the hardwood floor.

I barely look down at him before my eyes are back on Hud's. He steps closer to me. "Are you okay?" His hand reaches out softly to grab my arm.

"What the hell are you doing here?" I spout the words out with more venom than necessary, my tension still high and reeling from

Jerry. That, and I'm mad. *Don't you be my knight in shining armor when you pretend I don't exist.*

"I'd say, saving your ass, for one. They asked me to check on you."

"Well I don't need saving, or checking on."

Jerry scrambles to steady himself and stands, his height overpowering mine and very apparent as both men tower over me.

"You sure about that?" Hud grabs Jerry by the collar without taking his eyes off mine and drags him out the door with him. The massive front door slams shut for the first time today, leaving peace and quiet behind it, and I sink against the entryway wall to the floor trying to catch my breath.

My heart is still drumming, and I don't know if it's from the fear of what could have happened to me with Jerry or if it's from being rescued by Hud.

"Touch her again and I'll rip your fucking arm off." I've got Jerry Denison's back pinned to his truck bed.

"I was just playing, Hud." He dobs his split lip on his shoulder.

"She didn't like your game."

He glowers back. "She's a grown woman. She can decide for herself—"

I fist his shirt with both hands, pulling him in close. "Did I stutter?" My face is in his. "Don't touch her."

It's no secret that Jerry considers himself a ladies' man. "Okay," he finally says. "What's she to you?"

"A friend."

He snickers and spits to his side. "Sure."

"I mean it, Denison: she's off-limits." Stalking away from the son of a bitch, I reach for my cell and head back to the shop, scrolling through messages. Yep. There it is.

CalCoop: When U 🏠

HudBass: Soon

CalCoop: Have to go. Anderson in Austin. Will U check on 🦉

HudBass: Wren?

CalCoop: 👍

HudBass: 😠 👍

His text came through when we drove through Rockridge. They wanted me to check on her, and it's a good thing I did because Jerry's the kind who thinks if a woman shows some skin, she's asking for it. I get mad thinking about what the fucker might've tried if I hadn't shown up when I did.

And was she grateful I pulled him off of her? Hell, no. She tore into me like a fighting hen… *'I don't need you to take care of me.'* Wrong. She damn sure needed someone to take care of her.

HudBass: WTF?

CalCoop: ❓

HudBass: She bit my head off

CalCoop: 💩

Did they *not* tell her?

HudBass: Did she know I was assigned the task?

CalCoop: No man!  **Stealth**

HudBass:  

CalCoop:  

I shove my phone back in my pocket, cursing under my breath because Connor popped me on our trip about my language. Fuck. I mean duck. I've got to clean up my potty mouth if I'm going to raise him. And I'm going to raise him. One way or the other. Rosalee Gardner's an unfit mother. I'll prove it if I have to.

And VoltEdge is an unfit company. I'll prove that, too. In Houston, I did a Zoom meeting with three former VoltEdge employees. Each has a lawsuit against the company. Each was fired after reporting the company to the EPA for dumping toxic waste from their plant in Mississippi. All are part of the Fifth Circuit Court of Appeals. My FOIA request paid off.

VoltEdge has scanned most of this part of Texas looking for manganese. I don't know if they found it on my property, and I can't make them show me the report. But when it comes to court, my lawyer can subpoena their results, and we might be able to show they don't want my land for a plant—but to mine it. That won't be nearly as popular.

"Hud?"

My eyes follow the soft, Southern voice to see Mrs. Sanderson with her curly, almost blue hair standing in the garage. I fixed her air conditioner a while back. "Did my fix not work?"

She pushes her glasses up on the bridge of her nose as she dips her head sheepishly. Too cute. A seventy-year-old woman stands in front of me, avoiding my eyes like a little kid caught with her hand in the cookie jar. "No. I mean, yes, it worked, but..." She grimaces, "Now, my car has a shimmy all of a sudden."

I tuck my chin with a suspicious grin. Mrs. Sanderson isn't too much taller than Connor. She has to stretch tall to see over her steering wheel. "All of a sudden? Don't suppose you ran over a curb or something."

That's a sheepish grin if I ever saw one as she knits her brows together and hum-haws. "Not a curb. But I hit a pothole I didn't see." She winces. "I thought I'd lost my tire."

I chuckle. "Bring it in. I can get right on it."

"Thank you, Hud. I don't know what we'd do without you."

"Thank you, Mrs. Sanderson. Have a seat. Help yourself to a soft drink while I check it out. It shouldn't take long."

My apartment over the garage faces Main Street with a covered balcony across the front, which offered a straight line of sight to Wren's second-floor window over the cafe. Sometimes at night, I like to sit out here on the porch under the ceiling fan and drink a beer. Or whiskey. Unwind from the day.

Those days are gone. My lifestyle is changing with a kid. I'm drinking iced tea. A bitter little snicker sneaks up my throat. Iced tea is fine for lunch, but I like a beer after supper. Oh, well. Small price to pay to have Connor with me.

On the other hand, not much has changed regarding my line of sight with Wren. Her move around the corner puts her a little farther away, on the other side of the four-way, but I still have a straight line of sight. Lights are on, on the second floor over there.

Connor's in the living room watching some nonsense on YouTube, and I'm stretched out with my feet propped on the porch rail after supper. I made Hamburger Helper. No desire to go over to Martha's, which pisses me off, because before Rosalee showed up, I didn't have to cook. Martha fed me.

She still would. I just don't want to go over there.

I stick my head in the living room. "It's about bedtime, buddy."

His eyes leave the TV to plead with mine. "Aw, Dad, come on. Thirty more minutes. It's summer." He has perfected the puppy dog begging eyes.

"Have you had your shower?" It was my mother's rule growing up. Shower before bedtime so you don't get the sheets dirty.

"I went swimming, Dad. I'm not dirty."

Guess it's my rule now, for my son. "You need a shower before bedtime. And you need a haircut. I'll take you tomorrow. We can both get one."

He shakes his head with frightful eyes. "Momma wants my hair to get long."

"What?"

"She thinks it'll look good long."

My ticker takes it up a notch. I'm going to have to have my frigging heart checked if this shit keeps up between Wren and Rosalee. My son with a ponytail? "Do you want it to grow long?"

He hikes his shoulders. "I don't know."

"I'll tell you what. Jump in the shower, wash your hair and everything else and then you can watch TV until ten. Deal?"

He's off.

Fucking Rosalee. Long hair might fly in Austin, but he'll get picked on in school here with long hair. Vogel Springs isn't particularly contemporary. But, how a person wears their hair is their own personal expression. I'll let him decide.

This time, I resume my spot on the porch with a beer in hand. Screw it. I can still drink a beer now and then. Just not too many.

The lights go out on the second floor of the Vogel House.

"Night-night, Wren, you ungrateful little maneater." I shake my head. She is so naive. I think she really thought she could handle Denison today. She may be a little spitfire, but she's a minnow. Jerry's a barracuda—a carpenter, strong as fuck. I can take him, but she can't.

Wait. The upstairs lights come back on in Vogel House.

I straighten. What's going on over there?

I stand. She's got her hands over her mouth—she's running.

"Connor!" I yell.

No answer. I stride to the bathroom and open the door. He's in the shower. "Son." He sticks his head out of the shower curtain.

"I've got to check on Wren real quick. I'm locking you in, okay? Don't leave."

"Okay. I can watch YouTube, right?"

"Right."

*T*hat *bitch!* Doesn't appear when I'm next to being accosted, but she's up and at 'em, banging every kitchen cabinet and slamming all the drawers.

That or a worker, has their days and nights mixed up and already started downstairs.

Or, maybe… I'm dreaming before I ever fall asleep. Which one is more logical?

"Show yourself, Matilda! This isn't funny anymore. I'm exhausted." I grab a roll of velvet curtain material Anderson has propped on the wall and run down the stairs in my bare feet, boobs bouncing at record speed. Ow.

At any rate, I have on my pajamas, if you can call them that, in case it is a worker… No… Can't be.

I look down at the thought, double-checking myself in my vintage lavender baby doll pajama set. The shorts, more like bloomers, are as thin as panties, and the ruffle sewn around the hem of the upper thigh isn't substantial enough to make them more than that.

Perfect for a sweltering summer night with no air conditioner is the open back that connects two flaps of material to a single button at the nape of my neck. The rest gaps open, exposing my entire back.

Not ideal for bumping into workers—especially one Jerry Denison. Yikes.

Do they have meth heads in Vogel Springs? I make a mental note to ask Rosalee.

Anderson would have high-fived me for that intrusive thought if he were fucking here right now. Maybe some wayward youths from Rockridge are used to this being an abandoned house and haven't gotten the memo yet.

Good night. This fabric spool is heavier than I thought it would be. Good luck swinging it.

It sounds like a final cabinet door slams as my feet hit the bottom step, and now there's pounding at the front door.

This ghost is relentless. She's like Poltergeist level.

The pounding at the door picks up louder. "Wren! Open up." The deep, familiar voice shouts on the other side of the door as if there is a fire I'm unaware of.

"Hud?" I race through the entryway, fabric spool draped across the back of one shoulder, and swing open the heavy front door. I jump at the sight of the height of him, even though I recognized Hud's voice. I guess, in the horror movie in my head, I didn't expect him to actually be there. I didn't know what to expect.

"Wren. Are you okay?"

"She's mad, and banging around down here, destroying every-thing on the first floor to spite me." I take a deep breath, but there isn't one there. I breathe again, trying to catch my breath.

"Hey."

"What?" I must be staring up at Hud, dumbstruck.

A yard of velvet unrolls above my head from the spool draped behind me and hoods my face. I sway backward under the weight of it, until I feel a strong hand cover the back of my waist and scoop me upright.

A heavy weight releases from my shoulder and back, and with it, my own personal velvet curtain is removed.

Hud leans the spool against the doorway.

I take a deep breath, and this time, it flows in and out of my chest.

"Were you playing dress up Scarlett, or velvet is the new weapon to fight off intruders?" His eyes chase mine until I'm back focused on him.

"Not an intruder. Her." I point toward the kitchen, where a cabinet slams on cue. "See. The ghost. She's been at it for the last fifteen minutes."

"Matilda Vogel?" Hud raises the sexiest damn eyebrow I've ever seen, and I don't care if he's making fun of me right now. The expression on his chiseled face is worth it.

"You know her?"

"Well, not personally, but..." Hud rakes his eyes over my scant attire and clears his throat. "May I?" He motions toward the en-tryway.

"Of course." I step out of his way. "I hope she listens to you better than she listens to me." I call out to Hud as he struts effortlessly into the kitchen. Not wanting to be left alone, my feet pitter-patter swiftly behind him.

"Careful," he calls over his shoulder. "There are nails, screws, and splinters all over the place. You're barefoot."

I continue to tiptoe behind him, unwavering, darting my eyes at each cabinet we pass, hoping to catch Matilda in the act.

Instead, I catch Hud walking straight through the kitchen toward the parlor or sitting room attached to the dining room. He continues to the massive stained glass window in the back of the room.

The window is not only extraordinarily large for the room, it sits at an odd height, higher than I could ever reach.

As we step closer, I notice the window is open about a foot from the bottom. The sound of a cabinet slamming closed bangs yet again, and I cringe as my eyes close at how loud the banging is.

I look back to the kitchen and then to Hud in complete confusion.

"Not there." Hud shakes his head while pointing to the kitchen. "There." He points to the open stained glass window.

I step in front of Hud to look up, still very confused. "I don't understand."

Large, gentle hands fall on each side of my waist, his warm thumbs press into my bare skin from the open back of my pajama top as he lifts me.

I can smell him behind me, this close. It's the smell I've missed, the one that felt like a dream the day it reappeared and encompassed me in the alley behind Mueller's Cafe when Hud was so determined to prove it mattered to him what I thought.

I shake those thoughts loose to focus on what's in front of me.

Hud has me level with the open bottom of the stained glass window, and I lean forward to peek out. I should consider that my ass is in his face as I bend through the window to get a better look.

Instead, I'm mesmerized by two large, arched wooden shutters equally massive to the window. I never noticed them.

I guess this is the back of the house at the realization that I've never been out there and seen it from the other side. I peer left and right at the swaying shutters on each side and above me at the black night sky.

The stars are high and bright like they were that first night he drove us to Rockridge.

My mind goes back there at the feeling of once again being hoisted up in his arms. His hands pressed against my skin, holding me securely. It's hot out, so my goose bumps betray me as I look out at the night, my skin coming alive under his touch.

A gentle summer breeze picks up and caresses my face, blowing my hair back. I close my eyes and breathe it in. The wind picks up, and the shutter to the left of me bangs against the side of the house.

Instantaneously, one hand leaves my waist and shoots out beside my face, grabbing the other shutter before it hits me, slamming into its natural spot, on its way to close.

I don't know how or when Hud had the time to cradle me onto his right shoulder with one arm.

"Woah." I slide down him slowly until my feet touch the floor. My bare legs, covered in only my thin pajama shorts, feel every inch of the rough texture of his jeans against me.

The whole thing feels surreal or in slow motion.

I take an appropriate step away from him.

"There's your ghost." His voice is low and confident as he watches me with suspicion of his own. I look down and blink at the floor, then raise my face with a serene smile. I had been so enchanted by the beautiful window design and falling prey to Hud's arms once again, that I hadn't made the correlation he was trying to show me.

I shake my head as my smile fades.

"What?" He crooks his head down, seeking the expression on my face. "It was just the shutters beating in the wind this whole time. They've got to be latched down so they—"

"No... I know." I interrupt his explanation. "It's just so beautiful. I can't believe I didn't even know it was there. Talk about a hidden gem. Who puts a design feature so stunning on the back side of the house where no one else will see it?"

"In fairness to our forefathers, there may have been a dirt road or trail that went through the town on the other side, making that the front view of the house. That, or the original Vogels had it put there just for them. For when they were working their land."

"Just for them?"

"What did you see when you looked out, before you saw the shutters flying toward you?"

"Miles of night sky over acres and acres of land, and a patch of pecan trees in the distance."

"Right. So imagine if you were out there working those acres and you looked back toward home at what you'd see."

I breathe in the visual of what Hud suggests.

"I like that idea best. That they put that there just for them."

Hud turns to walk back through the kitchen toward the front door. We left it open with my fabric spool barricading it. He lifts it from the door frame and hands it back to me.

"Guess you think I'm pretty silly? Believing in ghosts."

"She's real, alright. She just wasn't banging your cabinets tonight." Hud laughs, and I punch him in the arm. He steps out of the doorway onto the wrap-around porch, and I leave my trusty fabric spool behind to walk him out.

Crickets chirp around us, and the tiny town looks so big to me from this porch. Like I can see the whole thing, yet it stands up tall to me, just as tall as Vogel House. I like that feeling.

The Dollar General is dark, but the lights from the Pit Stop stream diagonally over to us, reminding me that Hud's about to return to them.

"The porch needs a swing. Too big not to have one." He leans against the column by the steps.

"I know. I think Anderson is working on it."

"I'll see what I can do." Hud looks down at his shoes, then back up to me, tracing me from my feet and back to my eyes. My breath hitches, and a million butterflies swell into flight. "You could've told me you were staying."

"You could've asked."

"Fair enough."

My hands are behind my back, pressing against the column opposite of Hud's as I look away and out into the night. "Would it have mattered?"

"It might've made some things different." His voice comes out quiet, serious.

"Like what things?" My voice is unrecognizable to me, as I don't think I had decided to say that out loud. After a beat, I bring my eyes up to his. Hud takes a deep breath and looks back to his shop.

Right. I get it. It wouldn't have made that much of a difference. "Look, thanks for coming by and helping me out, but really, you shouldn't have to. I didn't stay to be your problem or to cause you problems or to..." I take a sidestep to the front door. "Really. I'm just here for Anderson. You don't owe me anything."

"Wren." He says my name like he means it. Still, nothing follows it.

"I won't make trouble for you here. I mean, I'll stay out of your way," I continue in the only way I know how.

"Is that what you think I want? For you to stay out of my way?" Hud takes a step closer to me, his body towering over mine as I stand barefooted, looking up at him. He tucks a strand of hair behind my ear. The heat between us is palpable. "That's what you think is going on here, between you and me?" Another step closer, and his hand finds its way to my bare back again. My nipples harden, feeling his fingers on my skin.

I suck in a breath and fight away the sting of tears. "Hud, you barely said goodbye to me. It was more like, 'peace out' or 'good luck,' and the moment you found out I was staying you ran for the hills..."

"Houston. I went to Houston. This is the Hill Country, not Houston. Goddamn it." Hud steps back, dropping his hand away. He runs his fingers through his dark hair. "You and everyone else in this town. You just go and start your own fucking think-tank before you know what's really going on."

"Then why can't you tell me?" I almost whisper it.

"Wren, I've got more going on than is fair to explain to anybody, least of all somebody who—"

"Who what, Hud?"

Hud lets out a miffed sigh and shakes his head. In two strides, he clears the porch steps. "Holler if you need anything." Somehow, he manages to shout behind him without looking back.

And before I take a second breath, he's halfway back to the shop.

The sun pours through Matilda's naked bay window, and I blink out of a squint to force my eyes open. The two seconds of silence I experience make me wonder if I didn't wake up early naturally to the sun's rays.

Fat chance.

A *vroom, rattle, rattle, chug, chug*—repeat. Then, chugging full throttle becomes the new background noise of dawn. I'd slam the pillow back over my head, but that sound woke me up enough to get up for good.

I took a bubble bath to put me back to sleep after Hud left last night, so I only have to get dressed in my trusty old staples of jean shorts and grab a thin summer top to exist in the three-hundred and seventy-five-degree heat.

I've got popping out of bed and getting dressed to see who I have eagerly working before their scheduled time or who's knocking to be let in down to a science.

In less than five minutes, I'm on the first floor, fully clothed, with basic hair and makeup, digging through Anderson's Nespresso flavors.

Lately, I've existed between the best of both worlds—a caramello espresso Altisso, and Martha's strong cafe drip. I press the power button and almost miss the faintest knock at the door before the machine gets going.

I clomp over to the door—uncaffeinated—to see which worker awaits me. At first glance, there's no one.

"Hey ya' Wren." The big voice booms from a small figure smiling up at me, and I can't help but drop down to hug Connor.

"Where have you been, buddy?"

"Dad took me to an Astros game. Now we're back. He said to come on in and grab a water, that you wouldn't mind. But I thought I should knock to make sure you're decent. I never get up this early, so I could understand if you weren't either."

"You, sir, are welcome here anytime."

"I haven't seen the place yet. Well... not for real." Connor attempts two over-exaggerated winks. "Don't tell Dad, but some friends and I snuck up to the porch and peeked in a couple of times on the way home from the pool, but that's before anybody owned it again, so I don't think we transgressed."

"Trespassed." I nod with a smile to correct him.

"Same thing, right?" Connor questions my correction, wise beyond his years.

My head tilts and an eyebrow hikes in thought. "Actually, yeah, kind of." I can't hide my smile. Connor is one uniquely charming fellow. "Well, you shall have a proper tour then, sir." I curtsy and spread my arm wide to welcome him.

We walk toward the kitchen as Connor's excitement rises over each power tool the contractors have left, and I point out what will become what when we're done with all the work. I pause in the kitchen at my perfectly curated cup of espresso. "Would you like some tea, sir? Or, would you prefer a bottle of water?"

In response to my curtsy, he bows. "Umm. Thanks anyway, madame, but I think the bottle of water will do." We giggle as I toss him a cold one from the ice chest.

"You got a lot of good ice in there and only water? If I'm gonna be coming around a lot more often with Dad working on stuff here, too, I could bring us some Mountain Dew. I got a bunch of extra cans at the house."

"I'll take em'. Hey, what's your dad working on here?" I step toward the kitchen window as I hear the engine sound that woke me circling nearby.

"Uncle Cal asked him to bring his tractor and get started on your backyard. Your friend is gonna' make grapes grow into wine next to the pecan trees. Hey, can I go see Matilda's room?"

"What? You know about Matilda?"

"Everyone knows about Matilda," Connor shouts as he races up the stairs. My instinct wants to shout, 'be careful,' but I'm not an authority figure. I'm this kid's friend, and I kind of like that about us.

I run up the stairs just as fast behind him as he marvels at the space and begins to tell me all the old haunted Vogel House stories about my infamous roommate.

We laugh until my stomach hurts and hear what I've come to understand as Hud's tractor engine roaring back our way.

"Bet we can see my dad from up here." We both run out of my room and across the hall to one of the vacant rooms with a window facing the back acreage.

Another thrill races through me at the idea that guests staying in this unfinished room will have a view of our baby vineyard one day.

I clear my throat as Connor's little arm shoots across my face to point at his dad, because, right now, this is a room with a view of Hudson Bass shirtless on a tractor.

I force my jaw to stay closed as he waves up at Connor on the turn before us.

His grey eyes sparkle up at us from underneath his sweaty ball cap, as if those could captivate me right now with the sheer amount of tan, chest, abs, and biceps on display for me for the very first time.

Cal asked you to come over with your tractor. I'll just bet.

And, my God, when the man's back turns to us... where do you get shoulders like that? And what's that dripping down his back along with sweat?

Is that a tattoo going down his spine? Hudson Bass, aren't you full of surprises? I dart my gaze back down to Connor. "What?"

"I said, my dad has his shirt off already. He must be hot. Don't you think we should bring him a bottle of water?"

"So hot." I feel my cheeks flush even though I know Connor has no idea where my mind is. "I mean. It's so hot out there your dad's got to be thirsty. Let's go... Race ya to the kitchen?"

You don't have to challenge Connor Bass twice.

We race down the stairs like two eight-year-olds, and yes, I truly have to fight to let him win as I can't seem to get outside to Hud fast enough. Have I not learned my lesson with this guy?

What the hell am I playing at? Or fishing for? Or—am I being desperate?

I wait for Connor to reach into the ice chest for Hud's water bottle, and the tractor comes my way again. Shamelessly, I stare out the kitchen window at its operator, and I'm confirmed that I do not care if this is desperate. It's hot. It's summer. Anderson would say it does that to people, and anything under the heat of a long, hot summer is forgivable.

"It's true," he'd say. "They made a movie about it in the late fifties."

Ugh, get out of my head, or I need to get out of his, and outside with Hud before I explode or Connor asks me why I'm drooling.

Connor waves from his dad's lap as the tractor approaches me again. Hud tickles him, and I watch my little friend buckle over in sheer, mouth-open-wide laughter.

I set two more water bottles that I just ran back in to grab on the back porch rail, in case anybody needs one. The tractor slows as it reaches the porch, and Hud kills the engine so Connor can hop off.

I walk toward them as if it's the most natural thing to do, and reach out to lift Connor off so Hud doesn't have to climb down from the tractor.

"Your turn, Wren. Maybe Dad will let you drive."

"Oh... no, I don't think..." I try to stifle the idea. I'm sure the last thing Hud needs is me getting in the way of him finishing in this heat.

"She knows how to drive a car, Dad..."

"Not quite the same thing buddy." Hud winks at his son.

Connor smiles at me, motioning toward the tractor. "Sorry, Wren. You can't drive it by yourself, so you'll have to ride like I do."

Hud leans down and extends an arm, lending me a hand to step up. "You heard the little man. Your turn, Baldwin."

I can't even make eye contact with Hud as I grab his hand.

Why am I so nervous? I slide into the seat, trying not to invade his space, but the seat is much smaller than I would have assumed.

"I hope you don't mind a little sweat," he says in my ear.

Scandalous.

His voice invading my space, my stupid senses. The goosebumps and butterflies are all on deck and ready to go full speed ahead.

He leans forward, his cheek pressed to mine as he starts the tractor, and I feel his hot breath on the side of my face. Jesus. He smells so good. Even better sweaty.

I'm about to crawl out of my skin. *Sit down.* Just sit all the way down carefully and be still. That is all you are responsible for right now, I coach myself, as I ease down further in the seat and he starts to drive.

His arms close in as he reaches around me to steer the tractor. I swallow a quick breath and try to adjust in the seat so that I'm not leaning too hard on him or pushing him off his own tractor with my ass.

How can this seat be this small?

The jostling of the tractor isn't helping my dilemma, and I'm afraid I've yet to fully sit down or back into the seat.

"Hey." I barely hear him shout behind me over the engine noise.

"What?" I turn my cheek toward him.

He leans close, his lips brushing my cheek as he says, "Steady now. You keep wiggling like that and we're going to have a problem I don't think we want to handle in front of Connor."

My pulse spikes at his words, and I must be red all over. I've never been so embarrassed and turned on at the same time.

I lean forward immediately to sit up better, then drag back, arching away from him. "What's better, scooting up, or back like this?" I demonstrate.

Hud leans in again to meet the cheek that I turn his way, only this time he brings his lips to my ear. "I think you got your answer."

I let out the breath I was holding in and try not to pant as I melt into the seat... into his lap.

His right hand steers as we turn toward the back half of the acreage, the farthest away from Connor we'll be before heading back to him.

Hud's left hand falls to the side of my waist, landing on my hip, and I feel his ample erection behind me. Whatever Hud was holding back last night, he is certainly not withholding on this tractor.

For a split second, I don't know what to do, but I sit still and feel my stomach flip over and over at the experience of him being so rock hard behind me.

I bite my bottom lip, and slide the back of my blouse up, leaning my bare back into his bare stomach and chest—as much as the tractor will allow.

His sweat smears across the exposed section of my back, and I arch my head to his shoulder.

"Fuck, Wren." His fingers dig into my waist.

"I want to smell like you." I look back and mouth to his face.

Hud's hand tightens around my hip and he pulls me into him, pressing my ass to him as best he can.

I adjust to the bulge in his jeans, amazed at his ability to control the tractor with one hand.

His breath quickens behind me, and I become more impressed with his self control when I see the tractor make the turn that Connor is counting on in the distance.

His face drops down to my shoulder and he traces up my neck with his nose, drinking me in. If only I knew how to turn the damn thing off, I would've stopped the tractor in the back of the field, turned to face him, and...

Connor's little figure is waiting for us on the porch... him cheering my tractor ride comes into view and is quite sobering.

Hud scoots me forward, off him, and his left hand returns to steering with his right as I slide the back of my top down.

I can't get off this tractor. No way in hell can I hide what she's done to me. And I hate like hell this ride is over. What I really wanted to do was drive her straight to the pecan grove, pull her into my lap, and slide inside of her.

But Connor was watching and waiting.

"Thanks for the ride." Wren smiles over her shoulder at me tauntingly, her little dimple showing, as I bring the tractor to a stop near the house. As she steps down, her eyes twinkle with mischief, a devilish little grin playing on her lips. "That was fun."

"We'll do it again sometime." She knows what she did to me. I wonder if I did the same to her.

"My turn again?" Connor bounces on his toes, waiting to climb back onto the tractor.

"Not yet, son. I need to make some hay first. I'll come back and get you." He gives me his pouty face, and it makes me grin. "I promise. I'll get you in a few minutes. Gotta make some headway first."

"Awww," is the last I hear as I turn on the mower and put the tractor in gear, trying to focus on the job at hand to get rid of this hard-on, a gift from the little maneater herself.

Yeah, I wanted to give her a taste of her own medicine. Look what it got me.

Her cheeks flushed red when I whispered in her ear. I'm not sure why. Wren Baldwin knew exactly what she was doing to me, wiggling her tight little ass against my crotch.

I got to thinking after I left her last night, about what Cal said a few days earlier. *She wants you.... give her a reason to stay...*

I'd asked him why a woman like Wren Baldwin would ever stay in Vogel Springs, and he'd yelled, 'You know less about women than I do... because she wants you.'

And then, somehow, I knew he was at least half right. Why else would she drag that pink suitcase down the middle of Main Street, right in front of my shop, if it wasn't to tempt me? If she'd wanted to avoid me, she'd have snuck out the back door of Martha's and down the alley to Vogel House. I wouldn't have been the wiser about her staying in town. Not for a while, anyway.

She's trying to get under your skin, Cal had hollered at me, and fuck if he's not right. I *do* know less about women than a gay man. I let that conversation roll around and around in my head as Connor slept beside me, and my eyes popped open wide with a new realization: Wren Baldwin has been intentionally tempting me.

I made up my mind right then: two can play that game. But keep your heart in check, I warned myself, because that woman would be happy to add another broken heart to her collection.

I threw back the covers, dragged poor Connor out of bed before daylight, drove to the homeplace, and loaded the tractor and cutter on the trailer. I had them unloaded and running not long after daylight.

My fucking dick rises to attention every time Wren parades in front of me, no matter what she's got on. But damned if last night—seeing her in baby doll pajamas, having my hands around her tiny waist, lifting her up so she could see out the window, her wiggling her ass in my face—if I didn't almost have a stroke trying to keep my cock from busting through my jeans.

She had to know it.

You want to play games, you little maneater? Game on.

I shucked off my T-shirt earlier than usual. Ordinarily, working in town, I'd leave my shirt on out of common courtesy. It might offend some women. But I'm not on Main Street. I'm driving a tractor in the middle of a hay pasture with a Tasmanian Devil trying to see how hard she can make my cock. So let's see if I can't give her a taste of her own medicine.

Besides, I like to feel the sun on my skin.

Shit, her bare skin against mine a few minutes ago. Fuck. Both of us sweaty, my hand on her hip...

Stop it, man. If you want your dick to deflate, stop thinking about her.

There's a nice breeze out of the south. I inhale a lung full of the morning air. Nothing but her perfume smells as good as fresh-cut hay, and even that's a close race.

I told Anderson, when he asked if I'd help him clear the land, that he could bale hay off his property and sell it. This is bluestem. It can grow six feet tall. It's already shoulder-high on Connor. Oh, shit. *Bluestem.*

It's probably full of chiggers. I didn't think to warn Connor or Wren. Or myself.

What am I doing with my shirt off? Damn, nothing itches worse than a chigger bite. You can't even see the little fuckers that burrow into your skin. A groan escapes my throat. I can hear it above the tractor engine. We're all going to be eaten alive by chiggers.

Shit. Dammit. Hell. That's what you get for playing games, dickhead.

Not a damn thing any of us can do about it right now.

My gaze goes back to the white rock hills that surround Vogel Springs. A man can roll a tractor easy enough here, if he takes his eyes off the uneven land he's working. You can't afford to let your mind wander. This grass is so high that if I don't keep my eyes peeled, I could run over a sharp boulder and puncture a tire. Mess up my mower blades.

Focus on the task at hand.

It'll take a hell of a lot of work to turn this into a showplace, which is what Anderson says he intends to do.

I'd guess there's a hundred acres, and Anderson wants to turn the twenty closest to the house into a vineyard. I told him it was a good idea. There are lots of vineyards in the Hill Country, but I'd think that means plowing, cultivating, and working in fertilizer. Maybe even irrigating it.

We don't hit water here for several hundred feet, but once you reach it, it's the best water there is. Full of minerals.

But who knows what grapes need? I never tried to grow a grape.

My hard-on finally gone, I pull back up to the house to see Connor jumping up and down and I wave him over, turning off the mower and the tractor motor.

Wren is up on the porch, her hand wrapped around a porch post watching me.

You like what you see, darlin'?

I cup my hands and holler. "Get in the shower!"

"Why?" She marches my way in her trademark platform sandals, swaying those hips.

"Chiggers. As tall as this grass is, me cutting it, with the breeze blowing—we've all probably got chiggers."

"Oh, no, chiggers? Really, Dad?" That boy knows about chiggers. Panic spreads across his face.

"Sorry, buddy, but yeah. Get in the shower. Make it as hot as you can stand it, and use as much soap as you can, and scrub hard."

He takes off lickety-split. "Wait, you don't have the keys." I reach into my jeans pocket, pull them out, and toss the shop keys to Wren. "Would you mind getting him inside and upstairs? Lock him in, and I'll get to a breaking point soon."

"Sure." She takes the keys, her eyes on my eyes, not the keys.

Despite the chiggers, I catch a grin taking over my face. *You do like what you see, don't you? I damn sure like what I'm looking at.* My cock takes notice, remembering her sweaty back up against my chest, her hips in my crotch just a few minutes ago.

I clear my throat, "You need to shower, too. Hot as you can stand it."

She nods. "I never had chiggers."

"And you never want 'em. Scrub hard."

Hud

Chapter 29
great escape

Twenty acres of bluestem this tall? This is a two-day job. The sun has climbed high, scorching the earth and everything on it. Shading my face with my forearm, I glance overhead. Gauging where the sun is? It's eleven o'clock, and I started at daylight. As I pull up to the Vogel House, turning everything off, I stand, take off my ball cap, and pull on my T-shirt, tugging it down.

My skin can take a lot of sun, but I've had more than my share today, and I made my point.

As I run my fingers through my sopping-wet hair, Wren approaches with a smile that confirms my suspicion.

I jump to the ground about the time she holds up an icy cold water bottle. "You've got to be thirsty."

"I am, thanks." I tilt my head back and drain that bottle dry, wiping my mouth with the back of my hand. Our gazes catch and lock tight. I can lose myself in those eyes.

I offer the empty back, and my eyes drift to Connor, whose arms are red from scrubbing so hard. I wink at him. "You wanna ride again, son?"

When Connor was little, he got chiggers in his privates. Guess it scarred him for life because he grimaces and shakes his head. "Chiggers, Dad… I don't know."

It brings the heartiest laugh I've had in I don't know when. I ruffle his hair and pull him against me. "Nobody likes them, but we've all got to live with them."

"Yuk." He careens his neck back to meet my eyes. "I'm ready for a haircut, Dad. I'm tired of hair in my eyes, and it's too hard to wash and comb. It gets tangled."

"Whatever you decide." He's too close, leaning too far back to see me, so I figure I'll make it easy on him. I reach down and pick him up. With our eyes level, Connor rests his arm on my shoulder. "First, Dad, I'm hungry."

"You didn't get much breakfast, did you?"

"Pop Tarts."

Wren clears her throat. "I'd make sandwiches but Anderson's left me high and dry. The kitchen is being remodeled."

"Martha's!" Connor chants. "Martha's!"

What the hell? I've avoided Martha's since Rosalee showed up. Fuck her. "Fine with me."

Wren smiles. "I'll buy since you're working."

I snicker. "Not on your life, darlin'." She doesn't even glower at me for using that nasty word. "I'll buy, but first let me wash some chiggers and dirt off me, too. I'll make it quick and meet y'all there."

Wren reaches into her shorts pocket and pulls out my shop keys. Once again, our gazes seem to lock and hold. "I had Connor call me when he was ready. I set him free and locked your shop back up."

"Thanks." I tuck the keys in my jeans and head for the shop. "Tell Martha I want the usual."

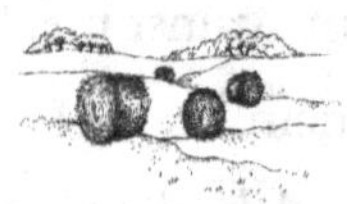

When I walk into Martha's, the place is buzzing. High noon. Connor and Wren have a booth by the windows. Her eyes twinkle as Wren watches me slide in beside Connor, directly facing her.

"Hud," she asks, "How come your shop is closed?"

"Anderson asked me to shred the bluestem. I've been slow the last few days. Anybody needs me, they know my number."

"How come it's been slow?" Connor asks.

I'm not going into that here and in front of Wren, but before I can come up with some lame excuse, a voice beside me snarks, "I'll tell you why his business is slow."

Tilting my head to the voice, I see Nick Wheelan glaring down at me. "Not the time or place, Nick." I cut my eyes at Connor and Wren. "Anything you want to say to me, do it when I'm not eating lunch with my son and a friend."

Nick's gaze narrows as he stares at me a beat longer. His focus moves from me to bounce between Connor and Wren. "You're right." He tips his ballcap to Wren. "My bad. Ma'am. Connor."

As Nick walks away, Wren's eyes are full of questions that I'm not prepared to answer. The next thing I know, Genevieve clomps a glass of water on the table before me. "You're not Mr. Popular anymore, are you Mr. Ass?" She clears her throat with a giggle. "I mean Mr. Bass."

"Genevieve!" Martha's voice booms from a few feet away as she stomps across the ancient hardwood floor to our booth. "If you want to keep your job, you'll apologize."

I'm doing my best to glare a hole through Genevieve as I tell Martha, "I don't need an apology. I consider the source."

Martha's fists swing to her hips, her eyes on Genevieve, not me. "Maybe you don't, Hud. But I do. No one will insult my customers and work here. Genevieve, apologize or leave and never come back." She aims her arm at the front door, and her voice is loud enough to travel through the cafe.

"I apologize," Genevieve sneers. "What would you like to order, Mr. Bass?" She pops the B.

"I already ordered for him," Wren snaps. "And you know it." Her cheeks are crimson. Her eyes are eviscerating Genevieve, too, as she lowers her voice. "Really? In front of his son?"

Go, girl.

Connor's eyes ping between Genevieve, me, and Wren.

Enough. "Martha, I'm sorry. We didn't mean to cause a scene." I lock eyes across the table with Wren, signaling, and scoot out of the booth, forcing Genevieve to step back. "We'll eat somewhere else."

Martha tweaks her mouth to one side. "This will never happen again, Hud. I promise you."

I stand and squeeze her shoulder as Connor climbs out of the booth behind me. "It's not your fault. We'll be back, don't worry."

"I have a great idea." Wren is all smiles as we re-group on the porch outside the cafe. I'm not sure which one rebounds the fastest, her or Connor. "Let's drive into Rockridge and have a burger."

"Sure." I fish in my front pocket for my truck keys.

"No." She tosses me her keys, and I catch them mid-air. "Let's go for a spin in the Maserati."

"Oh, boy!" Connor squeals. "And a haircut?" He peers up at me.

"Son, if you want a haircut, you can have a haircut."

Chapter 30

"intimate" domain

The alarm clock responds with 2:00 a.m. as I stare at it, and it stares back unmoved since the last time I looked. It appears even Matilda has deserted me.

Isn't this the witching hour?

Rolling onto my back, I find a splotch to stare at on the ceiling instead. It's so hot it's hard to sleep, and my mind keeps wandering back to the other day with Hud and Connor.

Everything was great, with the exception of what happened in Mueller's. But Hud and Martha go way back. That'll work itself out with Connor's next milkshake.

Connor.

I never dreamed I'd be riding with those two the next time I had my top down in my Maserati. By the time we made it to the burger joint, I was starving. I ate everything on my plate, including raw onion, which I tried not to belch up from the passenger seat as Hud drove us home.

We got a haircut.

I smile at the ceiling. They got a haircut. The relationship between man and his barber... I giggle out loud to Matilda, replaying the conversations in my head. I don't think I've ever watched a grown man get a haircut.

That was absolutely not on the docket with my father.

When I think about it... all the time I spent disappointing the man, we really didn't spend any time together at all. Not like that, not like Hud and Connor.

Hud let Connor pick any cut he wanted. An army buzz cut was high on the list due to the sweltering heat, but I must say I was relieved when the modified fauxhawk won. He looked adorable.

I think driving home with those two, I smiled so much my face hurt. I'd gone from no Hud in sight, but electricians, plumbers, roofers, and handsy carpenters, to a sweaty, almost dry hump on a tractor and the greatest day ever with two gentlemen I am finding myself very fond of—to the disappearance of Hud yet again.

At what point did I ask one question too many?

I dropped them off. Connor ran up to play video games and I walked Hud to the door. I wasn't trying to pry, but come on... the shop has been closed for days.

That throw-down at Martha's... How dare someone speak to him that way in front of his son? That is *not* the Vogel Springs I landed in or have come to know, and I guess I just needed some answers.

Martha had alluded to issues with his land and some company pursuing him. I didn't understand the extent until that moment in the cafe.

When I asked Hud that night, he answered me, but when I tried to throw supportive words his way by asking how they could do that to him of all people... I mean, isn't this town obsessed with the guy?

If Anderson were here or Matilda could speak, the response would be, "Apparently not as obsessed as you are, Wren Baldwin."

Good night. Maybe I did embarrass myself by asking. It's none of my business. I just don't get how Hud and I can be so close, and that says a lot about two practical strangers. So close on so many levels and so distant on the most common or obvious ones. The easy stuff. Maybe that's just it.

Hud doesn't see it as easy. In fact, when I brought up the conversation in the cafe, that's where the answers turned bitter.

Is it Rosalee?

My questioning him about the land and what's happening in this town with him... went unanswered by him and Martha. I understood Martha at the time. After all, I was a complete stranger then. But Hud?

It's clearly public knowledge if people are boycotting his shop.

Why is it hard to discuss with me?

My heart sinks. Unless it reminds him of Rosalee. Her snickering in the cafe with Genevieve was as if they were on the wrong side against Hud.

Maybe that's what's hard about the whole thing. Rosalee and Connor are not my domain to ask about, and I overstepped prying into Hud's business. I shake my head, shuddering at the thought.

I haven't quite landed on the issue without having all the information, but I've put enough of the elements together to determine that I can't be a priority for him.

I suppose I'm bold enough to wish I was enough of one for him to tell me that.

The most I got from him concerning the town and Rosalee was that intense look in his eyes when he said, "Money. Money changes anybody's mind."

Not his, though. I know better. I don't know how I know, but I know there is no dollar sign worth what is his. I just don't know why he won't let me express that.

The overhead light flickers on and off above my head. "Yes. I know Matilda. Bed time."

Construction is well underway when I yawn and blink my eyes open. I turn to my alarm clock, and this time, it offers 9:36 a.m. What?

How did I oversleep? I couldn't sleep, then I'm down for the count? Awesome.

Who let all the people in?

The power tools are in full swing, blasting louder than the AM radio the guys play while they work. I fly into my shorts, throw my hair into a messy ponytail, and descend the stairs.

"Is that bacon frying?" I can't hear my favorite sound, but I smell it. Our kitchen has been demolished, so there's not a chance. I'm now hallucinating.

"Well, if it isn't Sleeping Beauty." Anderson stands between the living room and kitchen construction with a stack of to-go boxes on top of the ice chest. "I bought break-fast."

I drop my forehead to the wall beside me and tap it a time or two.

"Oh my, I'm gone for a little over two days and you lost your hair brush?"

"Three and a half days, but who's counting? How was it?"

"The usual. My mom pretended to listen while she trimmed her roses and interrupted me to ask Rupert to add another person she forgot about to the guest list of her upcoming charity event, and my dad and brothers drove me to the new property and showed me their pet project, all the while changing the subject when I mentioned mine. Yay. But I brought money."

"Did they mispronounce Vogel Springs?"

"Honey, they didn't even let me say the words. If it's not something that can be prepped, powdered and franchised into more, it's not worth their time."

"Well, you're worth my time, apparently. I've been up at the crack of dawn every morning but today."

"Our clocks must be in sync, and you would have to be worth it for me to come around with that hair. Good God, did we not hang a mirror up there?"

"Shut it." I smile up at Anderson as he swings his arm over for a hug. I'm pissed at him, but I've never been happier to see him.

"How's my room and my vineyard coming? Do we have pecans yet?"

I can't help but laugh. "Stunning. I suddenly realize, I'd do better with Connor running this place. I think an eight-year-old has more patience and a general guideline of how things work and grow than you do."

"Connor, uh? If an apple doesn't fall far from the tree, I take it you've seen a lot more of daddy apple tree? Do tell."

"Save it. What a dirty trick. I didn't need looking after."

"She's right. I heard she held down the fort on her own very nicely while we were gone." Cal turns the corner in one stride, holding a drink carrier with three coffees. "Hi, baby girl. Are you the iced caramel latte?" He hands me a rare, foreign, but familiar drink with a plastic lid and straw.

"My absolute hero. I'm the iced anything you've got there with a lid and a straw. Where'd you score this?"

"Cal stopped in Rockridge on his way in." Anderson volunteers.

"It's not a Starbucks, but it's a wannabe, and sometimes, they try a little harder." Cal laughs. It's a contagious laugh, like Tiny's, and I find myself so happy to be surrounded by these two again.

"It's coming along." Cal peeks around at the construction and then into one of the breakfast take-out boxes.

I've learned, after hanging around this one, that NFL players are the same as 'growing boys.' They never get enough sustenance. I sip my caramel latte.

Anderson moves to the back parlor window, which I discovered through Hud. He's tall enough to be able to see out of it. He raises it and looks out. "Where are my grapes or the ditches to plant them in?" Anderson pouts.

"So, those have to be plowed after it's all mowed and the hay is baled." Cal joins Anderson at the window and looks out easily. "Wow. Hud's got a lot done already."

"Yes. But where is he today? I want my grapes growing." Anderson pouts again to Cal specifically.

Jesus. I've never seen him do that with anybody but me. I hope Cal can handle it.

"Hud got a call early this morning to fix a transmission. Which is amazing given the current temperature, and he'll resume work on Vogel House when his real job is completed."

Anderson perks up and smiles.

Something inside me snaps.

Sally come-lately-to-the-party shoots off like a rocket and fires one off. "What current temperature? The land issue? The boycott on his shop? Would someone please tell me what the fuck everyone else seems to know, but me?"

The construction noise pauses for a moment, and if this were a cartoon, a wren would fly straight into a glass window, smack down, and slide to the floor.

I peel myself proverbially off the floor and nod, signaling the construction workers to continue.

Cal and Anderson share a look, and their gazes land on me together. "Chickie? Do you need a spa? You want a little spa day break? Honey, go up stairs and brush your hair and Daddy will take you to lunch."

"Anderson!" Cal shouts at him on my behalf. "I'm sorry, Wren, no one meant to leave you in the dark. We should talk. If I've learned anything recently with Hud, it's that secrets don't make friends. As I said to him... It just all happened so fast. You and Anderson..." Cal looks over at Anderson, and my best friend smiles back so genuinely it makes my heart flutter.

"The eminent domain on Hud's land. Rosalee and Connor. The Vogel House bought and becoming a B&B run by you two, then over half the town turning their back on their own. I'm sorry, Wren. This is new terrain for all of us, I think."

I nod at Cal.

He's the only one or thing that's made sense since we opened the door to Vogel House, and he's here. Helping us. He means a whole lot to Hud, and somehow, he's become a fixture that means a lot to my best friend, too.

I let his words sink in, remembering how warm and welcome he and Tiny made me feel.

His honesty at this moment is a reminder of that. And the truth of what Hud is experiencing is the complete opposite, which is an abnormality for him and Vogel Springs.

Everything in me wants to ask how I can help, even though that's what got me in trouble with Hud in the first place. "You're right, Cal. It is a lot. I know we have a lot to catch up on here today, but could we do lunch?"

"Bitch, I just bought a five-star breakfast."

"Hush, Anderson." Cal and I almost shout it at the same time.

"I know Tiny is waiting to see us all. She'd be offended if we went anywhere else." Cal winks at me.

"Thank you, Cal. I would be delighted to."

"Fine. But we work out after, and I mean Lucille Ball style. We'll be stomping grapes." Anderson saunters off, and Cal and I shake our heads at my delusional bestie.

Wren

Chapter 31

you say it best...

L unch with Tiny was cathartic. I should check myself before I wreck myself calorically... clearly, all of my momentous moments in Vogel Springs revolve around food.

Except for Hud. But he's MIA. So...

I shut the door on the electrician, which ends my day. It's just after seven, so it's not dark out yet, and Anderson and Cal are long gone for the night. After lunch at Tiny's, they returned to Vogel House for an hour or two so that Anderson could sign off on some of the progress with the main contractor.

Then Anderson announced he had a few errands to run, and he and Cal would get dinner while they were out, and that was my cue to realize they wouldn't be back today.

It's okay, though. Anderson's been gone a few days, and so has Cal. They haven't seen each other in a bit, so it's cute that they want to hang out. That, and somebody has to be here to open and lock up.

Excitement should rip through my veins at the thought of an evening alone with no roaring power tools in the background.

The truth is, it makes me sad.

Anderson and I are in this together. I trust that. Just... unfortunately, not at this initial stage. So I don't have my best friend to entertain me.

With that missing, I recognize the void I've felt since the day Hud, Connor, and I headed out of town together. I begin to trudge upstairs to find a distraction when I consider a walk instead.

Yeah, I want to walk the acreage we were on and look up at the stained glass window from where the vineyard will be.

I slip out a back door, a smile already reaching my face as I see our own hay bales in the distance. I can't wait to walk the place. In terms of those chigger things Hud and Connor mentioned, I can only hope they were an exclusive obstacle the day he mowed.

There's nothing pleasant about the idea of whatever those are making their way up my skirt.

My phone buzzes, and I raise it to see a text from Hud.

HudBass: Hey

My heart stops.

My feet plant themselves in the grass beneath my sandals.

This is a first, since my car was fixed. I think that's the first and last time he texted.

Uncertain what I'm supposed to respond with, other than something lame like, 'Hey yourself,' I do nothing. I slide my phone back into my skirt pocket when it goes off again. Jeez. This is more nerve-wracking than Matilda.

HudBass: RU Home?

HudBass: At front door

WrenB: I just left. Taking a walk on grounds.

Ping!

HudBass: Out back?

WrenB: Yes

My heart pumps again, only to skip a beat, and my stomach starts its somersaults. He's not coming out here, is he?

Within seconds, I hear his long strides through the grass behind me.

"You shouldn't be out here alone." Hud delivers his first words to me in two days.

"It's not dark yet."

"Still. After Jerry—" Hud stops himself and continues to follow me.

"Is there something you need?" My eyes look up to his, and I don't know how to be anything but earnest when I'm with him.

"Yeah... Yes, Wren, there is." Hud's voice is low and calm, and if that statement wasn't loaded, I don't know what is.

I want to push him further. I want to ask him what he needs, but I can't bring myself to say anything. I keep walking at a steady pace further out into the field.

"What are you doing out here?"

"I told you, I'm going for a walk."

"Why?"

Now look who's full of questions.

"I want to walk as far as I can to the end of the land and turn around and see the stained glass window."

Hud stops in his tracks, and I keep walking. After a few more strides, I turn and look at him. "Where's Connor?"

Hud pauses a moment longer then brings his grey eyes to mine. "He's with Rosalee. She took him to a movie."

Now, I'm the one halting in the middle of the field. After a long stare-off, I bring my lips up to a half smile, sigh, and shake my head before turning away from him and continuing my walk.

I come upon Hud's tractor. I guess it's parked where he finished working. I stop beside it. My back is still to him.

I hear Hud approaching behind me, and dammit if all the butterflies don't soar through me all at once. I take a deep breath, and feel him directly behind me. He's close, but he's not touching me, and I'm not sure what he wants from me.

A cicada kicks off the orchestra, with crickets joining in, and I start to notice mosquitoes drifting around me and the hint of a firefly or two in the distance. It's incredible how nature kicks on, like an air conditioner or a car starting.

"I'm sorry. I know you wanted to talk." Hud closes the gap between us but doesn't touch me. I take a deep breath, feeling the heat behind me.

"But, I just..." Hud doesn't finish his thought, and for a moment I wonder if I'm going to be left out in this field alone.

The fighter in me screams, *'You just what?'* I've been down that road with Hud before, and it got me nowhere. I take another deep breath and let it land.

Still, nothing from him, but he hasn't moved. He places a large hand on the small of my back and I shiver on contact. An electricity moves through me I cannot explain.

I boldly turn to face him, bending my neck back to look directly at him and whisper, "Lucky for me..."

His eyes widen in surprise as he stares down at me, then his brows furrow together in confusion.

I step away from him, toward his tractor, and turn back to him. "I think you do your best talking on the tractor."

Hud's face changes and he rushes toward me. I feel his arms move around me and his hands around my waist, and when I meet his eyes, I smile and shake my head, then nod toward his seat. "Tractor."

He takes an obedient step up to the seat and swings his other leg over. Then he sits, legs spread open, waiting for his prize.

I climb up and attempt to throw a leg around. Hud grabs me by the waist and lifts me onto his lap so I can straddle him.

I lean in to kiss him, but his lips find mine first. They cover mine and devour me. One soft peck, to catch his breath, then his mouth is back to mine, separating my lips and demanding I open for him.

His tongue slides in to meet mine, and the slow exchange between us is anything but gentle. It's sensual, raw, and hungry.

I begin to rock my hips back and forth on Hud's lap, with each tongue lashing. My stomach dives when I feel him get hard beneath me, and I ache for him down to my core.

I don't think I've ever gotten wet just from kissing someone, but this isn't kissing. This is...

Hud bites my tongue in mid-kiss. He holds me there, his eyes open, and find mine as he sucks the fuck out of my tongue.

A soft moan of surprise escapes me before I can stifle it, and my eyes don't leave his.

I roll my hips into the bulge in his jeans. It's rough against my satin panties, and he feels so unbelievably good. My breath quickens, and in mid-search for air, he grabs my chin. "Let me look at you." He demands it of me as he tilts my head gently away. I arch backward, giving into his demand, and lay back on the steering wheel.

Hud breathes deeply, looking at me. His cock is so hard beneath me I could burst. He lifts my blouse and moves his hands up and down the flesh of my stomach, the back of my waist, beneath my bra.

Without looking around to see if there is anyone to see us, Hud's fingertips slice through the center front clasp of my bra and he releases me.

I gasp as his hand props my back forward, sitting me up and closer to him. His hands slide underneath my blouse, squeezing handfuls of my breasts.

He groans, and the sound of it has me trembling inside. I let out a breathy moan of pure need.

"Fuck, Wren. What are you doing to me?" He lifts my blouse with his head and goes underneath, his mouth replacing the hands that cover my breasts.

"Hud, Please."

"Please what?"

"Please," I beg until he closes my mouth with his. His tongue against mine has me almost bouncing in his lap. He spreads his legs as wide as he can in the tractor seat, and I feel his hand reach between us to find me.

A frenzy unleashes in my lower abdomen when his finger hooks inside the crotch of my satin panties, and he pulls my arousal out with it. His finger glistens with me on it and he shocks me when he touches it to my bottom lip, bringing my lip down and opening my mouth for me to taste it.

I lick myself off his finger.

"Is that what I did to you, Wren?"

I nod, looking deep into his eyes, still sucking on his finger.

"Fuck." He slides his finger back in me and quickly into his own mouth as if he can't wait anymore. His eyes grow large while on me, and he pulls my face to him. His mouth is by my ear. "I want to lay you out on the grass and taste you right here and now."

I shake my head again. "I said tractor."

He lets out a guttural laugh that becomes a groan. And my lips find his. I bite his bottom lip and move to his ear. "I want to see what I do to you."

Hud brings my hands to his belt buckle, and I don't hesitate to undo it, unbutton, unzip his jeans, and reach through the final barrier.

I find the opening in his boxers and place my hand over his girth. My lips purse together, and I take a deep breath as I reach further down and pull him out. He's so big in my tiny hand, and so hard I'm salivating at the sight of his perfect cock.

This is wild. This is something on a whole other level.

Hud looks at me, his gaze locked onto mine.

I pant back at him, stroking him softly, adrenaline pulsing through my veins.

"Wren," he pleads as he says my name, and he takes his fingers and slides my panties to the side. I move back on top of his lap and slide myself back and forth on him, smearing my wet up and down the length of his shaft.

Boldness of another level comes over me, and I can't tell if it's him or me, but I can't stop it.

I want him so badly, it's uncontainable.

"I fucking need you, Wren. I need you now."

I whimper as I feel his hands slide up the side of my thighs, up my skirt to my waist. Hud lifts me off his lap. He nods toward his cock, and I reach down and hold it in place as he slides me back onto his lap, lining my center with his tip.

My panties are still pushed to the side, and I've only pulled him out of his jeans and boxers, but the sight is so erotic, my lower abs convulse on the way down, and I shake as we make contact for the first time.

Without a second thought, he lowers me down onto his cock, and my breath hitches as I stretch to take him in.

I lick my lips and bite down on them, prepping to take more of him in, when my eyes return to his. Grey gems sparkle back at me, wide and anticipating. They haven't left mine.

"God, Wren. *FUCK.*"

I suck in a breath and slide the rest of the way down, leaning into him to keep my balance on the tractor. And once he fills me completely, I arch back, one hand on his shoulder, the other bracing his side as I begin rolling my hips into Hud. Relishing how he feels inside me, I moan without stifling it. His hands move to my hips to aid my thrusts. I look around as I'm riding Hud, and the sun has gone down. Night has fallen all around us.

I cry out when he pushes me down harder onto his cock, hitting me in just the right spot. The barrier between my underwear and his jeans creates friction in places I hadn't experienced before.

What is happening? A wide-eyed part of me can't believe we're really doing this, while the rest of me demands it's second nature and there is no limit to how shamelessly my body feels attached to Hudson Bass.

Hud watches me above him. His hands roam under my blouse and he lifts it up, exposing my breasts to him. He pushes me to go faster, and I bounce on top of him, getting more and more turned on by the way he watches me on top of him.

"You're so fucking beautiful, Wren."

Pleasure pulses through me. It hasn't stopped pulsating since we started. Then I feel his thumb on me, massaging above where his massive cock slides in and out of me. Everything is heightened with him, and I'm almost afraid of the intensity of my own orgasm approaching. I have never experienced sex like this. I've never been so needy for something... I'm aching for him.

Hud studies my face as I very nearly tremble on top of him, my walls stretched to the max to take him, and clenching up and down his thick shaft.

"Come for me, Wren."

"No."

"What?"

My cheeks flush in raw ecstasy as I bounce above him unapologetically, and I try to catch my breath as I shake my head, no.

Hud sits up in his tractor seat and scoops me up with him, his eyes wildly tracing mine. He cradles the back of my head and neck gently with one hand and squeezes my ass cheek rough, and barbaric as he presses me deeper onto him with the other. He groans, and I tighten around him. Tears swell in my eyes, and I feel him deeper than I've ever felt anyone.

"Steady now," he whispers in my ear. "Let it go."

With his words, on his demand, I come undone on his cock. He thrusts deep inside once more from below me, then lifts me quickly off him to come on my inner thigh.

Hud

Chapter 32

i never knew

My knees are weak and the shirt I wore is stuck to my skin with sweat. "Shit, Wren." I need air.

What just happened?

I tilt my head back, sucking in the night air, and reach under the seat to pull clean rags out of the toolbox, wiping my cum off of her leg, then my jeans. "Sorry for the mess." But I'm not sorry for that. What we did. I thought I knew everything there was to know about sex. I didn't. I never experienced sex like this.

Wren holds herself with one hand on the steering wheel and giggles. "Thanks for the mess." I feel her eyes adore me.

God help me, it feels so good to see her let her guard down.

Cleaned, with my jeans zipped, I pick her up by the waist and set her back in my lap, wrapping both arms around Wren and pulling her tight against my chest. I never came like that in my life. She'll be the end of me. I cut my eyes to see her nestled against me. It could damage her hearing, my heart pounding so loud against her ear.

Again, what the fuck just happened? I didn't plan this. In the back of my mind, I wanted it, yeah…. Shit, what am I saying, 'In the back of my mind.' I always wanted this. But when my feet mindlessly carried me to her front door, I didn't know this would happen. I would've come prepared. She'll think I'm a thoughtless jerk.

I've driven this tractor for years. I never dreamed of having sex on it.

Running my fingers through her long, soft hair, I comb it off her face and neck, where it stuck with sweat, and whisper in her ear, "I think we just had a first."

I feel her smile against my chest. "Told you, you do your best work on a tractor."

I chuckle. "Next time we'll go for the backseat of a car. I do pretty decent work there, too."

"Oooh, the Cabrio," she purrs. "It hasn't been initiated." Wren tilts her head back to peer up at me with triumph in her eyes. "So you do want me, Hudson Bass. Admit it."

I pull her tighter to me. She's so little. *Watch out you don't smother her.*

I tuck my chin to look into her eyes. "Want was never in question, was it?"

"It was to me." She has a pouty puppy face, like Connor, which brings another laugh gurgling from deep in my gut.

"Dammit, Wren I manhandled you the second or third day you were here. You mean to tell me you wondered if I *wanted* you?" I can't stop the laugh. "Jesus. How could you doubt that? I'm sorry I did that by the way. You just… I just…"

Once again, the words won't come as I softly shake my head.

With two hands, Wren pushes against my pecs so her back leans against the steering wheel, far enough for her to look into my eyes. "Why do you always do that?"

"Do what?"

"Hold back."

I moan. "It's complicated." I'm not going to be the weak fucker who begs her to stay. And I know she'll leave. It's just a matter of time. I remind myself, 'guard your heart with this one.'

"And I'm an intelligent woman," she snaps.

That's the exact tone she used on me that first day when I called her darlin'. This is going downhill fast. "That you are," I smile back. "Very intelligent."

She hops off my lap with a huff. Her dander's up. "Dammit, Hud."

"What?" I feign innocence, trying to throttle a smile, as I take in the beauty before me. God, she's heaven to see and touch.

Wren tosses her hair, sucks in, and blows out a quick breath. "Nothing."

I take it 'nothing' is kind of like 'fine,' which means she's as mad as a hungry badger. "We're not ending this night this way." I grab her shoulders and pull her back into my lap, slanting my mouth over hers, my tongue demanding access as I cup her face in my hands, and she softens against me, our tongues playing with each other again.

My cock is ready once more as she whimpers into my mouth, and I rub my face up her neck to whisper in her ear, "Have no doubt. I. Want. You. But I've got to go. Connor will be home any minute, and I've got to be there when she drops him off."

I should've expected this. But I didn't. I look over my shoulder from underneath the hood of a Kia to see four men standing shoulder to shoulder in my garage, silhouetted by the sun shining outside the open bay doors.

"What can I do for you?" I ask, unable to recognize any faces. Yet.

I walk toward them.

"You said to talk when you weren't having lunch with Connor." Nick Wheelan looks left and right around the shop. "Where is he?"

I wipe my hands on my rag, walking toward Nick. He was Connor's soccer coach when he was six. "Swimming. Say what you've come to say, Nick, and leave. I'm busy."

"I'll say it." James Fairplay steps forward. He's a wimpy, balding banker in Rockridge. "What you're doing isn't right." He purses his lips.

"Says who?"

Fairplay cuts his eyes left and right. "Us. All of us. A company wants to put a manufacturing plant here, and not only are you keeping them from doing it, the county's gonna raise our taxes to fight you to make it happen. It means—"

"I know what it means. Would it interest any of you to know that VoltEdge stands accused of dumping toxic chemicals? The waste from their manufacturing plant in Mississippi?"

They look at each other and mutter among themselves. "Bullshit, Hud. You're making that up," Nick spits.

"I don't make shit up and you know it. This will play out in court."

"You're really going through with it?" One of the other men demands.

I don't know him, nor do I give a flying fuck if he's the governor's son. I take a step closer. "Yes. Now I've got work."

One of the four snickers. "Enjoy it while you've got it. We're putting a full page ad in the Sunday paper asking Citizens for Progress to boycott your shop."

"Have at it."

As we all go our separate ways, I turn back to them, cup my hands, and holler. "Any of you idiots ask yourselves why my land is the only land in this county they want? Seems to me there's plenty to go around."

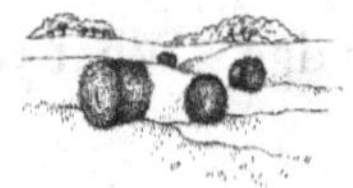

HudBass: Hey

Ping!

WrenB: Hey!

My thumbs hover over my cell phone. How do I say this? I haven't been able to get her out of my head. I knew once would never be enough. Finally, I find the emoji and hit send.

HudBass: 🚜 ❓

I wait like a high schooler as three dots hover over her name. She types something then backs it out. My eyes stay glued to the fucking screen as Wren texts something else, then backs it out again. Fuck.

Ping!

WrenB: A little b4
sunset

I'd high-five but there's no one to high-five. Connor's spending the night with buddies he made at the swimming pool, and Cal is so far up Anderson's ass I hardly ever see him. But fuck, yeah, me and Wren at sunset on a blanket in the grass. Doesn't get any better than that.

Shit. What about chiggers? Damn chiggers.

I do a quick search for chigger repellent. There it is. DEET will repel mosquitoes and chiggers. But she's a snowflake. She might not want to put DEET on her skin. I search organic alternatives to DEET, come up with options, and pull out my cell phone.

HudBass: Do U have peppermint, lemongrass or eucalyptus oil?

WrenB: Whatever for?

HudBass:  Chiggers

WrenB: On it!!!

I put my cell phone on the charger, lock the shop, and head for the shower.

"Well, what are you doing here?" Anderson asks as he opens the front door to Vogel House, which is still in chaos with his renovations maybe a third of the way through. "Do come in and ignore the mess. Are you here for a check?"

"Check?"

"Yes. I owe you for your work." I follow him as he strolls through a large open space, what I assume was once a living room.

My eyes find Cal. "You didn't tell him I don't charge my friends?"

He walks over and we slap backs. "Good to see you, bro. And yes, I told him. But he insists on paying."

It rankles me some. I'm no charity case. I can do a friend a favor. "I'm not in need of money."

"Come sit down and tell us all about it." Anderson leads us into the kitchen, which now has a large bar and floor and lawn chairs. I spot a refrigerator in the corner.

"Well, the truth is, I told Wren I'd teach her to drive the tractor."

The two share a smirking glance. I don't care. "She likes to ride the tractor. Since I finished the twenty acres by the house, I was going to move on toward the pecan orchard. I'll bale everything after it cures. Anderson, you ought to get five or six big bales an acre. Do the math. That's around five grand for these twenty acres alone."

Anderson throws one shoulder forward. "I insist on paying anyone who does that much work."

"I'm good right now, Anderson. Glad to help."

Ping!

WrenB: RU downstairs?

HudBass: 👍

WrenB: Do they know?

HudBass: 👍

HudBass: Dress for 🚜 ride

Cal twists off the top of a beer and offers it to me. "What's the latest, bro."

"I had some visitors this afternoon." I take a long tug on the bottle. "They're taking out a full page ad in the Sunday paper. Citizens for Progress calling for a boycott of Bass Pit Stop."

"Those bitches." Anderson stomps his foot and stands. "We'll take out a full-page ad that says "Citizens For Owner's Rights.""

And I have to laugh. Damn, it feels good. He doesn't know me, but Anderson Sofitel would damn sure do it. "That might not be the best idea for someone just opening up a new business here."

He refills his wine glass. "We don't rely on local business. Our customers will come from far and wide. Vogel House is a destination B&B in the Texas Hill Country."

I take another long drink of the cold beer. "VoltEdge has several whistleblower lawsuits from former employees who say they were terminated in retaliation for reporting the company dumped toxic waste from their plant in Mississippi."

"No!" Anderson is so demonstrative he makes me chuckle, and seeing, watching him, I understand Wren better.

"Yeah, I met with them when I went to Houston. And I found out something juicier."

"Oh, do tell," Anderson is all eyes and ears, sipping his wine while Cal, in his usual style, listens, going slow on his beer.

"They've been using satellites to scan for manganese all over this part of Texas. They need it to make electric car batteries. I'm beginning to wonder if they didn't find some on my land. Why else is it that they're so focused on having mine? I mean, there's manganese in Mason County and Llano and the Trans-Pecos. It's not that far-fetched."

"So they want to mine your land?" Wren is beside me. Her gaze is intense. "Then they'll stop at nothing. Do you own the mineral rights to your land?"

"Yes."

"So even if they take your land by eminent domain, they'll have to pay extra for the minerals."

My brows climb on my forehead. "Are you a lawyer?"

She hum-haws. "I worked for a lawyer." Her eyes drift strategically to Anderson. "A land lawyer."

Anderson's gaze locks with hers, and it's the most serious look I've seen the two share. Surprising. I never guessed. Something I never thought of, and she knows it, just like that. "But I don't want to sell."

"Then don't. I'm just saying, even if you lose in court, you can get your pound of flesh out of VoltEdge for the mineral rights."

She's smart. That's sexy as hell. I stand and down my beer. "Are you ready?"

"Oh. My. Gawd." Anderson grimaces as his eyes scan Wren from head to toe. "What are you wearing? Long sleeves and jeans? You look positively—country."

She swings her shoulders defiantly with her chin high. "I don't want to get chiggers."

Anderson sucks in air as his mouth sags. He takes a full step back. "What are you talking about *chiggers*?" He cuts his eyes at Cal then back at me and Wren, offended as hell written on his face. "What on Earth—"

Cal tips his head back and lets out a raucous laugh, the kind that keeps on coming, enticing me and Wren to join in. He grips Anderson's shoulder. "Anderson, chiggers are microscopic mites that live in tall grass, and if they get on you they'll eat you alive. Relax."

"Well I never heard of such." Anderson gulps his wine, his cheeks the color of the merlot in his glass.

"I get to drive the tractor." Wren claps her hands, sounding like Connor. "This will be so much fun. Later, guys."

Anderson cuts his eyes at Cal and groans. "A tractor ride. How unromantic."

And all I can do is chuckle inside, watching her ass as she sashays out the door.

"Wait," she says when we get outside. She scurries to her car and returns with a bottle of wine. "I stashed it in a cooler." She looks at what I'm holding in my hand. "What's that?"

"Connor's backpack. I brought a sheet for us to sit on. You got a corkscrew?"

Her smile fades. "I can't go back in and get one."

I dig in the backpack, pulling out a corkscrew. She grins at the sight. "I came prepared this time."

As we walk to the tractor, Wren clears her throat. "Speaking of being prepared."

I feel the heat in my face. "Yeah, about that. I bought protection."

She peers up at me with surprise in her eyes. "Bought? As in you didn't have any?"

"I didn't have any."

Her hand covers her mouth, and she emits a little moan, wagging her head. "Oh, Hud, tell me you didn't buy condoms at the Dollar General. Everyone in town will know."

A laugh escapes from my chest. God, she's funny. So demonstrative, like Anderson. "No, I drove to Rockridge." I fish in my hip pocket and hand her a folded piece of paper. "My test results from the clinic, to put your mind at ease."

She stops mid-stride, her face matching the color of Anderson's merlot as she stares at the paper, then lifts her gaze to mine. "You didn't have to do that."

"Yeah, I did. For your sake. What I did was pretty stupid the other night. Are you on birth control?"

"Yes."

This is getting too deep. "Hop on." I offer her my hand and help her onto the tractor. "The sun is getting low."

I start the tractor, showing her how the gear shift works. "You drive it just like a car, only you don't have a cab around you. You turn this thing over, you're probably done for. And this is hill country. Nothing out there is flat or even, so drive slow." I aim my arm up ahead. "When you get to the end of the mow line, I'll take over."

She glances back at me. "Why?"

"Because you can barely see over the steering wheel and you don't know what's in front of you in the tall grass." I lean near her ear. "And I know the fastest way to the pecan grove."

No argument.

She takes off with a smile, wiggling her ass into my crotch, her gaze dead ahead. "This is so cool." She almost squeals.

Yes, it is.

Hud

Chapter 33

ruined

Riding across a bumpy pasture with her ass nestled in my crotch, by the time we reach the pecan grove, I'm about to have a heart attack or bust out of my jeans, whichever comes first. She makes me so hard I can't have much blood in my brain, hence no oxygen, which explains why I'm a mindless fucker anytime I'm around her.

But my hard-on's got to wait a while longer. She wants to watch the sunset.

I grab the backpack as I jump off the tractor. "Slather up with your oil while I fix us a spot."

"What about you?"

"I'll be alright." I don't plan on being in the grass. Somehow, I didn't think the stench of bug spray would add to our experience.

I make quick work of spreading the blue checkered sheet beneath the canopy of a pecan tree old enough that its tap root is locked into the Edward Aquifer, judging by the size of its trunk and canopy.

We have an unobstructed view of the western sky, which is all but cloudless. The late-day sun is a softer version of its earlier, angry self, having mellowed into a glowing orb as it sinks into a apricot-colored horizon.

I spread my legs, like on the tractor, and Wren sits against me, between my legs. I think we both like this newly discovered position, with her ass up against me.

Wrapping an arm around her middle, I draw her close. It feels so natural. So right. "See those wispy clouds?" I point at pink and purple swirls high above the horizon. "That's what old-timers call mare's tails. They're supposed to mean the weather is changing."

She stares at the sky with childlike wonder. "Is it true?"

"Hell if I know." I slip my hand under her baggy shirt and pull her even closer, my hand wandering across her satiny skin.

She goes soft in my arms, nestling her back into my chest, her head against my shoulder, and whispers, "I love your touch."

My fingers dig into her skin as I whisper back, "You have no idea what you do to me." She can't.

I grasp her thighs and pull her ass into me, so she can feel my erection and I slide my hand inside her jeans. Feeling.

Feeling all of her that she will let me. Nestling my face in her shoulder, I inhale her, prompting Wren to tilt her head back, her eyes studying mine.

I cannot resist those pretty, pink lips that caught my eye the minute I laid eyes on her.

A groan escapes from deep inside me as I take her chin in my hand, trace those luscious lips with my thumb, and pull her into a kiss. My tongue demands access to her mouth. When she gives it, the kiss becomes almost frantic with desire, each of us starving for the other.

I unsnap the bra, taking her breast in my hand, teasing her taut nipple. "I've got to have you."

She whimpers into my mouth. "I want you, too."

I reach back and yank my T-shirt over my head, lay back on the sheet, and pull her on top of me. I want to feel her skin on mine, her breasts pressed into my chest... and more.

My hands slide inside her jeans, gripping her ass. "You've got to take these off."

She sucks and nibbles up my neck, whispering, "So do you."

Wren straddles me, unzipping my jeans, and I answer by yanking her oversized shirt over her head, the final light of day caressing her bare porcelain skin.

Look at her.

She's a living watercolor painting, sitting on top of me with her thick, wavy golden-blonde hair cascading below her shoulders, her perfect, perky breasts tempting me. I take them in my hands, teasing her nipples, eating her up with my eyes.

Her head tilts back as a little mewl escapes her throat, and those tits reach out for me.

I've got to have them. I pull her to me and take one in my mouth, suckling, teasing the other with my thumb, and Wren moans, rolling her hips into me.

"Fuck, Wren." I thrust hard against her, my jeans still on, as I take the other breast into my mouth.

"Wait." She's breathless.

Wren slides off me, and I lift my hips as she jerks my jeans down and reaches into my briefs, freeing my aching dick, and before I know what's happening, she has my cock in her mouth, swirling her tongue and sucking hungrily.

Once again, I surprise myself, hearing the animalistic growl that escapes my throat. Her tiny hand is gripping and pumping my shaft as she takes me deep into her mouth, sucking and twirling her tongue. When she teases my tip, I almost lose it.

I all but rip the jeans and panties off her, yanking them free, sliding my hand between her legs, finding her as wet as I am hard. "You're ready. For me."

"Yes."

I tease her clit and slide two fingers inside of her, curling them to find that sensitive spot, and she rewards me with the sexiest moan ever. More. She wants more.

"I've got to taste you." I lift and pull her to straddle my face, grip her waist, and hold her tight against me as I plunge my tongue inside of her.

The moan becomes a groan of pleasure as she slides her hands through my hair. "Oh, Hud. Please."

It's time.

I roll her onto her back, rest my weight on my forearms, and fist my cock to her entrance. She lifts her hips to meet me, and just as I'm poised to finally thrust inside of her—I stop.

Fuck! Dammit! Hell!

"I've got to get the condom in the backpack." What a mind-less, fucking idiot I am with her. Shit. Every time I'm with her my brain clicks off.

She grips my chin in her tiny hands, forcing me to meet her gaze. "Hud, you're clean and I'm clean and I'm on birth control." She hikes her hips into me.

"Are you sure?"

With wide eyes, her gaze locked onto mine, she nods. "Yes. I want you. Now."

I take my time to savor this sight in this waning light of day. Wren, on her back beneath me with a hopeful, hungry look of expectation as my cock is poised at her entrance. I drink in her angelic face and beautiful skin, her graceful neck, perfect breasts, and tiny waist.

This. I want to imprint this vision on my brain. I will still see this when I am a dying man.

I slide the head of my dick inside her, and she thrusts her hips into me.

We groan together in agonized ecstasy.

Slowly, I push as deep as she can take me, watching pleasure spread across that gorgeous face. She moves her hips, adjusting to me filling her up.

I pull out slowly and drive in deeper and harder, and Wren meets each thrust. She can't take any more of me.

We begin to move together, with perfect rhythm, like dance partners, as my thrusts become harder and faster.

"Oh... Hud." The breathless urgency in her voice tells me she's almost there, her little hands spread wide, caressing my shoulders, moving down to the small of my back.

She's breathing heavily, her hips meeting each thrust as I pump harder and faster. I'm not in control anymore as her fingernails dig into the flesh of my ass.

"Hud!" It's something between a wail and a moan as her body quivers and her walls throb around me. Wren's thighs grip my waist, squeezing tightly as her orgasm rolls through her, and at last, my cock explodes, buried as deep inside of her as she can take me, my release rippling through me in waves... again... and again. I've never... experienced... anything... so powerful.

I nuzzle my head in her neck, whispering her name, "Wren."

At last, I roll onto my back, bringing her on top of me, our skin slick with sweat. I grab a handful of her thick hair, stuck to her neck, holding it in a ponytail as I confess, "You're ruining me."

She smiles against my skin. "Do we need to get back? It's almost dark."

"I have headlights, but yeah, I guess we do."

We'd been too intensely focused on each other to hear the chorus of cicadas around us or notice the curtain of fireflies twinkling like low-hanging stars. An owl hoots in the distance before a pack of coyotes yip on the horizon. "It can be danger-ous to drive a tractor at night." I whisper. "Besides, your best friend will be wondering."

"Yeah."

I wrap her in my arms, not willing to let go just yet, and she nuzzles her face in my chest. For a few long minutes we just breathe together, listening to nature's symphony of the hills.

I can feel her little rabbit heartbeat against me, and I'm sure she feels mine drumming against her.

"Hud?"

"Um-hum." I am so relaxed with her in my arms, I could go to sleep right here.

"When you said earlier that you didn't have condoms the other night, were you just... out? Or do you not... ?"

"I outgrew chasing tail years ago. So no, I don't keep a condom in my back pocket or glove box."

"No relationships? I mean, since Rosalee?"

"None that took. And that one didn't take either, remember?"

Silence. She says nothing.

My gaze wanders about the star-filled sky, waiting for her to say... something. Anything. Maybe she's wondering if this one will take, and I want to tell her it already took. I'm fucking mad for her. But chickenshit that I am, I can't bring myself to say it. I'm too afraid of what will happen to my heart if she knows and still leaves. "Wren?"

She whispers against my skin, "I think it's time to get back."

Wren
Chapter 34
Lessons Learned

El MONTE SAGRADO SPA & RESORT: Hello Miss Baldwin. Checking in to see how you enjoyed your last visit. A reminder, you have an unused credit at the spa and we are happy to book your next visit.

KENDRA FROM PILATES: Hey, girl! Thinking of coming to class this week. Jake broke up with me. Want to get a Monster Juice after?

It's as if I never left or don't exist anywhere but here. I scroll through my latest messages, determined to catch up on anything that isn't Anderson or Hud. And there really isn't much of anything that isn't Anderson or Hud.

Hud. My God. What on planet Earth or Vogel Springs am I doing?

I'm so sore I can barely walk, and boy do I ever keep coming back for more.

My extended family includes an additional gay bestie who happens to be an NFL player, his aunt who raised him, an eight-year-old boy I'm so fond of I have to remind myself not to use the "L" word, his friends at the swimming pool, one very special cafe owner, and if I'm not careful, the Dollar General clerk and I might have enough in common to drive into Rockridge and get a pedicure one day next week. At least we keep promising we will. I don't know what's happening to me.

I was sure about Vogel Springs the day I committed to staying for Anderson and Vogel House. If I'm honest, I was sure about Vogel Springs when Hud carried me in his arms out of that no-vacancy Rockridge motel and brought me to Martha's.

The question is... am I sure about Hud?

The more absorbed I become in this place, the closer I'm getting to him and, well, everyone here I care about.

I know the answer I can't say out loud. I was never not sure about Hud. I'm certain of him. I'm just not sure what we're doing.

Wren Baldwin, if there was ever a time not to look a gift horse in the mouth... and when they say it's the gift that keeps on giving... again, my God.

I've never experienced anything like this. Good sex is just good sex, and after two or three times, in combination with getting to know someone, well, it usually just becomes sex.

With Hud, it's an event.

It's mind-blowing. There's always a surprise element, and I've never experienced orgasming Every. Single. Time. He makes me afraid of it sometimes. That's how crazy-good it feels.

I run out of Vogel House with Anderson pointing a finger and shaking his head and hip at me, like I'm some fucking teenager trying to sneak into a back seat.

If my initiation into Vogel Springs is Hud having me in every nook and cranny we can think of, then so be it. I just can't wait until we finish what we started that first moment in the garage at the shop.

Did I mention I can't get enough? And I know Anderson is onto me. I don't care. As long as he doesn't ask me questions I can't answer.

I don't want to know the answer if the risk is losing any ounce of this. I want every inch, drop and shred of what Hud is offering me, even if I don't know what he's offering, or for how long.

It doesn't matter. I can almost come undone during the day when reminded of his smell, his hands on my body, the way it feels when he holds me—and hold me, he does.

No one ever—well… it's never been like this. This is real. It's not something you make up in your head and want to be that way with some jerk who's just not supplying it.

Hud feels this way every time. Whenever he touches me and looks at me, I can tell how much he wants me. I may not know the why or for how long I get to have it, I just know I hope it never stops.

I haven't talked to Anderson about it because I don't know what I would say. We've been so busy with the Vogel House and him going back and forth to Aunt Tiny's. He's been trying to solicit her to run our kitchen when we open.

He promised she could be boss and hire whoever she wanted to do the potato peeling, onion chopping, and dough rolling.

She laughed and said she'd have to work double to teach any-body our age how to do it right. I've grown to know and love her as much as I do Martha.

"Cal said it should be ready in fifteen if you don't mind running over to grab it." Anderson appears in front of me from the kitchen. He's been droning on and on about the renovations, and I think he just finally asked me something.

"What?"

"Okay. We're done here."

"No. I was listening. I just didn't hear what you said."

"Bitch, please. A. If you were half the trollop I am, you'd be better at sneaking around. B. Even if you haven't gotten physically caught, your daydreaming is a dead give away." Anderson's face says more than the load he just spoon-fed me.

"Oh, please. You call what you and Cal are doing sneaking around? Just because we haven't talked about it or you two haven't come out of the closet together doesn't mean we don't know that you're practically living together at Tiny's." I wasn't ready to have this conversation, but leave it to Anderson to push anybody's buttons.

"I take it this 'we' is you and your new boyfriend?"

"Don't say that. It's not funny."

Thank God a knock on the front door stops the insanity. Anderson bypasses me faster than his short attention span.

"Who is it?" I mumble.

"The kitchen guys. They're coming to re-measure and take instruction from Tiny." Anderson answers the door. "Come on in guys, and get started. Tiny will be here any minute."

I nod and wave at the men, recognizing a couple of new ones as they pass us with toolboxes and backsplash samples.

"So you finally convinced her?"

"No. A promise of her own kitchen did. She's designing it. Cal's on his way over with her. He ordered us burgers to go from Mueller's, if you want to run over and grab. Martha said they'll be ready in about—"

Anderson's phone pings in his hand, and he brings it to his face to check. His eyes fade and his brows pinch together. Then I watch as he turns back to me with a blank expression, as if he forgot what he was just talking about.

"No dice. I'd know that look anywhere."

"You mean you're not in the mood for a burger?"

"I mean the text. Anderson? Who messaged you?" I step closer to him. I don't know why I'm so nosey, or who it's from, but I know the message has to do with me.

"I swear. I don't respond to these people. I haven't, and I won't. I promised you I wouldn't. You can scroll through and see." Anderson hands me his phone with reluctance.

I look down at the message he just received.

PhillipHughes: Just tell me she's OK. I need to know how she is

My face feels paralyzed as all the blood drains from it and my heart pounds in my ears. I toss the phone back to Anderson like a hot potato.

I don't understand my reaction as much as I understand the concern on Anderson's face as I take two steps back and try to catch my breath.

"Wren. Don't let it ruin your day, or any good thing you have going." Anderson's eyes plead with mine as I back toward the door.

Stepping into the bright sunshine, the beautiful day and the inkling of hope it brings are so foreign to the feeling in the pit of my stomach.

I don't cross the street to Mueller's immediately. I need a second. I run around the porch to the back of Vogel House and step into the mowed grass. Warmth surrounds me, and all my senses awaken as I stop and turn to stare at our stained glass window.

Our window, because Anderson and I bought the place. Ours, because Hud showed it to me, and it's the first thing that feels special and partly mine, that others who are invited can see.

I take a deep breath and stare into the colorful design, watching the sun hit it in all the right places. The design distracts me from my current state when I squint up to notice a bird in the top right corner of the stained glass. I never noticed it before, perched on a branch, but with its wings spread, as if it just landed above the rest of the scene. The sun's rays almost spear through it, and it takes my breath.

My heart rate steadies as I stare up at it. I'm calm now. The acid is gone from the back of my throat and I force myself to think of Phillip.

I may not have realized, but he's been a far scarier ghost than Matilda—a ghost from my recent past that sent me fleeing the life I'd been living the previous two years.

As reassurance settles over me, and the forced thought of Phillip stings less than seeing the message he sent Anderson, I begin to settle on a thought: It wasn't Phillip and what he did or even my father forcing his hand that made me run.

I'm not running from *them*. I'm running from who I am with them.

To love and trust someone with everything you think you have, and have them look at you and tell you, it's not enough—that they're choosing something else—that's not about them. It's about me.

I've been running from myself the entire time.

Phillip's text was just a ghost. His concern for me, or whatever his intent behind it is, doesn't do anything for me. Standing out here in the middle of a field that's done plenty for me, I see that.

I don't believe Phillip would be nefarious in getting in touch with Anderson. He may have cowered to my father in every way that counted, in terms of our relationship or lack thereof, and yes, he hurt me deeply—more deeply than I'd ever been hurt when he didn't choose me—but I don't think he would do my father's bidding to find me.

It could have been a genuine concern, but I recognize that now as his own ego. It has nothing to do with me.

The sun moves behind a cloud and pierces its way back out again. I smile as it falls on my face. I've never felt I belonged anywhere, and I know it's too soon to feel this way, but not even the reminder of Phillip can shake the sense of security Vogel Springs gives me.

It's funny, thinking about being in this same position with Phillip not long ago, with unanswered questions. However, when he didn't give me answers I chased them.

Hud leaves a lot unanswered. But I don't feel like I need to know. His actions speak louder than words.

I wonder if mine do.

Phillip finally obliged with answers, but they were all lies. Promises he wouldn't keep.

Hud has never lied to me. Not once. My heart knows and feels the difference.

I never felt this way with Phillip.

I thought I did at the time, but being with Hud is living. Everything before him was just making do.

A small part of me wants to run. It's not fear. It's the part of me that's learned the lesson.

When people respond to something you confide in them with, 'lesson learned,' then they give you that look. I hate that. I've always despised that expression. It implies our journey through life is learning what *not* to do at every corner—that life is merely a succession of lessons. For what? When do you stop learning the lessons and start living?

Martha's lunch grill must be kicking into high gear. The smell drifts over and reminds me of the task at hand. I turn away from my safe haven and begin my walk to the cafe with that pragmatic, ready-to-run voice still trying to negotiate with examples.

I spent over a year and a half, on and off again, with Phillip. I was by his side, at his beck and call in what felt like mutual understanding and affection. All the while, it was really a covert relationship that never saw the light of day or the inside of my father's office, other than behind closed doors when everyone had gone home and we fucked on his desk for fun.

I thought we were a secret because of me. I didn't want to make trouble for Phillip while he was on the partner track and Daddy's favorite. Sleeping with the boss's daughter might not have fared too well with the other partners, especially when you consider Philip had the perfect wife and two small children the firm adored.

There's always more to a story than you get in the beginning.

He was legally separated. Allowed to date. They both wanted out. Married young, and it just didn't take, blah, blah. Phillip agreed to keep things a secret, even though it wasn't as unsavory as it sounded and didn't have to be one... no one was having an affair.

I didn't want to jeopardize his reputation with senior partners, and Phillip was being sensitive to me and making sure I didn't tarnish my already-estranged relationship with my father. I had just gotten back in his good graces. Whatever that means. Truth be told, it's a place that doesn't exist.

Looking back at all the secrecy that made sense at the time, I can't help but wonder if it isn't a lesson I've already learned. As insatiable as my feelings are for Hud, they're a secret. Am I making the same mistake over again?

Wren

Chapter 35

secret handshake

Mueller's is jam-packed and Martha is in her element. I've never seen someone move so fast and auction off plates and new orders with hands behind her back, her chesty voice, and a pencil behind her ear.

I smile over at the table of workers I let in earlier this morning at Vogel House.

My smile fades quickly when I clock slimy Jerry Dennison sitting among them.

The cafe bell dings and the sound I could never tire of brings my smile back, along with the familiar face it lets in. "I knew it. Maserati. I heard the rumors, but I thought, surely, I'd hear from Hud if it were true." Travis, my tow-truck driver, is grinning wildly at me, and something in me wants to hug the guy.

I'm somewhere between proud and embarrassed that my adventure has brought me full circle for him to see. "So it's true? You never left? You're at the Vogel House now?" Travis steps to the counter to place his order.

The guy is so loud that everyone is staring, but I'm so tickled to see him that I don't care. "Yup. Me and a buddy of mine from Austin."

"Guess you saw something in these parts you liked." He aims his thumb over his shoulder. "I just dropped a tow off to Hud and he didn't say a word. That prick." Travis shakes his head and looks up at the menu board.

My mind races back and forth between 'Hud didn't say a word,' and the information about a tow being dropped off. A comfort settles in my soul, and I'm so glad Hud at least has that business coming in. I never thought I'd say this or even think it out loud, but... thank God for Travis.

The bell chimes behind me again, and all eyes meet Cal's.

"Dang, chickie, I wasn't sure if Martha got behind, or you flew away with our burgers." Cal approaches with a smile and an intricate, special dude-type handshake for Travis. "Bro, where have you been the last couple of weeks?"

"Workin' man. Shit, it's like old home week in here today," Travis repeats the signature handshake back to Cal.

"When is it not?" Cal smirks at the two of us, glancing around at the prying eyes of the rest of the town having lunch.

"Cal, your burgers are all set, let me grab the boxes." Martha swings around the corner with dirty plates that she's running back to the kitchen.

"Bro, I bet cousin is fired up with her here. It's got to ruffle Hud's feathers that this one stuck around." Travis says that one a little too loud.

"Yeah, but in a different way than you'd think." Jerry Denison tosses cash by the crumpled napkin on his plate and stands to leave, shaking his head at the rest of us. His fading busted lip is still present.

Rosalee halts in front of Cal, Travis and I at the counter, having spun away from the kitchen window with a large tray of sandwiches. "Excuse me." She looks me up and down, avoiding Travis and Cal.

Clearly, she caught on to what Jerry was referencing.

Oh, well. She doesn't scare me. The only good thing she has going for her is Connor, and that's all I care about.

Cal cuts his eyes to Rosalee, watching her walk away from us. He turns back to me with a strange look on his face.

I guess I don't know Cal well enough to read his thoughts, but something changes the air in the cafe for a second. Rosalee places sandwiches down on the corner window table where I usually sit. She lifts her head from her customers and peeks across the street at Hud's open garage, and a sharp sting shoots through my heart.

A pickle drops from my burger onto my chin, and I grab my greasy napkin to wipe my face. Tiny winks at me and we look over at Cal and Anderson, as their laughter from Cal's field impersonation of his biggest rival's touchdown dance permeates the room.

My gaze drifts down and I wonder if they're aware they're sitting so close together that their knees are touching on our make-shift chairs, ala milk crates we stole from Martha's. Maybe they aren't a secret, or they don't care if we know.

My eyes lift and catch Cal's. He tilts his head at me funny. The same contemplative look he had at the cafe when Rosalee copped an attitude with me is back.

Anderson stands to take everyone's to-go boxes and trash as Tiny follows him into the unfinished kitchen, talking about the kind of gas stove she likes and how many burners they will need.

Breaktime must be over, except for Cal, who's made it his job to stare at me. "Could I talk to you, Wren? Outside?" His voice is firm, and it occurs to me that I've never heard Cal so serious before.

I must appear startled by the question as Cal nods and raises an eyebrow at me for confirmation.

"Of course." Oh no. Oh, God. My stomach churns, and I'm about to be nauseous.

Is this about Hud? I haven't seen him or heard from him today, other than seeing the shop door open and knowing he was busy from bumping into Travis. Oh no.

Stop it, Wren. You're proving the lesson-learned section of your brain is right. This is why you don't jump, leap or fuck your way into feelings like this with no "talk" or commitment whatsoever.

It's moments like these, when an acclaimed NFL player has to sit you down and tell you how naive you've been that seconds that emotion.

Okay. Relax.

That last part brings me back from my spiral, and I follow Cal out the side parlor door leading to a section of the back porch.

We settle, and I'm not sure whether to sit, stand, or cry. Cal leans against a porch rail, folds his arms across his chest, and asks, "You alright?"

"Yeah." I nod profusely and add a smile, overcompensating for potentially not being all right. "You?" I ask him.

"Never better, actually." He raises a huge smile, and the Cal I know is back. "Look, I need to talk to you about something that is none of my business. The thing is, Hud is my business. I've made him my business since we were kids. Honestly, I've never seen him more alright in my life."

I raise a confused eyebrow.

"If he wasn't going through the literal nightmare he's going through with his land and business right now, I'd say this is the happiest I've ever seen him, and I know that's due to you."

Shit. Is it too late to feign bashful? "I don't know what you're talking about. I'm sure he's over the moon to have Connor all summer."

Cal smiles and shakes his head at me. "Connor. Yes. It does mean a lot to him to have him around anytime he can get him." Cal's face goes back to that serious, odd look I have only become familiar with today.

"Look, when I said this was none of my business, I meant me butting in about you and Hud is none of my business, so please forgive me if this feels like that. The truth is, I'm really stepping in to tell you something that isn't mine to tell. I think it's worth it though—you're worth it—and I know you're worth it to my best friend."

"Cal. What's going on?"

"Just bear with me here. Let me get this out, Wren." Cal pushes his hands forward in a halting motion.

"I'm about to tell you—or not tell you something—but heavily imply it. Something that I can't even tell Anderson, and maybe this is too soon and TMI, but Anderson and I don't keep secrets from each other." Cal runs his fingers through the top of his braids, pulling them back.

I look up at him and can't hide my earnest smile, nor the tear that falls down one cheek as my heart swells from what he revealed of his affection for my best friend.

"Yes, this happened fast. All of us happened fast. It's uncanny, and one fine day we'll have a bonfire and talk and laugh about it. But right now, a few things feel fragile, and they're too real and far too damn crucial to break. I know how Hud feels about you, whether he's conveyed it or not. And I think I know how you feel about him."

I suck in a breath and take a half-step toward Cal, but he halts me again.

"I'd never get in the way of nature taking its course with you two, but if it means making you understand how much my best friend needs you right now, even if he can't or won't communicate it, I have to."

Cal averts his eyes from mine, peering out at the bales of hay. "I got in the way of nature taking its course years ago, and it taught me something about my best friend that I should've already known." His eyes meet mine. "See, Hud's not just a good man, he's an exceptional man. I learned that the day I overstepped."

"What are you talking about, Cal?"

"I know something about Hud that may explain his guarded behavior. This fear of losing his land or his livelihood or Connor is a little more high stakes for him than the normal single parent."

Cal turns his head left and right, making sure no one is within earshot, as he quietens his voice and leans close. "After she popped up pregnant, insisting it was his, and after almost two years of Hud being a diaper-changing daddy with his money going out the window to her, not the baby, I got tired of her shit. I had a DNA test done behind Hud's back, thinking I was protecting my best friend." Cal brings a hand from the arms crossed at his chest to trace his thumb over his mouth.

My eyes refuse to blink as I shake my head in disbelief at what I think is coming.

"I'm not going to tell you what the results were. Only two people alive know what was on that paper." He hikes one shoulder. "Maybe three. Maybe Rosalee. She doesn't know I did the DNA test, but I'm assuming the calculated criminal she is, she either knows for sure or knew it was a possibility, and went with turning a blind eye to get child support out of the man she knew would pay.

"I'm sharing this with you because I trust how much you care for Hud. I trust you will keep this to yourself for Hud and Connor. But I wanted to share with you the mistake I made in not trusting. Bottom line is: Hud didn't want or need to know what I revealed to him. It didn't change the way he felt about his son one fucking bit. But now you see what Hud has on the line. Connor's more than your average case of a high school sweetheart ex, slash mother-of-your-child-turned-drug addict custody battle."

The tall man takes a long, deep breath before bringing his gaze to meet mine. His eyes shine with the threat of tears, and I know it cost him dearly to tell me this.

"Cal." My heart bottoms out right there, and it's all I can do to reach up and hug the man who cares for Hud as much as I think I do. As much as I want to, if given the chance.

"Wren. You don't have to do anything with this information. In fact, I pray you don't. It's just knowledge to help gauge your compass when you feel lost or in the dark about anything pertaining to Hud in these initial stages." Cal releases me and looks at me in earnest.

"I've over-shared, but again, Hud is my business, and I am choosing to trust you. I'm also confident I've overstepped, and I promise I'm not trying to put pressure on you to stay or deal with more than you prefer to handle. But if you're in the business of handling things... then hang in there through this rough patch. I promise you. He's worth the wait."

"**D**ad, can I go swimming this afternoon?" Connor asks with a mouthful of syrupy waffles.

His dad's gotten pretty good at frying bacon every morning and making homemade toaster waffles with syrup, if I do say so myself. It's become a routine.

Sometimes, we have fried eggs and toast but the kid loves waffles and syrup, which is running down his chin.

Most mornings, Connor noses around the shop, watching over my shoulder, asking questions and learning. He spends almost every afternoon at the pool, having befriended every kid in Vogel Springs. He's soaked up so much sun, his hair is sun-streaked, lighter than I remember it ever being, and his skin is bronzed, making his blue eyes pop even more than they normally do.

It makes me feel good. Connor Bass is happier than I've ever known him to be—not that he wasn't happy to start out with—it's just that now, joy oozes from every pore.

I want to get him signed up for school. Here. I haven't crossed that bridge with Rosalee.

"I thought we might go to the home place this afternoon."

He stops watching YouTube long enough to glance at me with curiosity. "Cause you're through baling hay?"

"Yeah. Time to run the baler back and get the plow."

My work in the shop has been slow but steady. Travis drags in a tow ever so often, and my friends still trade with me, although the full-page ad in the Sunday paper achieved what the Citizens for Progress wanted.

Not long ago, people from all over the county brought me cars to fix. Not since the ad. The boycott has given me time in the early mornings and evenings to make progress on Anderson's grape vineyard.

That tall bluestem made him a lot of good hay.

"What time, Dad?"

"Depends on whether anything comes into the shop. I promised Ted I'd check his suspension." I study my son, who is gobbling his second helping of waffles with his gaze pinging between me and the TV. "Has your mom said anything about school?"

He shakes his head, dabbing the syrup from his face with a paper towel.

"Do you want to start school here? In Vogel Springs?"

That got him.

"Yes." He jumps up, wrapping his arms around me, nuzzling his cheek into me. "Yes, yes, yes!"

I scruff his hair. "I'll talk to your mom." My eyes drift across the street. The cafe's not busy. "Guess this is as good a time as any."

Connor's out of the apartment, bounding down the stairs before I can open my mouth. "Wait!" I yell down the stairwell.

His eager face peeks back at me.

"Let me ask. Maybe it'll go over better."

He scowls. "She better say yes."

Sure enough, Martha doesn't have a single customer. Rosalee and Genevieve are sitting at a table folding napkins when Connor and I walk in.

Rosalee glances up, her eyes on Connor. "Hey, sweetie." She smiles and opens her arms wide. "Give me a hug."

He races to hug his mother, pulls back with an enormous smile, and blurts out, "I want to go to school here, Mom."

Oh, shit. I need a fire extinguisher with the flames Rosalee's shooting at me. I grip Connor's shoulder. "He was supposed to let me ask. Can he?"

Her gaze narrows, laser-focused. She'd like to disembowel me. "We'll talk later."

"Why, Momma, why?" Connor's shoulders sag. "I love it here."

I squeeze his little shoulder reassuringly. "Son, go ask Martha if she'll let you have a blueberry muffin."

He peers up at me and at his mother. He gets it. "Okay."

"Genevieve, would you give Rosalee and me a minute?"

Unbelievable. She cuts her eyes from me to Rosalee, who nods.

As Genevieve stalks away from the table—I'm sure she'll stay within earshot—Rosalee hisses, "You snake. Ambushing me that way."

"Wasn't intended to be an ambush." I lean in close, so fucking Genevieve can't overhear, my voice barely above a whisper. "He wants to stay with me and I want him to stay with me and we both know, Rosalee, you don't want the responsibility of looking after Connor full time."

"You had no right to cut his hair." She spits her words.

"So sue me."

Her hand flies high, but I'm prepared this time, catching her wrist before her open palm meets my cheek. "I've had about enough of that. Connor *wanted* a haircut. Now make up your mind about school, for your son's sake. Your parents can't take care of him anymore. I told you, I'll keep sending you child support."

I release her wrist, my gaze slicing through Rosalee as I holler over my shoulder, "Connor, let's go!"

Connor slams through the swinging kitchen doors, a half-eaten muffin in one hand, the other half falling out of his mouth as he yells, "Bye, Martha! Bye, Mom."

She glares at me. "Fuck you, asshole."

"I think it's high time for an old-fashioned Texas barbecue." Anderson's voice rings from the kitchen of Vogel House as Connor and I walk through the soon-to-be lobby. It's come a long way. There are so many people in and out of this old house that the front door is left unlocked during the day.

"I've heard all about your famous barbecue, Tiny Cooper. It's time I tasted it."

"She can make a mean brisket," I say as we enter the almost-finished-being-renovated kitchen that has Tiny Cooper's imprint all over it.

"Hud, honey." She turns with open arms, hearing me, but her gaze falls on Connor. "My gracious, child. Look how you've grown." She ushers him to her. "Get over here and give me a hug."

Connor buries his face in Tiny's loving bosom and I side-hug her shoulders. "Good to see you, Tiny."

She looks me up and down, dimples showing in her plump cheeks. "What brings you to Tiny's kitchen?"

My wandering eyes betray me as Anderson snaps. "She's not here."

"I'm going to take the hay baler home and come back with the plow. You still want to cultivate the twenty acres, right?"

"Yes, I do. But I won't let you do any more work without paying you."

I shake my head and Anderson's brows hit his hairline. He waves his hand, dismissing me. "Then no more work. Period. I will not take charity any more than you will. And you've done far too much work, Hudson Bass, for it to be a favor anymore. No more—I pay, or no more work. Shoo."

We all erupt in laughter, even Connor. "Okay. So moving forward, I'll accept your pay."

"How about a reward for what you've already done?" Anderson asks. "I hear from Cal that you have a beautiful little lake and a fabulous rock barbecue pit at your home place." He clears his throat. "Which I have never seen because I have never been invited to see it."

He glances around the room. "You're taking your hay-thingie home. Why can't we take the afternoon off, all of us, and have an old-fashioned barbecue?" He peers at Tiny. "What do you say? You, me, Cal, Wren, Hud and Connor."

"Can I bring Marcos, Dad?" Connor peers up at me with his trademark begging eyes.

"Sure."

Anderson claps his hands and prances in a circle. He's entertaining as hell. "It's done, then. What do we say, four o'clock, the Bass home place?" He waves at me. "Hud, you grill or smoke or whatever it is you heterosexuals do to meat. We'll bring everything, including good wine. Of course it won't be from my vineyard yet, but still... gotta' leave em' with something to look forward to."

It brings another bubble of laughter throughout the room. Connor and I exchange glances. "Wine at a barbeque?" I snicker and Connor grimaces and shakes his head, so I place our order. "We'll have Mountain Dew and beer."

"And I say it'll be hotter than hell." Cal strolls into the kitchen, resting his massive hand on Anderson's shoulder. "But whoever gets too hot can cool off in the lake. I'm in."

"Thank you, children, for the invitation but I think I'm going to pass." Tiny says. "It's too hot outside for an old woman this time of year. Besides, I might miss my program."

"What program?" Connor asks.

"On TV," Cal answers. "The Price is Right."

Tiny shakes her shoulders with pride, beaming. "I've been watching The Price is Right since Bob Barker was young. Now I've got Drew to keep up with."

Again, my gaze drifts around the room. Fuck, where is she? I don't smell her or hear her.

"I told you, she isn't here," Anderson quips, and by the look on his face, he's challenging me to ask where Wren is. It's been a couple of days. I need my fix.

I don't ask. He said she was invited. She better be there. Hooking up the trailer, I pull my phone from my pocket.

HudBass: Where R U?

WrenB: Leaving yoga in Rockridge

HudBass: BBQ 4 pm?

WrenB: Yum!

It's our secret code.

HudBass: Maybe 🚜?

WrenB: 🖤

Two days and I miss her. What the fuck am I saying? I missed her on day one.

Hud

Chapter 37
dirty trick

Wren laughs. She's having fun with the two boys while I get the fire going. "No, you turkeys. Like this." She stands barefooted near the water's edge with her hands in a prayer position, raises her right foot, and presses it flat to the inside of her left thigh, demonstrating some yoga pose for Connor and Marcos.

They watch with their mouths open.

She smiles, taunting her audience. "It's called the tree position. Now try again."

They both try, I think, for the third or fourth time and fall on their faces.

"No fun." Marcos dismisses Wren with a flick of his wrist and peers at Connor. "Last one in!" The boys race for the cool water, splashing.

Wren approaches, her eyes twinkling as she inspects the barbecue set up under the shade of a live oak, which includes half a dozen lawn chairs, our ancient stone grill and a weathered picnic table, which she covered with a blue and white checkered plastic tablecloth. "How long 'til we eat?"

I lift the lid and peek at the coals. "Forty minutes, maybe more."

She spreads her arms, her head on a swivel, admiring the landscape, and it feels good to see her appreciate the place. Her Maserati is parked nearby. Wren shuttled the two boys out here in her low-riding car, following me with the trailer and baler. I guided her over the Bluetooth on how to straddle ruts.

Wren inhales a deep breath of the country air, scented by cedar, and raises a brow, tucking her chin. "And exactly why haven't I been here before?" Her gaze intensifies and her voice quietens. "I see now why you can't bear the thought of selling it."

My eyes leave the chicken I'm marinating in a covered tin pan, and my jaw flexes. "I won't sell it, Wren." I glance around and point. "See that skeleton of a house over there?" Her eyes follow my aim and she nods. "My ancestors built that rock cabin right after the Civil War. This land isn't leaving the Bass family."

We're fast approaching a hearing on the land, a motion to quash, filed by my attorney. That shit is something I try not to think about, like I try not to think about what it's going to do to me when she leaves.

I turn my back to Wren and swallow a lump rising in my throat, reminding myself that day is coming, too. The Vogel House renovation is progressing at an amazing speed.

She says, "I think I'm going to get in the water with the kids."

That spins me around.

She reaches to shirk off her tank top, and just like it does every fucking time she disrobes, my heart stops as I watch her. Shit. No matter how many times I tell myself to guard my heart, I know that fucking guard has been demolished. By her.

She taunts me. "Wanna get in with me?"

I check the grill again. We've got time.

I smile at her, and she knows exactly what's on my mind.

Off come her shorts, leaving her wearing a one-piece bathing suit covering the parts of her I may love most. "Race you." She takes off for the water.

I yank off my T-shirt and run after her, scooping her up along the way, carrying her as I wade waist-deep with her giggling like the boys.

She swishes her legs, "Put me down."

I toss her in the deep water.

"Me next, Dad!"

"No, me!" Marcos croons.

Here come the boys for their turn as Wren's head bobs above the water. "I'm going to get you for that." She loved it. I can tell. She yells, "Get him, boys!"

I stand tall playing King of the Hill as all three of them wade through the water for me, trying to wrestle me down. They can't.

One after the other, I pick them up and toss them in the deep, and every time, they bob up and come back for more, all of us laughing.

"Well, look at that." It's Anderson. He and Cal stand at the water's edge. "Isn't this just *Little House on the Prairie*?"

Cal has been showing him around the place.

"Cal, check the fire, will you?" I call.

Dutifully, he heads to the grill.

"Boys, get up here." Anderson summons them with a wave. "I have a surprise from your Aunt Tiny."

They're gone, leaving me and Wren in the water. Alone. "Let's swim."

A few minutes later, we're treading water on the backside of a cedar-covered peninsula that juts out, offering a little cove of privacy.

"The water is so cool. And clear." She paddles closer, treads water for a minute, and grins. "Clear enough that I can tell you're happy to see me."

"You have no fucking idea."

She giggles. "Oh, yes I do."

Under the water, she unbuttons my shorts and slides her hand inside, gripping my erection. "We need to get rid of that before the boys see."

"No shit." I grab her waist and pull her to me, moving us to where I can stand chest-deep in the water. She can't.

I reach and pull her legs around my waist. A grin commands my face as I pull the straps of the bathing suit off her shoulder and cup one breast in my hand, teasing her nipple. "You want a tractor ride?"

She cuts her eyes to where the men and boys hover around the picnic table and grill. They're a hundred yards away, on the other side of the cedars, and they've forgotten us for a few minutes.

"Always," she coos.

I slide her bathing suit to the side, and even in the cold, clear water, I feel her warm silkiness on my fingers. My dick gets even harder.

I turn us so even if someone walks down the bank, all they can see is my back as I slide two fingers deep inside of her. I have learned the exact spot that brings her to the brink, so I curl my fingers, massaging it.

"Oh, Hud," she breathes out. "Damn you. You know my body too well." Her head falls back, the way it always does.

God, I love what she does to me. Seeing what I do to her.

I unzip my shorts, free my cock, place it at Wren's entrance, and slowly slide deep inside of her. As always, she is so wet, so warm, especially in this cold water, and so fucking tight. I moan. "Shit, baby."

She rises up and glances over my shoulder. "I can't see anyone."

"I know." I drive into her hard, and she catches her breath.

"Hud, hurry, before they see."

"They aren't going to see." Maybe it's the fear of being caught or the excitement of doing something so forbidden in broad daylight with a crowd across the way, but my dick is already about to explode. It won't take me any time. I've got to get her off first.

She lays back, floating on top of the water, holding onto me with her legs around my waist. My hand is big enough to grasp her waist and pull her into me, my cock driving deep as I continuously stroke her clit with the other, and Wren moans that beautiful sound of her agonized ecstasy that I've come to cherish.

I pull her into me feverishly again... and again... careful to stand straight in the water, making her body do the work so even a nosey neighbor won't see me thrusting into her.

Shit. We're making waves.

"Oh, Hud," She moans as her pussy quivers around my cock, her legs tighten around me and an animalistic growl escapes my throat as her throbbing walls milk my release.

"What the hell's going on over there!" That's Anderson, yelling from the other side of the lake. "Hello? Where are you two? Where's Wren?"

Fuck. Not now.

He has the worst timing of any man alive.

I suck in an irritated breath. "She's trying to see how long she can hold her breath underwater," I call over my shoulder while she tucks in my dick and zips up my shorts. I wink at her as she smiles gloriously and I turn my head to again yell over my shoulder. "You made me lose count. She'll have to start over!"

Wren buttons my shorts before she ducks under the water and bobs up beside me as if she really has been underwater, swimming to where they can see her. "Anderson, you made him lose count!"

"Well, get over here!" he hollers through cupped hands. "Cal says it's time to put the meat on!"

My meat is done.

But Wren is as chirpy as her namesake. "I'll race you back." She wiggles her shoulders confidently and dives in.

How is it that women rebound from sex faster than men? She's treading water, waiting for me to race her.

"I won't let you win."

"Fine." She takes off swimming across the lake while I take in another deep breath, watching her glide gracefully through the water. I can give her a head start and still win.

She's in the deep middle—and goes under.

What the fuck? Are you messing with me?

I begin wading toward her. She doesn't come up.

"Wren?" I yell.

Nothing. No Wren.

"Wren!" My voice carries through the countryside.

Nothing.

I swim like crazy, diving under the water where I saw her go under, searching for her with my heart about to explode in my chest. I can see clearly as I swim in a circle. Nothing. Fucking nothing.

I swim deeper. Where is she? No, God, no!

I come back up for air—and Wren's wading out of the water in front of her applauding audience. "Gotcha." She walks backward, laughing.

"Don't do that! You scared me!"

"I won!"

Now I'm pissed, swimming like a madman to shore as they all watch with amusement. I stomp over to her as she turns up a soda and grins.

Our gazes are latched. "That wasn't funny."

She's still giggling. "I thought it was."

Fuck, they're all having a ball at my expense.

I tower over her, mad enough to pick up something and throw it. "I thought you got a cramp. I thought you were drowning." My heart is still throbbing in my chest as I drip water all over everyone. "You scared the shit out of me."

Anderson's head tilts back, and he guffaws as he elbows Cal. "Now, I just wonder why Wrenny would have a cramp?"

Busted.

"That was absolutely delicious." Anderson pats his stomach, stretches his legs, and leans back in his chair. We're sitting in a circle of lawn chairs—some of them, like Anderson's, more posh than others—having polished off the fixings. Except for Tiny's homemade ice cream. Not even the boys had room for it.

Cal and I are drinking beer, Wren and Anderson are sipping wine, and the boys are off exploring.

Anderson holds up his almost-empty glass, waving his arm in front of him. "Hud, do you realize this land is perfect for a vineyard?"

I finish my beer and head for the cooler to pull out another. "Never thought about it. My people have always grazed sheep and goats. A few head of cattle."

"Well, over there," he aims his arm at the remains of the original home place, "there are grapevines. Someone raised grapes here at one time."

"I didn't know."

"You need to check into it."

Ping! My phone alerts.

"Travis may have a tow." I stride to the picnic table and grab my phone.

Rosalee: I want Connor tonight

HudBass: We're at homeplace

HudBass: Can it wait til tomorrow?

Talk about bad timing. A scowl overtakes my face.

HudBass: He has a friend w/him

Rosalee: Drop him off. I want my son

Rosalee: Now.

I don't want to waste the money, or I'd chunk the cell phone in the lake.

"Hud? What is it?" Wren asks.

My eyes meet hers. "Rosalee wants Connor."

"Well fuck her," Anderson chimes in.

"You can. I have no desire." And they laugh. But I didn't mean it to be funny. "Connor!" I cup my hands, calling. He and Marcos wandered off when I told them they couldn't get back in the water until their food settled.

I turn in a circle, bellowing, "Connor!"

"Yessir." They come running from a nearby cedar stand. He is such a good kid.

"Your Mom wants you."

He glances at Marcos. "Do I have to?"

I hand him my phone. "Call her and ask."

He takes the cell phone and calls his mother on speakerphone, all of us watching and listening as Rosalee's voice comes across loud and clear. "Dammit, Hud, I said no."

"Mom. It's me," Connor says, his eyes pleading with mine. "Please let me stay. Marcos is with me."

"Sorry, kiddo," she says. "We're going to see Granny and Pappa. They asked to see you."

His blue eyes are frozen, locked onto mine. He's torn. He loves her parents. But he's having so much fun. "Can we go tomorrow? Please?"

And there comes the Rosalee I know so well. "Give the phone to your father," she bites out.

Obediently, Connor hands it to me and turns to Marcos, wagging his head, the two of them trudging back toward the cedars.

"Get his butt back here ASAP," Rosalee barks. "I'm ready to leave work."

I shoot the phone the finger. Connor and Marcos have walked off. They don't see, but the others do. Wren's eyes drift to meet mine.

"Okay." I click off the phone. "Fuck," I say under my breath.

Wren's hazel eyes are still locked with mine.

"We need to talk, bro." Cal stands and strides toward the water.

I follow. "What?"

He signals to the phone as if it were Rosalee. "How long have we both known that she-devil? She's got something up her sleeve, demanding him back like that."

I rub my forehead, feeling it sunburned. "I'm going to sue her for custody. I've been so busy with the land lawyer, I haven't had time to get in touch with a family lawyer."

"You better." He tucks his chin, looking down at me. "Cause we both know her. She's got a bee up her ass and—"

I cut him off, nodding. "This morning, Connor told her he wants to go to school here."

He shakes his head, turning in a circle. "Fuck, man. She's gonna take him and run."

My stomach twists. "By God, she better not." I glance around the barbecue. "It'll take thirty minutes to an hour to clean up this mess. I can't drop everything to run him back right now."

"We'll take the boys." Anderson stands and volunteers, glancing at his watch. "I need to get back and lock up the house, anyway. It's getting late."

Wren says, "I'll help you clean up."

I turn to Cal. "After you drop off Marcos and take Connor to her, get Rosalee to the side and tell her this for me. She better not do something stupid."

Wren

Chapter 38

feels like home

Watching the boys drive off with Anderson and Cal registers in more ways than one. Rosalee texting Hud out of the blue that way, demanding Connor. I get it. I know she's his mother. It's a rough, unsettled time, and maybe even uncharted territory for her, with Hud having him the majority of the time.

But Connor had a friend over. How insensitive can she be?

I toss the folded tablecloth I bought on the porch next to the BBQ tools that Hud rinsed off, as I reach for the last box of condiments we packed up from the table. I'm not sure where he wants these, but I know the ketchup and mayo have to go in the fridge.

I wait by the porch steps of the stone house, watching Hud approach with the ice chest. My stomach flips as the other reason watching the car of our friends, Connor and Marcos, drive away hits home. It's a selfish reason—home.

This will be the first time I've been home with Hud or to his home. And this is the real one, apparently, not just his spot above the Pit Stop. I've never been invited there alone with him, either.

With their exit, we're alone for the first time, that's not sneaking away to be alone. It feels like something new and different, and I want it.

I just can't know if he does. After all, he didn't invite me out here with the plan of ending up alone with me.

Hud carries the ice chest onto the concrete porch and leaves it. He lifts the box of condiments from my arms and clears his throat as he turns the knob to open the front door. He's still upset about Rosalee, and I don't blame him. I'd want to claw her eyes out. The keys land on an end table, interrupting the silence of the cozy, dark house, and I wonder if I should offer to go. I don't want to push him or overstay my welcome.

"Do you want a shower? Get cleaned up from the lake and sun?"

I smile back at him, dumbfounded, as he flips the lights on, and I look around the old house.

"We've still got dessert we didn't get to, right?"

"What?"

"Homemade ice cream... Tiny sent?" Hud walks past me, back out the front, and grabs a metal container with a plastic lid from the ice chest. I watch him pass back by me into the kitchen to put it in the freezer. "We can clean up and have some."

"I love it."

"Homemade ice cream?"

"No. Yes. Yes, I do, but I meant your place. I love this place —your house." What in the entire fuck is happening to me? I sound like a talking doll whose batteries are going out. You'd think we'd never been alone together. Why am I so nervous?

Hud looks me over as if he's trying to figure me out. "It's my parents' old place. I love it too, so I've kept it up, and made it mine and Connor's as much as I can, but I'm at the shop the majority of the time. I thought that might change soon, until Rosalee's bullshit."

"I'm sorry."

"It's not your fault. I don't care that she inconveniences me, it's him. I don't like it when she uses him to get at me. He's not leverage."

I can't look at Hud. We've never spoken about his private life or anything substantial. I'm afraid I'll scare it away. My eyes drift up to the large oil painting on the living room wall. A corner of my mouth rises, and I shake my head. "That's an original Windberg."

"The Texas painter? Yeah, it was my parents'. I think it was a gift for my mom once."

"Most people just have his prints." I stare back at the bluebonnets in the iconic windmill scene and trace the painting to the open cattle gate with the broken fence.

"What, are you? Eighty?" Hud tries to hold back his widening smile, and I can tell he's trying to assess the situation.

"No. Just a fan."

"Of old-timer's oil paintings from the 60's?"

"Hey. You're the one with it hanging in your living room."

"I told you. It was my mother's."

"Mine belongs to my father. It hangs in his law office. It's a windmill scene too, but at night. Against an all-black skyline with no stars. Instead of the blue bonnets, there's snow covering the ground. It reflects like light across the painting and you don't know you're missing the stars. It's haunting and beautiful. I can't tell you how many times I've sat in his office and stared at it, wondering how we could both be so captivated by this one painting, yet have nothing else in common."

Hud stands beside me and stares at the painting with me. An awkward silence passes, and it feels like he wants to ask me more, but he doesn't. With his eyes still on the painting, I hear a low grumble in his chest, and his throat clears for the second time since we've been in his house alone together.

"Sounds like your dad doesn't deserve an original Dalhart Windberg." We both burst out laughing, and the tension dissipates. "Come on. I'll get you a towel and show you around."

From the living room, he leads me through the dining room and into the kitchen. It's the old-fashioned kind with a table in the middle.

Behind it is a much larger room, the den, he calls it, with a rock fireplace sprawled across the back wall. Off the den is a primary suite.

"Dad added all of this on when I was a teenager." He points. "That was my parents' room."

He guides me into a hallway that opens to the den and living room.

"That's Connor's room." Hud points to the right as we pass a doorway and continue to the end of the hall. "And this is me."

"You don't sleep in the other room?"

"My parents' room? I will, someday soon. I just haven't re-vamped it yet. My room, the one I grew up in, is right beside Connor, while theirs is way across the house. He's brave as hell, but he's still young. With moving around so much between his grandparents, my shop apartment, and whatever excursion Rosalee takes him on, I feel like I should be close enough he can holler in his sleep and know I'd hear him."

My heart melts, and I go from trying to sneak a peek at Hud's style of linens and his taste in bedroom furniture, be it a modern set he recently purchased or what was left over from his adolescence... to turning and looking up at him to see if he's real and still standing there.

After what Cal implied about Connor, this makes me understand Hud's heart even better, and I'm blown away by who he is.

Slow down, Wren. There is so much more you don't know.

Tonight, I don't care. I know his heart, and I—

He tosses me a towel from atop his dresser. I didn't even see him move behind me and flip on the light.

"The top drawer is full of T-shirts unless you prefer to eat ice cream in your only semi-dry-by-now lake clothes. Shower's in the back."

I take the towel and nod, and just like that, he walks away, leaving me to the shower. I assume he's going to shower in the other bathroom.

What the hell is happening here?

Okay. Let's do the math. The air changed the moment we stepped into the most perfect house on the most beautiful land, which is so perfect for him and Connor. If I thought Martha and Tiny felt like home... Jesus, I've already bonded with his deceased mother over our taste in art.

Speaking of art, he drops a small nugget about Rosalee and Connor, and I drop a big fat steamy oil painting of a turd about my father.

Nice one. A can of worms I am relieved he did not open.

My Maserati is parked outside, which leads me to believe he could reasonably expect me to drive away in it shortly after ice cream, yet he offers me a shower and a T-shirt. Okay, said shower and T-shirt do not suggest I'm driving home anytime soon.

However, said sex we've been having—crazy, insatiable, any-chance-we-can-get, including in-public sex—suggests that we would absolutely shower together. *Enough.*

I practically dive into the shower and fumble with the water, letting it get hot enough while standing under it like the complete lunatic I am. I can't afford to take in any more of Hud without knowing what to do with the information I've got, so I resolve not to look around and bask in things like his pine and mint shower gel that smells like a wake-up call and the large bar of soap that smells like him.

Dammit.

I finish and dry off. My jean shorts smell like lake and barbeque smoke, and my swimsuit is still a bit damp, so I opt for the T-shirt.

The T-shirt with no bra and no panties?

Well, it's a long, baggy one that comes halfway to my knees. And let's be real. The guy's not only seen everything underneath it, but he's tasted it, too. I grab my suit and shorts in one hand and confidently exit his room in a dark green Lake Greeson, Arkansas, T-shirt.

"I told you it didn't need chocolate syrup." Hud watches me lick the last spoonful of Tiny's homemade vanilla out of my coffee mug. He explained he has proper ice cream bowls, but he and Connor prefer eating ice cream out of coffee mugs so you can hold the handle and really focus on your spoon work. That, and Connor says the handle keeps your hand from freezing.

"This is the greatest thing I've ever tasted." I dip my spoon in to scrape a last potential drop.

"Yeah, Cal and I've been spoiled on it since the first summer Tiny made it for us. Like I said, it doesn't need any topping whatsoever, but if you want to lose your mind, like catnip-level, you can put that old-school Smucker's pineapple ice cream topping on it." Hud blows air out and makes a sound effect, as he scrapes his own last drop, and puts his spoon in his mouth upside down to lick it.

Before I know it, he's grabbed both of our mugs and is rinsing them at the sink. I stand from the living room couch and contemplate what I should do next.

He hasn't mentioned anything, much less made a move or even been flirty during ice cream. He has to know I'm buck-naked under his shirt.

If not sex, my hunch could be right that things got too real with Rosalee's call and my bizarre mention of my father and a creepy oil painting.

I should just go.

This is Hud and Connor's domain. This is this man's home. He was polite to follow through with dessert, but I should politely say good night before it gets more awkward for me, and he looks over and wonders why I look like I thought I was invited to a slumber party.

Hud comes back from the kitchen and looks at me. Still, nothing. He's not saying anything. I sidestep toward my belongings. "Well. I guess I should get going." Again, nothing. I smile and reach toward my clothes. "Get out of your hair."

Hud moves to me. He stands above me. My heart races when I look up at him, the same way it does anytime I look up at him, and he's looking down into my eyes this way.

He walks me to the wall, his large hands catching my upper back as it lands against it. Hud traces down the inner part of my arms and leans in, trapping me there.

He's a constant gentle giant, so when he dominates me in the act, I can't fucking stand it. It's the hottest thing I've ever encountered.

"Out of my hair?" He cocks an eyebrow. "That's interesting. You usually can't wait to run your fingers through it."

I stifle a whimper as he traces me with his eyes. "Unless you don't plan to stay." Something changes in his face. My eyes blink in recognition, and I can't help but sense it's a much deeper question.

My eyes flicker on his until our gazes lock solid. I bite my bottom lip and breathe deeply, for fear my heart is about to pound out of my chest.

He smells like soap and this cologne I can't place—but have fucking craved since the day I smelled it on his shirt, when he ravished me in the shop.

One hand presses the wall by my head, supporting his stance above me, while the other slides down my face, my collar bone and toys with the sleeve of his shirt on me. "Stay with me tonight, in my bed." He kisses tenderly down my neck to my shoulder, leaving me breathless. I'm already panting for him.

My quick breaths turn into words. "So you can do unthinkable things to me in your childhood bedroom?"

Hud presses his finger to my lips to shush me. My eyes widen, and he slides it inside my mouth, and I swirl my tongue around his warm flesh, sucking his finger as he slowly removes it from my mouth.

"So I can make love to you."

Before we can make eye contact again, he scoops me up bridal-style and carries me. I drop my ear to his chest and close my eyes to the pounding of his heart as he walks us down the hallway to his room.

It's dark in his room, with no light on, and I can barely make out the slate grey color of his duvet cover until he pulls it back and lays me down on lighter grey sheets. They are almost a silver color like his eyes. Damn.

He lays me down in the middle of his king-sized bed. I feel my wild hair fall all around me, and he watches me adjust into his pillows. He lifts his shirt over his head and tosses it to the side. His tan skin, chiseled chest, and the deep V-line below that dips into his jeans are all on display for me.

He slowly kneels on the bed.

His hands strategically slide the hem of his T-shirt I'm wearing up past my ribs. He's careful not to touch my skin as he pulls it over my head to expose my entire body to him.

I draw in a breath while staring up at him as I shiver. Goosebumps spread over me as Hud hovers above me. A piece of his dark hair falls below his temple as he explores my face, my naked body below his for the taking.

He doesn't say a word. He just stares into me.

His lips fall to my face and he gently separates my lips with his own, finding my tongue and intertwining it with his to a rhythm that makes me moan.

My hands fall above my head and I feel his big hands wrap around my wrists. His tongue grows heavier in my mouth, chasing mine faster, and I arch my back up to feel him. I want to feel him so badly. My nipples are so hard they scrape against his firm chest, but that's all he allows them to do, just graze him.

He leaves my mouth and takes his to my ribs, just below my breasts. He's teasing me.

With my newly freed hands, I slide my fingers down his bare chest until I meet his belt buckle and begin unbuckling. He shakes his head as if to tell me not yet, so I bring my hands back to my neglected breasts and place them where I want his.

He fucking growls at the sight and removes his belt immediately. He lets me unbutton him and take him out. I can't get enough of the feel of his hot flesh and heavy cock in my hand.

"Wren," he warns. Then he dips a finger into me and I'm so wet I'm visibly dripping from it.

He groans and slathers my arousal onto the tip of his cock. I'm almost convulsing underneath him. I want him on top of me so badly. I reach for his cock again, but he lowers himself onto me.

His lips are on mine, his tongue diving for mine, and his hands squeezing my breasts until I feel my nipples want to burst. I whimper when his wet mouth finds them. He doesn't stay too long before he traces his mouth down my belly button where my panty line would halt him, only he looks up at me hungrily with grey eyes that make me tremble—and then he does.

His tongue shoots up my slit and through to my core, and I cry out for him to do—I don't know what—because he's got me ready to come undone, fucking me with his thick tongue like this.

I fist his hair, then the sheets, and my head pushes deeper into his pillows as I suck in a breath.

The moment extends when Hud lifts me slightly off the bed, tilting my hips up in one gentle shove, and his tongue licks me from top to bottom. Oh my God. I cry out at the sensation as he handles me like I'm something that belongs to him, working his masterful tongue over every inch of his property.

"Hud..." My eyes beg him to come to me. I'm shaking and I don't know what to do without him close to me now. Grey eyes rise from between my legs and he gives my body back to gravity. The palm of his strong hand spreads wide across my lower abdomen as he presses me back onto the bed and gingerly pulls two fingers out of me.

He slowly makes his way back to me. Finally, I feel his hard cock pressed to my naked thigh as he leans into my ear and says, "I want all of you, Wren Baldwin."

My eyes widen in a frenzy and I arch my back, bucking my hips to find him. We meet and he pushes all the way inside me. My walls stretch to accommodate him without a hitch, and he fucks me like I was made to take him. He moans while thrusting deep inside me and my walls tighten around him at the sound of it.

My stomach tightens, and he brings his hand down me above his thrusts. He pushes deeper into me, and I can't take it anymore. I beg and I beg until I come undone again on his throbbing cock. I feel him about to explode in me and my core aches for the sensation. Hud doesn't pull out.

He pulls me closer to him, lifting me from the bed with one arm tightly around me as he releases inside me. I feel every bit of it as my head drops back to the pillow and he collapses on me, out of breath, as my own chest heaves beneath him. "Hud," I whisper like a statement as I close my eyes to rest, holding him to me.

Night fell at some point, and we slept straight through it in that position, only moving after that for him to spoon me or for me to lay my head on his chest. I turn away from him, and he pulls me back to him in his sleep.

My heavy eyelids flicker, opening slowly, as I feel him hard behind me. I tilt my hips down to glide my wet slit up and down him. I can't help it. He woke me with it. I line myself up to his tip and lean forward, then push onto him. He grabs my hip and sinks all the way into me and I scream his name when he fills me. I couldn't rest until I found him again in the night, and it's not something I think I will ever tire of doing.

Hud rolls to his back and I climb up to ride him. I pause on the way up, salivating for him. I slide my mouth over his cock and lick myself off him, watching his face the entire time. His hooded eyes nearly roll back in his head before he pulls me up and onto his cock. I sit up and let him watch me ride him, the early morning sun threatening to rise and peek through his curtains.

Arching into it, I roll my hips into him faster and faster, then I fall to his chest kissing him wildly while I keep up the pace. Hud grabs my chin gently and lifts it, bringing me to see his face. He stares into my eyes while I thrust until we both explode together. A moment later, he tries to hold me again, but this is my turn.

I push him to roll to his side, away from me, so I can spoon him. I adjust the sheets, slide toward his back, and wrap my arms around him. The sun makes its way through to us, and that's when two words come into view written down the length of Hud's spine. *Steady now.*

Chapter 40
coming into focus

"Hud?" Wren mumbles at my back. "When did you get this?"

The early morning sun filters into the bedroom as Wren spoons me, both of us spent from our night and morning of passion. "Get what?"

"This." She traces a manicured fingernail down my spine.

Oh. *That.* It's in her face.

I roll over, using my fingers to brush hair from her forehead and eyes. "I lost my parents in a car wreck when I was twenty-five. My mother died instantly, but Dad lived a few days. Long enough to ask me to never sell the land. Several months later, Rosalee disappeared with Connor." I pause, trying not to relive it. "It's... not a time I like to remember."

She strokes my face and whispers, "I'm so sorry."

I study her eyes, which are studying mine, and I take my time to adore the sprinkling of freckles dotted across her little nose and cheeks. "Anyway, my dad said that to me all my life. 'Steady now,' the first time he let go and I rode a bicycle without training wheels.

'Steady now,' the first time he gave me the reins and I rode a horse by myself or drove the tractor or car. 'Steady Now' was my father's mantra any time you had to do something you didn't think you could do. So when I lost them all—Mom, Dad and Connor—I don't know." I pause for a deep breath. "I needed it permanently embedded onto me."

She smiles sweetly, resting her hand on my chest. "I love it. It's so you."

My eyes drink her in. Wren, lying beside me in bed, like a dream. I allowed myself to fantasize about this—waking up with her in my arms—but I can't say I ever believed it would happen. I've resigned myself to take what I can get while I can get it, savoring one day at a time, still knowing, somewhere in my gut, that she will drive away someday.

I'll face that when it comes. "Thank you."

"Thank you for what?" she asks.

I pull her to me and kiss her soft lips for the millionth time since we've had this unexpected gift of being together alone all night—being able to fall asleep in each other's arms. "For everything. For just... being you."

Her fingers trace my brow line, and she runs her fingers through the hair falling on my forehead, combing it back as she says, again, "I'm sorry."

"For what?"

"For everything that's pressing on you now. The stuff with your land. Rosalee."

I roll to my back, resting my head on my folded arm, staring at the ceiling. "My first hearing is tomorrow. It's a motion to quash. My lawyer says we have to go on record asking the judge to throw out the case, but he doesn't think the judge will do it. He's under too much political pressure."

I cut my eyes to see her. "And Cal thinks Rosalee may try to take Connor and run." She props up on one elbow, watching me as I say, "I'll fucking kill her if she does."

"Hud, you can't say that."

"I know. But I can think it. No, I wouldn't kill her-kill her. But I'll spend my last dollar to make sure she never sees him again if she does something like that." And it hits me like a tidal wave. "Fuck!"

The hair on the back of my head tingles.

I sit up in bed and throw off my covers. "She knows my last dollar—all the money I have—is tied up fighting for the land." I bolt out of bed, my heart thundering. "I need coffee."

Stalking into the kitchen, I put on a pot to brew with my mind spinning like a top.

Wren is behind me. "Talk to me, Hud."

"I know what she's doing." My jaw aches, I'm clenching it so tight, as my gaze wanders the room, gathering the pieces of her evil fucking plot as the puzzle comes into focus. It's finally as clear as the August sky.

"She didn't come back here to look after her parents. She hasn't been looking after them. She's been here, watching me." I grip Wren's tiny shoulders as reality sinks in. "Rosalee came here when Genevieve told her VoltEdge wanted my land, expecting me to sell it for an ungodly amount of money, and she'd get her cut for Connor.

"Child support is based on the father's income. She'll demand ten, twenty, fuck a hundred times more child support if I sell the land. Now that she realizes I'm not going to sell it, knowing that if I lose in court I won't have squat, she's more pissed off than anyone in the county that I haven't agreed to sell."

I pour us both a cup of coffee while it's still brewing. "Yesterday, Connor asked her if he could stay with me and go to school here." My eyes leave hers, darting around the air high in the room. They won't be still. "Cal's right. Rosalee just ran off with Connor to force me to sell the land. 'You want him back? Sell the land.' I guaran-fucking-tee you, that's what she did. She. Wants. Money."

Wren gasps, her eyes like little moss green saucers. "She wouldn't."

"Why didn't I snap on this earlier? Cal kept saying it, and I felt it in my gut: Rosalee was up to no good, but neither of us realized she was this Machiavellian. Wren, I need to get to town."

"I'll hurry," she says.

"Do you mind locking up? I'll leave you the key. I want to get back."

She stands on tiptoes and kisses me. "Go."

Why the hell didn't I unload yesterday? Screw it. I unhook the trailer. I can't deal with the vineyard now, anyway. "Dammit," I groan.

Never put off until tomorrow what you can do today. That was one of my mother's favorite sayings. I should have that tattooed on my forehead. Not only should I have unloaded the baler yesterday, I should've gotten my suit out of the cleaner in Rockridge for the hearing tomorrow.

I dial my Bluetooth.

"What is it?" Wren asks without saying hello, and I can read the concern in her voice. She does care.

"Will you do me another favor?"

"Anything."

"Will you go into Rockridge and pick up my suit? I need it for court tomorrow. It's at Empire Cleaners. I took it in last week—a black suit, black slacks, white dress shirt and tie. I'll pay you back."

"Of course I will. I'll bring your clothes and your house key to the shop later."

We say goodbye. Next call, Cal, who answers, "Yo, brother."

"I figured it out."

"You're on speaker. Tiny and Anderson are here."

"Rosalee didn't come here for her parents. Whether her mother broke her hip or not, she'd have come back anyway, once she heard VoltEdge wanted to buy my land. She has dollar signs in her eyes. If I sell, she can get a million times more child support for Connor."

"I knew it didn't feel right. Dammit, now she's got him. I gave him to her. Fuck. She's going to say, if you want him back, sell the land."

"That's what hit me a few minutes ago. And my first court hearing on the land is tomorrow. She couldn't have timed it better."

"Let us make some phone calls." Anderson interjects from somewhere across the room. "Maybe we can help."

"How? About what?"

"We have resources," he yells from wherever he is.

I don't have any idea how Anderson or Cal can help, but I bite out, "Keep it legal."

"One quick question," Anderson says, now obviously standing by Cal's phone. "Do you have the names of the officers of Volt-Edge? The CEO?"

"I've read it, but I can't recall it now. Why?"

"Like I said, we have resources."

Mueller's is hopping when I pull up to the shop. I don't even open up the shop. I stalk straight to the cafe, searching the crowd for Rosalee.

Martha uses her back to push through the swinging doors from the kitchen with a tray full of food. Our gazes catch as I stand near the counter. "She's not here," Martha bites out as she bustles past me. "Serves me right for giving her another chance."

My eyes find Genevieve taking an order. I've got sense enough not to cause a scene with this breakfast crowd so I pour myself a cup of coffee and wait, watching Gene-fucking-vieve Landry like a hawk.

Now what?

My heart drums as I pull out my cell phone and begin texting.

HudBass: Where's Connor?

No response. Not even the three dots that show me she's received the text and is responding. Just nothing.

My gaze narrows as I glance back up at Genevieve.

As she turns from the table where she's taking an order, our eyes meet and she stands still, staring. A faint smile lifts the corners of her mouth.

I may commit murder right here in the cafe.

My phone rings, and I snatch it on the first ring. Before I can say hello, I hear Wren. "Hud, listen to me for just a second. Please."

"Okay."

"Steady now."

I close my eyes, sucking in a chest full of air, almost feeling her hand stroking my cheek as she says, "It'll be alright. We'll get this figured out. Okay?" Her voice is so smooth.

"Thank you," I say quietly. "I needed that." Silence lingers on the line as I walk outside the cafe, where there are no ears. "Rosalee isn't at work."

I hear Wren draw in a quick rasp. She lets it out slowly. "Well, she's conniving but I don't think Rosalee is stupid. She won't just disappear with him, knowing you have the right to see him. She'll have to show her hand."

"Maybe. I'm supposed to meet with the lawyer at one o'clock, to get ready for tomorrow."

"Do you think she knows you have the hearing tomorrow?"

"I don't know how she would."

"Court dockets are public record. While I'm in Rockridge, I'll swing by the courthouse."

"And do what?"

"Snoop. I'll go to the District Clerk's Office, ask to see the filings on your case and while I'm there, I'll chat up the clerk and casually ask about who all has been checking on the case. Blah, blah, blah. You'd be surprised how much information a little schmoozing can get you."

"You'd do that?"

She giggles. "Goofy. For you, anything. I'll see you in a bit."

Chapter 41

an ultimatum

I've got not one customer. Not one frigging customer. Just as well. I'm not sure I could concentrate enough to change someone's oil.

I pull out my phone again, checking. Rosalee still hasn't responded, which I knew. There's been no ping.

I call her mother, Vickie. For the first time since Connor arrived, she answers. "Hello, Hud." Guess she read the caller ID. "How's Connor? I miss that boy so much."

And that tells me all I need to know. Rosalee lied when she told him she was taking him to see her parents. Where the fuck did she take him?

"How are you doing, Vickie? Getting any better?"

"Yes, thank you for asking. I'm healing. Stan's not improving, of course." She sighs in resignation. "So we may stay here, where they can help me take care of him, even after I get back to normal."

"Vickie, has Rosalee said anything about Connor? School? Anything?"

"No, Hud, I'm sorry. I've barely seen her."

A vision of my hands around her neck flashes before me, and I blink it away. "I thought she came back to help take care of you."

"So did I, Hud. So did I." She speaks haltingly, swallowing tears. "I lost my daughter... a long time ago."

I can't burden her with my suspicions. But I owe her this. "Vickie, Rosalee can't get her hands on your money, can she? With you not at home and all?"

"No, Hud. Stan was smart enough years ago to write Rosalee out of our will. Everything goes to Connor."

Internally, I groan. "Does she know that?"

"I don't know. She may suspect it."

"Get well, Vickie. Give Stan my best."

The doorbell jingles and Cal strolls into the lobby with a million questions on his face as I hang up the call with Vickie.

"Connor is her ace in the hole." I nod at the phone. "That was Vickie. One, Rosalee did not take Connor to see them. Two, Stan wrote Rosalee out of their will. Everything they have goes to Connor. But what they didn't think about is the fact that she's his legal guardian. Once they're gone, she'll still control everything until he turns eighteen. By then, it'll all be gone." My heart rate won't slow down. This fresh cup of coffee probably isn't helping, but I can't keep myself from guzzling it.

Cal takes a seat across from me. "In the meantime, she doesn't have shit. Just your child support and what she earns from the cafe."

"She didn't show up for work today."

"I'm doing some research."

"What? Tell me."

He fiddles with his fingernails before his gaze meets mine. "I've got a buddy with the Texas Rangers. Not the baseball team. Law enforcement. It's off book, but he's checking to see if Miss Rosalee has any skeletons rattling around out there. Maybe she's got charges pending somewhere. You never know."

I lean back in my chair, resting my head in my hands, peering at the ceiling again. "I don't know. I guess it's possible, but for some reason, I don't see Rosalee being arrested."

"Shit, Hud. If she's in that drug world, she may very well have spent a night or two in jail. Something you can use in a custody battle."

Ping!

Rosalee: My son is with me.

My gaze volleys from the phone screen to Cal, then back to the phone.

HudBass: WHERE?

Cal comes to look over my shoulder as we watch the three dots hovering... backing out... then *Ping!*

Rosalee: We need to talk alone.

HudBass: OK. Where?

I squeeze the phone in my hand. Waiting.

Rosalee: Be there in a minute

HudBass: BRING CONNOR!

I watch the screen. The three dots hover... and back out. Gone. I realize I'm about to crush my phone in my hand before I ease my grip.

Cal bends lower over my shoulder. "Show me that phone number." He grabs a posted note and scribbles as I show him her contact information. "I'll be back. I don't need to be here when she walks in."

I head back to the coffee pot as he heads toward the door.

In the bathroom, I splash cold water on my face and stare at my reflection in the mirror. Those are my father's eyes looking back at me. And there it comes, clear as if he was in that mirror talking to me eye to eye. Dad's deep voice says, "Steady, now son. You can do it."

When I step into the lobby, she's sitting there.

She had her hair fixed, her roots covered, wearing makeup. Maybe she's been clean a while, because her skin's not as pruney as it was the day she arrived. She looks more like the Rosalee I once knew.

Her blue eyes latch onto me, like I'm a cougar on the prowl, as I stride to her. "Where's Connor?"

She smiles up at me with her head tilted back. "With friends."

"Did he enjoy seeing Stan and Vickie?"

"Of course. He had a ball."

Where can I hide the fucking body? "What do you want to talk about, Rosalee?"

She purses her lips, blinks a time or two, stares at me for a long beat, and says, "I want you to sell the land."

"Not happening."

"Then, it'll be a while before you see your son."

"You can't do that."

"I absolutely can. I talked to a lawyer. I am his custodial parent. We don't have joint custody, Hud, remember? I can move to Idaho if I want to, and you still have to send child support wherever I live. He goes where I go."

"Rosalee, you don't want him. Not really."

Her gaze narrows into two little topaz-colored slits. "I want you to sell that land and I want you to support your son in the manner he deserves. Your child support isn't much."

"It's what the court set."

"Yes." She stands. "And think what the court will set when you sell the land."

I fucking knew it. My volume pegs out. "Get this through your thick skull. I'm not selling land that's been in my family for more than a hundred years."

She sneers and tsks. "Too bad you missed your chance to kiss your son goodbye."

I snatch her upper arm as she turns to leave. "Give him back."

She tries to jerk her arm away, but my grip is too tight.

Rosalee glares up at me defiantly. "He was never yours, Hud. He's been on loan this summer. I'll give you until that hearing tomorrow." She points with her free arm out the door, toward Rockridge. "You can go in there and tell them you've decided to sell the land, or accept the fact that because of your stubborn pride, you lost your land and your son."

Wren

Chapter 12

6 degrees

I text Anderson a "911" as I merge onto the highway on my way back to Vogel Springs. I dropped the suit off as soon as I retrieved it so Hud could at least have that peace of mind. I wanted him to see it hanging there when he finished meeting with his attorney. One small problem solved.

Then, I headed back to Rockridge to do recon.

I didn't find out much, except the judge's name for tomorrow's hearing.

My Bluetooth rings, and Anderson's name appears in all caps across the screen.

"Hello."

"Oh, now she says hello, the generally accepted format of a greeting. Bitch! If you or Cal text me 911 one more time today, I better receive a paycheck from Vogel Springs dispatch."

"Anderson... I..." My voice shakes like a child's, and I feel stupid like he knows I fell too fast, and he's going to tell me I'm just messing up again.

"Your boy needs our help."

My head bobs up and down as if he can see me, and a tear streams down my face at how understanding Anderson is.

"Meet me at Vogel House in fifteen?" I say it as tear-free as possible.

"Matilda's room, STAT. We've already started."

I can almost feel Anderson's wink through the Bluetooth. *That's* why he's my true blue. I think I'm crying because I know he seldom receives the amount of understanding he gives others. Sure, he's rich and happy. But Anderson chooses to be happy. Money doesn't make his success, his outlook does. His generosity. My best friend has dealt with as many heartaches as anyone, probably more, as we are both the odd man out in our upstanding families.

Money doesn't heal heartbreak. It just makes it easier and allows you the means to celebrate it. Or, in my case, run from it.

I race up the stairs to the second floor of Vogel House to find Anderson holding court with my tank tops.

"We've got to drive into Austin, chickie. Did you buy every color the DG had to offer? And this one... *Hellooooo*, early 90's throwback. Is that neon green?"

Anderson smooths my bright green Dollar General spaghetti strap tank on the bed and places a note card on it.

"It was hot, and I wanted some color. What's all this?" My eyes scan my summer wardrobe, each top placed neatly across the bed like people, with a notecard for a name tag.

"As you know, I'm a visual learner." He sweeps his arm across the bed of tank tops. "This, love, is VoltEdge. Starring from left to right, each person who may or may not be in that courtroom, but who *is* trying to demolish your leading man. It's our job to name them and see what we can do."

"God bless you Anderson, and both of our wretched families."

"There's not much they're good for, but this is certainly an opportunity to showcase their talents." Anderson breathes into an upside-down smile and raises his eyes the way his mother would.

"Cal. Where's Cal, has he heard from Hud? You said he 911-ed you." I let my tote bag slide from my shoulder and toss it to the floor.

"God you're cute when you're in love. Cute, but psycho." Anderson waves a jazz hand across my face like the sun is coming out. "Psycho, but cute."

I slap his hand away from my face. "The 911?"

"Don't you worry about my leading man. He's well past your God-forsaken Rockridge, and on the other side of Austin by now, handling Rosalee's ass. Let's just say he saw a man about a horse, and that man was not a state trooper, but a Texas Ranger."

"Does he have something on her?" I'm chomping at the bits at just the sound of her nightmare name.

"Don't doubt 'the beat' baby."

"Isn't that an on-the-field touchdown nickname?"

"On the field or off the field, Cal hath never let-eth me down." Anderson makes prayer hands and bows at me. I chunk a discarded piece of my wardrobe at him. "Wait, you didn't take the opportunity to go to Austin with him?"

"And leave my little Wren to her own devices in love?"

I run and hug Anderson tightly.

"That, and there's like a million floor samples coming tomorrow, as well as work on my vineyard I can't neglect."

"You *do not* have a vineyard—yet. You don't even have a seed or the ground tilled to plant one."

"Yea of little faith. Okay. What did you find out?"

"Umm. The judge. Judge Reece Holt."

Anderson pulls out his phone and begins texting feverishly. "Okay, now. VoltEdge. You take from yellow to pink, and I'll take from aqua to black. There are six representatives thus far who pertain to this case, or are the vultures circling Hud. Two of each of these groups are legal counsel, and odds are—"

I interrupt, finishing his thought. "They were invited to your mom's last charity function, or my dad either shook their hand last week or crushed them in a mediation."

"Yes. Are you scared?"

"Of what?"

"Hudson, when he finds out you have superpowers."

"I don't have superpowers. My dad does." I look up at Anderson and sadly determine he's being serious.

"I'm just saying, this would be like me secretly being a scout for the NFL draft pics to Cal. To Hud... you, us, what we can find out and do here—"

"It's what has to be done. Who cares, if it lets him keep his land?"

"Okay. I was just checking before we went full-on Erin Brockovich, but in, like tinted black town cars, with taste in clothing. Actually, after handling these tank tops, I think Erin Brockovich is the appropriate reference for you here."

I reach for a pencil and extend my hand to slug Anderson's shoulder.

"Wait. It's my brother." Anderson scans through the messages, and my stomach sinks when he shakes his head. "The judge. Reece Holt is the guy he thought he was. It's political. He always sides with big business."

"So Hud's lost this hearing before he walked in, even though we know the eminent domain from their end is absolute bullshit?"

A yawn escapes my entire face as I wake from a seated position where I collapsed on my array of tank tops and apparently nose-dived into the Google search on my laptop.

Wiping the drool from my keyboard, I stretch to glance out the window. If Vogel House had a resident rooster, it would be crowing about now.

"Wrenny-Pooh!"

Scratch that. We do have one.

"I've got something for you!" Anderson crows on his way up the stairs.

It better be coffee.

"I have the names of the conglomerate directly responsible for Hud's case." Anderson passes me a steaming mug of coffee, and I slide off my bed.

"Yes, I know. VoltEdge, and you're looking at them." I fan the notecards of names we added to the tank tops throughout the night.

"Yes, and darling, VoltAge is a sister company to VoltEdge. Edge makes lithium-ion batteries for electric cars and Age makes alkaline batteries for consumer products. They are also sister companies with the ones that manufacture lithium-io-dide batteries for pacemakers, as well as New Age Minerals, their manganese and lithium mining company. Ring a bell?"

"All Brightstar Industries. Okay? So? This is just one small part of..."

Anderson shakes his head at me profusely. "Neon Green tank top. Read the name tag."

"Augustus." I zero in on the name I penciled in at three in the morning. "Yeah, but he's only VoltEdge."

"Augustus... what? Say it," Anderson coerces.

"Augustus Sinclair. So what? His daddy threw him a little bone. Are you saying the apple doesn't fall far from the tree?"

"No, honey. Read. It. I'm saying you were right last night when you found him affiliated. The apple is the tree." Anderson shoves a document in my face, and there, in black and white, BrightStar Industries, wholly owned by Archimedes, Inc.

And the CEO of Archimedes is… Geoffery Harrison Sinclair.

My father's biggest rival.

"Brightstar Industries, AKA VoltEdge, is Geoffery Sinclair. My folks' people confirmed it for me first thing this morning." Anderson does a tango with himself across my floor.

"Oh my God. That's why I put the neon green tank top in the no show pile. I racked my brain trying to figure out why CEO of VoltEdge, Augy Sinclair, would be on the list for the hearing. Why would he show up with his legal counsel for something so small potatoes…"

Anderson fills in the blanks. "Because it's not small potatoes. Geoffrey didn't throw anybody a bone. He sent his son. It's in his name so people won't do the math and put eight and eight together. Hud's being sued for his land by your father's archnemesis himself."

I glance back down at the paperwork and the name that is responsible for ruining Hud for his own gain, but also the name that might be what saves us. My father and Geoffery Sinclair's rivalry goes all the way back to college.

Daddy could crush him with his hands tied behind his back on a case like this, even without the scary truth of what Brightstar is guilty of in going after Hud's land. My father could find multiple ways to spin this into a massive touché against Geoffrey, without blinking an eye.

He would jump at the opportunity to take him down so easily and unexpectedly.

"Anderson." My eyes widen as I stand and face my best friend in the middle of the shit show we've created in my bedroom.

"Wren, Hud can't win this case without—"

"My Daddy."

Chapter 43

pop tarts & heartache

I pause on the steps of the courthouse, taking a minute to look up at the empty blue sky. Some things a man has to do alone. Stand on your own two feet, as my father would say.

They all offered to be with me in the courtroom, but I don't know how to explain it, even to myself, much less them, but this was something I had to do on my own. It's me, my lawyer, the county attorney, and VoltEdge.

I won't drag Wren, Anderson, Cal, and Tiny in here with me any farther than they already are, like I can't drag them into this fight for Connor.

It's me and Rosalee.

I tilt my head at the sky, feel the warmth of the sun on my face, and whisper a plea for strength. We lost, like we thought we would. Judge Holt denied our motion to quash the county's lawsuit, clearing the way for trial. It won't be long. He agreed to fast-track it.

I glance at my cell phone, which was turned off in court. I turn it on.

Nothing from fucking Rosalee. She made it clear she knew about today's hearing, so she'll be texting soon. Walking for the truck, I hear her voice in my head—yesterday's edict: 'You go in that courtroom and agree to sell or you will never see your son again.'

A nasty snort escapes me. Sorry, Rosalee. That wasn't an option. The window to sell closed. It's sink or swim. Win or lose everything. Reality hit hard when Judge Holt cleared his throat, pounded that wooden mallet on his bench, and said, "Motion denied."

My scalp prickles. Rosalee's right: I'm on the brink of losing my land and my son.

I lose the suit jacket and sling it over my shoulder as I walk toward the truck, loosening the tie and unbuttoning the top of my dress shirt so I can breathe.

The truck's like an oven. It's a hundred degrees, and I've got a dark leather interior. I start the ignition and turn the air conditioner on full blast, standing outside until the interior cools enough so it won't fry my ass when I sit down.

"Hud." My lawyer, Brad Tennison, is jogging toward me. "Listen." He purses his lips and digs the toe of his leather loafer into the concrete when he gets here.

"Say it, Brad."

He's considered the best real estate attorney in these parts, which is why I hired him. But we're up against the county and VoltEdge. His dark eyes meet mine. "I think we need to hire some hard hitters. Big time land experts. There's a law firm in San Antonio I can call, but the best in the nation is in Dallas."

"How much?"

"Hell, Hud, I don't know. Do you want me to make the calls?"

"Yeah. At least find out what they think and how much they'll charge."

I don't do it often, but I feel like getting drunk. One night, just suck the bottom out of a whiskey bottle. I indulge myself. Driving from Rockridge to the shop, I stop by the liquor store and load the fuck up. Why not?

I've had the shop closed all day, and I had almost no business yesterday.

If this keeps up, I'm not going to have the money to pay Brad, much less some high-powered law firm from Dallas or San Antonio. And I've still got fucking Rosalee demanding money.

I punch my Bluetooth. "Call Rosalee Gardner."

"Calling Rosalee Gardner," the female voice croons back.

I think I'm going to rename the contact Rosa-fucking-lee Gardner. Let me hear that name come across Bluetooth.

"Did you do it?" she snaps before I can say hello.

"Too late. The window to sell closed. It's not an option, Rosalee. You can't squeeze blood out of a turnip." Of course, I knew that yesterday.

She hisses. "You selfish son of a bitch. Why didn't you sell it earlier?"

I refuse to respond to that. "I want Connor back. Your game didn't work. I'm not going to be rich. The father of your son is a mechanic who owns a small-town garage, and that's what child support is based on."

"Fucker," she spits.

I yell into the Bluetooth. "Bring my son back!"

Click.

Driving into Vogel Springs from Rockridge, I pass the Vogel House, full of cars and trucks. Anderson, Cal, and Wren—all their cars are there, along with the worker vehicles. Lately, mine would've been there, too, with me on the tractor.

I don't know. Something about being hovered over right now feels... suffocating. Being watched with pitying eyes. I just don't want it right now. I need to deal with this alone. I can't explain it, not even to myself. My need to do this alone. But it hits me as I unlock the side door to the shop, how selfish that is.

They want to be here for me.

Trudging through the dark garage, I leave the closed sign on the front door and the lobby dark. I'm not opening today.

My chest aches walking into the apartment, seeing Connor's crap strewn everywhere. Pop Tarts and Oreos, the waffle iron and waffle mix. His syrup bottle. The YouTube logo on TV—I never had any of that here before he came to live with me.

I grab his T-shirt off the couch and smell it—and I'm carried back to the first time I held that boy in my hands, wailing, so tiny. Seven pounds, some-odd ounces. Fuck. The memory makes my knees weak. I sink down on the couch. Even then, I knew I didn't love his mother. I wasn't about to marry her or give her my name. But I loved him.

Connor wasn't two years old when Cal came to me with papers saying, 'The boy's not yours.' It was the only time in my life I wanted to put my hands around his neck and choke Cal Cooper.

"What do you mean he's not mine?" I'd yelled at him, and he tapped his forefinger on the paper. "That's a DNA test. She was fucking someone else, bro. The. Boy's. Not. Yours. You don't owe her child support."

The world fell out from under my feet.

I knew all along there was a chance. After high school, Rosalee and I drifted apart. On again, off again, as I went to college, and she kept partying, getting wilder and wilder.

We didn't have a commitment. Hell, I wasn't exclusive to her, either. We weren't together anymore. But I figured I probably was the father. I believed with everything in me that he was my biological son.

I remember thinking about it back then, staring at the fucking paper Cal tapped, and I realized—almost two years in? His DNA test didn't mean a flying fuck to me. From the moment that boy opened his eyes to this world, he saw me as his father. And I saw him as my son. You don't take that away because of some piece of paper.

What is a father? Fatherhood. What does it mean? Is it as cut and dried as genetics? DNA?

Fuck, no. Fatherhood is commitment. It's an unshakable, unspoken vow that says nothing and no one on earth is more important to me than you, my child. And it hits me, sitting in the living room of my apartment, holding my eight-year-old son's T-shirt, that this is all on me.

I. Am. His. Father.

It's on me to get him away from that trainwreck of a mother who has him.

"Hey, bring us up to date," Anderson says, seeing me walk through the lobby of Vogel House.

"We lost. We knew we would." I hold up a bottle of whiskey and one of vodka. "Let's drink to the demise of my life. Outside. I just don't feel like sitting inside."

My eyes scan the room.

"She's not here," Anderson quips. "She's running a quick errand. Now, sit down and tell me all about it."

"Like I said, the judge denied the motion to quash and fast-tracked the trial."

"Oooh. Judge Holt fast-tracked it." Anderson purses his lips. "Hum." He taps his finger to his chin.

"What are you doing, Anderson? What have you got up your sleeve? What did you mean, *we've got resources*?"

He waves his hand at me dismissively and stands from where he's sitting on a barstool. "Do you trust Cal?" His gaze bores into me.

"With my life."

"Do you trust Wren?"

My breath hitches. "... Yes..."

Fire spews from Anderson's eyes. "Now what's that hesitancy I just caught?"

"I trust Wren cares and she knows how much I care. But I also trust Wren Baldwin will blow this joint when you wrap this up here." I stand and show him my palm. "And that's something I can't deal with right now, on top of VoltEdge and Rosalee. Leave that hornet's nest alone, Anderson. I mean it."

He exudes a giant huff. "Very well. Trust this: they're both working on your behalf. Right now."

"Where are they?"

"Cal's upstairs on the phone."

"And Wren?"

"I'm here." She's behind me. *Did she hear what I said about her leaving?*

I turn to face her. "Hey," I smile and nudge my head toward the bar, where Anderson set the liquor bottles I brought in. "I brought booze and I need a drink. Want to join me?"

She smiles. "Always."

"You two go sit on the porch and I'll play host," Anderson says. "Shoo. Get out from under my feet."

I walk to the bar, open the whiskey, and take a long chug before he can mix drinks, wiping my mouth on the back of my hand. "I needed that."

"So… it didn't go well today?" Wren strokes my arm as we sit alone on a new wicker loveseat she bought for the porch. She's doing all she knows to show me her support.

"That's an understatement." I suck in a deep breath, peering out over the pasture dotted with bales of hay. "Not only did I lose, I found out it's too late to agree to sell even if I wanted to. I'm losing everything."

Silence lingers like an anvil as I finally breathe out, "Rosalee was right. Because of my stubbornness, I'm going to lose the land and my son."

For the first time since I lost my parents, I close my eyes, fighting tears, and Wren strokes my back.

For some reason, her sympathy isn't what I want or need right now. I shift my shoulders at her touch, and she recoils. "I don't need pity right now, Wren." I hear the bite in my words as I straighten and face her. "I need to fix the mess I created."

Anger overtakes her voice. "You didn't create this mess, Hudson Bass. VoltEdge did when they tried to take your land and Rosalee did when she took your son." She stands before me, on the verge of stomping her foot. "You aren't to blame here."

In my heart, I know I am. My stubbornness.

Ping!

I snatch my phone from my back pocket. "It's Rosalee," I growl, staring at the screen, holding it where Wren can see.

Rosalee: Dad it's me. Will u come get me?

My heart rate shifts into hyperdrive.

HudBass: Yes. Where?

Rosalee: I don't know. A friend of Mom's

My fucking heart explodes. I hear it pounding from my chest into my ears.

HudBass: ON MY WAY

My eyes meet Wren's. "I've got to go."
She clutches my forearm. "Where, Hud? He doesn't know where he is."
Ping!

**Rosalee: Don't bother asshole.
I'm coming to you.**

She caught him with her cell phone. My arm trembles, the phone in my hand shaking as I text back.

HudBass: BRING MY SON

"Warn Cal and Anderson," I tell Wren, feeling my pulse pounding in my neck.

She runs inside as I sit still, going through the scenarios in my head. Rosalee knows I'm not going to be a millionaire. What's her next play?

I stride across the side porch for the front, heading to the shop to wait for Rosalee and, hopefully, Connor as Cal steps through the front door, blocking my way. "Slow down," he demands.

"She's coming. I need to get to the shop."

Cal barks, "Will you give me just a minute?"

"Why?"

"Because you're not thinking straight."

Anderson is at Cal's side, holding out a drink for me, and I shake my head. "That window passed, too, buddy. I don't need to drink right now."

"Very well," Anderson says, sculling the drink in his hand. "Now listen. And trust."

Against all instincts, I can't stifle the grin that comes with Anderson's command. I nod as Wren appears, standing beside her best friend.

It's me facing a wall of Cal Cooper, Anderson Sofitel, and little Wren Baldwin, but before they can say whatever it is they want to say, Rosalee pulls up in front of Vogel House and stops her car.

Brazen. Wherever she's got him, it's not far from here.

She stalks toward the porch, with all of us standing on it, her eyes drifting from me... to Wren... back to me. It's an ugly glare. "I figured you'd run to your support group for help. Hudson Bass, can we speak alone?"

"Say it to everyone," Cal spits out.

"I've got this," I tell him, striding past the group to meet Rosalee on the lawn. "Where's Connor?"

"I told you, you won't see Connor until I get my money."

"And I told you, I don't have any money."

She aims her arm at the shop. "Yes. You. Do. You may've pissed away your family land, but you own that, and it's worth plenty."

"How the fuck do you think I could pay child support if I lose my business?"

"You already lost your business with the boycott, you idiot. But you own that whole block. Sell it. I want a quarter million dollars. You give me that, and I'll give you primary custody of Connor."

My gaze narrows, the wheels in my mind spinning. "A quarter million dollars and you'll get the fuck out of his life and mine? Forever?"

She glowers for a long, hard minute, chewing on her lower lip before she spits out. "I'll retain visitation rights."

"Fuck no. For a quarter million dollars you relinquish all rights."

Finally, she snarls. "Okay."

Fucking whore of a mother. "Done. Bring him to me."

She wags her freshly manicured finger. "Not until I get the money." She turns to stalk back to her car, then faces me again. "Hurry. I'm ready to get out of this fucking one-horse town."

They all heard. How could they not? I mount the stairs to see three stunned faces.

"I can't believe she would sell her son." Wren's eyes, her voice, and the frozen look on her face register her astonishment. "What kind of woman does that?"

Anderson sneers and points at the taillights of Rosalee's car. "That kind." He claps his hands. "Okay. One problem solved, onto the next."

I cut my eyes at Anderson. "One problem solved? I've got to get my hands on a quarter million dollars. Now."

We walk inside. Wren watches me silently as I head for the bar and turn up the bottle of whiskey, taking two long chugs, enjoying the burn as it slides down my throat. Clunking the bottle on the bar, I yell, "Fuck!"

I slap the bar. "Fuck! Fuck! Fuck!"

How can life turn upside down so fast? It does that to you. I remember the night I got the call about my parents.

"We can get the money, bro," Cal says.

And one more time, anger roils inside of me. "No. This is my fight. I'm not going to run to my friends and ask them to fix it for me."

"Goddammit, Hud!" In an uncharacteristic display, Anderson slaps the bar as he yells, "Are you trying to make this harder than it has to be? Cal, me, Wren—we can loan you the money to get full custody of your son and you can pay us back. The money is not an issue."

Wren's eyes plead with me. "Can we talk?"

Wren. Sweet, beautiful, sexy Wren. She wants, with everything in her, to fix this. But she can't. "Yeah, we can talk."

On the porch, she peers up at me. "Hud, like you said the first day we met, my car cost three-hundred-thousand-dollars. That's more than she's asking to give you full custody of Connor. He's worth a whole lot more to me than my car. Let me do this. For you. I have the money. Not even Cal and Anderson have to know."

I feel my jaw tighten. "I can't do it. Thank you, but no."

"Why?" Her eyes, her whole body show her exasperation.

"Because a man's got to stand on his own two feet, for one thing. But the real reason is, I'm his father. He is my responsibility."

Something crosses her face, her eyes—and for a nanosecond, I wonder... *does she know?* I explode. "Connor Bass is my son. I gave that boy my name. There's no greater promise a man can make than to give another person his name." I tap my chest. "He's my child. My responsibility. I can't look myself in the mirror if I let my friends fix this."

Tears fill her eyes. I think I scared her, but I meant every word.

Realizing how hard I bit at her, I soften my voice. "It's not the end of the earth. I'll either mortgage or sell the business and property in town. I'll take a job like most people have, and life will go on for Connor and me."

She takes me in, her gaze locked onto mine, through a treacherously long stretch of silence, and slowly nods with the corners of her mouth tugged down. "Life goes on for Connor and you."

"Yeah."

She glances away, staring at the pasture. "You'll give up everything... for your son."

The way she says it. It's not a question. It's a declaration.

"Wouldn't you? If he was yours?"

She chews on the inside of her cheek as she keeps... nodding... her gaze locked onto the pasture. Her teary eyes come back, finally meeting mine again. "Wow." She inhales sharply and exhales slowly. "You're a good father, Hudson Bass. Mine might throw money at a problem, but he'd never sacrifice anything—much less everything, for me."

Wren

Chapter 15

walk of shame...
wearing dior

I don't know how long I've been on the road, just that I've been driving since I left Vogel House. First, in the opposite direction of Dallas, maybe to prove to myself I still could. Even though I know my car won't stop until I reach Dallas, I had to entertain that pragmatic part of my brain. The part that learned the lesson.

It's the part that heard Hud say no to my money, as if he wanted no part of my help. And the part that clocked when he made it clear there was nothing in the world that mattered to him as much as Connor. Rightfully so.

Still, that part of my brain suggests that therein lies my answer. This is the same trap I fell into with Phillip, and there is no room for me in their equation either.

Hud's done nothing wrong, and there is no comparison between him and Phillip. I would never make this situation about me. The trouble with relationships and me is that they are seldom... about me.

Anderson would second that.

My Bluetooth rings, and his name pops up. I don't answer. Anderson's been calling repeatedly since I drove off without saying goodbye. I know he's just trying to check on me or make sure I'm not really running.

Am I?

It is an option with a much more sane potential outcome. Anderson's name flashes across my screen again, and my mind flashes back to the porch steps, the look on Hud's face, and how it felt watching him walk away from me.

Maybe that was the right move, if not the inevitable one.

Ugh. This place still smells the same way it did when I was eight. I smelled that orange Starburst-flavored tile cleaner mixed with the fresh Easter lily-scented air fragrance that smells of funerals and death to me for the last two years and never really noticed it.

Now that I've been away—really away—it's a scent that invades my senses. That, and the smell of leather couches, are the smells that represent the person they belong to and always have.

Standing in the front lobby, I search for my ID. I didn't save my old badge, but my license with his name on it should suffice enough for security to warn him I'm in his building. A mildly recognizable young woman smiles, halting me from digging for my wallet.

"Good morning, Miss Baldwin. Go right on in."

Hmm. Guess she didn't get the memo. I only saw her a few times during my stint at the desk because the attorneys don't have to enter through the main lobby open to the public. All legal personnel, and certainly the boss's daughter, have access to a separate top-floor entrance.

As I stand in front of the lobby elevator leading to the high-rise offices, I can't help but wonder, if I no longer have access... am I still the boss's daughter?

Ding.

A small chuckle rises from the back of my throat as the elevator opens for me. That's not the sound of the bells that follow me around Vogel Springs, and it makes me miss—I almost said... home.

My eyes raise to catch shocked expressions. Either these people never expected to see me again, and this will be a bigger surprise than I thought—or the Dior girl was right when she handed me this pantsuit in a size smaller than I would ask for, boasting, 'Deep teal is the new navy, and with you're coloring, and those pointed-toe slingback pumps, a show-fucking stopper.'

Let's go with the latter.

I smile and cock an eyebrow high as I glide to my destination. Daddy always did say, "Clothes make the man." Lucky for him, in his circles, they do. Otherwise, he would have nothing else to offer.

Too bad Armani doesn't specialize in compassion, character, merit, loyalty... My list would continue, but my thoughts and air are hijacked when I spot Phillip crossing toward a conference room.

I freeze as my confidence melts to the floor. Please don't let this Dior pantsuit be enough of a show-stopper to have him do a double take.

It is.

Phillip walks back around the corner where he disappeared and tilts his head toward the apparition that is me, less than thirty feet from him.

My confidence may have melted, but my pride and stance have not.

I walk through the initial sighting, and just as his eyes land on me for a second time, I turn down my father's hall without making eye contact.

A show-fucking-stopper. My confidence is back, and even the daunting, ornate hallway that leads toward the senior partner's den of iniquity doesn't slow my stride. My father's office is the focal point, of course.

His secretary tries to keep her jaw intact as she stares at me the way I envision I would have looked at Matilda had the little deviant ever decided to show herself.

"Wren... uh... he's..."

"I'll just take a seat, Erin. I'm happy to wait." I save her from my father's excuses. What a rotten job she has, keeping track of that bastard. Imagine not knowing what to say to someone's daughter... deciding which lie to tell.

"I'm certain he won't be long," I say it with a level of pretension.

Who is she kidding? As soon as she picks her jaw up off the floor and tells him I'm out here, he'll lose his mind and want to hide me in his office as soon as possible.

I catch my reflection in the glass window to the left of me. I do look sharp. I look like I speak his language, which is the point of today.

I had a Brazilian blowout before I came, and my hair is sleek and straight, the way he always requested when we went into court.

My father hates my wavy locks. He says it looks wild and unkempt.

He means me. I'm wild and unkempt because I disagree with him.

"Wren. Uh, he'll…" His secretary ducks out of his office and sashays back toward her desk for safety. Her throat clears while she searches for the rest of the words. I stand and nod, crossing in front of her to walk in. I would offer her a smile, but I have no generosity left for these people.

He's facing his view. His back is to me. His hands are in his pockets as he stares at the Dallas skyline. "Sit," he says without looking back at me.

Never.

Daddy 101: Never sit while your opponent is standing. And if he thinks I'm letting an outfit that would knock even his judgmental socks off fade into the background, then I've got more of the upper hand than he thought.

A beat goes by before Daddy turns to face me. "Well, you can take the girl out of a courtroom, but you can't take the courtroom out of…" His words trail off as he reaches for a glass and pours himself a scotch. He does not offer me one. I stand still, staring through him as he takes his time and a sip. "If I didn't know better, I'd say you were back for your old job."

"Lucky for us both you're a clever man," I finally speak.

He offers a cocky half-smile. "I like to think I'm intelligent enough to get my way."

"Is that what they call it these days?"

He takes the hit with no rebuttal and moves to his desk as if to keep working. "I assume you're here because you want something. By all means," he extends his hand, inviting me to sit across from him. "I'd love to hear this."

I still don't sit. I stay right where I am.

My father put distance between us my entire life. I'd like to keep it.

"I've brought you a gift." I take two confident strides forward, out of necessity, and slap a dark navy file folder on his desk.

One brow rises as they both pull together in confusion. His black eyes dart back up at me before he opens it gingerly, as if it's a bomb that could go off or one of those prank cans with silly string.

My father is an extremely handsome man who looks nothing like me.

Maybe that's our disconnect. I'm told I'm the spitting image of his own mother. She had hazel eyes and my hair, making me one of those rare cases where two people with brown eyes have a kid with light eyes. Even his eye color couldn't dominate when it came to me.

He looks like Andy Garcia, save the actor's charming smile that makes Andy's eyes dance. My father only shares his intensity. That fierce look where black eyes deadpan through anything that gets in his way.

I can't resist watching as he reads the names affiliated with the case. The initial flicker of recognition and increased interest blazes through his corneas as he lands on VoltEdge, then... he removes his glasses, closes the file, and looks up at me like I just won first prize at the sport he was best at. Probably because I just did.

"Dare I ask what's in it for you?" He can't help it.

"Well, I didn't expect you to thank me first."

"The landowner?"

I don't respond.

He persists. "A friend or pet of yours? Can we all rejoice that you've gotten over your schoolgirl crush that almost cost my best attorney his career?"

"To put it in your terms, if you do this—if you take the case that will allow you to crush your biggest rival with little effort on your part, if you win—"

"Which I would win. You know this or you wouldn't bring it to me."

"Yes, and he wins. He keeps his land. If you win, and you make certain he wins, I'll stay away."

"You'll stay away from what, my darling daughter? You can't even say his name without giving yourself away." His gaze drifts past me, and I look over my shoulder to see Phillip standing outside the glass window of my father's office.

His six-foot trim frame towers above the secretary's desk, demanding to be let in, until his eyes meet mine, and he locks them in an all-too-familiar gaze. His sandy brown hair is slicked back above soft brown eyes that plead with mine. For what, I don't know anymore.

He's annoyingly youthful and Ivy League looking, even with a premature dusting of salt and pepper about his temples announcing his mid-thirties encroaching.

A flood of emotions rush over me, the result of the dirty trick Daddy meant it to be.

Only, these feelings are not from Phillip. They are from the man who doesn't see me or know me well enough to know the most important name in the world to me is in that folder. "You just worry about the two names that matter most in that file, Geoffery Sinclair and Hudson Bass." I pivot to walk straight out of his office.

"Wren," My father calls after me. I see in the window reflection that the folder is back open and in the middle of the thick document. "You don't have to, you know… stay away. You could come back, take your LSAT, and work."

"For you? Or with you, Dad?"

"Did you do this? Did you find the discovery on Sinclair?"

I halt in my tracks at his door, with Phillip staring at me from less than three feet away on the other side of the glass. I don't look back at my father. I stare directly at Phillip as I say, "Don't ask questions you already know the answer to, Daddy. It's unbecoming."

I'm flat on my back underneath an old SUV when the lobby bell jingles. Ordinarily, I wouldn't hear it. But then, ordinarily, I'd be playing music, and Connor would be asking a million questions like, 'What's that thing, Daddy?' 'What does this thing do?' Or, 'How does that work?' If not Connor, a customer might be on tiptoes peering over my shoulder talking about the weather.

I'm not playing music, and no one else is around. Bass Pit Stop is as silent as a damned tomb.

The owner of this Rogue, a new customer, brought it in first thing this morning, saying it has a bad shimmy. Now I know why. His suspension is shot to hell.

"Yo!" Cal's familiar greeting rings through the almost-empty garage.

"Back here," I yell.

Next thing I see is his long legs standing near mine, him saying, "Yo, bro. Need to talk."

"I need to get this job out."

"C'mon, man. Take a break."

I roll out from under the vehicle, mad at the world. "I don't need a break. I need to work." I'm still flat on my back, looking at a long-legged giant with cornrows.

His gaze narrows as he tucks his chin and hikes one brow. "I've got some news for you." And he smiles.

It's the kind of broad smile I needed to see. I'm on my feet, wiping my hands with a rag I pull from my hip pocket. "What?"

"Come see what my Ranger friend found out." He takes big steps toward the office, and I follow. Cal taps his forefinger on papers he placed on my desk—the same way he tapped that fucking DNA test years ago. "Read that."

I feel my scalp tighten. I'm not sure I want to.

But I do, and my eyes widen, one line at a time, as I read. "You've got to be shitting me."

"I wouldn't." He grins.

"She's wanted?"

"Rosalee was popped for possession of methamphetamine a year ago in Dallas. She had a little over a gram. That's felony possession—two to ten in the pen. She never showed for trial, so now there's a bench warrant for her arrest, on top of the possession charge."

I'm still processing it. "What does that mean? Exactly?"

He points at the paper with a satisfied smile. "Means, if they can find her, the law will pick her up. When they do, Connor is in your custody, man. You don't have to pay her a fucking dime."

Cal's brows draw into a unibrow as he glances left and right. "Tell me you didn't sell this place already."

My focus is on the print-out. "No. I talked to a realtor." My gaze moves to join his. "Can I take this to a family court and get custody of Connor now?"

"I'd think so."

I sink into my desk chair, almost ashamed to look at him. He saved me. "I don't know how to thank you."

"Just lookin' out for family, man. No thanks needed."

Family. I think of how terrified my son must be, not knowing where he is. He's frightened and miserable, or he'd never have texted me to come get him. "I don't want to traumatize Connor any more than he already is, with cops swooping in and arresting his mother."

Cal nods. "Let me talk to my Ranger. He won't be the one to pick her up. It'd be the local sheriff's office, acting for Dallas if... and I mean *if* they can find her miserable little ass."

"Yeah. Now we need to find her and Connor."

Our gazes catch as we say together, "Genevieve."

Mueller's Café isn't particularly busy when we walk over, which makes me wonder again: Is my slowdown in business because of the boycott or the season?

And it hits me: it's both. It is summer. People are on vacation. But it's also that the people who normally come to Bass Pit Stop to have their car fixed aren't biding their time in Vogel Springs, eating at Martha's, or browsing the shops. What affects one of us affects all of us. My defiance is costing Martha Mueller, too.

She smiles, seeing us, as she sets two glasses of water on the table. "Hud, Cal. Good to see you. What can I get you, boys?"

Martha Mueller's the only person I know who can call Cal Cooper 'boy' and get by with it.

"Chicken fried steak," we say together—again.

"Right up."

Before she can turn, I ask quietly, "Have you heard anything about Rosalee?" I cut my eyes at Genevieve. "Maybe from her friend?"

Martha's mouth puckers. "Lots of texting and phone conversations but nothing I can get a whiff of." As I nod, Martha asks, "Connor?"

"With his mother."

She shakes her head and tsks as she heads to the kitchen with our order.

"Watch her," Cal says, tilting his head at Genevieve, who has her back to me, taking an order. About then, she turns around, our gazes catch, and she averts her eyes as she stalks to the kitchen to place the table's orders.

I try not to be conspicuous, talking to Cal and keeping her in my peripheral vision. It's not long until she slips her phone from her apron. "She's texting her."

"Um-hum." Cal cuts his eyes her way. He'd have to turn around to see her. "Keep watching."

Genevieve shoves the cell phone into her apron and goes about her business as Martha returns to our table, setting down two glasses of iced tea, asking, "Where's Wren?"

My gaze zooms from Martha to Cal. "I was wondering that, myself." I haven't seen her car at Vogel House or heard from her since that night—the night she offered to pay Rosalee's ransom demand and I declined.

I couldn't. A man can't take that kind of help from anyone, much less from the woman he's sleeping with, and look himself in the mirror.

Cal chews on his lips, answering Martha with his eyes on mine. "Haven't seen her."

"You haven't seen her?" We ask together, Martha and I.

He shakes his head slightly. "Neither has Anderson. He's been calling, and she hasn't picked up."

I shove back from the table, straightening in the booth. "What the fuck? Where is she?"

"Man, your guess is as good as mine." Cal takes a long sip of his drink, his eyes still on mine. "She slipped out early that next morning, after y'all talked on the porch. She just took off."

Dammit.

I peer out the window at my lifeless shop, and my mind drifts back in time.

No, fuck, no. So many memories with her. Her fainting in Rockridge, me carrying her in my arms, manhandling her in the garage that day, getting caught. The first time we had sex on the tractor. The night she let me make love to her, waking up with

Wren Baldwin's arms wrapped around me, spooning. We were perfect. She was perfect.

And that last night, when she tried to comfort me about the land hearing and Connor by caressing my back—what did I do? I rebuffed her touch and refused her offer to help.

I rest my head in my hands as I groan. I told her, 'It's no big deal, life will go on with Connor and me,' and she looked at me like she was trying to climb behind my eyes to read my mind, repeating, 'for you and Connor.'

It wasn't a question; I remember that. And I said, 'Yeah. Me and Connor.'"

How big a fool can one man be? I stare at the table. Stupid dumb fuck.

"Look." Cal pulls me from my morbid trance.

"What?"

He tilts his head. "Genevieve. Sneaking out the back door." He swings his legs around and slips out of the booth. "I'm going to see if I can't catch an earful."

I don't follow. My gut is too empty. I've all but lost my family land, I can't find my son—but thanks to Cal, we have a prayer of getting him back—and I just pissed away the best relationship I ever had. There's never been a woman who makes me feel the way Wren makes me feel. It was a new kind of high.

Cal told me, 'Give her a reason to stay.' Instead, I gave her a reason to leave. I as much as told her there was no room for her in our lives.

Shit. Dammit. Hell.

I look up, as Cal slips back in the booth. "She's talking to Rosalee."

"How do you know?"

"Cause I opened the back door a slip and listened. Genevieve didn't see, her back was to me, but I heard her say, 'He's here, with Cal,' and a minute later, she asks, 'Are you still at Jerry's?'"

My brows hit my hairline. "Jerry's? As in Denison? That motherfucker's got my son?"

Cal clenches his jaw and twists his neck. "Only Jerry I know of around here."

"I'm going to kill him."

I'm on my feet, two steps toward the door, when Cal's monster claw grips my arm. "Sit down, man. Let the cops handle it."

Maybe the hardest thing I ever had to do, call the cops instead of pounding the fuck out of Jerry Denison.

I'm waiting in the Bass Pit Stop parking lot when Bill Farnsworth pulls up in his sheriff's patrol unit and Connor jumps out, running to me with open arms. "Daddy!"

I scoop him up, trembling, and lift him high, squeezing him tight as he sobs into my chest. "Where have you been?"

"I don't know." His arms are around my neck, my hands are splayed across his back, as my son cries into my neck, and I hold him as tightly as I can without cutting off his air, whispering into his ear, "Steady, now, son. I've got you. You're with me, and I won't let you go. Never again."

He gulps out between heavy sobs. "Mamma left with some men."

My heart hurts in my chest—not for her. For him. "It'll be alright, son. Your mamma had some business she had to take care of. You'll see her again."

I just hope the fuck the next time he sees her, I'll have legal custody.

I peer down at Connor, nestled against me in bed, and pet his back. He's safe now.

He's getting too big to sleep in the same bed as his father. It's been fine for the summer, but he's mine now. Or he will be. We need to move back to the home place, where he'll have a room of his own. Space for his games and toys.

The home place. It's more important now than ever that I not lose it.

Staring at the ceiling, I see Wren in my head, staring at Mom's Windberg painting. She fit there. She's gone.

I slip out of bed, move to the kitchen, and grab a beer, sitting on the porch facing Vogel House. Her bedroom is dark. *You lost her.* Even if, out of some miracle, I win the lawsuit and keep the land

I've lost Wren—and it's too late to tell her what was on the tip of my tongue day after day.

I sink my head back, staring at the ceiling fan. 'Never put off 'til tomorrow what you can do today.'

Why did I never tell her I loved her?

Easy answer: because you're a coward.

I was so fucking afraid of getting my heart broken that it got broken anyway—because I didn't have the courage to say, 'I love you.' If I ever see her again, it'll be the first thing I say to her. And I'll beg her to stay.

Wren

Chapter 47

all the old familiar places

"**W**ren. Wait! We can't end like this." Phillip races to me and puts his hands on each side of my face, forcing me to look up at him.

"We already did when you chose my father."

"I chose my family, Wren."

"Your family, that you pretended to be leaving. The marriage that was so over you just couldn't keep your hands off me? Get your fucking hands off me!" I push out from under him and walk two steps away. "You chose your career, don't pretend otherwise."

"And you wouldn't know what it's like to have to." Phillip turns away from me now.

"Oh. Because my daddy handed one to me? Wow. I love that you think me that cheap. Trust. It cost me. You don't know it yet, maybe because I love you more than you love me, but it cost me t his—" I motion my hand between the two of us. "It cost me you."

Phillip rushes to me. Hot tears splash down his face onto my cheeks and he's squeezing me so tightly I can't breathe. I want it to feel good.

I want it to be the embrace that reminds me... win or lose, even though I lost... he still loves me.

But it isn't that. And no matter how tight Phillip holds me, it doesn't erase the fact that he isn't choosing me. He's letting me go.

He presses me closer to him, the familiar place I've relied on for the last year and a half feeling foreign for the first time.

It's not a moment of passion. It's a moment of fear. Phillip is afraid of my father and the choice he just made. As he should be.

If there is one thing I can count on with my father, it's that he only understands strength. Not weakness. Phillip is weak. He's Daddy's sacrificial lamb now, not me. Funny. I guess this brought me freedom from both of them.

It hasn't even crossed my mind to consider what I'll do or where I'll go when I don't return to the office Monday morning, but I'm not worried about that. The answer is... anywhere but here.

"Let me go before you say something we can't come back from." Phillip knows what I mean. It's been on the tip of both our tongues since my father laid down the law and made him choose. The idea that this doesn't have to end. Thank God he didn't insult me by suggesting it. I step away from him and turn to leave.

"Wren. This can't be it?" He says it like a child. One that does want to have his cake and eat it, too. My entire body sags and I feel as if my soul deflates. I draw in a deep breath and walk away.

I can't get out of Dallas fast enough.

This is it. And it has to be because I find myself second-guessing as I slink away ashamed.

I didn't do anything wrong, so why do I feel ashamed?

Because if he had asked me... If he had said those words, "It doesn't have to end..." What would I have done?

The fact that I would have considered it makes me more ruthless than my father, that, or more sacrificial. It's one thing when you are a lamb and someone sacrifices you, but to choose that for yourself?

No way. My father and Phillip had a lot more in common than I did with either of them.

I start my Maserati, pull out, and don't look back.

It had been a little over nine months since that moment I drove away from my father and Phillip the first time and didn't look back.

I swore then I would never come back, but it couldn't be helped. As I speed down the highway in my Dior suit, with two more hanging in the back for Hud's upcoming trial, I can't help but look ahead.

My only fear is that I'm looking at a future that may not include me. Had Hud and I already had the conversation that Phillip and I had those nine painful months ago? That night on the porch of Vogel House, he specified that he and Connor would move on.

Why didn't that sound an alarm in my head? Because he chose Connor for all the right reasons, I surmised that it wasn't necessarily about me.

Or maybe I'm just too dense to recognize he was, in fact, purposely leaving me out of the equation. And that was his way of telling me.

It doesn't matter.

I'd help him anyway on principle. I chose to stay and become a part of Vogel Springs. He's friends with the people I love. Even if I'm not allowed to love Hudson Bass anymore, I'll still help him save his land.

Who am I kidding? I'm irreversibly in love with the man. I have never known physical or emotional love like the kind I experience with Hudson Bass, and I chose him the day I fell apart in his arms in Rockridge, and the town chose me.

I can't know where Hud stands, especially now that I've gone behind his back and gotten my father to take the case. He doesn't tell me what I need to know, but he has one thousand percent shown me up until the off-day he lost Connor. I couldn't explain it to anyone if they put a gun to my head, but I hold onto the time he said, 'Don't ever doubt I want you. I absolutely do.' Somehow that feels like the truth.

I shrug as I take the exit to Vogel Springs and speed through the four-way stop to Vogel House. Grabbing my garment bags and keys, I'm making a conscious effort not to look over at Bass Pit Stop.

I've tortured myself enough for one day. I can't go down the rabbit hole of what-ifs. I've got to keep forging ahead with the plan.

Anderson sits at a the bar with its newly-finished marble countertop, on a plastic-covered barstool, sipping a glass of wine. "And?" he says, as he looks me over.

I nod and toss my keys next to his wine bottle.

"Don't you ever scare me like that again. I felt like a girl waiting for three days for the guy to text, to see if we were going out again. Only this is my business and the rest of our lives."

"Okay. That's rich."

"Fine. And, I'd say you clean up good, but I'm not ready to compliment you just yet. Were we right?"

"Spectacularly. The case is practically won in that folder, and by the time Daddy's done with it..."

"Hudson Bass will ride again." Anderson toasts the air dramatically and chugs his wine.

"That's the idea." I turn to walk toward the stairs. I'm exhausted and want to peel this suit off of me.

"And when Phillip's done... Is Phillip done?" Anderson's eyebrow almost quivers as it rises. Even his facial expression is afraid of what his question suggests.

"I didn't speak to him. I will keep it professional during the trial, but I greatly look forward to his return to Dallas with my father." I take the first step up.

"Wait a minute. He's here? They came and your father brought Phillip?"

"They have suites in Marble Falls. We meet with Hud's local guy tomorrow. It's a test, Anderson. You know Daddy never takes a proposition without a counter move."

"And Phillip is his counter?"

"We'll see." I look over my shoulder at Anderson as I take another step, dragging myself up the banister. "He has a suite there for me as well, beside Phillip, for going over the case."

"Yet, you came home."

"Yes."

"Good girl."

"Now, can I please go to bed so I can make this happen tomorrow? Tell me I haven't been gone so long I have to shove Matilda off my cot."

"She's missed you as much as we have, I'm sure."

"And Hud?" I stop halfway up the flight and turn to look down at Anderson.

"As you know, he got Connor back. That's all I know, kid."

"That's what counts. That's what matters most." I tap the banister twice and march the rest of the way up the stairs in silence.

Chapter 18
paydirt

"**H**ud, call me back, man. We hit paydirt."

It's late morning when I replay the message Brad left on my cell phone. He called while I was on the phone with a customer. I couldn't click over, so I sent him straight to voicemail and then got busy with that suspension.

Listening to it, my heart skips over a ray of hope and I call him right back. "What's up?"

He took the call on the first ring, chirpy as a little parakeet. "Remember, I told you about the law firm in Dallas that's the best in the country?"

"Yeah."

"I just got off the phone with them. They're on our case. This is great news, buddy!" I have a visual image of Brad jumping up and down like Connor does. He's a little guy.

"Can I afford them?"

"The main man has a personal interest in this case. He's taking it at no charge."

"Are you shitting me?"

"It's my understanding he and Geoffery Sinclair go way back. Bitter enemies."

"Sinclair? Isn't he the CEO of VoltEdge?"

"No. He's the father of the VoltEdge CEO, Augustus Sinclair. Apparently, they hate each other. He says you have a strong case, and he jumped at the chance to knock him down a peg. Are you going to look a gift horse in the mouth?"

I snicker. "Hell, no." Maybe the stars are finally aligning in my favor.

"Can you come to my office this afternoon?"

"Yeah. What time?"

"Three o'clock."

"I'll be there."

Brad's assistant smiles when she sees me walk into his office a few minutes early. I cleaned up to meet my new legal team. Slacks and a dress shirt. "Hey, Hud, don't you look nice?"

"Thanks."

"They're running a few minutes behind and Brad's on the phone with a client. You want some coffee?"

"Yeah, thanks, Jenny." We went through school together. I think Jennys' got three or four kids now.

"Wait in the conference room and I'll bring it to you."

I don't know who he is or why he's doing it, but I've got to thank this Dallas lawyer who's joining the team for free.

A little knot twists in my gut. Nothing's ever free.

I look up as the conference room door swings open and Brad ushers in two men—an older man with black eyes and salt and pepper hair. Movie star-looking. He has to be the main guy, the one with a hard-on for Sinclair.

Beside him is another man who looks maybe thirty-five, with light brown hair. Preppy.

Brad says, "Hudson Bass, meet Warren Baldwin and Phillip Hughes."

I stand, shaking their hands, and in walks the prettiest woman I've ever seen. My gaze freezes on her, looking like a million-dollar corporate lawyer. Her normally wavy hair is straight. And that suit she has on. Now, that's a woman who drives a Maserati.

"Baldwin." My eyes move from her to her father. They look nothing alike. "I didn't put it together."

My ticker's already shifted into overdrive. I want to say a million things to her, but nothing comes out. Brad has no idea what's between me and Wren. Do the two new suits?

The younger guy takes Wren by the elbow, guides her to the conference table, and pulls out a chair for her. Fucker.

"Did you hear me?" Baldwin says.

Not with the fucking ringing in my ears. "Sorry. No. What?"

"I said you have a strong case."

"Good."

Baldwin starts thumbing through papers in a file, jabbering, but I can't take my eyes off of her. She doesn't seem to notice. What the hell is going on?

He clears his throat loudly, gaining my attention. "Mr. Bass, the initial information you gathered was very useful. It gave us our starting point. We've already bought the same satellite imaging of your property that VoltEdge has and it proves you do have a rare deposit of manganese on your land, which answers the question: Why your land?"

Baldwin tweaks his mouth to the side and scratches his ear. "It's not a large deposit, though. Not big enough to justify the expense of opening up a mine and building a refinery. But... if you're looking at this part of Texas to build a production facility, near all the new electric car manufacturing plants, why not build it on the only land around that has a manganese deposit? Just in case..."

The guy beside Wren jumps in. "This is clearly corporate over-reach. It's not about what's best for the people of this county, it's about what's best for VoltEdge." He and Baldwin exchange glances. "With that company, it always is."

He slides papers across the big table toward me. "What you found out about claims against their facility in Mississippi, we found similar whistleblower claims in other facilities as well, almost all about illegal discharge of toxic material and firing employees in retaliation for reporting the discharges. They will ruin this pristine part of Texas if they get a toehold here."

I shuffle through all the wrongful termination claims.

It's the best news I've heard since this nightmare began, except for the son of a bitch who leans back and spreads his arm across the back of Wren's chair. *Isn't that cozy?*

I make myself look away from them to her father. "I'm impressed. So, you think we have a chance?"

"You have better than a chance," Baldwin says. "We can win this."

My gaze goes back to Wren. "You did this?"

She's straight-faced. Businesslike. "You got it started with your research with the USGS and your meetings with the whistleblowers in Houston."

Yeah, she's from this corporate world. She's totally in her element. Too damned comfortable in it.

I feel a million miles away from her. Where's the woman in blue jean cut-offs wiggling her ass into my crotch on the tractor?

The cocksucker at her side smiles like he just hit a home run. "Wren found out something much more valuable."

And that's your grand slam because...? I feel flames shooting out of my eyes. "I'm sorry, It's Phillip, right?" *Yeah, screw it. My voice has a bite to it.*

"Yes."

"What did you find out, Wren?"

"Guess who has stock in VoltEdge." Now she slides some papers my way, and it's a little like the day I read the print-out on Rosalee. Only this time my jaw actually drops.

"Son of a bitch." I look from the paper to Wren, to the douche almost cuddling her, and then her father. "Judge Nelson owns shares in VoltEdge?"

Baldwin doesn't answer. Wren does. She smiles, cutting her eyes at the fucker Phillip then over at me. "And three of your county commissioners."

My eyes widen as I shove back from the table. "Are you serious?" Yeah, my voice is louder than it should be.

Baldwin snickers. "I know how Geoffery Sinclair operates. As soon as I learned VoltEdge was pulling out all the stops to get your land, my people started digging. VoltEdge is a publicly traded company. Their shareholder information is public record."

Cocksucker, I mean Phillip, interrupts. "Four men we know of—your county judge and three of your four commissioners, all own shares in VoltEdge. If VoltEdge profits, they profit."

Wren's father takes command of the room again, standing. "I have no doubt Sinclair gifted those shares to these men when they learned of your manganese and targeted your land."

I don't know what I'm maddest about. The railroad job that I just learned the commissioners have pulled on me, or seeing this dickhead with his fucking arm still around Wren's chair.

I want her to slap him.

But she doesn't.

I stand, too. "That's all illegal, isn't it? Like... conflict of interest?"

"Absolutely. When we show it to the judge, he'll have to make the right decision. But on top of that, we think we can get you punitive damages, if you want to go after them."

"In what way?" I ask.

"They've cost you business, haven't they? Took money out of your pocket. Hurt your reputation. A man's good name is worth something. If this thing actually goes to trial, we'll ask VoltEdge and the county to pay all lawyer fees plus punitive damages to cover the harm they've inflicted on you and your family personally, and especially on your business." He waves his arm. "Hell, we'll ask for that even if it doesn't come to trial."

I offer my hand to Wren's father. "Thank you."

He flashes a satisfied smile. "Trust me. It's my pleasure." He begins gathering his papers. "We have to be in court first thing in the morning. Get some rest, Mr. Bass, and be ready for it."

"Will I testify?"

He lifts his head and our eyes meet, lock and latch. He's sizing me up as I am him. Those are sharp fucking eyes. He clears his throat and says, "I can't imagine, with what we have, that it will come to that. Judge Holt will have no choice but to throw this case out."

When I turn around to ask Wren if we can talk—she and fuck budget have disappeared. They're not in the goddamned room.

She's back. I swore if I ever saw her again, I'd tell her I love her, that I'd ask her to stay—but how could I, in that room? And now she's gone.

Where'd she go?

I hightail it for Vogel House with my heart racing as fast as my truck.

Connor's in Dallas with Marcos and his family, at Great Wolf Lodge and Six Flags. After all he's been through, the kid needed a fling before school starts. When they asked if he could come along, the timing was perfect, with the trial. He'd be miserable sitting in a courtroom all day.

Pulling up at Vogel House, no Maserati. My heart thuds to the floorboard.

I pound on the door. It's not a knock.

Anderson opens the door. I don't give him a chance to invite me in. "Did you know she was back?"

"Well, hello to you, too. Yes, I knew."

"Where is she?"

Anderson scans me from head to foot. "You clean up nicely, Mr. Bass. Follow me, I can see you need a drink." He sashays into the kitchen and I follow like a damned puppy dog expecting a treat. "To answer your question, I assume Miss Wren Baldwin is in Marble Falls, with them, working on your case."

"How long has she been back?"

"She drove in last night. What's your poison? Whiskey, gin, vodka, beer?"

"Whiskey, thanks. Did you know what she was doing?"

He lifts his brows, holding a whiskey bottle mid-pour as he stares a hole into me. "Did I know she was diving back into the shark tank to save your ass? Yes. Well... not at first. She did just drive off and she did avoid my calls, but my Wrenny came through like she always does. I figured she was taking what we found to her father."

"What we found?"

He reaches for two glasses. "You really can be clueless, Hud. Wren, Cal, and I all worked on your behalf through the Rosalee ordeal and your land crisis. She and I worked together to get the names of all the corporate officers of VoltEdge."

He finally begins to pour. "Same circles, you know. When she found the name Geoffery Sinclair, it was like striking gold. We actually high-fived. If there is one man on this Earth who Warren Baldwin hates, it is Geoffery Sinclair. She knew dangling that in front of her father would be like throwing chum in the water." He cuts his eyes at me and he's dead serious. "Her father really is a human shark."

I believe it.

He holds out the drink to me. Finally.

I take it, scull it, and hold the glass out for more. "Is she going back to Dallas and work for him?"

"God, I hope not," he says as he pours me another. "But that's something you'll have to ask her." His brows twist, and Anderson nails me with a steely stare. It's a 'don't fuck with me glare,' as he starts in. "Let's get this straight between you and me. Don't even think about turning down this help. You have no idea how hard it was for her to have to walk back into that office. She made that sacrifice for you, Bucko."

"Was it hard because of her father or that douche bag who had his arm around her?"

"Both." Anderson freezes and slowly twists his neck to peer at me. "Phillip?" He purses his mouth.

"Pretty boy, thirty-five ish, light brown hair, looks like a tennis player or rower."

"That's Phillip alright." He puts his hand over his mouth as his eyes get big. "He had his arm around her? In front of her father?"

"Close enough. Around her chair."

"Hum." His mouth puckers.

"Spill." I snatch the whiskey bottle and help myself.

Anderson tweaks his mouth to the side, scratches an eyebrow, and finally outs with it. "Let's just say, there's history there. Not quite a year ago, it came down to Phillip having to make a choice. Suffice it to say, he did not choose our Wrenny."

My fuse ignites at the thought of him hurting her, them all cozied up today, and I slap the bar open-handed. "That simple son of a bitch didn't choose her? And he's a lawyer? You're telling me I have Phillip the Fucker to thank for Wren being here?"

"She was on the run."

"Goddammit!" I turn in a furious circle like a madman, trying to think. "Then he can't love her. Not like I do. I'll be damned if I'll lose her to a man who let her go."

Anderson flashes a slow, cunning smirk with his chin tucked tight. "Are you saying you love her?"

"Well fuck, yeah, Anderson. And you say I'm slow? From that first day, when she fainted and I carried her to my truck, Wren Baldwin has owned my fucking heart. I was too afraid she'd break it to let her know." I take a step closer, my gaze as fiery as his was earlier. "Let's get this straight between you and me: I'd give up the land before I'd just let her go. That idiot Phillip isn't going to get her back."

Hands clap in the shadows of the kitchen. "Told you."

My gaze follows the voice to see Cal standing in the corner with his arms now folded over his chest, grinning at Anderson. "I called it. I know him."

"How long have you been there?"

"Long enough." He strides across the room and squeezes my shoulder. "Finally, you admit what I've seen all along. I never heard you talk about anybody the way you do her."

"Because there's never been anybody like her. Never will be."

Can I sleep? Hell no. My blood pressure is higher than the Vogel Springs water tower.

I don't need to get wasted and stumble into court in the morning, so I take a hot shower and go to bed early, lying on my back with my hands behind my head, staring at the ceiling. My eyes won't be still.

I move to the living room and sit like a zombie in front of the TV, not hearing a word they're saying.

I head to the porch, sitting with my gaze glued on Vogel House. It's dark upstairs.

Back to bed. I still can't sleep for the echo of my callousness that night, telling Wren life would go on for Connor and me. Like she didn't matter.

When she repeated it, self-absorbed son of a bitch that I am, I still didn't get it.

It was such a fucking slap in her face the night after we made love. Dammit! She thinks I rejected her.

If I get a chance to make this right, I'll get on my knees if I have to.

I turn onto my side, staring through the open bedroom blinds at Vogel House.

Screw it. I tromp into the kitchen, pull a beer out of the fridge and down it, standing with the fridge door open.

I open a second beer and carry it to the porch, sitting with my feet propped on the railing, watching Vogel House, listening to a barn owl and cicadas, watching a stray cat scurry down the middle of Main Street.

Son of a bitch! Headlights shine on Vogel House.

I help myself to a third beer and return to my lookout. It's not long until a light comes on in Wren's bedroom. She didn't spend the night in Marble Falls with Daddy and dickhead after all.

Maybe now I can get some sleep.

Wren

Chapter 19

courtroom jitters

I don't miss this. The smell of old wood and new carpet. Even when there is no carpet, something in every courtroom smells like it. It's the pomp and circumstance I marvel in.

I get that from my father. If there isn't a show... you put one on. It's how you win.

The hum of the courtroom. People buzzing on one side, while the other side sits silently, staring straight ahead. The curiosity. The expectation. The hope.

It used to be my favorite part. My daddy plays into it all so well. Warren Baldwin is at his best in front of an audience.

The double doors open behind us. More onlookers shuffle in, only these aren't onlookers; they're family members here to support Hud. Martha's eyes scan the courtroom, and she smiles brightly when they land on mine.

See. I'm doing this for her, too.

Hud's land, this life in Vogel Springs. It matters.

Cal and Tiny arrive next, with Hud helping Tiny get seated next to Martha and Anderson. Then, I watch as Cal slaps Hud on the back and gives him a loaded nod of encouragement.

I thought it was the emotion at seeing everyone show up for Hud... but it wasn't my eyes that watered. It was my mouth. Watching the six-foot-plus, masculine God of my sex dreams walk toward me in a black suit, white dress shirt, and tie had me unable to sit right.

Good Lord, Hud.

Talk about cleaning up good. I didn't think the object of my affection could get any hotter. Is that the suit I picked up for him? What the entire—

My father shifts in his chair before me and clears his throat. Hud's eyes drop to mine in a nanosecond, and I bat my eyes to open them better and look up and smile when I feel a hand on my shoulder pulling me away and back to my reality.

Phillip motions me toward him and whispers something I can't make out. I lean into Phillip for him to repeat it, but my eyes stay focused on Hud's as he stares down at me before he turns, sitting beside Daddy in the seat directly in front of me.

I feel the urge to check and make sure I'm not drooling. His thick thighs fill out his long-legged suit pants, and my mind couldn't help racing to all the parts that fill out his tall, lean body, making the fabric stretch across his biceps and broad shoulders where he just stood before me.

"Wren!" Phillip whisper-shouts, and I realize I'm literally leaning at him per his request—but I haven't taken my gaze off Hud's back.

I tilt my head to look inquisitively at what Phillip is asking, but something feral comes over me as my head shifts toward Hud's shoulder. My temple practically rests on it, and I drink in Hud's freshly showered scent. The scent makes my ovaries quiver while Phillip asks me which file I put my father's copy of the mineral rights document in.

He knows. He's just trying to... truthfully, I can't say I know what Phillip is playing at.

I give him an answer and Hud glances at him. Phillip straightens immediately, nodding at Hud to acknowledge his arrival.

A spark flickers in my lower abs. *Calm down, fellas.* You don't have to get out a ruler. Trust me. I know who'd win.

"All rise." I look up as everyone stands around me, and we prepare for the bailiff to introduce the judge and begin the session.

Locking my gaze on what's in front of me, Hud's back, I continue spiraling down the many ways I've missed him and the thoughts drumming up from the way he looks in his suit. Because I'm dreading—*'Warren Baldwin and Phillip Hughes in defense of Hudson Bass.'*

That.

They don't deserve to have their names next to his, but I'm damn grateful they're here.

If I never thought I would tire of hearing my father's name called out next to my former object of affection, Phillip Hughes, let me say for the record, I'm exhausted.

It's only been a few days and we've fallen into the same routine of the way Daddy likes to work. The way Phillip and I worked so well together under his wing. It's an easy routine to fall back into when someone dangles a carrot over your head, showing interest in giving me my old job back, plus talk of the career I didn't complete being made available to me.

But next to Phillip? The very opposite of what my dad wants or wanted.

Why is he pretending it's okay for us to be in the same room together? For Phillip to trip over his feet to sit next to me and open my bottle of water? He's baiting me.

I know my father's tricks better than he does.

I've seen them all play out in courtrooms just like this one, and he's learned nothing new. The world doesn't require a man like him to have to.

Someone's watch beeps on the other side of the aisle as the county attorney's opening statement drones on and on about what this means to the town and its progress.

My father yawns. The oldest trick in baseball, yet every pitcher and batter does it to their appointment.

I worried it would be difficult to be this close to Phillip again, and it is, just not for the reasons I thought. For the most part, I've ignored any unraveling thread or remnants of our past, my mind has been so worried about the case and Hud.

Hud. My eyes flutter to his collar and the back of his neck, where his dark hairline meets tanned skin. He shouldn't have to be here, sitting next to Phillip. Seeing these two universes collide is an anomaly I don't want to face again.

My heart sinks as my eyes drift to my father, sitting on the other side of Hud, and I fear I've invited the devil to the most holy, serene, unadulterated place there is.

"This is not a complicated case. It's a case of owners' rights and corporate overreach." Daddy turns to charm the room after dropping his plan of attack on the judge. Classic debate style. My father delivers upfront. He tells you what he's going to do to you, then he shows you how.

Still, they never see it coming.

It's the same ideology of hiding something in plain sight.

Forgetting the pissing contest I'm responsible for in front of me, I turn to the smiling faces behind me. Martha, Tiny, Cal, and Anderson couldn't look or feel more like family if they signed up for it themselves. Warmth replaces the turmoil in my stomach, and I'm able to shut the familiar tone of my father's courtroom voice out of my head.

Wren

Chapter 50

chambers

The bailiff walks a sticky note to the judge as my father takes his seat after delivering his opening statement.

A ten-minute recess is called, and hearing the rush of the crowd stirring to their feet and feeling the air of the men in front of me swish my direction, I all but book it to the double doors to exit.

Setting my sites on a hidden alcove that promises a water fountain, I take a deep breath and slow my steps. Sure enough, behind the pillar... said water fountain.

I lean in and push the throttle forward, catching the first splatter of water on my bottom lip when hands wrap around my waist and pull me from it.

Hud props my back against the pillar, facing away from the crowds' view and towers above me. His pupils dilate as his grey eyes fall on mine and I stare up at him. The droplet of water dripping from my bottom lip draws his eyes down to it. He grabs my chin firmly and slides his thumb delicately across the bottom of my lips, catching it. "I thought you left." Hud's voice is smooth and low, his face is close.

"I live here."

Hud's eyes close, and he stifles amusement. He blinks back up at me, silver eyes probing mine, as his hand leaves the wall above my head and twists one of the smooth strands of my straightened tresses. "You changed your hair."

"I straightened it."

"I don't like it." Hud brings his cheek to mine and drinks me in.

"I don't either," I whisper in his ear as my breath hitches. My heart starts beating so fast that I know he can hear it.

Hud looks down at my rising chest. A small smile lifts one corner of his mouth, and then it dissipates. A more serious expression meets mine and Hud pulls himself away from me. He takes a step forward, putting him in sight of the crowd gathered down from the water fountain. "No matter what happens. Whatever the outcome... I want you to have this. It's yours to keep. It's been yours since you got here."

I gasp as his hand slides a slim square box into my pocket.

His hand grips my hip, fingers pressing the top of my thigh and panty line as he ensures the little box is in place.

My stomach flips at his touch. I have no idea what he means or what it is, but I want to touch him so badly, and I don't mean appropriately.

His brows pinch together as he turns back to look at me, his hands cruelly to his sides. "Don't open it now. Later." And he walks away.

When I catch my breath and catch up with the last of the crowd filtering back into the courtroom, I'm late to my seat. I scootch through, disturbing all in my row, with the bailiff silencing everyone.

Daddy stands. "Judge, may we approach the bench?"

This is what he lives for.

It's what he came here to do.

But it's the part I'm worried about. What if we're wrong? What if I was wrong and it doesn't work?

It has to work. After all this, it just has to.

Wait a minute... *How could Hud think I left for good? Does he not know I—*

Daddy hands the judge a file of documents and the courtroom stirs.

Hud looks back at me and our eyes lock.

"Counsel." The judge addresses my father and the other attorneys who have approached the bench. It's inaudible, but they're whisper-arguing up there—Daddy and the other attorneys—as Judge Holt clears his throat loudly, announcing, "We'll discuss this matter in chambers."

His gavel drops, and so do my organs as I watch my father follow Judge Holt into his chambers.

I'm terrified now that it is no longer in my hands and that it is my father I have to put all my trust into.

The side door from the judge's chambers pops open almost before it closes all the way.

Damn it. They weren't in there long enough for the judge to make a decision.

Judge Holt walks to his bench, standing, telling the packed courtroom, "Ladies and gentlemen, in lieu of another recess, I'm going to call lunch, to allow me time to review the documents presented by the defense. Bailiff."

The Judge looks my dad in the eye and turns back to his chambers. A rush fills the courtroom as chatter and opinions fight to be heard, and I feel the energy of our friends approaching to flood Hud with support. He's looking straight ahead, and I want to reach out and grab his forearm and pull him back to me.

Someone grabs mine instead. My head swivels to the side at Phillip's touch, my body recognizing it on every level and my brows pinch in confusion. I try to relax my face to address him.

He asks, "Can we talk? It's important." Phillip's hand has not left my elbow as he leads me to the side.

I go willingly—almost enthusiastically—as I'm concerned we missed something with the case.

Phillip strategically leads me around the crowd, edging us to the exit. I look back to find Hud, but all I see is our group enveloping him and Anderson's eyes on mine.

He quirks an eyebrow, and I give him a reassuring one back.

In mere moments, I'm standing in a conference room adjacent to the courtroom.

Wow, I've got to hand it to Phillip, he certainly did his research. The door closes behind us, and Phillip runs his hands through his hair.

Oh God. Is it worse than I thought, did Daddy do something to kill the case?

"Wren," Phillip's voice is firm as if telling me to brace myself.

"What did he do?" I lunge toward Phillip, tears searing my eyes. My hands are on Phillip's suit jacket as if I could pick him up and throw him.

He looks down at me in surprise. His eyes soften as he shakes his head slowly. And then it occurs to me, that's not what he was dragging me in here to talk about.

"Not... your dad, Wren. It's not the case."

I take a half step back, my hands slowly loosening their grip on the tailored fabric as I slide them down. Phillip drops his hands over mine, pausing their release. "Wren, the case is fine. I called you in here because I'm not. I need you to know I was wrong, that I made the wrong choice... that if I had it to do over again—"

I release my hands and almost fly away from him, pacing across the room like a cannonball darting from one wall to the next. "You want a do-over?" I am livid.

Phillip all but shushes me. "I said if I had it to do over."

"Oh, that's rich. Why do I feel like this is the same speech your wife got when I left and you came crawling back to appease my father's wishes?"

"Don't you dare cheapen us that way. I loved you and you know it. I made a life choice, not a romantic one." Phillip is the one yelling now.

"Thank you for enlightening me. I'm so glad to know they are two separate categories." I turn my face away from him.

"You were right, Wren. About him."

"I told you. Win one too many cases with the monster, and you'll see. Although I can't blame you. I all but begged for him to work his magic here today."

"It's the fucking fact that you had to beg—that you had to grovel to that bastard. It's not the cases, Wren, it's not the sport. I signed up for that part. It's him. What he did to you."

Phillip takes two strides closer to me, and I feel his heat behind me. He's respectfully not touching me. But he's too close to be respectful.

"When you left, it destroyed me. Everything that could have gone south for me at the office and personally at home—*did*. Erissa didn't even want me back. She was seeing someone new. It was in the early stages, but still. She was moving on, the way you and I should have been allowed to. My world caved in, and your dad was the one there to pick me up. I was just too impaired to catch on to the fact that he was the one who had his hand on my back pushing me down."

I turn to look at Phillip. He's standing closer to me than I thought.

"He made it seem like it wasn't about you, Wren, that his goal was to get you out of the picture, and get me back to good—fuck! As if you were so wrong for me."

"I get it Phillip." I place a consoling hand on his arm. "I'm used to this, remember? It has never been about me when it comes to Daddy."

"You don't get it. It's been about you from the start." Phillip puts his hand on the arm I reached out, and I take a step back for safe measure. "He knew where you were, Wren. The entire time you've been in this Podunk town. He pretended to let you go at first, to almost force you out. Then he watched me beg and plead to find you. I must've called Anderson fifty-five times a month. Talk about loyalty, good God, that man didn't falter.

"He never answered. Not even a confirming text. I just continued to message him once I realized he didn't block me, hoping for a weak drunk moment. Anything to let me know you were safe. Your father said nothing to me. He watched me agonize, and he behaved as if you were gone for good, and he could care less."

I slide my hands in my pantsuit pockets out of habit, taking a courtroom stance as if to question Phillip over all the new discoveries. My hand lands on the slim box, burning a hole in my pocket, and a million butterflies engage from my core up to my chest.

I take a breath, almost overwhelmed with the surge of emotion and hope the box brings.

"Go back to when you said he knew where I was..."

"The warranty on your Maserati. When it was called in, they called your father."

My blood turns cold at the thought that I was found out. All this time, I've been watched from afar and under his thumb, exactly where he wanted me.

Hud's box presses against the top of my thigh. "I swear to God, Phillip, if he does something to ruin Hud's case..."

Phillip's head dips down, and he shakes it from side to side, taking the hit on the name I say with such conviction.

"You're telling me he used me to get you where he wanted you, and now he's using you to pull me back?" Fire burns in the backs of my corneas.

"No. No, he's not Wren. I'm pulling you back. I want you back."

I cross the small room in three quick strides, daring the heel of my pumps to betray me. I would crawl away if they did. "Wait," I spit out as I dramatically bring my hand up to halt Phillip from closing the gap I forged between us. "On what planet... with what rationale would my father allow you to be this close to me, to assume this position, and allow you to be what brings me back, when he would *never* allow us to be together?"

"I told you. It's not me he wants. It's you. Two words, Wren. Self-sacrifice. That's what he's banking on. What did you do when he gave me the ultimatum?"

"That doesn't matter, Philip, it was an ultimatum for you. You made the choice that ended us," I say, free of malice, as I turn my head away from his heated stare.

"And you ran. Without an ultimatum from your father, you made it so easy for me. You took away any option of me going back or changing my mind. You self-sacrificed your job, your father's good graces, and you sabotaged any hope of us. You gave up. Gave us up."

"I still don't see how this gets me back to..."

"Do you love him?" Phillip steps closer, closing that gap.

"What?" My voice sounds petulant, like a child's.

"Hudson Bass." With one hand safely to his side, he smooths the collar of my suit out behind my neck and gingerly lifts a caught strand of hair away with the other. It's casual, not quite platonic, but more familiar than anything else.

It's kind. His face softens with every inch closer to me, and his eyes begin to plead, and that feels like a betrayal to me as I stand with my hand wrapped around Hud's gift in my pocket.

"If I were you, that would be the first thing I figured out before your father figures out how to make you give *him* up." Philip turns his back to leave. "I meant what I said, Wren. If I had it to do over, if you gave me a chance right here and now, regardless of your father, it will be a very different choice."

Hud

Chapter 51
verdict

S itting alone at the lawyer's table, I peer at the door to the judge's chambers. Warren and Brad, the county and VoltEdge lawyers—they've all been back there for what feels like an eternity.

I glance around the courtroom, where people are milling, whispering, speculating, waiting.

My stomach's somewhere on the floor, where it dropped when Wren disappeared with Phillip, God knows how long ago.

He doesn't think I know what he's doing? He's trying to win her back.

Not like there's anything I can do about it right now.

"Hudson! Stop cracking your knuckles!" Anderson chides me in a whisper-shout. "It makes my skin crawl every time you do it."

The enormity of Cal's hand squeezes my shoulder. "You've got this, bro. Relax."

I nod and glance over my shoulder at them. "Wren really came through."

"Wrenny always does." Anderson smiles and snipes. "Never doubt her."

I face them. "Warren may be a shark, and Phillip may be a douche, but the team of Baldwin, Baldwin and Hughes is impressive as hell. VoltEdge and the county attorney are as outmatched as a Mazda trying to race a Maserati."

Anderson swishes his shoulders. "Agreed. Everyone in this courtroom saw it."

"I have her to thank." She did this. For me.

And fuck if I haven't gone and lost her. She and Phillip. They just... fit. But I'm not rolling over and playing dead.

The door to Judge Holt's office swings wide and out file the suits. Stone-faced, all of them.

My gut takes a left-handed twist. I can't read him. Warren Baldwin is a poker player. I can't tell—did we win? He doesn't look smug.

"All rise!" the bailiff commands.

Judge Holt makes his way to the bench, scowling. "Be seated."

All the people who had been waiting in the hallway are back inside. Phillip appears at my side. That means she's back, too.

It's the moment of truth. The moment we've all been waiting on.

Brad rests his hand on my shoulder.

Judge Holt overlooks his packed courtroom and clears his throat. "I have never been a part of such a politically-charged case. I have reviewed the evidence." He glares at the county attorney. "All of the evidence. The court rules in favor of the defendant, Hudson Bass."

Everyone behind me cheers. The other side of the courtroom, packed shoulder-to-shoulder with members of the Citizens for Progress, either groan, or moan, or silently glare. At me.

"Silence in the courtroom!" The judge and bailiff roar together. Everyone obeys.

Judge Holt clears his throat loudly again and taps his gavel on the bench. He puckers his mouth and shakes his head slowly, glowering at the other table. "This case should never have come to trial. I'm going to take this moment to publicly admonish the members of the Friedensburg County Commission and VoltEdge for pursuing this matter under the guise of eminent domain when it is a blatant case of corporate and personal greed.

"And I'll go further." He casts his gaze on the audience behind the VoltEdge lawyers. "You Citizens for Progress. Know what bandwagon you're jumping on next time, before you set out to ruin a man's business."

He pounds his gavel on the desk and stands, looking squarely at me. "This case is dismissed with prejudice. Mr. Bass, your land is your land. Neither the county nor VoltEdge can ever try to take it from you again."

It's followed by another raucous courtroom eruption, and I damn near break out in tears as Warren Baldwin shakes my hand and grips my shoulder. "Congratulations, Hud." He winks and pulls his mouth near to my ear. "They bought off everyone but the one who mattered most: the District Judge."

I pull him into a back slap. "I can't thank you enough."

He grins like a shark. "I told you, it's my pleasure."

Brad pats my back, and we shake hands as I glance over his head and around the room, searching for Wren, wanting to pick her up and thank her.

But one more time, I can't find her.

Martha's arms are around me, and she presses her head to my chest. "It's over, Hud. It's finally over. Praise the Lord."

I kiss the top of her head, holding her shoulders. "Thanks, Martha."

Now Tiny's got an arm around my waist, holding tight, while Cal pulls me into a side hug, and Anderson, I swear, is prancing and applauding, high-fiving someone I'm sure he doesn't even know.

And I just keep... searching the courtroom... for her.

"Congratulations." Phillip offers his hand and pulls me close, but that's not a triumphant smile I'm looking at. "You win, man."

I grip his shoulder, smiling. "Well, so did you."

Our gazes latch, and Phillip's eyes narrow as he leans in, his voice barely above a whisper. "I'm not talking about the land. We both know the land was never as important as her."

My face freezes as we share an inappropriately long, drawn-out stare, and I fight the need to shove my fist into his face, thinking about his mouth being on hers.

Our hands are still clasped together. "You're damned right I know it." I need to rub salt in the wound. "I'd never choose anything over her. Not even the land."

"Yeah." His pretty boy mouth draws down at the corners. "Maybe you better let her know that."

Fucker.

It feels forever before the crowd disperses and I make my way home, but I have to admit, I basked in the victory and the congratulations from so many friends.

I got a last glimpse of Wren walking with her father and Phillip toward their cars. She's leaving with my heart.

I want to share this victory with my son, but Connor is still in the Metroplex with Marcos' family, so I drive to the Pit Stop, taking it all in as I park, and I'll be damned if I don't almost laugh out loud, envisioning the day Wren scurried across this parking lot that first day. How could I have known she'd change my life?

It wasn't many days ago I was getting ready to sell this place. I'd all but accepted that I lost the land.

My guardian angel, wherever he or she is, took care of my son, my business, and my land. What about Wren?

If this has reinforced one thing I already knew, it's that you never give up, not even when you think you've lost. I won't. I'll find her, and even if she turns me down, she'll know that I'm not Phillip. She and Connor. They matter more to me than anything.

I throw a few things in a bag and head for the home place. After damn near losing it, I want to be there something fierce. I may have everything there before Connor gets home. He's going to have his own permanent bedroom. A place for his things, where he can bring his friends.

Driving down the long caliche lane, as the homeplace comes into view—*what the hell?*

I chuckle out loud, a smile commanding my face. My Vogel Springs family. They do love a party. The barbecue is already fired up, the picnic table is covered in another blue and white checkered cloth, and I spot a tin tub full of ice and beer.

They must've planned this—maybe win or lose. Getting out of the truck, turning in a circle, I can't count all the cars.

What I don't see? The Maserati.

Wren

Chapter 52

change of address

Both hands press tightly on the restroom sink counter as I stare at myself in the mirror. The water I splashed on my face trails a line from my forehead to my chin as it deletes my heavy makeup on its way. I stand and quickly blot it away.

Get it together, Wren. You'll miss the verdict.

I don't like being in this position.

It's a position I grew up in—being my father's pawn—one of the eight least valuable pieces on the chess board, and I have played every one of them for Daddy since I was old enough to speak. Phillip hasn't played them all yet.

I'm not certain he knows which piece he is today.

That makes me more nervous. Especially when he suggests he's not playing at all.

So I was right about Phillip... he did love me. Apparently, he thinks he still does.

My freshly manicured acrylic nail taps profusely on the marble counter like a petrified rabbit. I take a deep breath and wring out my shaking hands. None of this matters.

He still didn't choose me, and I don't mean to be selfish, but it may be the one thing I inherited from my father... what killed it for me with Phillip. Not being chosen.

Only, how could I not see my father coming?

I was raised on this tactic. My mother self-medicates between hair appointments and facials to navigate such. Damn it if I didn't give him a win and an in. I swing my hands from trying to trap them in my pockets, and out flies the slim box I've coveted since Hud slipped it to me.

I slide on my knees to grab it and keep it from landing under a stall.

Thank God there's no one in here to witness me crawling on the tile floor in a three-thousand-dollar pantsuit while I lose my mind contemplating three men who have the absolute worst communication skills.

My hands tremble again as I lift the slim square box to remove the lid and my heart nearly explodes.

I can scratch Hud's name off the list of poor communication skills.

A delicately linked gold bracelet holding one heart-shaped charm glistens up at me, telling me everything I need to know. I gasp as I remove it from the box and stare at the thick, full heart that dangles before me.

"It's yours to keep. It's been yours since you got here."

Hud's words from the water fountain replay in my head, and my brain, body, and soul respond.

He gave me his heart.

The man was on the brink of losing everything—his land, his son, his business—and he gave. Me. His. Heart.

I never asked Hud for anything for fear of losing him, like I lost Phillip, yet when he was down to having nothing to give, he gave me everything—the same way Vogel Springs did when I had nothing to offer.

Nervous energy ricochets through me, and I don't think I can be still or cool enough to pull this off. I smile at the familiar faces surrounding me and nod as I hand Travis, the tow truck driver, a beer from the kitchen refrigerator.

He winks back at me and gives me a real nod and genuine smile of recognition for what he thinks is about to ensue.

"Stop it, you. You're gonna make me pee myself, I'm so nervous."

"Wouldn't be the first time we'd been close to that outcome together." Travis lifts his beer in a toast and squeezes through the throng of people filling his cousin's house. The yard is full of well-wishers, too.

My eyes search the friends and family I've found here at Vogel Springs, and I can't help but think of my own.

My father's face when he left. When I told him, with absolute certainty, I would take my LSAT and the look on his face. It was the same look he had when he shook Hud's hand for the first time. A look of uncertainty. A look that sprung a leak in his otherwise strategic expression and one that suggested he may have been one-upped or out-served.

No. I don't think he saw Hud coming, and if he doesn't believe me about the LSAT, he'll be happy to discover some time from now that, although Vogel Springs lacks a nail salon, an airbrush tanning studio, and so much more... it may just find itself with one damn good law practice.

I'll need something to do after decorating, while Anderson and I watch our grapes grow.

Anderson. I hear his claps and shouts from outside on the porch. He's louder than everyone else. It must be time. He's here.

Waiting in the kitchen, my stomach turns somersaults and my heart takes off faster than my Maserati ever could as I shift the heart that hangs from my wrist to make it more visible.

"For he's a jolly good fellow... for he's a jolly good—" The singing crowd follows Hud inside and halts when he does.

I bite my bottom lip as I watch his eyes start at my wedge sandals and red toenails, tracing up my legs to my favorite jean shorts. Then he takes in my pale purple tank top and, finally, my face.

I raise my bracelet-clad wrist to nudge one of my freshly dried waves away from my face and watch his eyes swell when they meet mine.

Hud vaults to me and lifts me by my waist. I wrap my legs around him as he spins me. "Your hair is back," he says as we stop spinning, and his eyes re-discover me.

I nod and hum back at him as I stay cradled in his arms, legs still wrapped around his waist.

"And so are you," he says almost as a question.

"I never left."

Hud's smile reaches a height I haven't seen, and his eyes dart to my wrist, which presents what dangles from his shoulder. He inspects the heart bracelet, and his grey eyes twinkle back at mine as he rolls his bottom lip, conjuring his next thought.

The crowd cheers and claps as he spins me one more time. "Put me down, you'll make me dizzy."

Hud brings his mouth to my ear. "Can't right now."

Now it's me smiling so big I can't contain it as I feel him rock hard beneath my jean shorts.

He whispers, "Stop it. You keep smiling at me like that and I've got no chance. You'll have to tell all the people we love to leave."

I peek over his shoulder at the crowd of our friends, who have started dissipating to give us a small amount of space. "Don't tempt me," I growl in his ear, as I slide down to stand before him.

I take a half step back to reach for him a beer, and his hand wraps around my forearm. He steps closer, and there is so much electricity between us that I think these people really will have to leave.

"Wren." Hud's voice is low, and I don't recognize the fear in it. "I can't believe you'd do this for me. You gave up everything to go to your father. Anderson said he could have cut you off financially."

I feel my brows pinch together, and my voice comes out so committed to its cause that I almost sound angry. "I don't need his money, Hud. You can always earn more money. You can't make more land. I couldn't let you lose it."

Hud looks down at his feet, then charges back at me, grabbing my upper arm. "But why? Why, Wren, would you do that for me?" He's practically shaking me as he pleads with me.

My eyes close as a tear drops down my cheek, and I hate that I'm remembering the heartache from the last time I was this vulnerable with someone.

I lift my eyes to Hud's, tasting more tears on my lips, and when I see his grey eyes lost and searching for me, I can't help but tell him the truth. "Because I love you," I say without fear.

Hud's mouth crashes into mine so fast I see stars behind my eyes. He kisses me feverishly, lifts me off the tiptoes of my wedge sandals, and squeezes me so tight I almost can't breathe.

He all but whimpers into my mouth as he presses my face and my body to his and dives back in for more. His kisses are starved for me as if he didn't think he'd have them again.

How could he not know?

I use my upper body and arms to practically climb up him and kiss him back just as hard, knowing we have to stop.

With his hands tangled in my waves of hair, me latched onto him for life... our friends and neighbors will call the police, we look so crazed.

"Hu-d," I whisper, breathless in his ear. He lets out a deep sigh into my mouth and slowly loosens his grip, lowering me to my feet.

He stares back at me for the longest. Silver eyes, dark and deep in thought. An inquisitive but knowing expression coats his face as he studies me more. "Does this mean…" he starts to ask.

"Well, I call Vogel Springs my home, and you gave me your heart, but only you can tell me where I'm supposed to sleep ton—"

"Here. Every night. I'm asking you to stay, Wren."

"Why?"

"Because I love you, and I don't want to be without you."

"And when Connor's back?"

"He has his room. And if Vogel House can spare you a few days a week, I'm going to need someone to remodel ours."

Epilogue Anderson

ONE YEAR LATER

As I toss the stack of last month's bridal magazines into Martha's garbage, her creased 11-lines shoot disdain my way.

"Oh, please," I huff. "Don't act like you recycle."

"Tiny and I had pages circled in some of those!" She reaches for them, and I swat her hand.

"It doesn't matter. We've lost her."

"To what? The other side?" Martha squints at me. The old broad is toying with my emotions. I draw the line at her version of sarcasm.

"I'm not sure what yet, but something is definitely wrong with our Wrenny-Poo."

"Hmm. I don't see it."

"She's canceled every appointment, Martha. She still hasn't returned for her final dress fitting. She doesn't respond to any of my texts about the reception. Amarillis By Morning put out an APB on her and tracked me and Cal down at Vogel House because she still hasn't stopped in to approve her bouquet design."

424

Shit. That reminds me of the center layout floral design I saw in *The One In White* November edition, and I rise with no explanation to pick through the trash.

Slapping the partially wet front cover down on the four-top Martha and I occupy before the lunch rush, I brush off a few coffee grounds. "What?"

Martha's side eye is as vicious as my own.

"There's a venue in an ad, and I want to copy their table layout and centerpieces for the Vogel House dining room."

"Always an agenda."

"Come hook or crook, honey. And don't you forget it."

Our laughter fills the empty café with Martha's shaking chest settling as her eyes land across the street, on Bass Pit Stop. A beat passes through her laser focus on Hud's place. "I don't know. I just don't see it. Hud and Connor have been happier than I've seen them."

"No kidding. So has Wren, when I finally do lock her down for bookings and details."

Martha points an index finger in my face. "Now, the church is already handled. I set that up with the pastor and Ladies' League myself. No charge, by the way. Hud's family and mine go way back with the United Methodist of Vogel Springs, if you will. He was an acolyte when he was a little boy." She smiles, proud as punch.

"Bet he hasn't set foot in there since."

"Well, he and Wren both are about to. All that's left is your end."

I mimic Martha's move and stare over to the busy Pit Stop. "Trust me. Vogel Häus is handled. It will be the most beautiful reception this town has attended."

"Are you still changing the name? What's the matter with house?"

"And your last name is Mueller. Häus is German. It's a German town. I'm simply preserving the historical home's roots."

"Ah, and it's a home now, too. Again. What's wrong with H-O-U-S-E?"

"You stay out of it. You still haven't determined if this is a diner or a café. It says 'café' on the sign, but the whole town says they're going to the 'diner.' Or is that just my poor interpretation of the lingo here in Hicksville? You know, the way dinner is lunch and lunch is supper."

"The Hicksville you love," she sneers.

"Yes. And I love all of this for our girl!" I motion to a magazine spread with lush bouquets of peonies dripping down the aisle, and an arch we hadn't considered. My short attention span dives back into wedding planner mode, and the potential of my best friend running from the best thing that ever happened to her, including the town we both call home, fades away.

THREE MONTHS LATER

My mother does the honors and clips a blue barrette into the back of one of my braids. The rest of my strawberry blonde tresses drop down my back in their natural waves. Something Martha and I insisted on against Mom and Anderson's better judgment

Mom's not quite acclimated to the quaintness of Vogel Springs, but this week's the most I've seen her and Dad together in the last five years.

"Wren. You're shaking, darling. This isn't like you." My mother's shrill-but-always-calm voice spills over the vanity from behind me.

Right. Usually, I'm a good little soldier when I'm getting my way, or Daddy's getting his.

"You couldn't be more beautiful. And this dress—well, even your dad will be impressed. And we both know that's no easy feat. I must say, as much as I don't understand this... town or this,

Hudson of yours, they seem to have both worked wonders on your rebellious nature."

"You're just glad Anderson's here to keep me honest from your end."

"That is a plus. Otherwise, I fear I've lost my only flesh and blood to hay bales and tractors."

I clear my throat, trying not to choke on the thought of Hud and me on a particular red tractor. "I'm just worried, that's all."

"Oh, now don't be. Your father couldn't be more pleased."

"Not about him. About us. You, me, Daddy, and Anderson, all in one room. One wedding reception together. We're too much. This place is real. It's genuine. Hud's real, Mom. He and Connor are the most important things in the world to me, next to Anderson."

I see her flinch, as the sting hits her—that my best friend, and possibly this town, are more beloved to me than she is.

She takes the hit and bends down to look at me. "Money has let your father, me, and certainly you, for that matter, get by with a lot. Some might say anything we want. And you'd be wise not to forget that. I understand you want this now... and I'm okay with that. As long as..." A single tear runs down her cheek as the faint sound of the background music from the chapel changes to the song before my wedding march.

"Mom... I have to—"

"I'm okay with it, as long as you count me. Consider I'm a part of you, too. You're stronger than me, Wren. You always have been. It's why you run when things get tough. It's not because you're weak. It's because you're not complacent, like I am. You run from the things you simply won't stand for, and I like to think that little bit of rebellion caused by your father's antics comes from me. You're the part of me that would be strong if I had it in me, Wren. You're my backbone and my pride and joy. The only good parts of your father and me. Just remember that's what got you to Vogel Springs and Hud. You can be ashamed of your father and me, most certainly... but that—the best parts of us... of you—that's nothing to be ashamed of."

The wedding march begins, and she rises to exit. White noise fills the room as the door shuts, and I hear her and Anderson outside.

"Where is she?" Anderson's muffled voice carries to the mirror I stare into. "I need her out here two songs ago!"

"She's fine," My mother's shrill, annoyingly collected harrumph responds. "Hudson, you may knock, but you can't go in. Let the mother of the bride observe one more superstition, if you will."

"Yes, ma'am." Hud's deep voice registers a low hum that seems to vibrate through the door and into my chest. "I've got her."

He might as well have told my mother, "She's mine," and every fiber of my being flies to the door, despite the heavy white material that surrounds my bodice and hips.

"Hud," I whisper into the solid wood door. "We don't have to do this part. Not like this."

"Shh. We do have to do this part."

"But, my daddy, and Anderson—I just don't want all this pushed on you. I know who you are, Hud, and I love every shred of you. I know this isn't you. It's not what you want."

"I've never wanted to show off anything in my life. Never wanted attention. But as far as I'm concerned, a love like ours deserves this much attention. If not more."

Both shock and heat rush through me, as his strong silence is suddenly loud. "Don't do it for your dad or Anderson, or Martha, for that matter. Hell, she's standin' up front right now in her Sunday best and hat, passing out programs with Connor—you better believe it!"

I laugh so hard at the truth of his statement that I can't help but snort in my twenty-thousand-dollar dress.

"Do it for me," he finishes.

"What?" My eyes widen, and something swells in my heart that I thought couldn't get warmer or bigger than it already is.

"For me, Wren. I want to show you off to the whole damn world, with God and everybody watching. I want my son to see what true love is... a love so big the whole damn town had to come get a piece of it. A love he'll feel every day, just by being near us. That's a love that doesn't hide at the Justice of the Peace—"

"Hud, I did that for you. In case all of this was too much."

"And I did that for me because I wanted you to be my wife so damn bad I couldn't wait. The Justice of the Peace didn't prove anything but to you and me, and I'd marry you there again tomorrow. But I'd also do this."

God, if I can't feel his touch on my face. Every bone in my body melts for this man.

"Wren. This wedding does nothing but prove how big our love is. A love so damn big you can't run from it, and I can't hide it."

I can't believe my fear of losing him to my parents and Anderson's dream wedding caused him to think I had cold feet.

We're already married!

This is ridiculous. To think I could still scare him off with a designer wedding gown, my dad's pomp and circumstance, and Anderson's over-the-top-designer-slash-wedding planner extraordinaire. Hud's got a heart so big. He's not just doing this for me and the coveted dress I said yes to... he's doing this for Martha. too. I've never seen her smile as much as she has the last two months. She looks ten years younger.

And for his son. Connor.

Our son.

Tears stream down my makeup, and my breath remains caught in my throat, rendering me speechless. I knew he loved me. But I didn't know he loved me this much. This stubborn, brooding, normally emotionally unavailable man let me in.

I have never been loved by anyone like this.

The idea that I get to give to Connor what Anderson and I were never shown gives me a purpose I never knew I could be worthy of.

Hud gulps, and there's a tremble in his voice as if he's pleading with me. "Look, I got a business in the dead center of town, with a neon light begging for people to stop in, but you know I'm a private man. I also have a home, our home on the outskirts of town in the middle of hundreds of acres, and as far as I know, only two people have the keys to it."

On the verge of swooning, my mouth opens to praise what he just said to me. All of it. Only a beat of silence halts me.

A low mumble from Hud breaks the tension. "Well, Cal has a key. You know. Emergencies."

Holding my breath and tongue a moment, I let out a defeated sigh and sheepishly add, "Anderson. I gave him one. Just in case."

"Cal also gave one to Tiny... ages ago. Just... in case." Hud reluctantly offers.

Another beat goes by as we contemplate the level of privacy our homestead provides.

Hud clears his throat. "And Martha. For when she has to pick up Connor."

Our quiet laughter crescendos into the door shaking between us. Our hands still grip the knobs on both sides.

"I love you, Mr. Bass."

"I love you more, Mrs. Bass."

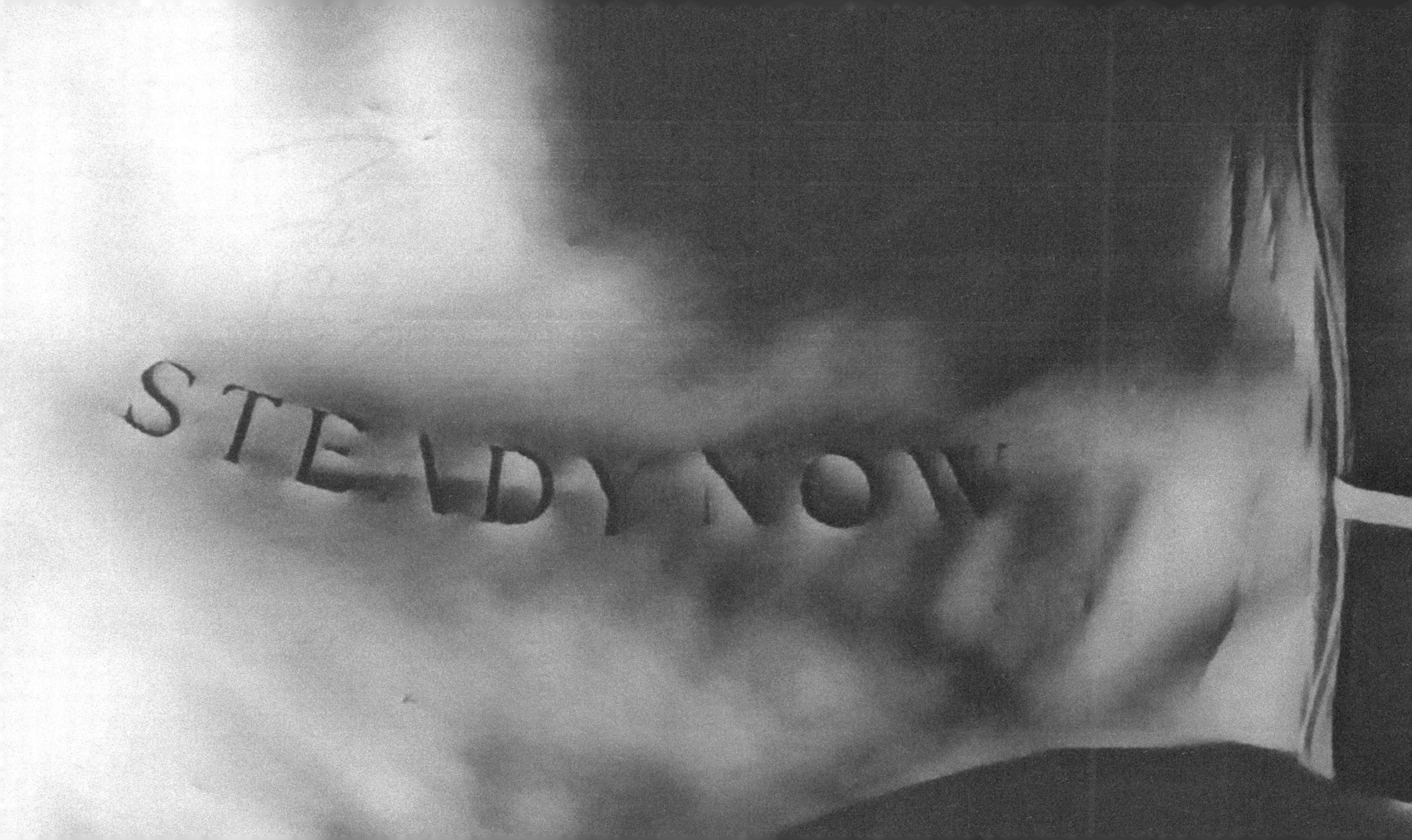

STEADY NOW

Liberty Stowe

Liberty Stowe is a Contemporary Romance Author who hit the map with her debut Small Town Romance, *Steady Now.*

Still dancing at the Pink Pony Club or home, visiting... rocking on her grandparents' porch swing. With a heart split between the Piney Woods and the Hill Country, her mind often wanders to the footprints she left across West Texas and the nails left in the walls of all her Manhattan, Birmingham, and LA apartments. Love life: A Lana Del Ray song about Video games and Diet Mountain Dew, and a handmade spoon ring that could never truly be misplaced. If her Small Town Contemporary romance books had a voice... Yola or Sierra Ferrell. And there's never enough time to throw the dog his ball as many rounds as he wants or to water all the flowers she'd like to grow.

libertystowe.com
TikTok & Instagram: @authorlibertystowe
Facebook: Author Liberty Stowe

RETURN TO

VOGEL SPRINGS

Book 2...

THE VOGEL SPRINGS COLLECTION

www.ingramcontent.com/pod-product-compliance
Lightning Source LLC
Chambersburg PA
CBHW010603310726

48969CB00010B/2550